# THE UGLY LITTLE BOY

By Isaac Asimov and Robert Silverberg
NIGHTFALL

# ISAAC ASIMOV
## and
# ROBERT SILVERBERG

---

# *The Ugly*
# *Little Boy*

---

A FOUNDATION BOOK

*DOUBLEDAY*

*NEW YORK*
*LONDON*
*TORONTO*
*SYDNEY*
*AUCKLAND*

A FOUNDATION BOOK
PUBLISHED BY DOUBLEDAY
a division of Bantam Doubleday Dell Publishing Group, Inc.
666 Fifth Avenue, New York, New York 10103

FOUNDATION, DOUBLEDAY, and the portrayal of the letter F
are trademarks of Doubleday,
a division of Bantam Doubleday Dell
Publishing Group, Inc.

ISBN 0-385-26343-0

Printed in the United States of America

For Martin Harry Greenberg
—with a double measure of affection

And, alone in the dim emptiness of the sleeping forecastle he appeared bigger, colossal, very old; old as Father time himself, who should have come there into this place as quiet as a sepulchre to contemplate with patient eyes the short victory of sleep, the consoler. Yet he was only a child of time, a lonely relic of a devoured and forgotten generation. . . .

—JOSEPH CONRAD, *The Nigger of the Narcissus*

# THE UGLY LITTLE BOY

# PROLOGUE

# *Silver Cloud*

SNOW HAD COME IN during the night, a fine dusting of it, thin as mist, traveling on the western wind. It was snow that must have come a great distance. The scent of the sea was still on it, rising now from the bleak broad tundra as the warmth of the early morning sun began to go to work on it.

Silver Cloud had seen the sea once, a long time ago, when he was a boy and the People still hunted in the western lands. The sea was huge and dark and restless, and when the sunlight struck it in a certain way it gleamed like strange liquid fire. To enter it was death, but to look upon it was wonderful. He would never see it again; that much he knew. The lands bordering the sea were held by the Other Ones now, and the People were in retreat, steadily moving closer and closer each year to the place where the sun is born. And even if the Other Ones were to disappear as suddenly as they had come, Silver Cloud understood that he would have no hope of returning to the coastal territory. He was too old, too lame, too close to his end. It would take half a lifetime for the tribe to retrace its eastward path, perhaps more. Silver Cloud did not have half a lifetime left. Two or three years, if he was lucky: that was more like it.

But that was all right. He had seen the sea once, which was more than anyone else in the tribe could say. He would never forget the scent of it, or its great surging strength. Now he stood on the high ground overlooking the encampment, staring out at the unexpectedly snowy plains—opening his nostrils wide, breathing deeply, letting the musky odor of the sea rise to him from below on the fumes from the melting snow. For just a moment he felt young again.

For just a moment.

A voice behind him said, "You mentioned nothing about snow last night when we made camp, Silver Cloud."

It was the voice of She Who Knows. Why had she followed him up here? He had come up here to be alone in the quiet time of the dawn. And she was the last person he wanted to be bothered by in this private moment.

Slowly Silver Cloud swung round to face her.

"Is snow so unusual that I need to give warning every time it's on the way?"

"This is the fifth week of summer, Silver Cloud."

He shrugged. "It can snow in the summertime as well, woman."

"In the fifth week?"

"In any week," said Silver Cloud. "I remember summers when the snow never stopped, when it came day after day after day. You could see the bright summer sun shining through it, and still the snow fell. And that was in the western lands, where the summers are warmer than they are here."

"That was a very long time ago, before I was born. The summers are getting better everywhere, so they all say, and it seems to be true. —You should have let us know that snow was coming, Silver Cloud."

"Is that so very much snow? It's only a light little dusting, She Who Knows."

"We could have put out the sleeping-rugs."

"For such a little dusting? Such a trifle of snow?"

"Yes. Who likes awakening with snow in the face? You ought to have told us."

"It didn't seem important," said Silver Cloud irritably.

"You should have told us anyway. Unless you didn't know it was coming, of course."

She Who Knows gave him a long hostile look, full of malice. She was becoming a very annoying woman as age bit deeper into her, Silver Cloud thought. He could remember a time when she had been the beautiful slender girl Falling River, with cascades of thick dark hair and breasts like summer melons. Everyone in the tribe had desired her then: he too, he would not deny that. But now she had passed her thirtieth winter and her hair had turned to white strings and her breasts were empty and men no longer looked at her with desire, and she had changed her name to She Who Knows, and was putting on lofty airs of wisdom as though the Goddess had entered into her soul.

He glared at her.

"I knew that the snow was coming. But I knew also that it wouldn't be worth mentioning. I felt the snow in my thigh, where the old wound is, where I always feel the oncoming snow."

"I wonder if you really did."

"Am I a liar? Is that it?"

"You would have told us, if you knew snow was coming. You would have liked having a sleeping-rug over you as much as anyone else. Even more so, I think."

"So kill me," Silver Cloud said. "I admit everything. I failed to feel the snow on the way. Therefore I failed to give the warning and you woke up with snow on your face. It's a terrible sin. Call the Killing Society, and have them take me behind the hill and hit me twelve times with the ivory club. Do you think I'd care, She Who Knows? I've seen forty winters and a few more. I'm very old and very tired. If you'd like to run the tribe for a while, She Who Knows, I'd be happy to step aside and—"

"Please, Silver Cloud."

"It's true, isn't it? Day by day you grow ever more bright within with great wisdom, and I simply grow old. Take my place. Here. Here." He undid his bearskin mantle of office and thrust it brusquely in her face. "Go on, take it! And the feather cap, the ivory wand, and all the rest. We'll go down below and tell everybody. My time is over. You can be chieftain now. Here! The tribe is yours!"

"You're being foolish. And insincere as well. The day you'll give up the feather cap and the ivory wand is the day we find you cold and stiff on the ground in the morning, not a moment before." She pushed the mantle back at him. "Spare me your grand gestures. I don't have any desire to take your place, now or after you're dead, and you know it."

"Then why have you come up here to bother me about this miserable little snowfall?"

"Because it's the fifth week of summer."

"So? We've already discussed this. Snow can come at any time of the year and you're perfectly well aware of that."

"I've looked at the record-sticks. We haven't had snow this late in the year since I was a girl."

"You looked at the record-sticks?" Silver Cloud asked, taken aback. "This morning, you mean?"

"When else? I woke up, I saw the snow, and it frightened me. So I went to Keeps The Past and asked her to show me the sticks. We counted everything together. Seventeen years ago it snowed in the fifth week of summer. Not since. —Do you know what else happened that summer? Six of our people died in the rhinoceros hunt and four were killed in a stampede of mammoths. Ten deaths in a single summer."

"What are you telling me, She Who Knows?"

"I'm not telling you anything. I'm asking you if you think this snow's an omen."

"I think this snow is snow. Nothing more."

"Not that the Goddess may be angry with us?"

"Ask the Goddess, not me. The Goddess doesn't speak much with me these days."

She Who Knows' mouth quirked in exasperation. "Be serious, Silver Cloud. What if this snow means that there's some sort of danger lying in wait for us here?"

"Look," he said, gesturing grandly toward the valley and the plains. "Do you see danger out there? I see a little snow, yes. Very little. And I also see the People awake and smiling, going about their business, starting forth on another good day. That's what I see, She Who Knows. If you see the anger of the Goddess, show me where it lies."

Indeed everything seemed wonderfully peaceful to him down there. In the main encampment the women and girls were building the morning fire. Boys too young to hunt were wandering about nearby, rummaging through the light covering of snow to gather twigs and bits of withered sod to be used as fuel. Off to the left in the domain of the Mothers he saw the babies being given their morning meal—there was Milky Fountain, that inexhaustible woman, with an infant at each breast, and Deep Water was leading the toddlers in a circle game, pausing now to comfort a small boy—Skyfire Face, it was—who had fallen and barked his knee. Behind the place of the Mothers, the three Goddess Women had built a cairn of rocks to serve as a shrine to Her and were very busy at it: one of the priestesses setting out an offering of berries, another pouring onto the bloodstone the blood of the wolf that had been killed yesterday, a third kindling the day-fire. Over on the other side Mammoth Rider had set up his workshop and was already turning out flint blades, which he still made with perfect workmanship despite the palsy that was steadily overtaking his limbs. Moon Dancer and one of her daughters sat behind him, at work on their usual task of chewing hides to make them soft enough to turn into cloaks. And far off on the horizon Silver Cloud saw the men of the Hunting Society in the field, fanning out over the tundra, spears and throwing-sticks at the ready. The uneven long line of their footprints still showed, a bare suggestion of them, anyway, the dark outlines of heels and splayed toes proceeding outward from the camp in the rapidly vanishing snow.

Everything seemed peaceful, yes. Everything seemed normal and regular, a new day dawning in the life of the People, who were as old as time and would endure until the end of days. Why should a little midsummer snow cause any concern? Life was hard; snow was a commonplace thing and always would be, all the year round; the Goddess had never promised anyone that the summer would be free from snow, however kindly She had been in that regard in recent years.

Strange that he hadn't felt it coming toward them the night before, though. Or had he, and not paid close attention? There were so many aches and pains these days; it was harder and harder to interpret each one of them.

But all seemed well, nevertheless.

"I'm going down now," he said to She Who Knows. "I just came up here for a little quiet time alone. But I see that I'm not going to be allowed to have it."

"Let me help you," she said.

Furiously Silver Cloud brushed away the hand she had extended toward him.

"Do I look like a cripple to you, woman? Keep your hands to yourself!"

She shook her shoulders indifferently. "Whatever you say, Silver Cloud."

But the track down from the high ground was rough and troublesome, and the light coating of melting snow hid some of the small treacherous rocks from view and made them slick and slippery beneath his feet. Before he had gone ten paces Silver Cloud found himself wishing his pride had allowed him to take She Who Knows up on her offer. That would have been impossible, though. Nobody minded if he limped a little, but if he started needing assistance on a gently sloping path like this they might begin thinking it was time to help him to his final rest. Old people were revered, yes, but they couldn't be coddled beyond a certain point. In his day he had helped other old ones to their final rest, and a sad business it was, too, making nests for them in the snow and standing by until the chill had carried them into their last sleep. He wanted no such help for himself: let his time come when it came, not an hour before. It would be soon enough anyway.

He was panting a little when he reached the bottom of the hill, and he felt warm and sweat-sticky beneath his cloak of thick gray fur. But the descent hadn't been too bad. He was still strong enough to hold his own.

Cooking smells reached Silver Cloud's nostrils. The laughter of children and the piercing cries of infants drifted through the air. The sun was climbing swiftly. A sense of well-being pervaded his spirit.

In three more days it would be time for the Summer Festival, when he would have to dance in the circle and sacrifice a young bullock and rub its blood on the chosen virgin of the year. And then take her aside and embrace her to insure the success of the autumn hunt. Silver Cloud had been a little uneasy as the time of the Summer Festival approached, thinking that he was getting a bit too lame to do a proper job of dancing, and perhaps might bungle the sacrifice of the bullock as he had once seen another aging chieftain do long ago; and as for the embracing of the virgin, he was a trifle uncertain about that part too. But in the warmth of the morning all those fears dropped away. She Who Knows was becoming a quavering old fool. The snow signified nothing. Nothing! This was a fine bright day. For the People a glorious summer lay ahead, unfolding in ever-increasing warmth.

A pity that the Summer Festival wasn't to be held today, Silver Cloud thought. While his spirit was in this upward-turning phase; while his body was, for the moment at least, experiencing a little rush of renewed vigor. The dancing—the bullock—the embracing of the virgin—

"Silver Cloud! Silver Cloud!"

Hoarse breathless voices, ragged exhausted gasps, coming from the open fields beyond the place where the Goddess Women were tending their shrine.

What was this? Hunters returning so soon? And in such haste?

He shaded his eyes and looked into the sun. Yes, it was Tree Of Wolves and Broken Mountain, running toward the camp with all their might and calling his name as they ran. Tree Of Wolves was waving his spear about in a frantic, almost crazy way; Broken Mountain didn't seem to have his weapons with him at all.

They came staggering into camp and fell practically at Silver Cloud's feet, wheezing, moaning, struggling for breath. They were two of the strongest and swiftest of the men, but they must have run at full tilt all the way back from the hunting field and they were at the end of their endurance.

Silver Cloud felt a great uneasiness coming over him, driving away that all-too-brief moment of joy and peace.

"What is it?" he demanded, giving them no time to catch their breath. "Why are you back this early?"

Broken Mountain pointed back behind him. His arm was trembling like an old man's. His teeth were chattering.

"Other Ones!" he blurted.

"What? Where?"

Broken Mountain shook his head. He had no strength left in him for words.

Tree Of Wolves said, with a tremendous effort, "We—didn't—see —them. Just their tracks."

"In the snow."

"In the snow, yes." Tree Of Wolves was on his knees, head hanging downward. Great racking movements almost like convulsions ran through him from his shoulders to his waist. After a moment he was able to speak again. "Their prints. The long narrow feet. Like this." He drew the shape of a foot in the air with his fingers. "Other Ones. No doubt about it."

"How many?"

Tree Of Wolves shook his head. He closed his eyes.

"Many," said Broken Mountain, finding his voice again suddenly. He held up both his hands and flashed all his fingers—again, again, again. "More than us. Two, three, four times as many. Marching from south to north."

"And a little west," said Tree of Wolves somberly.

"Toward us, you mean?"

"Maybe. Not—sure."

"Toward us, I think," said Broken Mountain. "Or us toward them. We might walk right into them if we don't take care."

"Other Ones out here?" Silver Cloud said, as though speaking only to himself. "But they don't like the open plains. This isn't their kind of country. There's nothing for them here. They should be staying closer to the sea. Are you sure about the feet, Tree Of Wolves? Broken Mountain?"

They nodded.

"They are crossing our path, but I think that they won't come toward us," said Tree Of Wolves.

"I think they will," Broken Mountain said.

"I think they don't know we're here."

"I think they do," said Broken Mountain.

Silver Cloud put his hands to his face and tugged at his beard—hard, so hard that it hurt. He peered into the east as though if he only looked intensely enough he would be able to see the band of Other Ones marching across the track his people meant to take. But all he saw was the rising glare of the morning.

Then he turned and his eyes met those of She Who Knows.

He expected that she would be looking at him in a smug, self-righteous, vindicated way. The unexpected midsummer snow had been a bad omen after all, hadn't it? And not only had he completely failed to predict its coming, he had also utterly misinterpreted its dire significance. *I told you so,* She Who Knows should be saying now. *We are in great trouble and you are no longer fit to lead.*

But to his amazement there was no trace of any such vindictiveness in She Who Knows' expression. Her face was dark with sorrow and silent tears were rolling down her cheeks.

She held her hand out toward him and there was something almost tender in the way she did it.

"Silver Cloud—" she said softly. "Oh, Silver Cloud."

She's not simply weeping for herself, Silver Cloud thought. Or for the danger to the tribe.

She's weeping for me, he realized in astonishment.

# CHAPTER ONE

---

# Loving

## [1]

EDITH FELLOWES smoothed her working smock as she always did before opening the elaborately locked door and stepping across the invisible dividing line between the *is* and the *is not*. She carried her notebook and her pen although she no longer took notes except when she felt the absolute need for some report.

This time she also carried a suitcase. ("Some games for the boy," she had said, smiling, to the guard—who had long since stopped even thinking of questioning her and who waved her cheerfully on through the security barrier.)

And, as always, the ugly little boy knew that she had entered his private world, and he came running to her, crying, "Miss Fellowes— Miss Fellowes— " in his soft, slurring way.

"Timmie," she said, and ran her hand tenderly through the shaggy brown hair on his strangely shaped little head. "What's wrong?"

He said, "Where's Jerry? Will he be back to play with me today?"

"Not today, no."

"I'm sorry about what happened."

"I know you are, Timmie."

"And Jerry—?"

"Never mind about Jerry now, Timmie. Is that why you've been crying? Because you miss Jerry?"

He looked away. "Not just because of that, Miss Fellowes. I dreamed again."

"The same dream?" Miss Fellowes' lips set. Of course, the Jerry affair would bring back the dream.

He nodded. "The same dream, yes."

"Was it very bad this time?"

"Bad, yes. I was—outside. There were children there, lots of them. Jerry was there, too. They were all looking at me. Some were laughing, some were pointing at me and making faces, but some were nice to me. They said, Come on, come on, you can make it, Timmie. Just take one step at a time. Just keep on going and you'll be free. And I did. I walked right away from here into the outside. And I said, Now come and play with me, but then they turned all wavery and I couldn't see them any more, and I started sliding backward, back into here. I wasn't able to stop myself. I slid all the way back inside and there was a black wall all around me, and I couldn't move, I was stuck, I was—"

"Oh, how terrible. I'm sorry, Timmie. You know that I am."

His too-large teeth showed as he tried to smile, and his lips stretched wide, making his mouth seem to thrust even farther forward from his face than it actually did.

"When will I be big enough to go out there, Miss Fellowes? To really go outside? Not just in dreams?"

"Soon," she said softly, feeling her heart break. "Soon."

Miss Fellowes let him take her hand. She loved the warm touch of the thick dry skin of his palm against hers. He tugged at her, drawing her inward, leading her through the three rooms that made up the whole of Stasis Section One—comfortable enough, yes, but an eternal prison for the ugly little boy all the seven (Was it seven? Who could be sure?) years of his life.

He led her to the one window, looking out onto a scrubby woodland section of the world of *is* (now hidden by night). There was a fence out there, and a dour glaring notice on a billboard, warning all and sundry to keep out on pain of this or that dire punishment.

Timmie pressed his nose against the window.

"Tell me what's out there again, Miss Fellowes."

"Better places. Nicer places," she said sadly.

As she had done so many times before over the past three years, she studied him covertly out of the corner of her eye, looking at his poor little imprisoned face outlined in profile against the window. His forehead retreated in a flat slope and his thick coarse hair lay down upon it in tufts that she had never been able to straighten. The back of his skull bulged weirdly, giving his head an overheavy appearance and seemingly making it sag and bend forward, forcing his whole body into a stoop. Already, stark bulging bony ridges were beginning to force the skin outward above his eyes. His wide mouth thrust forward more prominently than did his wide and flattened nose and he had no chin to speak of—only a jawbone that curved smoothly down and back. He was small for his years, almost dwarfish despite his already powerful build, and his stumpy legs were bowed. An angry red birthmark, looking for all the world like a jagged streak of lightning, stood out startlingly on his broad, strong-boned cheek.

He was a very ugly little boy and Edith Fellowes loved him more dearly than anything in the world.

She was standing with her own face behind his line of vision, so she allowed her lips the luxury of a tremor.

They wanted to kill him. That was what it amounted to. He was only a child, an unusually helpless one at that, and they were planning to send him to his death.

They would *not*. She would do anything to prevent it. Anything. Interfering with their plan would be a massive dereliction of duty, she knew, and she had never committed any act in her life that could be construed as going against her duty as she understood it, but that didn't matter now. She had a duty to *them*, yes, no question of that, but she had a duty to Timmie also, not to mention a duty to herself. And she had no doubt at all about which the highest of those three duties was, and which came second, and which was third.

She opened the suitcase.

She took out the overcoat, the woolen cap with the ear-flaps, and the rest.

Timmie turned and stared at her. His eyes were so very big, so brightly gleaming, so solemn.

"What are those things, Miss Fellowes?"

"Clothes," she said. "Clothes for wearing outside." She beckoned to him. "Come here, Timmie."

## [2]

She had actually been the third one that Hoskins had interviewed for the job, and the other two had been the preferred choices of the Personnel people. But Gerald Hoskins was a hands-on kind of chief executive who didn't necessarily accept the opinions of those to whom he had delegated authority without taking the trouble to check those opinions out for himself. There were people in the company who thought that that was his biggest fault as a manager. There were times when he agreed with them. All the same, he had insisted on interviewing all three of the women personally.

The first one came with a three-star rating from Sam Aickman, who was Stasis Technologies' Personnel chief. That in itself made Hoskins a little suspicious, because Aickman had a powerful bias in favor of hard-edge state-of-the-art sorts of people. Which was just the right thing if you happened to be looking for an expert in implosion-field containment, or someone who could deal with a swarm of unruly positrons on a first-name basis. But Hoskins wasn't convinced that one of Sam's high-tech types was exactly the right choice for this particular job.

Her name was Marianne Levien and she was a real tiger. Somewhere in her late thirties: sleek, lean, trim, glossy. Not actually beautiful—that wasn't the most precise word for her—but striking, definitely striking.

She had magnificent cheekbones and jet-black hair that was pulled back tight from her forehead and cool glittering eyes that didn't miss a thing. She was wearing an elegant business suit of deep rich brown with gold piping that she might have picked up in Paris or San Francisco the day before yesterday, and an oh-so-underplayed little cluster of pearl-tipped gold strands at her throat that didn't strike Hoskins as the sort of jewelry one usually wore to a job interview, especially one of this sort. She looked more like an aggressive youngish executive who had a slot on the board of directors as her ultimate target than like his notion of what a nurse ought to be.

But a nurse was what she was, fundamentally, even if that seemed a very modest designation for someone of her professional affiliations and accomplishments. Her résumé was a knockout. Doctorates in heuristic pedagogy and rehabilitative technology. Assistant to the head of Special Services at Houston General's childrens' clinic. Consultant to the Katzin Commission, the Federal task force on remedial education. Six years' experience in advanced artificial-intelligence interfacing for autistic kids. Software bibliography a mile long.

Just what Stasis Technologies, Ltd. needed for this job?

So Sam Aickman seemed to think, at any rate.

Hoskins said, "You understand, don't you, that we'll be asking you to give up all your outside projects, the Washington stuff, the Houston affiliation, any consulting work that might require travel. You'll basically be pinned down here on a full-time basis for a period of several years, dealing with a single highly specialized assignment."

She didn't flinch. "I understand that."

"I see that in the last eighteen months alone you've appeared at conferences in São Paulo, Winnipeg, Melbourne, San Diego, and Baltimore, and that you've had papers read on your behalf at five other scientific meetings that you weren't able to attend personally."

"That's correct."

"And yet you're quite sure that you'll be able to make the transition from the very active professional career outlined in your résumé to the essentially isolated kind of existence you'll need to adopt here?"

There was a cold, determined glint in her eyes. "Not only do I think I'll be completely capable of making the transition, I'm quite ready and eager to do so."

Something sounded just a little wrong about that to Hoskins.

He said, "Would you care to expand on that a bit? Perhaps you don't fully grasp how—ah—monastic we tend to be at Stasis Technologies, Ltd. And how demanding your own area of responsibility in particular is likely to be."

"I think I do grasp that, Dr. Hoskins."

"And yet you're ready and eager?"

"Perhaps I'm a trifle less eager to run around from Winnipeg to Melbourne to São Paulo than I used to be."

"A little touch of burnout, maybe, is that what you're saying, Dr. Levien?"

A shadow of a smile appeared on her lips, the first sign of any human warmth that Hoskins had seen her display since she had entered his office. But it was gone almost as quickly as it had appeared.

"You might call it that, Dr. Hoskins."

"Yes, but would you?"

She looked startled at his unexpected sally. But then she drew a deep breath and reconstructed her all but imperturbable poise with hardly any show of effort.

"Burnout might be too extreme a term for my current attitudinal orientation. Let me just say that I'm interested in repositioning my energy expenditures—which as you see have been quite diffusely manifested—so that they're allocated to a single concentration of output."

"Ah—yes. Exactly so."

Hoskins regarded her with a mixture of awe and horror. Her voice was a perfectly pitched contralto; her eyebrows were flawlessly symmetrical; she sat splendidly upright with the finest posture imaginable. She was extraordinary in every way. But she didn't seem real.

He said, after a little pause, "And what is it, exactly, that led you to apply for this job, other than the aspect of allowing you a single concentration of energy expenditure?"

"The nature of the experiment fascinates me."

"Ah. Tell me."

"As every first-rate author of children's literature knows, the world of the child is very different from the world of adults—an alien world, in fact, whose values and assumptions and realities are entirely other. As we grow older, most of us make the transition from that world to this one so completely that we forget the nature of the world we've left behind. Throughout my work with children I've attempted to enter into their minds and comprehend the other-worldly nature of them as profoundly as my limitations as an adult will enable me to do."

Hoskins said, trying to keep the surprise out of his voice, "You think children are alien beings?"

"In a metaphorical way, yes. Obviously not literally."

"Obviously." He scanned her résumé, frowning. "You've never been married?"

"No, never," she said coolly.

"And I assume you haven't gone in for single parenting, either?"

"It was an option I considered quite seriously some years ago. But my work has provided me with a sense of surrogate parenting that has been quite sufficient."

"Yes. I suppose that it has. —Now, you were saying a moment ago that you see the world of the child as a fundamentally alien place. How does that statement relate to my question about what led you to apply for this job?"

"If I can accept at face value the remarkable preliminary description of your experiment that I've been given, it would involve me in caring for a child who quite literally comes from an alien world. Not in space, but in time; nevertheless, the essence of the existential situation is equivalent. I'd welcome a chance to study such a child's fundamental differences from us, by way of obtaining some parallactic displacement that might provide additional insights for my own work."

Hoskins stared at her.

No, he thought. Not real at all. A cleverly made android of some sort. A robotic nursoid. Except they hadn't perfected robots of this level of quality yet—he was certain of that. So she had to be a flesh-and-blood human being. But she certainly didn't act like one.

He said, "That may not be so easy. There may be difficulties in communication. The child very likely will have a speech impediment, you know. As a matter of fact there's a good chance that it may be virtually incapable of speech at all."

"It?"

"He, she. We can't tell you which, just yet. You do realize that the child won't be arriving here for another three weeks, give or take a day or two, and until the moment it arrives we'll basically know nothing about its actual nature."

She seemed indifferent to that. "I'm aware of the risks. The child may be drastically handicapped vocally, physically, and perhaps intellectually."

"Yes, you may well have to deal with it the way you'd deal with a severely retarded child of our own era. We just don't know. We'll be handing you a complete unknown."

"I'm prepared to meet that challenge," she said. "Or any other. Challenge is what interests me, Dr. Hoskins."

He believed that. The conditional and even speculative nature of the job description had produced no reaction in her. She seemed ready to face anything and didn't seem concerned with the whys and wherefores.

It wasn't hard to see why Sam Aickman had been so impressed with her.

Hoskins was silent again for a moment, just long enough to give her an opening. Marianne Levien didn't hesitate to take advantage of it.

She reached into her attaché case and drew forth a hand-held computer, no bigger than a large coin. "I've brought with me," she said, "a program that I've been working on since the word came across on the computer network that you were open for applications for this position. It's a variation on some work I did with brain-damaged children seven years ago in Peru: six algorithms defining and modifying communications flow. Essentially they bypass the normal verbal channels of the mind and—"

"Thank you," Hoskins said smoothly, staring at the tiny device in her outstretched hand as though she were offering him a bomb. "But there are all sorts of legal complexities preventing me from looking at your material until you're actually an employee of Stasis Technologies,

Ltd. Once you're under contract, naturally, I'll be glad to discuss your prior research with you in detail, but until then—"

"Of course," she said. Color flooded her flawless cheeks. A tactical error, and she knew it: overeagerness, even pushiness. Hoskins watched her elaborately making her recovery. "I quite see the situation. It was foolish of me to try to jump past the formalities like that. But I hope you can understand, Dr. Hoskins, that despite this very carefully burnished façade of mine that you see I'm basically a researcher, with all the enthusiasm of a brand-new graduate student setting out to uncover the secrets of the universe, and sometimes despite all my knowledge of what's feasible and appropriate I tend to sidestep the customary protocols out of sheer feverish desire to get to the heart of—"

Hoskins smiled. Hoskins nodded. Hoskins said, "Of course, Dr. Levien. It's no sin to err on the side of enthusiasm. —And this has been a very valuable conversation. We'll be in touch with you just as soon as we've made our decision."

She gave him an odd look, as though surprised he wasn't hiring her on the spot. She had the good sense not to say anything else except "Thank you very much" and "Goodbye," though.

At the door of his office she paused, turned, flashed one final high-voltage smile. Then she was gone, leaving an incandescent image behind on the retina of Hoskins' mind.

Whew, Hoskins thought.

He pulled out a handkerchief and mopped his forehead.

[3]

The second candidate was different from Marianne Levien in almost every way. She was twenty years older, for one thing; for another, there was nothing in the least elegant, cool, intimidating, incandescent, or androidal about her. Dorothy Newcombe was her name. She was plump, matronly, almost overabundant; she wore no jewelry and her clothing was simple, even dowdy; her demeanor was mild and her face was pleasantly jolly.

A golden aura of maternal warmth seemed to surround her. She looked like any child's ideal fantasy grandmother. She seemed so simple and easy-going that it was hard to believe that she had the prerequisite background in pediatrics, physiology, and clinical chemistry. But it was all there on her résumé, and one other surprising specialty besides—a degree in anthropological medicine. For all the wonders of twenty-first-century civilization, there still were primitive regions here and there on the globe, and Dorothy Newcombe had worked in six or seven of them, in various parts of the world—Africa, South America, Polynesia, Southeast Asia. No wonder she had Sam Aickman's seal of approval. A woman who could have served as a model for a statue of the goddess of motherly love, and who was experienced besides in the handling of children in backward societies—

She seemed exactly right in every way. After the oppressive hyper-glossy perfection of the too-awesome Marianne Levien, Hoskins felt so much at ease in this woman's presence that he had to fight back a strong impulse to offer her the position right away, without even bothering to interview her. It wouldn't have been the first time that he had allowed himself the luxury of giving way to a spontaneous feeling.

But he managed to master it.

And then, to his astonishment and dismay, Dorothy Newcombe managed to disqualify herself for the job before the interview had lasted five minutes.

Everything had gone beautifully up to the fatal point. She was warm and personable. She loved children, of course: she had had three of her own, and even before that, as the eldest child in a large family with an ailing mother, she had been involved in child-rearing from an early age, caring for her many brothers and sisters as far back as she could remember. And she had the right professional background. She came with the highest recommendations from the hospitals and clinics where she had worked; she had stood up under the strangest and most taxing conditions of remote tribal areas without difficulty; she enjoyed working with disadvantaged children of all sorts and was looking forward with the greatest excitement to tackling the unique problems that the Stasis Technologies project was certain to involve.

But then the conversation came around to the subject of why she would be willing to leave her present post—an important and apparently highly rewarding position as head of nursing at a child-care center of one of the Southern states—for the sake of immuring herself in the secretive and closely guarded headquarters of Stasis Technologies. And she said, "I know that I'll be giving up a great deal to come here. Still, I'll be gaining a great deal, too. Not only the chance to do work of the kind I like best in an area that nobody has ever worked in before. But also it'll give me a chance to get that damned nuisance Bruce Mannheim out of my hair at last."

Hoskins felt a chill run through him.

"Bruce Mannheim? You mean the 'children in crisis' advocate?"

"Is there some other one?"

He drew his breath in deeply and held it. Mannheim! That loudmouth! That troublemaker! How on earth had Dorothy Newcombe gotten herself mixed up with him? This was completely unexpected and not at all welcome.

After a moment he said carefully, "Are you saying that there's sort of a problem between you and Bruce Mannheim, then?"

She laughed. "A problem? I guess you could call it that. He's suing my hospital. Suing me, I suppose I'd have to say. I'm one of the named defendants, actually. It's been a tremendous distraction for us for the past six months."

A sickly sensation churned in the pit of Hoskins' stomach. He fumbled with the papers on his desk and struggled to regain his equilibrium.

"There's nothing about this in your Personnel report."

"No one asked me. Obviously I wasn't trying to conceal anything or I wouldn't have mentioned it now. But the subject just never came up."

"Well, I'm asking you now, Ms. Newcombe. What's this all about?"

"You know what kind of professional agitator Mannheim is? You know that he takes the most far-fetched positions imaginable by way of showing everybody how concerned he is for the welfare of children?"

It didn't seem wise to get drawn into spouting opinions. Not where Bruce Mannheim was concerned. Warily Hoskins said, "I know there are people who think of him that way."

"You phrase that in such a diplomatic way, Dr. Hoskins. Do you think he's got your office bugged?"

"Hardly. But I don't necessarily share your obvious distaste for Mannheim and his ideas. As a matter of fact, I don't really have much of a position about him. I haven't been paying a lot of attention to the issues he's been raising." That was a flat lie, and Hoskins felt uncomfortable about it. One of the earliest planning papers dealing with the current project had said: *Take every step to make sure that we keep pests like Bruce Mannheim from landing on our backs.* But Hoskins was interviewing her, not the other way around. He didn't feel obliged to tell her anything more than seemed appropriate.

He leaned forward. "All I know, actually, is that he's a very vocal crusader with a lot of articulate ideas about how children in public custody ought to be raised. Whether his ideas are right or not, I'm not really qualified to say. About this lawsuit, Ms. Newcombe—"

"We've taken some small children off the streets. Most of them are third-generation drug users, even fourth-generation, congenital addicts. It's the saddest thing you can imagine, children who are *born* addicted. —I assume you're aware of the generally accepted theory that drug addiction, like most physiological addictions, very often arises from some genetic predisposition in that direction?"

"Of course."

"Well, we've been conducting genetic studies on these children, and on their parents and grandparents—when we're able to find them. We're trying to locate and isolate the drug-positive gene, if there is such a thing, in the hope that some day we can get rid of it."

"Sounds like a good idea to me," Hoskins said.

"It does to everyone except Bruce Mannheim, apparently. The way he's come down on us, you'd think we're performing actual gene surgery on those kids, not simply doing a little prowling around in their chromosomes to find out what's there. Purely investigative work, no genetic modification whatsoever. But he's slapped us with sixteen different injunctions tying our hands in every imaginable way. It's enough to make you cry. We've tried to explain, but he won't pay attention. He distorts our own affidavits and uses them as the basis for his next lawsuit. And you know how the courts are when it comes to accusations that children are being used as experimental subjects."

"I'm afraid I do," said Hoskins dolefully. "And so your hospital is spending its energies and resources on legal defense instead of—"

"Not just the hospital. He's named specific individuals. I'm one of them. One of nine researchers who he's charged with child abuse— literal child abuse—as a result of his so-called studies of our work up to this point." There was obvious bitterness in her voice, but a touch of amusement, too. Her eyes flashed a bright twinkle. She laughed until her heavy breasts shook. "Can you imagine it? Child abuse? *Me?*"

Hoskins shook his head sympathetically. "It does seem incredible."

But his heart was sinking. He still had no doubt that this woman was ideally qualified for the job. But how could he hire someone who was already in trouble with the dreaded Bruce Mannheim? There was going to be controversy enough over this project as it was. No doubt Mannheim would be poking his nose into what they were doing before very long in any case, no matter what precautions they took. All the same, to add Dorothy Newcombe to the roster would be asking for the worst sort of trouble. He could just imagine the press conference Mannheim would call. Letting it be known that Stasis Technologies had chosen to hire a woman who was currently defending herself against the accusation of child abuse at another scientific facility—and Mannheim would make *accusation* sound like *indictment*—to serve as nurse and guardian of the unfortunate child who was the pathetic victim of this unprecedented new form of kidnapping—

No. No. He couldn't possibly take her on.

Somehow he forced himself to go through another five minutes of asking questions. On the surface, everything remained amiable and pleasant. But it was an empty exercise, and Hoskins knew that Dorothy Newcombe knew it. When she left, he thanked her for her frankness and expressed his appreciation of her high qualifications and offered her the usual assurances that he'd be in touch soon, and she smiled and told him how pleased she had been by their conversation—and he had no doubt at all that she realized that she wasn't going to get the job.

As soon as she was gone, he phoned Sam Aickman and said, "For God's sake, Sam, why didn't you tell me that Dorothy Newcombe is currently on the receiving end of some kind of cockeyed lawsuit of Bruce Mannheim's?"

Aickman's face on the screen registered amazement verging on shock.

"She *is?*"

"So she told me just now. A child-abuse accusation stemming from the work she's been doing."

"Really. Really," Aickman said, crestfallen. He looked more abashed than amazed now. "Hell, Jerry, I had no idea at all that she was tangled up with that colossal pain in the neck. And we questioned her very thoroughly; let me tell you. —Not thoroughly enough, I guess."

"That's all we'd need, hiring somebody for this job who's *already* on Mannheim's hit-list."

"She's terrific, though, isn't she? Absolutely the most motherly human being I ever—"

"Yes. Absolutely. And comes with a money-back guarantee that we'll have Mannheim's legal vultures sinking their claws into us as soon as he finds out she's here. Or don't you agree, Sam?"

"Looks like you're going to go for Marianne Levien, then, is that it?"

"I'm not through interviewing yet," Hoskins said. "But Levien looks pretty good."

"Yes, doesn't she," said Aickman, with a grin.

[4]

Edith Fellowes had no way of knowing that she was merely the Number Three candidate for the job, but it wouldn't have surprised her to learn it. She was accustomed to being underestimated. There was nothing flashy about her, nothing very dramatic, nothing that registered immediate top-rank qualifications in anything. She was neither stunningly beautiful nor fascinatingly ugly, neither intensely passionate nor interestingly aloof, neither daringly insightful nor painstakingly brilliant. All through her life people had tended to take her for granted. But she was a stable, firmly balanced woman who knew her own worth perfectly well, and, by and large, she had had a satisfying, fulfilling existence—by and large.

The campus-like headquarters of Stasis Technologies, Ltd. was a place of mystery to her. Ordinary-looking gray buildings, bare and plain, rose from pleasant green lawns studded by occasional small trees. It was a research center very much like a thousand others. But within these buildings, Edith Fellowes knew, strange things were going on—things beyond her understanding, things virtually beyond her powers of belief. The idea that she might actually be working in one of those buildings soon filled her with wonder.

Like most people, she had only the haziest notion of what the company was or the way it had accomplished the remarkable things it had done. She had heard, of course, about the baby dinosaur that they had managed to bring out of the past. That had seemed pretty miraculous to her, once she overcame her initial reaction of skepticism. But the explanations on television of *how* Stasis Technologies had reached into the past to bring the extinct reptile into the twenty-first century had been incomprehensible to her. And then the expedition to the moons of Jupiter had pushed Stasis and its dinosaur into the back pages of the newspapers, and she had forgotten all about them both.

The dinosaur had been just another nine days' wonder, one of many in what was turning out to be a century of wonders.

But now, apparently, Stasis was planning to bring a *child* out of the past, a human child, a prehistoric human child. They needed someone to care for that child.

She could do that.

She wanted to do that.

She might just be able to do that better than anyone else. Certainly she would be able to do it very, very well.

They had said the job was going to be challenging, unusual, extremely difficult. She wasn't troubled by any of that. It was the unchallenging, ordinary, simple jobs that she had always preferred to avoid.

They had advertised for a woman with a background in physiology, some knowledge of clinical chemistry, and a love for children. Edith Fellowes qualified on all three counts.

The love for children had been built in from the start—what normal person, she wondered, *didn't* have a love for children? Especially a woman?

The knowledge of physiology had come as part of her basic nursing training. The clinical chemistry had been something of an afterthought—it had seemed a good idea, if she was going to work with sickly children, many of them premature or otherwise starting life under some handicap—to have the best possible understanding of how their troubled little bodies could be made to function more effectively.

Challenging, difficult job involving an unusual child—yes, it was her kind of thing. The salary they were offering was pretty phenomenal, too, enough to catch her attention even though the pursuit of money had never been much of a factor in her scheme of living. And she was ready for a new challenge. The all-too-familiar routines of children's-hospital life were beginning to pall on her now, even to make her a little resentful. That was a terrible thing, she thought, to resent your own work, particularly work like hers. Maybe she needed a change.

To care for a *prehistoric* child—

Yes. Yes.

"Dr. Hoskins will see you now," the receptionist said.

An electronically actuated door rolled silently open. Miss Fellowes stepped forward into a surprisingly unostentatious-looking office that contained an ordinary sort of desk, an ordinary data-screen, and an ordinary-looking man of about fifty, with thinning sandy-colored hair, the beginnings of jowls, and a curiously down-curved mouth that looked more sullen, perhaps, than it really should.

The nameplate on the desk said:

### GERALD A. HOSKINS, Ph.D.
CHIEF EXECUTIVE OFFICER

Miss Fellowes was more amused than impressed by that. Was the company really so large that the C.E.O. had to remind people of the identity of the man in charge by putting a nameplate in front of himself in his own office? And why did he think it was necessary to brag of having a Ph.D.? Didn't everybody here have an advanced degree or two? Was this his way of announcing that he wasn't simply a mere corporate executive, that he was really a scientist himself? She would have assumed that the head of a highly specialized company like Stasis Technologies, Ltd. would be a scientist, without having to have it jammed in her face this way.

But that was all right. It was possible for a man to have worse foibles than a little self-importance.

Hoskins had a sheaf of printouts in front of him. Her résumé, she supposed, and the report on her preliminary interview, and things like that. He looked from the printouts to her, and back to the printouts, and to her again. His appraisal was frank and a little too direct. Miss Fellowes automatically stiffened. She felt her cheeks coloring and a muscle twitched briefly in her cheek.

*He thinks my eyebrows are too heavy and my nose is a little off center,* she told herself.

And then she told herself crisply that she was being ridiculous, that this man had no more interest in evaluating the angle of her nose and the fullness of her eyebrows than he did in knowing what brand of shoes she might be wearing. But it was surprising and a little disturbing to be looked at so intently by a man at all. A nurse in uniform was generally invisible, so far as most men's interest went. She wasn't in uniform now, but over the years she had developed ways of making herself look invisible to men even in her street clothes, and, she supposed, she had been quite successful at that. Being studied this way now was something she found more unsettling than it should have been.

He said, "Your record is quite an outstanding one, Miss Fellowes."

She smiled but said nothing. What could she possibly say? Agree with him? Disagree?

"And you come with some very high recommendations from your superiors. They all praise you in almost identical words, do you know that? Unswerving dedication to your work—deep devotion to duty—great resourcefulness in moments of crisis—superb technical skills—"

"I'm a hard worker, Dr. Hoskins, and I generally know what I'm doing. I think those are just fancy ways of saying those two basic things."

"I suppose." His eyes fixed on hers and she felt, suddenly, the strength of the man, the singlemindedness of him, the dogged determination to carry his tasks through to completion. Those could be fine traits in an administrator. They could also lead him to make life maddening for those who worked with him. Time would tell, she thought. She met his gaze evenly and steadily. He said, finally, "I don't see any serious need to question you about your professional background. That's been very carefully gone over in your previous interviews and you came through with flying colors. I've got only two points to take up with you, really."

She waited.

"One," he said, "I need to know whether you've ever been involved in any matters that might be considered, well, politically sensitive. Politically controversial."

"I'm not political at all, Dr. Hoskins. I vote—when there's someone I think is worth voting for, which isn't very often. But I don't sign petitions and I don't march in demonstrations, if that's what you're asking."

"Not exactly. I'm talking about professional controversies rather than political ones, I guess. Issues having to do with the way children should or should not be treated."

"I only know one way children should be treated, which is to do your absolute best to meet the child's needs as you understand them. If that sounds simplistic, I'm sorry, but—"

He smiled. "That's not precisely what I mean, either. What I mean is—" He paused and moistened his lips. "The Bruce Mannheim sort of thing is what I mean. Heated debate over the methods by which certain children are handled in public institutions. Do you follow what I'm saying, Miss Fellowes?"

"I've been dealing mainly with weak or handicapped children, Dr. Hoskins. What I attempt to do is keep them alive and help them build up their strength. There isn't much to have a debate over in matters like that, is there?"

"So you've never had any kind of professional encounters with so-called child advocates of the Bruce Mannheim sort?"

"Never. I've read a little about Mr. Mannheim in the papers, I guess. But I haven't ever had any contact with him or anyone like him. I wouldn't know him if I bumped into him in the street. And I don't have any particular opinions about his ideas, pro or con."

Hoskins looked relieved.

He said, "I don't mean to imply that I'm opposed to Bruce Mannheim or the positions he represents, you understand. But it would be a serious complicating factor here if our work became the subject of hostile publicity."

"Of course. That would be the last thing I'd want also."

"All right, then. We can move along. My other question has to do with the nature of the commitment to your work that we'll be demanding of you here. —Miss Fellowes, do you think you can love a difficult, strange, perhaps unruly and even highly disagreeable child?"

"Love? Not merely care for?"

"Love. To stand in loco parentis. To be its mother, more or less, Miss Fellowes. And rather more than less. This will be the most lonely child in the history of the world. It won't just need a nurse, it'll need a mother. Are you prepared to take on such a burden? Are you *willing* to take on such a burden?"

He was staring at her again, as though trying to stare through her. Once again she met the intensity of his gaze with unwavering strength.

"You say he'll be difficult and strange and— What was the word? —highly disagreeable. In what way, disagreeable?"

"We're talking about a prehistoric child. You know that. He—or she, we don't know which yet—may very well be savage in a way that goes beyond the most savage tribe on Earth today. This child's behavior may be more like that of an animal than a child. A ferocious animal, perhaps. That's what I mean by difficult, Miss Fellowes."

"I haven't only worked with premature infants, Dr. Hoskins. I've had experience with emotionally disturbed children. I've dealt with some pretty tough little customers."

"Not this tough, perhaps."

"We'll see, won't we?"

"Savage, very likely, and miserable and lonely, and furious. A stranger and afraid, in a world it never made. Ripped from everything that was familiar to it and put down in circumstances of almost complete isolation—a true Displaced Person. Do you know that term, 'Displaced Person,' Miss Fellowes? It goes back to the middle of the last century, to the time of the Second World War, when uprooted people were wandering all over the face of Europe, and—"

"The world is at peace now, Dr. Hoskins."

"Of course it is. But this child won't feel much peace. It'll be suffering from the total disruption of its life, a genuine Displaced Person of the most poignant kind. A very small one, at that."

"How small?"

"At present we can bring no more than forty kilograms of mass out of the past with each scoop. That includes not only the living subject but the surrounding inanimate insulation zone. So we're talking about a little child, a very little child."

"An infant, is that it?"

"We can't be sure. We hope to get a child of six or seven years. But it might be considerably younger."

"You don't know? You're just going to make a blind grab?"

Hoskins looked displeased. "Let's talk about love, Miss Fellowes. Loving this child. I guarantee you that it won't be easy. You really do love children, don't you? I don't mean in any trivial sense. And I'm not talking now about proper performance of professional duties. I want you to dig down and examine the assumptions of the word, what love really means, what motherhood really means, what the *unconditional* love that is motherhood really means."

"I think I know what that love is like."

"Your bio data says that you were once married, but that you've lived alone for many years."

She could feel her face blazing. "I was married once, yes. For a short while, a long time ago."

"There were no children."

"The marriage broke up," she said, "mainly because I turned out to be unable to have a child."

"I see," said Hoskins, looking uncomfortable.

"Of course, there were all sorts of twenty-first-century ways around the problem—ex utero fetal chambers, implantations, surrogate mothers, and so forth. But my husband wasn't able to come to terms with anything short of the ancient traditional method of sharing genes. It had to be *our* child all the way, his and mine. And I had to carry the child for the right and proper nine months. But I couldn't do that, and he couldn't bring himself to accept any of the alternatives, and so we—came apart."

"I'm sorry. —And you never married again."

She kept her voice steady, unemotional. "The first try was painful enough. I could never be sure that I wouldn't get hurt even worse a second time, and I wasn't able to let myself take the risk. But that doesn't mean I don't know how to love children, Dr. Hoskins. Surely it isn't necessary for me to point out that my choice of profession very likely has something to do with the great emptiness that my marriage created in my—in my soul, if you will. And so instead of loving just one or two children I've loved dozens. Hundreds. As though they were my own."

"Not all of them very nice children."

"Not all of them nice, no."

"Not just nice sweet children with cute little button-noses and gurgly ways? You've taken them as they come, pretty or ugly, gentle or wild? Unconditionally?"

"Unconditionally," Miss Fellowes said. "Children are children, Dr. Hoskins. The ones that aren't pretty and nice are just the ones who may happen to need help most. And the way you begin to help a child is by loving it."

Hoskins was silent, thinking for a moment. She felt a sense of letdown building up in her. She had come in here prepared to talk about her technical background, her research in electrolyte imbalances, in neuroreceptors, in physiotherapy. But he hadn't asked her anything about that. He had concentrated entirely on this business of whether she could love some unfortunate wild child—whether she could love *any* child, maybe—as though that were a real issue. And on the even less relevant matter of whether she had ever done anything that might stir up some sort of political agitation. Obviously he wasn't very interested in her actual qualifications. Obviously he had someone else in mind for the job and was going to offer her some bland, polite dismissal as soon as he had figured out a tactful way to do it.

At length he said, "Well, how soon can you give notice at your present place of employment?"

She gaped at him, flustered.

"You mean you're taking me on? Right here and now?"

Hoskins smiled briefly, and for a moment his broad face had a certain absent-minded charm about it. "Why else would I want you to give notice?"

"Doesn't this have to go to some committee first?"

"Miss Fellowes, *I'm* the committee. The ultimate committee, the one that gives final approval. And I make quick decisions. I know what sort of person I'm looking for and you seem to be it. —Of course, I could be wrong."

"And if you are?"

"I can reverse myself just as quickly, believe me. This is a project that can't afford any errors. There's a life at stake, a human life, a child's life. For the sake of sheer scientific curiosity, we're going to do what some people surely will say is a monstrous thing to that child. I have no illusions about that. I don't for a moment believe that we're monsters here—no one here does—and I have no qualms or regrets about what we propose to do, and I believe that in the long run the child who is the subject of our experiment will only stand to benefit from it. But I'm quite aware that others will disagree radically with that position. Therefore we want that child to be as well cared for as possible during its stay in our era. If it becomes apparent that you're not capable of providing that care, you'll be replaced without hesitation, Miss Fellowes. I don't see any delicate way of phrasing that. We aren't sentimental here and we don't like to gamble on anything that's within our power to control, either. So the job is to be considered no more than tentatively yours, at this point. We're asking you to cut yourself loose from your entire present existence with no guarantee that we'll keep you on here past the first week, or possibly even the first day. Do you think you're willing to take the chance?"

"You certainly are blunt, Dr. Hoskins."

"I certainly am. Except when I'm not. Well, Miss Fellowes? What do you say?"

"I don't like to gamble, either," she said.

His face darkened. "Is that a refusal?"

"No, Dr. Hoskins, it's an acceptance. If I doubted for one moment that I was the wrong woman for the job, I wouldn't have come here in the first place. I can do it. I *will* do it. And you'll have no reason to regret your decision, you can be certain of that. —When do I start?"

"We're bringing the Stasis up to critical level right now. We expect to make the actual scoop two weeks from tonight, on the fifteenth, at half-past seven in the evening sharp. We'll want you here at the moment of arrival, ready to take over at once. You'll have until then to wind down your present outside-world activities. It *is* clear that you'll be living on these premises full-time, isn't it, Miss Fellowes? And by full-time I mean twenty-four hours a day, at least in the early phases. You did see that in the application specifications, didn't you?"

"Yes."

"Then we understand each other perfectly."

No, she thought. We don't understand each other at all. But that's not important. If there are problems, we'll work them out somehow. It's the child that's important. Everything else is secondary. Everything.

# INTERCHAPTER ONE

# *She Who Knows*

IT WAS THE MIDDLE of the day now and a sense of mounting crisis was affecting the whole encampment. The entire Hunting Society had returned from the plains, without having remained there long enough even to catch sight of game, let alone to do any hunting—and now its seven members sat in a morose huddle, fretting over the possibility of war and how it would affect them. The Goddess Women had unpacked the three holy bear-skulls and had set them up on the stone shelves above the shrine of the Goddess, and were crouching naked in front of them, anointed with bear fat and wolf blood and honey, chanting the special prayers that were supposed to bring wisdom in time of great peril. The Mothers had gathered all the small children under their wings as if they expected the Other Ones to attack at any minute, and the half-grown ones lurked at the edge of the circle, fearful and uncertain.

As for the older men, the wise and distinguished elders of the tribe, they had gone off by themselves to the little hill above the camp for a discussion of strategy. Silver Cloud was up there, and Mammoth Rider, and one-eyed humpbacked Fights Like A Lion, and fat, sluggish Stinking Musk Ox. On their decisions the fate of the tribe would rest.

When the Other Ones had moved into the tribe's hunting grounds in the western lands and it became clear that nothing the People did was going to make them leave, the elders had decided that the best thing to do was go east. "The Goddess has chosen to give the western lands to the Other Ones," Stinking Musk Ox opined. "But the cold lands in the east belong to us. The Goddess means for us to go there and live in peace." The others agreed. Whereupon the Goddess Women had cast the destiny-stones and had come up with a result that supported the opinion of the men.

So the People had migrated to this place. But now the Other Ones had turned up here too, apparently.

What do we do now? She Who Knows wondered.

We could go south to the warm lands, perhaps. But very likely the warm lands are full of Other Ones by now. Should we go up north where the terrible ice fields are, then? Surely the Other Ones are too tender to want to live in a place like that. But so are we, She Who Knows suspected. So are we.

She felt a great sadness. They had come a long way to this place. The strenuous march had left her weary, and she knew that Silver Cloud was tired also, and many of the others. It was time to rest now, and gather meat and nuts to store for the winter ahead, and replenish their strength. But it seemed that they would have to wander again, without any chance to rest, without a moment of peace. Why was that? Was there no place in this broad barren land where they would be allowed to pause for a time to catch their breath?

She Who Knows had no answers, not to that, not to anything, really. Despite the proud name she had given herself, She Who Knows was baffled by the problem of the eternally bothersome Other Ones, just as she was by the challenges and mysteries of her own existence.

She was the only member of the tribe who had no real place, no real function. Like most girls, she had grown up assuming that she would be a Mother, but she had waited too long to take a mate, preferring instead a free-spirited roving life, even going out to the hunting fields with the men sometimes. When in her twentieth year she finally did agree to take the warrior Dark Wind as her mate, a very late age for such a thing, nothing but dead babies came from her womb. And then she lost Dark Wind as well, to a black fever that carried him off in a single afternoon.

She still had much of her beauty then, but after Dark Wind died none of the unmated men of the tribe had wanted to have her—no matter how beautiful she might be. They knew that her womb was a place that killed babies, so what value could she have as a mate? And Dark Wind's early death argued that she was cursed by ill luck, besides. So she would remain forever alone, untouched by men, she who once had had so many lovers. She would never become one of the Mothers.

Nor could she join the Goddess Women, not now; it would be a mockery of the Goddess and all that she stood for that a sterile woman should serve Her, and in any case you had to begin learning the mysteries of the Goddess Women before the first blood came from your loins. It was absurd to have an aging woman of twenty-five who had borne and lost five babies in five years becoming a Goddess Woman.

So She Who Knows was neither a Mother nor a Goddess Woman, and that meant she was nothing at all. She did the ordinary things that any woman would do, scraping hides and cooking meals and caring for the sick and looking after children, but she had no mate and she belonged to no Society and that made her almost a stranger among her own people. The one hope for her was that Keeps The Past would die, and then she could become the tribe's chronicler. Keeps The Past was a woman like herself, not a Mother and not a priestess, and in all the tribe she was She Who Knows' closest friend. But although Keeps The Past was forty years old, indeed the oldest woman in the tribe, she was still vigorous and sleek. Whereas She Who Knows, eight years younger, was already turning into an old woman. She was starting to think that she was destined to shrivel and fade and die long before Keeps The Past yielded up her record-sticks and went to the Goddess.

It was a sorrowful sort of life. But She Who Knows took care to hide the sorrow that afflicted her from the others. Let them fear her; let them dislike her. She would not have them pitying her.

Now she stood by herself, as usual, looking around at the others in their groups. Each one was as helpless against the threat of the Other Ones as she was. But at least they were together, in the comfort of a group.

"There's the one we need!" Blazing Eye called out. "She Who Knows ought to come out and fight the Other Ones alongside us!"

"She Who Knows! She Who Knows!" the Hunting Society men called raucously.

They were mocking her, of course. Hadn't they always? Hadn't each of these men in his turn rejected her, in the days after Dark Wind's death, when she had hoped to find a new mate?

But she went over to them all the same, and stood grinning fiercely down at them where they huddled in a circle on the frosty ground.

"Yes," she said. "A good idea. I can fight as well as any of you."

She reached out, so quickly that she couldn't be stopped, and snatched up Blazing Eye's spear. He grunted in rage and jumped up to take it from her, but she deftly slid her hands along it to the hunting-grasp, and prodded the flint tip of its point against Blazing Eye's belly. He looked at her, goggle-eyed. It wasn't just the sacrilege of having a woman handle his spear that seemed to be bothering him; he appeared actually to think she was going to stick it into him.

"Give me that," he said in a thick voice.

"Look, she knows how to hold it, Blazing Eye," Tree Of Wolves said.

"Yes, and I know how to use it, too."

*"Give me that."*

She prodded him with it again. She thought Blazing Eye was going to have a fit. His face was bright red and sweat poured down his cheeks. Everyone was laughing. He made a swipe at the spear and she pulled it back out of his reach. Furious, he spat at her and made a demon-sign with his clasped hands. She Who Knows grinned.

"Make that sign again and I'll wash it away with your blood," she told him.

"Come *on*, She Who Knows," Blazing Eye said sourly. He was visibly struggling to control himself. "It isn't right for you to be touching that spear, and you know it. We're in enough danger as it is, without your committing evil acts."

"You invited me to go out and fight with the men," she said. "Well, if I do I'll need a spear, won't I? Yours is a perfectly good one. It will suit me very well. Make yourself another one, if you like."

The other men laughed again. But there was an odd edge on their laughter now.

She feinted with the spear and Blazing Eye, cursing, dodged it. He came forward stolidly as if to take it from her by sheer force. She warned him off with a serious thrust. Blazing Eye jumped back, looking angry and a little afraid.

It was hard for her to remember when she had last enjoyed herself so much. Blazing Eye was the strongest warrior of the tribe, and the most handsome man as well, with shoulders as wide as a mammoth's and wonderful dark eyes smoldering like coals under a splendid brow that jutted forth like a cliff. When they were young she had slept with him many times and she had hoped he would take her as his mate when Dark Wind died. But he had been the first to refuse her. Milky Fountain was the only mate he wanted, he had said. He liked the sort of woman who knew how to bear children, is what he had told her. And that had been the end of it between Blazing Eye and her.

"Here," She Who Knows said, relenting at last. She leaned forward and jammed the point of Blazing Eye's spear into the ground. Under the midday warmth, the last of the night's snowfall had disappeared and the earth was soft.

Blazing Eye snatched the spear up with a growl.

"I ought to kill you," he muttered, brandishing it in her face.

"Go ahead." She spread her arms wide and pushed her breasts outward. "Strike right here. Kill a woman, Blazing Eye. It'll be a fine achievement."

"It might bring us a little good luck," he said. But he lowered the weapon. "You ever touch my spear again, See Who Knows, and I'll tie you up on a hillside somewhere and leave you for a bear to eat. Do you understand that? Do you?"

"Save your threats for the Other Ones," she replied evenly. "They'll be harder to frighten than I am. And I'm not frightened at all."

"You saw an Other One right up close once, didn't you?" Broken Mountain asked her.

"Once, yes," She Who Knows said, frowning at the troubling memory of it.

"What did he smell like, when you were that close?" said Young Antelope. "He really stank, I'll bet."

She Who Knows nodded. "Like a dead hyena," she said. "Like something that had been rotting for a month and a half. And he was ugly. You can't imagine how ugly. His face was flat, like this, as if somebody had pushed it in." She gestured emphatically with her hands. "And his teeth were as small as a child's. He had ridiculous little ears and a tiny nose. And his arms, his legs—" She shuddered. "They were absurd and hideous. Like a spider's, they were. So long, so thin."

They were all looking at her in awe, even Blazing Spear. No one else in the tribe, not Silver Cloud himself, had ever come face-to-face with an Other One, so close that she could have reached out and touched him, the way she had. Some of them had seen Other Ones now and then at a great distance, just fleeting glimpses, back in the days when the tribe had lived in the western lands. But She Who Knows had stumbled right into one in the forest.

That had been years ago, when she was nineteen, still a wild girl then, who went her own way in all things. The men of the Hunting Society had forbidden her, at last, to accompany them on their patrols any more, and she had gone off by herself early one morning in a dark, scowling mood, wandering far from the tribe's encampment. At midday in a little glade of white-barked birch trees she had found a pretty rock-bound pool, and she had stripped off her robe of fur to bathe in its chilly blue water, and when she came out she was astounded to see an Other One, an unmistakable Other One, staring at her from a distance of no more than twenty paces.

He was tall—incredibly tall, as tall as a tree—and very thin, with narrow shoulders and a shallow chest, so that he looked more fragile than any woman, tall though he was. His face was the strangest face she had ever seen, with oddly delicate features like a child's, and extremely pale skin. His jaws looked so weak that she wondered how he could manage to bite all the way through his meat from one side of a piece to another, but his chin was unpleasantly heavy and deep, thrusting out below his flat, pushed-in face. His eyes were large and of a weird, washed-out watery-looking color, and his forehead went straight up, no brow ridges whatsoever.

All in all, she thought, he was astonishingly ugly, as ugly as a demon. But he didn't seem dangerous. He carried no weapon that she could see, and he appeared to be smiling at her. At least, she thought that was a smile, that way he had of baring those tiny teeth of his.

She was stark naked and in the full ripeness of her youthful beauty. She stood before him unashamed and the unexpected thought came to her that she wanted this man to beckon to her and call her to his side, and take her in his arms, and make love to her in whatever way it was that the Other Ones made love to their women. Ugly as he was, strange-looking as he was, she wanted him. Why was that? she wondered. And she answered herself that it was because he was different; he was new; he was *other*. She would give herself to him, yes. And then she would go home with him and live with him and become an Other One herself, because she was weary of the men of her own tribe and ready for something new. Yes. Yes.

What was there to be afraid of? The Other Ones were supposed to be terrifying demons, but this man didn't seem demonic at all, only strange of face and much too tall and thin. And he didn't appear menacing, particularly. Only different.

"My name is Falling River," she said—that was what she called herself in those days. "Who are you?"

The Other One man didn't reply. He made a sound deep in his throat that might have been laughter.

*Laughter?*

"Do you like me?" she said. "Everyone in the tribe thinks I'm beautiful. Do you?"

She ran her hands through her long thick hair, wet from her swim. She preened and stretched, letting him see the fullness of her breasts, the strength and solidity of her arms and thighs, the sturdiness of her neck. She took two or three steps toward him, smiling, crooning a little song of desire.

His eyes widened and he shook his head. He held his arm straight out at her with the palm facing her, and began making signs with his fingers, sorcery-signs, no doubt, demon-signs. He backed away from her.

"You aren't afraid of me, are you? I just want to play. Come here, Other One." She grinned at him. —"Listen, stop backing away like that! I won't hurt you. Can't you understand what I'm saying?" She was speaking very loudly, very clearly, putting plenty of space between one word and the next. He was still backing away. She put her hands beneath her breasts and pushed them outward in the universal gesture of offering.

He understood that, at least.

He made a low rumbling sound, like that of an animal at bay. His eyes had the bright sheen of fear in them. His lips drew back in an expression of what—dismay? Disgust?

Yes, disgust, she realized.

*I must look as ugly to him as he does to me.*

He was turning now, running from her, lurching helter-skelter through the birches.

"Wait!" she called. "Other One! Other One, come back! Don't run away like that, Other One!"

But he was gone. It was the first time in her life that a man had refused her, and she found the experience astonishing, unbelievable, almost shattering. Even though he was an Other One, even though she must have seemed alien and perhaps unattractive to him, had he really found her so repellent that he would growl and grimace and *run?*

Yes. Yes. He must have been only a boy, she told herself. Tall as he was, only a boy.

That night she returned to the tribe, resolved to take one of her own kind as a mate at last, and when Dark Wind asked her soon afterward to share his sleeping-rug she accepted without hesitation.

"Yes," she said to the men of the Hunting Society. "Yes, I know all too well what the Other Ones are like. And when we catch up with them I mean to be right there beside you, killing the loathsome beasts like the foul demons that they are."

"Look," Tree Of Wolves said, pointing. "The old men are coming down from the hill."

Indeed, there they came now, Silver Cloud leading the way, limping painfully and all too obviously trying to pretend that he wasn't, and the other three elders creaking along behind him. She Who Knows watched as they paraded into the camp, going straight to the place of the Goddess-shrine. For a long while Silver Cloud conferred with the three priestesses. There was much shaking of heads, then much nodding. And eventually Silver Cloud stepped forward, with the oldest of the priestesses at his side, to make an announcement.

The Summer Festival, he said, would be canceled this year—or postponed, at least. The Goddess had shown her displeasure by bringing a party of Other Ones uncomfortably close to their encampment, even in these eastern lands where no Other Ones were supposed to live. Plainly the People had done something improper; plainly this was not a good place for them to be. Therefore the People would leave here this day and would undertake a pilgrimage to the Place of Three Rivers, far behind them, where on their way east last year they had erected an elaborate shrine in honor of the Goddess. And at the Place of Three Rivers they would beseech the Goddess to explain their errors to them.

She Who Knows groaned. "But it'll take us weeks to get there! And it's in the wrong direction entirely! We'll be walking right back into the territory we've just left, where Other Ones are swarming everywhere!"

Silver Cloud gave her an icy glare. "The Goddess promised us this land, free of Other Ones. Now we have come into it and we find Other Ones already here. This is not as it should be. We need to ask Her guidance."

"Let's ask for it down south, then. At least it'll be warmer there, and we may find a decent place to camp, with no Other Ones around to bother us."

"You have our permission to go south, She Who Knows. But the rest of us will set out this afternoon toward the Place of Three Rivers."

"And the Other Ones?" she cried.

"The Other Ones will not dare to approach the shrine of the Goddess," said Silver Cloud. "But if you fear that they will, She Who Knows, why, then—go south! Go south, She Who Knows!"

She heard someone laughing. Blazing Eye, it was. Then the other men of the Hunting Society began to laugh, too, and a few of the Mothers joined in. Within moments they were all laughing and pointing at her.

She wished she still had Blazing Eye's spear in her hands. She would smite them all if she did, and nothing would stop the slaughter.

"Go south, She Who Knows!" they called to her. "Go south, go south, go south."

A curse came to her lips, but she forced it back. They meant it, she realized. If she spoke out angrily now, they might well drive her from the tribe. Ten years ago she would have welcomed that. But she was an old woman, now, past thirty. To go off by herself would be certain death.

She murmured a few angry words to herself, and turned away from Silver Cloud's steady stare.

Silver Cloud clapped his hands. "All right," he called. "Start packing up, everybody! We're breaking camp! We're getting out of here before it turns dark!"

# CHAPTER TWO

# Arriving

## [5]

F OR EDITH FELLOWES it was a tremendously busy few weeks.
The hardest part was the winding up of her work at the hospital. Giving only two weeks' notice was not only irregular, it was down-
right improper; but the administration was reasonably sympathetic
once Miss Fellowes let it be known that she was leaving with the
greatest reluctance, and only because she had been offered an opportunity to take part in an incredibly exciting new research project.

She mentioned the name of Stasis Technologies, Ltd.

"You're going to be taking care of the baby dinosaur?" they asked
her, and everybody chuckled.

"No, not the dinosaur," she said. "Something much closer to what
I know."

She didn't give any further details. Dr. Hoskins had forbidden her
to go into specifics with anyone. But it wasn't hard for those who
knew and worked with Edith Fellowes to guess that the project must
have something to do with children; and if her employers were the
people who had brought that famous baby dinosaur out of the Mesozoic, then surely they must be planning to do something along the
same lines now—such as bringing some prehistoric child out of a
remote period of time. Miss Fellowes neither confirmed or denied it.
But they knew. They all knew. Her leave of absence from the hospital
was granted, of course.

Still, she had to work virtually round the clock for a few days, tying
off loose ends, filing her final reports, preparing lists of things for her

successors, separating her own equipment and research materials from the hospital's. That part was strenuous but not otherwise burdensome. The really difficult part was saying goodbye to the children. They couldn't believe that she was leaving.

"You'll be back in a week or two, won't you, Miss Fellowes?" they asked her, crowding around. "You'll just be going on vacation, isn't that so? A little holiday? —Where are you going, Miss Fellowes?"

She had known some of these children since the day they were born. Now they were five, six, seven years old: outpatients, most of them, but some were permanent residents and she had worked with them year in, year out.

That was hard, breaking the news to them, very hard.

But she steeled herself to the task. Another child needed her now, an extraordinarily special child, a child whose predicament would be unique in the history of the universe. She knew that she had to go where she would be most needed.

She closed up her small apartment on the south side of town, selecting the few things she would want to take with her to her new home, storing away the rest. That was done quickly enough. She had no houseplants to worry about, no cats, no pets of any kind. Her work had been the only thing that really mattered: the children, always the children, no need for plants or pets.

But in her prudent way she arranged to maintain her lease for an indefinite period of time. She was taking very seriously Gerald Hoskins' warning that she might be let go at any moment. Or might want to resign, for that matter: Miss Fellowes knew she should allow for the possibility that the operation at Stasis Technologies would be uncongenial to her, that her role in the project would be unsatisfying, that she might discover very swiftly that it had been a gigantic mistake to have taken the job. She hadn't burned her bridges, not at all: the hospital would be waiting for her return, the children, her apartment.

During those final two weeks, busy as she was, she made several trips across town to the headquarters of Stasis Technologies to help prepare for the arrival of the child from the past. They had given her a procurement staff of three, two young men and a woman, and she provided them with an extensive list of things she would need—medicines, nutritional supplements, even an incubator.

"An incubator?" Hoskins asked.

"An incubator," she said.

"We're not planning to bring back a premature child, Miss Fellowes."

"You don't know *what* you're bringing back, Dr. Hoskins. You told me so yourself, in just about that many words. You may be bringing a sick child; you may be bringing a weak one; you may be bringing a child who'll fall ill the moment it starts to get modern-day microbes into its system. I want an incubator, at least on a standby basis."

"An incubator. All right."

"And a sterile chamber big enough to contain an active and healthy child, if it turns out that it's too big to live in an incubator."

"Miss Fellowes, be reasonable, please. Our budget is—"

"A sterile chamber. Until we know that it's safe to let that child be contaminated by our air."

"Contamination is unavoidable, I'm afraid. It'll be breathing our microbe-ridden air from the moment it arrives. There's no way we can conduct the Stasis under the germ-free conditions you seem to want. No way, Miss Fellowes."

"I want there to be a way."

Hoskins gave her what she had already come to think of as his patented no-nonsense glare. "This is one that I'm going to win, Miss Fellowes. I appreciate your desire to protect the child from all imaginable risks. But you have no understanding of the physical layout of our equipment, and you've simply got to accept the fact that we can't deliver the child instantly into a perfectly pure isolation chamber. We *can't*."

"And if the child sickens and dies?"

"Our dinosaur is still in fine health."

"There's no reason to believe that reptiles, prehistoric or otherwise, would be subject to infection by the microorganisms that carry the diseases humans contract. But this is a human being you'll be bringing here, Dr. Hoskins, not a little dinosaur. A member of our own species."

"I appreciate that fact, Miss Fellowes."

"And therefore I ask you to—"

"And I tell you the answer is no. Some risks have to be shouldered here, and microbial infection is one of them. We'll be ready with all possible medical assistance if a problem develops. But we're not going to try to create a miraculous magical 100% safe environment. We're *not*." Then Hoskins' tone softened. —"Miss Fellowes, just let me say this much. I've got a child myself, a little boy, not even old enough for kindergarten yet. Yes, at my age, and he's the most wonderful thing that ever happened in my life, bar none. I want you to know, Miss Fellowes, that I'm as concerned about the safety of the child that'll be arriving here next week as I would be for my own son Jerry's. And as confident that all will go well as though my own son were involved in the experiment."

Miss Fellowes wasn't sure that the logic of his argument was especially sound. But it was clear enough to her that he wasn't going to be shaken on this point, and that she had no leverage with him short of resigning. The possibility of resignation was something that she would hold in reserve, but it was pointless to threaten it now. It was the only weapon she had. She had to save it for the right moment, and this didn't seem to be it.

Hoskins was equally adamant about letting her have an advance look at the area where the child would be housed. "That's the Stasis zone," he said, "and we're running a non-stop countdown in there. Nobody can go in there while that's going on. Nobody. Not you, not me, not the President of the United States. And we can't interrupt the countdown for the sake of letting you have a sight-seeing tour."

"But if the accommodations are inadequate—"

"The accommodations are adequate, Miss Fellowes. More than adequate. Trust me."

"I'd still prefer—"

"Yes. Trust me."

Despicable words. Yet somehow she *did* trust him, more or less.

She still wasn't sure what kind of scientist Hoskins might be, or how good, despite that vague, boastful PH.D. on his nameplate. But one thing was certain. He was a tough administrator. He hadn't come to be the head man of Stasis Technologies, Ltd. by being a pushover.

### [6]

At precisely five in the afternoon on the fifteenth of the month, Miss Fellowes' telephone rang. It was Phil Bryce, one of Hoskins' staffers.

"The countdown's in its final three hours, Miss Fellowes, and everything's right on target. We'll be sending a car to pick you up at seven o'clock sharp."

"I can get over there on my own, thank you."

"Dr. Hoskins has instructed us to send a car to pick you up. It'll be there at seven."

Miss Fellowes sighed. She could argue, but what was the use?

Let Hoskins win the small victories, she decided. Save your ammunition for the big battles that surely lay ahead.

## [7]

A light rain was falling. The evening sky was gray and dreary, and the Stasis Technologies buildings looked uglier than ever, big barn-like structures without the slightest scrap of elegance or grace.

Everything seemed makeshift and hasty. There was a harsh, engineery feel about the place, cheerless and inhumane. She had spent her whole working life in institutional surroundings, but these buildings made even the most somber hospital look like the abode of joy and laughter. And the badged employees, going rigidly about their business, the closed-in faces, the hushed tones, the air of almost military urgency—

What am I doing here? she asked herself. How did I ever get drawn into all of this?

"This way, please, Miss Fellowes," Bryce said.

People began to nod and beckon to her. No announcements of her identity seemed necessary. One after another, men and women seemed to know her and to know her function. Of course, she was wearing a badge herself now, but no one appeared to look at that. They all just knew. *This is the nurse for the child,* they seemed to be saying. She found herself all but placed on skids as she was moved swiftly inward, down corridors that had a tacky, improvised look, into an area of the research center that she had never entered before.

They descended clanging metallic stairs, emerged into a windowless tunnel of some sort lit by glaring fluorescent lights, walked for what seemed like forever underground until coming to a steel doorway with the rippling moire patterns of a security shield dancing up and down over its painted black surface.

"Put your badge to the shield," Bryce said.

"Really, is all this necess—"

"Please, Miss Fellowes. Please."

The doorway yielded. More stairs confronted them. Up and up and up, spiraling around the walls of an immense barrel-shaped vault, down a hallway, through another door—did they really *need* all this?

At last she found herself stepping out onto a balcony that looked down into a large pit. Across from her, down below, was a bewildering array of instruments set into a curving matrix that looked like a cross between the control panel of a spaceship and the working face of a giant computer—or, perhaps, just a movie set for some fantastic and nonsensical "scientific" epic. Technicians, looking rumpled and wild-eyed, were racing around down there in an absurdly theatrical way, making frantic hand signals to each other. People were moving thick black cables from one outlet to another, studying them and shaking their heads, moving them back to their original positions. Lights were flashing, numbers were ticking downward on huge screens.

Dr. Hoskins was on the balcony not far away, but he only looked at her distantly and murmured, "Miss Fellowes." He seemed abstracted, preoccupied, hardly present at all.

He didn't even suggest that she take a seat, though there were four or five rows of folding chairs set up near the railing overlooking the frenzied scene below. She found one herself and drew it up to the edge for a better view.

Suddenly lights came on in the pit, illuminating the area just beneath where she sat, which had been completely dark. She looked down and saw partitions that seemed to make up an unceilinged apartment, a giant dollhouse into the rooms of which it was possible to look from above.

She could see what seemed to be a microwave cooker and a freezer-space unit in one room and a washroom arrangement off another. There was a small cubicle full of medical equipment of a kind that was very familiar to her—indeed, it appeared to contain all the things she had asked Hoskins' staffers to provide. Including the incubator.

And surely the object she made out in another room could only be part of a bed, a small bed.

Men and women wearing company badges were filing into the room, now, taking the seats alongside her. Miss Fellowes recognized a few of them as Stasis executives to whom she had been introduced on her earlier visits here, though she was unable to remember a single name. Others were completely unknown to her. They all nodded and smiled in her direction as if she had been working here for years.

Then she saw someone whose name *and* face were familiar to her: a thin, fine-looking man of fifty-five or thereabouts, with a small, fastidiously clipped gray mustache and keen eyes that seemed to busy themselves with everything.

Candide Deveney! The science correspondent for International Telenews!

Miss Fellowes wasn't much of a screen-watcher. An hour or two a week, sometimes even less; there were weeks when she didn't even remember to turn the thing on. Books were sufficient entertainment for her, and for long stretches of time her work itself was so fascinating that even books seemed unnecessary. But Candide Deveney was one screen person she did know. There were times, every once in a while, when some event of immense interest came along that she simply *had* to see, not merely read about—the landing on Mars, for instance, or the public unveiling of the baby dinosaur, or the spectacular nuclear destruction, high above the Eastern Hemisphere, of that tiny but deadly asteroid that had been on a collision course with Earth the year before last. Candide Deveney had been the on-screen face during those events. He was notoriously at the scene of every major scientific breakthrough. That he was here tonight impressed Miss Fellowes despite herself. She felt her heart beating just a little faster at the realization that this must indeed be going to be something of high importance if it was worthy of his being present here, and that she was almost close enough to reach out and touch Candide Deveney himself as the great moment approached.

Then she scowled at her own foolishness. Deveney was only a reporter, after all. Why should she be so awed by him, merely because she had seen him on television?

What was a more fitting reason for awe, she thought, was that they were going to reach into the remoteness of time and bring a little human being forth into the twenty-first century. And *she* was going to be a vital part of that enterprise. She—not Candide Deveney. If anything, Candide Deveney ought to feel impressed at being in the same room with Edith Fellowes, not the other way around.

Hoskins had gone over to greet Deveney, and seemed to be explaining the project to him. Miss Fellowes inclined her head to listen.

Deveney was saying, "I've been thinking about what you people have been doing here ever since my last visit here, the day the dinosaur came. —There's one thing in particular I've been wrestling with, and it's this matter of selectivity."

"Go on," Hoskins said.

"You can reach out only so far; that seems sensible. Things get dimmer the farther you go. It takes more energy, and ultimately you run up against absolute limits of energy—I don't have any problem comprehending that. —But then, apparently you can reach out only so *near*, also. That's what I find the puzzling part. And not only me. I mean, if you can go out and grab something from 100 million years ago, you ought to be able to bring something back from last Tuesday with a whole lot less effort. And yet you tell me you can't reach last Tuesday at all, or anything else that's at all close to us in time. Why is that?"

Hoskins said, "I can make it seem less paradoxical, Deveney, if you will allow me to use an analogy."

(He calls him "Deveney"! Miss Fellowes thought. Like a college professor casually explaining something to a student!)

"By all means use an analogy," Deveney said. "Whatever you think will help."

"Well, then: you can't read a book with ordinary-sized print if it's held six feet from your eyes, can you? But you can read it quite easily if you hold it, say, one foot away. So far, the closer the better. If you bring the book to within an inch of your eyes, though, you've lost it again. The human eye simply can't focus on anything that close. So distance is a determining factor in more than one way. Too close is just as bad as too far, at least where vision is involved."

"Hmm," said Deveney.

"Or take another example. Your right shoulder is about thirty inches from the tip of your right forefinger and you can place your right forefinger on your right shoulder without any difficulty whatsoever. Well, now. Your right *elbow* is only half as far from the tip of your right forefinger as your shoulder is. By all ordinary logic it ought to be a lot easier to touch it with your finger than your shoulder. Go on, then: put your right forefinger on your right elbow. Again, there's such a thing as being too close."

Deveney said, "I can use these analogies of yours in my story, can't I?"

"Well, of course. Use whatever you like. You know you've got free access. For this one we want the whole world looking over our shoulder. There's going to be plenty here to see."

(Miss Fellowes found herself admiring Hoskins' calm certainty despite herself. There was strength there.)

Deveney said, "How far out are you planning to reach tonight?"

"Forty thousand years."

Miss Fellowes drew in her breath sharply.

*Forty thousand years?*

[8]

She had never considered that possibility. She had been too busy with other things, things like breaking off her professional ties with the hospital and getting settled in here. She became aware now, suddenly, that there was a good deal of fundamental thinking about this project that she had never taken the trouble to do.

She knew, of course, that they were going to be bringing a child from the past into the modern world. She understood—although she wasn't certain exactly where she had picked up the information—that the child would be taken from the prehistoric era.

But "prehistoric" could mean almost anything. Most of Europe could have been considered "prehistoric" only three thousand years ago. There were a few parts of the world still living a sort of prehistoric existence today. Miss Fellowes had assumed, in so far as she had given the matter any real consideration at all, that the child would be drawn from some nomadic pre-agricultural era, possibly going back five or at most ten thousand years.

But *forty* thousand?

She wasn't prepared for that. Would the child they were going to hand her be recognizable at all as human? Had there even been such a thing as *Homo sapiens* forty thousand years ago?

Miss Fellowes found herself wishing she could remember a little of her college anthropology courses of long ago, but right at this moment only the merest shreds of information came to the surface of her mind, and those, Miss Fellowes feared, were hopelessly garbled and distorted. Before true human beings had evolved, there had been the Neanderthal people, yes? Primitive brutish creatures. And the even more primitive Pithecanthropus people had roamed the world before them, and something else with an equally intricate name, and probably some other kinds of pre-men or sub-men, too, shaggy little naked ape-creatures that could more or less be considered to be our distant ancestors. But how far back in time had all these ancestral people lived? Twenty thousand years ago? Fifty? A hundred thousand? She really knew nothing useful about the time-frame of all this.

*Great God in heaven, am I going to be taking care of an ape-child?*

She began to tremble. Here she was, fussing over incubators and sterile chambers, and they were preparing to toss something very much like a chimpanzee into her lap, weren't they? Weren't they? Some fierce hairy little wild thing with claws and teeth, something

that really belonged in a zoo, if anywhere, not in the care of a specialist in—

Well, maybe not. Maybe the Neanderthals and the Pithecan-
thropuses and all those other early forms of human-like life had lived a
million years ago and more, and what she'd be getting would be
nothing more than a wild little boy. She had coped with wild little
boys before.

Still, it sounded like such an enormous span of time, forty thousand
years. The vastness of it dizzied her.

Forty thousand years?

*Forty thousand years?*

## [9]

There was tension in the air. Now the chaotic ballet in the pit below
had ceased, and the technicians at the controls were scarcely moving
at all. They communicated with one another by means of signals so
subtle that it was almost impossible to detect them—a flick of an
eyebrow, the tapping of a finger on the back of a wrist.

One man at a microphone spoke into it in a soft monotone, saying
things in short phrases that made no sense to Miss Fellowes—numbers, mostly, punctuated by what sounded like phrases in code, cryptic
and impenetrable.

Deveney had taken a seat just next to her. Hoskins was on the other
side. Leaning over the balcony railing with an intent stare, the scientific reporter said, "Is there going to be anything for us to see, Dr.
Hoskins? Visual effects, I mean."

"What? No. Nothing till the job is done. We detect indirectly,
something on the principle of radar, except that we use mesons rather
than radiation. We've been running the meson scans for weeks, tuning
and retuning. Mesons reach backward—under the proper conditions.
Some are reflected and we have to analyze the reflections, and we feed
them back in and use them as guides for the next probe, fining it
down until we start approximating the desired level of accuracy."

"That sounds like a tough job. How can you be sure you've
reached the right level?"

Hoskins smiled, his usual quick one, a cool on-off flash. "We've
been at work on this for fifteen years, now. Closer to twenty-five, if
you count the work of our predecessor company, which developed a

lot of the basic principles but wasn't able to break through to real reliability. —Yes, it's tough, Deveney. Very tough. And scary."

The man at the microphone raised his hand.

"Scary?" Deveney said.

"We don't like to fail. *I* definitely don't. And failure's an ever-present default mode in our operation. We're working in probabilistic areas here. Quantum effects, you understand. The best we can hope for is likeliness, never certainty. That's not good enough, really. But it's the best we can hope for."

"Still, you seem pretty confident."

"Yes," Hoskins said. "We've had the fix on this one particular moment in time for weeks—breaking it, remaking it after factoring in our own temporal movements, checking parallaxes, looking for every imaginable relativistic distortion, constantly seeking assurance that we can handle time flow with sufficient precision. And we think we can do it. I'd almost be willing to say that we *know* we can."

But his forehead was glistening.

There was a sudden terrible silence in the room, broken only by the sound of uneasy breathing. Edith Fellowes found herself rising from her seat, leaning forward, gripping the balcony railing.

But there was nothing to see.

*"Now,"* said the man at the microphone quietly.

The silence ascended to a higher level. It was a new kind of silence, *total* silence, a silence more profound than Miss Fellowes had ever imagined could be achieved in a room full of people. But it lasted no longer than the space of a single breath.

Then came the sound of a terrified little boy's scream from the dollhouse rooms below. It was a scream of the most awful intensity, the kind of scream that made you want to cover your ears with your hands.

Terror! Piercing terror!

A frightened child, crying out in a moment of utter shock and despair, letting its voice ring forth with astonishing power and force—an expression of such overwhelming horror as could barely be believed.

Miss Fellowes' head twisted in the direction of the cry.

And Hoskins' fist pounded on the railing and he said in a tight voice, trembling with triumph, *"Did* it!"

[10]

They went rushing down the short spiral flight of steps that led to the operations room, Hoskins in the lead, Deveney just behind him, and Miss Fellowes—unasked—following the journalist. Perhaps it was a terrible breach of security for her to be going down there now, she thought. But she had heard the cry that child had uttered.

She belonged down there at least as much as Candide Deveney, she told herself.

At the bottom of the staircase Hoskins paused and looked around. He seemed a little surprised that Miss Fellowes had come down after him—but only a little. He said nothing to her.

The mood in the operations room had changed dramatically now. All the frenzy was gone, and most of the tension. The technicians who had been monitoring the time-scoop equipment looked utterly spent. They stood by quietly, appearing almost dazed. Hoskins ignored them too. It was as though they were mere discarded parts of the machinery, no longer of any importance to him.

A very soft buzz sounded from the direction of the dollhouse.

Hoskins said, "We'll go inside now."

"Into the Stasis field?" Deveney asked, looking uneasy.

"It's perfectly safe to enter Stasis. I've done it a thousand times. There's a queer sensation when you pass through the envelope of the field, but it's momentary and it doesn't mean a thing. Trust me."

He stepped through an open door in mute demonstration. Deveney, smiling stiffly and drawing an obviously deep breath, followed him an instant later.

Hoskins said, "You too, Miss Fellowes. Please!"

He crooked his forefinger impatiently.

Miss Fellowes nodded and stepped across the threshold. She felt the field unmistakably. It was as though a ripple had gone through her, an internal tickle.

But once she was inside she was aware of no unusual sensations. Everything seemed normal. She picked up the clean fresh smell of the newly constructed wooden rooms, and something else—an earthy smell, the smell of a forest, somehow—

The panicky screaming, she realized, had ended some time ago. Everything was quiet inside the stasis field now. And then she heard the dry shuffling of feet, a scrabbling as of fingers against wood—and, she thought, a low moan.

"Where is the child?" asked Miss Fellowes in distress.

Hoskins was examining some dials and meters just inside the entrance to the dollhouse. Deveney was gaping idiotically at him. Neither one seemed in any hurry to look after the child—the child that this vast and incomprehensible mass of machinery had just ripped out of some unthinkably ancient era.

Didn't these fool men *care?*

Miss Fellowes went forward on her own authority, around an elbow-bend corridor that led to the room with the bed in it.

The child was in there. A boy. A very small boy, very dirty, very scrawny, very strange-looking.

He might have been three years old—certainly not very much more than that. He was naked. His small dirt-smeared chest was heaving raggedly. All around him lay an untidy sprawl of loose earth and pebbles and torn-off tufts of coarse grass, all of it strewn around the floor in a broad arc as though a bushel load of landfill had been casually upended in the room. The rich smell of soil rose up from it, and a touch of something fetid, besides. Miss Fellowes saw some large dark ants and what might have been a couple of furry little spiders moving around slowly near the boy's bare brown feet.

Hoskins followed her horrified glance and said with a sharp thrust of annoyance in his voice, "You can't pluck a boy cleanly out of time, Miss Fellowes. We had to take some of the surroundings with him for safety's sake. Or would you have preferred to have him arrive here minus one of his legs or with only half a head?"

*"Please!"* said Miss Fellowes, in an agony of revulsion. "Are we just going to stand here? The poor child is frightened. And it's filthy."

Which was an understatement. She had never seen a child that was quite so disreputable-looking. Perhaps he hadn't been washed in weeks; perhaps not ever. He reeked. His entire body was smeared with a thick layer of encrusted grime and grease, and there was a long scratch on his thigh that looked red and sore, possibly infected.

"Here, let me have a look at you—" Hoskins muttered, stepping forward in a gingerly way.

The boy hunched low, pulling his elbows in against his sides and drawing his head down close against his shoulders in what seemed like an innate defensive stance, and backed away rapidly. His eyes were fiery with fear and defiance. When he reached the far side of the room and could go no farther, he lifted his upper lip and snarled in a hissing fashion, like a cat. It was a frightening sound—savage, bestial, ferocious.

Miss Fellowes felt a cold shock wave sweeping through her nervous system. *This* was her new charge? *This?* This little—animal?

It was as bad as she had feared.

Worse. Worse. He hardly seemed human. He was hideous; he was a little monster.

Hoskins reached out swiftly and seized both of the child's wrists, pulling his arms inward across his body and crossing them over his belly. In the same motion Hoskins lifted him, kicking and writhing and screaming, from the floor.

Ghastly banshee howls came forth from the child. They erupted from the depths of his body with astonishing force. Miss Fellowes realized that she was trembling, and forced herself to be calm. It was a frightful noise, ear-splitting, repellent, sub-human. It was almost impossible to believe that a boy so small could make sounds so horrendous.

Hoskins held him at arms' length in midair and looked around in obvious distress at Miss Fellowes.

"Yes, hold him, now. Don't put him down. Watch out for his toenails when he kicks. Take him into the bathroom and let's clean him up. That's what he needs before anything else, a good warm bath."

Hoskins nodded. Small as the child was, it didn't seem to be any easy matter to keep him pinioned that way. A grown man and a little child: but there was tremendous wild strength in the child, small as he was. And beyond any doubt he thought that he was fighting for his life.

"Fill that tub, Miss Fellowes!" Hoskins yelled. "Fill it fast!"

There were other people inside the Stasis area now. In the midst of the confusion Miss Fellowes recognized her three assistants and singled them out.

"You, Elliott—get the water running. Mortenson, I want antibiotics for that infection on his leg. In fact, bring the whole antisepsis kit into the bathroom. Stratford, find yourself a cleanup crew and start getting all this trash and filth removed from here!"

They began to snap to it. Now that she was giving the orders, her initial shock and horror were starting to drop away and some degree of professional aplomb returned to her. This was going to be difficult, yes. But she was a specialist in managing difficult cases. And she had been up against plenty of them during the course of her career.

Workmen appeared. Storage canisters were brought in. The workmen began to sweep away the soil and debris and carry the canisters off to a containment area somewhere in back. Hoskins called to them, "Remember, not a scrap goes outside the bubble!"

Miss Fellowes strode after Hoskins into the bathroom and signaled for him to plunge the boy into the tub, which Elliott was rapidly filling with warm water. No longer just one of a group of confused spectators, but now an efficient and experienced nurse swinging into action, she was collected enough to pause and look at the child with a calm, clinical eye, seeing him clearly as though for the first time.

What she saw overwhelmed her with new dismay. She hesitated for one shocked moment, fighting against the sudden emotions that swirled up through her unguarded mind. She saw past the dirt and shrieking, past the thrashing of limbs and useless twisting. She saw the boy himself.

Her first impression in that moment of chaos had been right. He was the ugliest boy she had ever seen. He was horribly ugly—from misshapen head to bandy legs.

His body was exceptionally stocky, very deep through the chest and broad in the shoulders. All right; nothing terribly unusual about that, really. But that long oversized skull! That bulging, sloping forehead! That immense potato of a nose, with its dark cavernous nostrils, which opened outward as much as downward. The great staring eyes framed in those huge bony rims! The receding chin, the short neck, the dwarfish limbs!

*Forty thousand years,* Miss Fellowes told herself numbly.

Not human. Not really.

An animal. Her worst-case scenario had come true. An ape-child; that was what he was. Some kind of chimpanzee, more or less. *That* was what they were paying her all this money to look after! How could she? What did she know about caring for little savage prehistoric apes?

And yet—yet—

Maybe she was wrong about him. She hoped so most profoundly. There was the glow of unmistakably human intelligence in those huge, gleaming, furious eyes of his. His skin, light brown, almost tawny, was covered only with fine golden down, not the coarse shaggy pelt that one would imagine an animal-child to have. And his face, ugly as it was—it wasn't really the face of any kind of ape. You had to look behind the superficial strangeness, and when you did you saw that he was really just a little boy.

A little boy, yes, an ugly little boy, a strange little boy, a *human* boy —a dirty little frightened child with bandy legs and a peculiarly shaped head and a miserable excuse for a chin and an infected cut on his thigh and a curious red birthmark on his cheek that looked like a jagged bolt of lightning—yes, yes, he wasn't at all like any child she had ever seen, but nevertheless she would try to think of him as a human being, this poor lost frightened child who had been snatched out of time. Perhaps she would succeed. Perhaps.

But Lord, he was ugly! Lord, Lord, Lord, it was going to be a real challenge to love anything that looked as ugly as this child did! Miss Fellowes wasn't at all sure that she would be able to do it, despite everything that she had told Dr. Hoskins when he had interviewed her. And that was a deeply troubling thought.

The tub was full now. Elliott, a brawny dark-haired man with huge hands and thick wrists, had taken the boy from Dr. Hoskins and was holding his squirming body half submerged. Mortenson, the other assistant, had wheeled in the medical tray. Miss Fellowes squirted half a tube of antiseptic soap into the bathtub and a yellowish bubbly foam began to churn up. The bubbles seemed to catch the child's attention for a moment and it stopped howling and kicking—but only for a moment. Then it must have remembered that something horrible was happening to it, and it went back to struggling.

Elliott laughed. "He's a slippery little bugger. Almost got away from me that time."

"Make sure he doesn't," Miss Fellowes said grimly. "My Lord, what filth! Careful—hold him! Hold him!"

It was a brutal job. Even with two men helping her, it was all she could manage to keep the boy under some measure of control. He never stopped squirming, wriggling, kicking, scratching, bellowing. Whether he thought he was defending his life or just his dignity Miss Fellowes had no idea, but she had rarely had such a reluctant patient as this. They were all splashed with soapy, dirty water now, and Elliott had stopped laughing. The boy had raked his arm with his fingernails and a long bloody line showed beneath the thick curling hair. Miss Fellowes wondered whether it might be necessary to sedate the child in order to get the job finished. She regarded that only as a desperate last resort.

"Get yourself an antibiotic shot when we're done," she said to

Elliott. "That's a nasty scratch. There's no telling what kind of prehistoric microbes that boy may be carrying under his fingernails."

She realized that she had forgotten all about her earlier demand to have the child arrive into a sterile, germ-free environment. Somehow that seemed like mere foolishness to her now. The boy was so strong, so agile, so fierce; and she had imagined a weak, vulnerable little thing—

Well, Miss Fellowes told herself, he was still vulnerable, regardless of the way he fought. They'd have to monitor him very closely in the first few days to make sure that he wasn't coming down with some bacterial infection to which he had no built-in resistance.

"Lift him out of the tub for a minute, Elliott," she said. "Mortenson, let's put some clean water in there. Lord, Lord, what a *filthy* little child!"

The bath process seemed to go on and on forever.

Miss Fellowes worked in silence and with a sense of rising outrage. Her mood was beginning to swing back the other way, toward annoyance, toward actual anger. She was no longer thinking of how stimulating it was to tackle a difficult challenge. What was uppermost in her mind now, spurred by the continued wild strugglings and outcries of the boy and the way she and everything about her was getting drenched, was the notion that Hoskins had tricked her into accepting an impossible assignment whose true nature she had not really understood.

He had hinted that the child wouldn't be pretty. But that was a long way from saying that it would be repulsively deformed and as intractable as a jungle animal. And there was a stench about the boy that soap and water was managing to alleviate only little by little.

As the battle continued, she had the strong desire to thrust the boy into Dr. Hoskins' arms—soapy and wet as the child was—and walk right out of this place. But Miss Fellowes knew that she couldn't do that. There was the matter of her professional pride, after all. For better or for worse, she had agreed to take this job on. She would simply have to go through with that. Hoskins hadn't tricked her in any way, she admitted to herself. He had told her that the work was going to be tough. He had said the child would be difficult, strange, unruly, perhaps highly disagreeable. Those had been his exact words. He had asked her if she was prepared to love the child *unconditionally* —regardless of the way its chin might recede or its brow might bulge. And she had said yes, yes, yes, she was prepared to deal with all that.

—And there would be the look in Hoskins' eyes, if she walked out now. A cold searching look that would say, *So I was right. You're only interested in looking after pretty children, eh, Miss Fellowes?*

She glanced over at him. Hoskins was standing apart from them, watching coolly from a distance with a half-smile on her face. The smile broadened as his eyes met hers, as though he was able to read her mind and could see the feelings of outrage and the sense of betrayal that were churning in it, and was amused by what he saw.

I *will* quit, she thought, as fury surged up in her all over again.

But not yet. Not until I have things under control here. To quit before then would be demeaning. Let me get this hideous little savage civilized a little first: and then Hoskins can find someone else to cope with him.

## [11]

The bathtub skirmish ended with a victory for the three adults over the small frightened child. The outer layers of filth were gone, at least, and his skin had taken on a reasonably presentable undertone of pink. His piercing cries of fear had given way to uncertain whimpers.

He seemed worn out by all his struggling. He watched carefully, eyes moving in quick frightened suspicion, going back and forth from one to another of those in the room.

He was shivering. Not so much from fear as from cold after his bath, Miss Fellowes guessed. Stockily built though he was, he was terribly thin—no spare fat on him at all, arms and legs like pipestems —and he was trembling now as if his dirt had been a useful layer of insulation.

Miss Fellowes said sharply, "Bring me a nightgown for the child!"

A nightgown appeared at once. It was as though everything were ready and yet nothing were ready unless she gave orders, as though Hoskins was deliberately standing back and letting her call the tune, to test her.

"I'd better hold him again, Miss Fellowes," the burly Elliott said. "You'll never get it on him all by yourself."

"You're right," Miss Fellowes said. "I won't. Thank you, Elliott."

The boy's eyes widened at the approach of the nightgown as if it were some implement of torture. But the battle this time was shorter and less violent than the one in the tub. Elliott seized each tiny wrist with one of his huge hands and held the short arms upward; and Miss

Fellowes deftly drew the pink flannel nightgown down over the gnomish head.

The boy made a soft interrogative sound. He slipped the fingers of one hand inside the collar of the nightgown and gripped the fabric tightly. His strange sloping forehead furrowed in a deep frown.

Then he growled and gave the cloth a quick, hard tug, as though to rip the nightgown off.

Miss Fellowes slapped his hand sharply. From Dr. Hoskins, behind her, came a sound of surprise. She ignored it.

The boy reddened, but didn't cry. He stared at Miss Fellowes in a curious way, as if her slapping him hadn't offended him at all, but rather seemed familiar and expected. His eyes were the biggest child-eyes Miss Fellowes had ever seen, dark and shining and eerie.

The splayed, stubby fingers of his hand moved slowly across the thick flannel of the nightgown, feeling the strangeness of it, but he made no second attempt to rip it away.

Miss Fellowes thought desperately: Well, what next?

Everyone seemed in suspended animation, waiting for her—even the ugly little boy.

A long list of things that needed to be done blossomed in her mind, not necessarily in order of importance:

Prophylaxis for that infected scratch of his.
Trim his fingernails and toenails.
Blood tests. Immune-system vulnerability?
Vaccinations? A course of preventive antibiotic treatments?
Haircut.
Stool samples. Intestinal parasites?
Dental examination.
Chest X ray. General skeletal X ray, too.

And half a dozen other items of varying degrees of urgency. But then she realized what the top priority of all must be, at least for the ugly little boy.

Briskly she said, "Have you provided food? Milk?"

They had. Ms. Stratford, her third assistant, wheeled in a gleaming mobile unit. In the refrigeration compartment Miss Fellowes found three quarts of milk, with a warming unit and a supply of fortifications in the form of vitamin supplements, copper-cobalt-iron syrup, and other things she had no time to be concerned with now. Another compartment held an assortment of baby foods in self-warming cans.

Milk, simply milk, that was the thing to begin with. Whatever else he had been eating in the place from which he had been taken—half-charred meat, wild berries, roots and insects, who knew what?—milk was a safe bet to have been part of a child's diet. Savages, she speculated, would be likely to go on nursing their children to an advanced age.

But savages wouldn't know how to handle cups. That much seemed certain. Miss Fellowes poured a little of the milk into a saucer and popped it into the microwave for a few seconds' worth of warming.

They were all watching her—Hoskins, Candide Deveney, the three orderlies, and everyone else who had managed to crowd into the Stasis area. The boy was staring at her too.

"Yes, look at me," she said to the boy. "There's a good fellow."

She held the saucer carefully in her hands, brought it to her mouth, and pantomimed the act of lapping up the milk.

The boy's eyes followed. But did he understand?

"Drink," she said. "This is how to drink."

Miss Fellowes pantomimed the lapping again. She felt a little absurd. But she brushed the feeling away. She would do whatever felt right to do. The boy had to be taught how to drink.

"Now you," she said.

She offered him the saucer, holding it out toward him so that all he had to do was move his head forward slightly and lick up the milk. He looked at it solemnly, without the slightest sign of comprehension.

"Drink," she said. "Drink." She let her tongue flick out again as though to show him once more.

No response. Just a stare. He was trembling again, though the room was warm and the nightgown surely was more than sufficient.

Direct measures were in order, the nurse thought.

She put the saucer down on the floor. Then she seized the boy's upper arm in one hand and, bending, she dipped three fingers of her other hand in the milk, scooping some up and dashing it across his lips. It dripped down his cheeks and over his receding chin.

The boy uttered a high-pitched cry of a kind she hadn't heard from him before. He looked baffled and displeased. Then his tongue slowly moved over his wetted lips. He frowned. Tasted. The tongue licked out again.

Was that a smile?

Yes. Yes. A sort of smile, anyway. Miss Fellowes stepped back.

"Milk," she said. "That's milk. Go on. Have a little more of it."

Tentatively the boy approached the saucer. He bent toward it, then looked up and over his shoulder sharply as though expecting to find some enemy crouching behind him. But there was nothing behind him. He bent again, stiffly, clumsily, pushed his head forward, licked at the milk, first in a cautious way and then with increasing eagerness. He lapped it the way a cat would. He made a slurping noise. He showed no interest in using his hands to raise the saucer to his face. He was like a little animal, squatting on the floor lapping up the milk.

Miss Fellowes felt a sudden surge of revulsion, even though she knew that she was the one who had pantomimed the lapping in the first place. She wanted to think of him as a child, a human child, but he kept reverting to some animal level, and she hated that. She *hated* it. She knew that her reaction must be apparent on her face. But she couldn't help it. Why was the child so bestial? It was prehistoric, yes—forty thousand years!—but did that have to mean it would seem so much like an ape? It was human, wasn't it? *Wasn't* it? What kind of child had they given her?

Candide Deveney caught that, perhaps. He said, "Does the nurse know, Dr. Hoskins?"

"Know what?" Miss Fellowes demanded.

Deveney hesitated, but Hoskins (again that look of detached amusement on his face) said, "I'm not sure. Why don't you tell her?"

"What's all this mystery?" she asked. "Come on, tell me, if there's some secret I'm supposed to find out about!"

Deveney turned to her. "I just was wondering, Miss—whether you're actually aware that you happen to be the first civilized woman in history ever to be asked to take care of a young Neanderthal?"

# INTERCHAPTER TWO

# Goddess Woman

THIS WAS THE FOURTH MORNING of the westward march, the pilgrimage back to the Place of Three Rivers. A dry cold wind had been blowing steadily out of the north ever since Silver Cloud had given the order to turn around and retrace their long path across the barren plains. Sometimes new gusts of thin, hard snow came whistling by, dancing in wild milky swirls overhead—and this in mid-summer! Truly, the Goddess must be angered. But why? What had they done?

By night the People huddled in crannies and crevices under a white moon that drenched the sky with rivers of chilly light. There were no caves here to crawl into. Some of the most enterprising ones found twigs and branches and flung little lean-tos together for themselves, but most were too weary after a day's marching and foraging to make the effort.

The day of the Summer Festival had come and gone, and—for the first time in memory—no Summer Festival had been held. Goddess Woman didn't care for that at all. "We will have famine when the cold months come," she said gloomily to Keeps The Past. "To neglect the Summer Festival is a serious thing. Has there ever been a year when we allowed the day to go by without the proper observances?"

"We aren't neglecting the Summer Festival," Keeps The Past rejoined. "We're simply postponing it until we can seek the guidance of the Goddess."

Goddess Woman spat. "The guidance of the Goddess! The guidance of the Goddess! What does Silver Cloud think he's up to? *I* am the one who provides the guidance of the Goddess. And I don't need to return to the Place of the Three Rivers in order to provide it."

"Silver Cloud does," said Keeps The Past.

"Purely out of cowardice. He's become afraid of the Other Ones and he wants to run away from them, now that he knows that they're ahead of us."

"Ahead of us and behind us both. We can't hide from them any longer. They're all around us. And there aren't enough of us to fight them. What are we to do? The Goddess must tell us how to deal with them."

"Yes," Goddess Woman conceded sullenly. "I suppose that's true."

"So unless you can advise us yourself, in the name of the Goddess, concerning the tactics we ought to follow—"

"Enough, Keeps The Past. I see your point."

"Good. Try to keep it in mind, then."

Goddess Woman uttered a sulky sniff and walked away by herself, over to the fire. She stood close, arms huddled against her sides.

She and Keeps The Past had been bickering for more years than Goddess Woman cared to think about, and they were not coming to like each other any more as the time went along. Keeps The Past thought she was something special, with her long memory (supplemented by her bundles of record-sticks) and her deep knowledge of tribal traditions. Well, she *was* special in her way, Goddess Woman grudgingly supposed. But she is not holy. *I* am holy. She is just a chronicler; but I speak with the Goddess, and sometimes the Goddess speaks with me.

Still, Goddess Woman admitted, as she opened her fur wrap to allow the warm pink glow of the fire to rise up and around her lean, stocky body, Keeps The Past did have a point. The Other Ones were a tremendous problem—those tall, agile, maddening flat-faced people who had come out of nowhere and seemed to be spreading everywhere, appropriating the best caves for themselves, the finest hunting grounds, the sweetest springs. Goddess Woman had heard horrifying tales occasionally from tribeless wanderers who had crossed the People's path, tales of clashes between the Other Ones and bands of the People, of hideous massacres, of horrifying routs. The Other Ones had better weapons, which they seemed to be able to manufacture in incredible quantities, and they were more swift afoot in battle too, it appeared: they moved like shadows, so it was said, and when they fought you it was as though they were on all sides of you at once. So far Silver Cloud had been able to avoid any of that, deftly steering the tribe this way and that across the great open plains to keep them away from collisions with the dangerous newcomers. But how long could he go on managing to do that?

Yes, best to make this pilgrimage and see if the Goddess had any advice, Goddess Woman told herself.

Besides, Silver Cloud had been very persuasive when it came to the religious side of the argument. The Summer Festival marked the high point of the year, when the sun was warm and the day was long. It was a celebration of the kindness of the Goddess, of Her grace and favor, a giving of thanks in advance for the benefits that She would bestow during the remaining weeks of the summer hunting and food-gathering season.

How could they hold the Summer Festival, Silver Cloud had wanted to know, when the Goddess was so plainly displeased with them?

More to the point, Goddess Woman thought: how could they hold the Summer Festival when Silver Cloud flatly refused to perform it? It was a rite that required the participation of a man, and only the most powerful man of the tribe at that. It was he who had to dance the dance of gratitude before the shrine of the Goddess. It was he who had to carry out the sacrifice of the bullock, he who had to take the chosen virgin in his arms and initiate her into the mysteries of the Great Mother. The other holy festivals of the tribe were the responsibility of the three Goddess Women; but there was no way they could carry out this one. The chief had to do it. If Silver Cloud refused to take part, the Summer Festival could not be held. That was all there was to it. Goddess Woman felt uneasy about that; but the decision belonged to Silver Cloud.

Goddess Woman turned away from the fire. It was time to set up the shrine for the morning rites.

"Goddess Women!" Goddess Woman called. "Both of you! Let's get to work!"

They had all had individual names, once. But now each one of the three priestesses was simply known as Goddess Woman. You gave up your name when you entered Her service. The Goddess had no name, and Her servants had no names either.

Goddess Woman was still able to remember the name of the youngest Goddess Woman, for she was Goddess Woman's own daughter, and Goddess Woman had named her herself: Bright Sky At Dawn. But it was years since she had spoken that name out loud. To her, and to everyone else, her daughter who had once been Bright Sky At Dawn was simply Goddess Woman now. As was the second-oldest Goddess Woman, whose earlier name was starting to slip from Goddess Woman's memory—it was either Lonely Bird or Runs Like The Fox, Goddess Woman was not sure which. Those two had looked very much like each other, Lonely Bird and Runs Like The Fox. One of them was dead and the other had become a priestess, and over the years Goddess Woman had come to confuse their identities in her mind.

As for her own birth-name, Goddess Woman no longer had any idea what it might have been. She had forgotten it years ago and she rarely gave it any thought now. She was Goddess Woman and nothing but Goddess Woman. Sometimes as she lay waiting for sleep she found herself wondering despite herself what her old name could have been. Something with sunlight in it? Or golden wings? Or shining water? There was brightness in it somewhere, she was fairly sure of that. But the name itself had slipped away forever. She felt guilty for even trying to think of it. Certainly there was no one that she could ask. It was a sin, a Goddess Woman using her birth-name in any way. Whenever she started to think about it she immediately made a sign of purification and asked forgiveness.

She was the second-oldest woman in the tribe. This was her fortieth summer. Only Keeps The Past was older, and by no more than a season or two. But Goddess Woman was strong and healthy; she expected to live another ten years, perhaps fifteen, maybe as many as twenty if she was lucky. Her mother had lived to a great old age, even beyond her sixtieth year, and her grandmother as well. Long life was a characteristic of her family.

"Will we do the full rite this morning?" the youngest Goddess Woman asked her, as they moved the stones about, assembling the shrine.

Goddess Woman gave her an irritated glance. "Of course we will. Why shouldn't we?"

"Because Silver Cloud wants us to leave here right after morning meal. He says we have to travel farther today than we've been doing the last three."

"Silver Cloud! Silver Cloud! He says this, he says that, and we hop like frogs to his commands. Maybe he's in a hurry, but the Goddess isn't. We do the full rite."

She lit the Goddess-fire. The second Goddess Woman produced her little wolfskin packet of aromatic herbs and sprinkled them on the blaze. Colored flames flared high. The youngest Goddess Woman brought the stone bowl of blood from yesterday's kill and poured a little onto the offering-altar.

From the furry bear-skin in which they were stored, Goddess Woman brought forth the three holy bear-skulls that were the tribe's most sacred possession, and put them out on three flat stones to shield them from contact with the ground.

The skulls had been in the tribe's possession for more generations than even Keeps The Past could say. Great heroes of long ago had slain those bears in single combat, and they had been handed down in the tribe from one Goddess Woman to the next. The bear was the Father-animal, the great kindling force that brought forth life from the Great Mother. That was why Goddess Woman had to take care not to allow the skulls to touch bare soil, for then they would fructify the Mother, and this was not the season for doing that. Any children who were kindled into life now, in mid-summer, would be born in the dark days of late winter, when food was at its scarcest. The time to kindle young ones was in autumn, so that they would come forth in the spring.

Goddess Woman laid her hands on each of the skulls in turn, lovingly stroking its upper vault, polished smooth and ice-bright by the hands of many Goddess Women of years gone by. She felt shivers running through her hands and arms and shoulders as the power of the elemental Father-force tingled upward out of the skulls and into her body.

She caressed the shining fangs. She fingered the dark eye-sockets.

The Father-force opened the way for her, admitting the Mother-force to her soul. One force necessarily led to the other; one could not invoke one without feeling the presence of the other.

"Goddess, we thank Thee," murmured Goddess Woman. "We thank Thee for the fruit of the earth and for the flesh of the beasts and most deeply do we thank Thee for the fruit of our wombs." Briefly she touched her breasts, her belly, her loins. She crouched and dug her fingertips into the hard frosty soil. Cold as it might be today, it was still the breast of the Mother, and she fondled it with love. Beside her, the other two Goddess Women were doing the same.

She closed her eyes. She saw the great arc of the Mother's breast stretching out before her to the horizon. She filled her soul with awareness of Goddess-presence, of Mother-force.

*Bless us,* Goddess Woman prayed. *Preserve us. Give us the grace of Thy love.*

She was pulled harshly from her meditations by the sound of raucous screeching laughter somewhere behind her. The boys of the tribe, playing their rough games. She forced herself to ignore them. They were of the Goddess too, however crude and cruel and foolish they might be.

The Goddess had created women for bearing children and giving nurture and love, and men for hunting and providing and fighting, and each had a role to play that the other could not venture to perform. That was the meaning of the Summer Festival, the coming together of man and woman in the service of the Goddess. And if boys were rough and irreverent—why, it was because the Goddess had made them so. Let them laugh. Let them run in circles and strike at each other with sticks when they caught up with one another. That was how it was meant to be.

When the lengthy rite was finished Goddess Woman rose and scratched the fire into embers with a stick and collected the holy stones. She gathered up the bear-skulls, kissed each one, tucked them away in their mantles of fur.

She caught sight of Silver Cloud standing at a great distance, arms folded impatiently as though he had been waiting in an ill-tempered way for her to get done with it. Closer at hand, Goddess Woman saw She Who Knows leading a band of the littlest children around in a circle, teaching them a song.

How pathetic, she told herself. She Who Knows, that barren woman, pretending to be one of the Mothers. The Goddess has dealt harshly with She Who Knows, Goddess Woman thought.

"Are you done finally?" Silver Cloud shouted. "Can we get going now, Goddess Woman?"

"We can get going, yes."

She Who Knows came over to her. A little gaggle of the smaller children tagged along behind her—Sweet Flower, Skyfire Face, and a couple of the others.

"Can I talk to you for a moment, Goddess Woman?" She Who Knows asked.

"Silver Cloud wants us to pack up and get on our way."

"A moment, that's all."

"A moment, then."

She was an irritating woman, She Who Knows. Goddess Woman had never liked her. No one did. She was clever, yes, and full of dark energy, and you had to grant her a certain grudging respect. But she was prickly and difficult. She had had a life full of troubles, and Goddess Woman felt sorry for her about that—the dead babies, the loss of her mate, all those things. But nonetheless she wished that She Who Knows would leave her alone. There was an aura of bad luck about her, of Goddess-displeasure.

She Who Knows said quietly, "Is it true what I hear, that there's going to be a special sacrifice when we get to the Place of Three Rivers?"

"There'll be a sacrifice, yes," Goddess Woman said. "How can we have a pilgrimage if we don't make an offering when we get to the Pilgrimage-place?"

"A *special* sacrifice."

What was left of Goddess Woman's patience was rapidly wearing thin. "Special how, She Who Knows? Special in what way? I have no time for riddles now."

"The sacrifice of a child," said She Who Knows.

Goddess Woman would not have been more startled if She Who Knows had thrown a handful of snow in her face.

"What? Who says such a thing?"

"I heard the men talking. We'll give a child to the Goddess at the Place of Three Rivers so that She will make the Other Ones keep away from us. Silver Cloud has already decided it. Presumably after discussing it with you. Is that true, Goddess Woman?"

Goddess Woman felt a pounding in her breast and heard a sound like thunder drumming in her ears. She felt weak and dizzy and she had to force herself with difficulty to remain upright and to keep her eyes level with those of She Who Knows. She drew her breath in deeply, filling her lungs, again, again, again, until some semblance of poise returned to her.

Icily she said, "This is madness, She Who Knows. The Goddess *gives* children. She doesn't want them back."

"Sometimes She takes them back."

"Yes. Yes, I know," said Goddess Woman, her tone softening a little. "The Goddess moves in ways beyond our understanding. But we don't kill children and offer them to Her. Animals, yes. Never a child. Never. Such a thing has never been done."

"The Other Ones have never been a serious danger to us before, either."

"Sacrificing children isn't going to protect us from the Other Ones."

"They say that you and Silver Cloud have decided that it will."

"They're lying, whoever they are," Goddess Woman said hotly. "I don't know anything about this plan. Nothing! —All this is nonsense, She Who Knows. It won't happen. I promise you that. There'll be no sacrifices of children around here. You can be completely sure of that."

"Swear it. Swear by the Goddess. —No." She Who Knows reached out and took Skyfire Face by one hand and Sweet Flower by the other. "Swear by the souls of this little boy and this little girl."

"My word should be enough," Goddess Woman said.

"You won't swear?"

"My word is sufficient," said Goddess Woman. "I don't owe you any oaths. Not by the Goddess, not by Sweet Flower's little backside, not by anything. We're civilized people, She Who Knows. We don't kill children. That should be good enough for you."

She Who Knows looked skeptical. But she gave ground and went away.

Goddess Woman stood by herself, thinking.

Sacrifice a child? Were they serious? Did they actually think it would serve any purpose? *Could* it possibly serve any purpose?

Would the Goddess countenance such a thing? She tried to think it through. To yield up a little life, to return to the Goddess that which the Goddess had given—was that any way of convincing Her that She must help the People in this time of need?

No. No. No. No. However Goddess Woman looked at it, she saw no sense in it.

Where was Silver Cloud? Ah, over there, looking through Mammoth Rider's new batch of arrow points. Goddess Woman went over to him and drew him aside. In a low voice she said, "Tell me something, and tell me honestly. Are you planning to sacrifice a child when we get to the Place of Three Rivers?"

"Have you lost your mind, Goddess Woman?"

"She Who Knows says that some of the men are talking about it. That you've already decided on it and that I've given my agreement."

"And *have* you given your agreement?" Silver Cloud asked.

"Of course not."

"Well, the rest of the story is just as true. Sacrifice a child, Goddess Woman? You couldn't possibly have believed that I would ever—"

"I wasn't certain."

"How can you say that?"

"You canceled the Summer Festival, didn't you?"

"What's wrong with you, Goddess Woman? You don't see any difference between putting off a festival and killing a child?"

"There are those who'd say that one is just as wrong as the other."

"Well, anyone who says something like that is crazy," Silver Cloud retorted. "I have no such intentions, and you can tell She Who Knows that I—" He paused. His expression altered strangely. —"You don't think that it could possibly do us any good, do you? You aren't suggesting—"

"No," said Goddess Woman. "Of course I don't. Now *you* sound like you've lost your mind. But don't be ridiculous. I'm not suggesting it in the slightest. I came over here to find out whether there was any truth to the rumor, that's all."

"And now you know. None. None whatever."

But there was an odd look in his eyes, still. Silver Cloud's outrage seemed to have softened and he had turned inward upon himself, somehow. Goddess Woman wasn't sure how to interpret that inward look. What could he be thinking of?

Goddess above, he couldn't seriously be considering the idea of sacrificing a child all of a sudden, could he? Did I put something monstrous into his mind just now?

No, she decided. No. That couldn't be it. She knew Silver Cloud well. He was tough, he was unswerving, he could be brutal—but not this. Not a child.

"I want you to understand my position very clearly," Goddess Woman said with all the force she could muster. "There may very well be some men in this tribe who think it could be useful to offer a child to the Goddess, and for all I know, Silver Cloud, they might be able to succeed in talking you into it before we reach the Place of Three Rivers. But I won't allow it. I'm prepared to bring the heaviest curse of the Goddess down on any man who even proposes such a thing. It'll be the bear-curse, the darkest one of all. I'll cut him off from every shred of Her mercy without any hesitation. I'll—"

"Easy, Goddess Woman. You're getting all worked up over nothing. Nobody's talking about sacrificing children. Nobody. When we get to the Place of Three Rivers we'll catch ourselves an ibex or a chamois or a good red elk, and we'll give its meat to the Goddess as we always do, and that will be that. So calm yourself. Calm yourself. You're kicking up a tremendous fuss about something that you know I'd never permit to be done. You *know* it, Goddess Woman."

"All right," she said. "An ibex. A chamois."

"Absolutely," said Silver Cloud.

He grinned at her and reached out to squeeze her shoulder fondly. She felt very foolish. How could she ever have imagined that Silver Cloud would entertain such a barbaric notion?

She went off by herself to kneel by a little stream and throw cold water against her aching forehead.

Later in the morning, when the tribe had resumed its march, Goddess Woman came up alongside She Who Knows and said, "I had a talk with Silver Cloud. He knew no more about this child-sacrifice scheme than I did. And he feels the same way about it that I do. That you do. He wouldn't ever allow it."

"There are those here who think otherwise."

"Who, for instance?"

She Who Knows shook her head vaguely. "I won't name names. But they think the Goddess won't be satisfied unless we give Her one of our children."

"If they think that, they don't understand the Goddess at all. Forget all of this, will you, She Who Knows? It's just so much empty talk. The talk of fools."

"Let's hope so," said She Who Knows, her voice dark with foreboding.

They marched onward. Gradually Goddess Woman put the matter from her mind. She Who Knows' refusal to name names had aroused her suspicions. Very probably there was nothing to the story at all, and never had been. Perhaps the woman had invented the whole thing; perhaps she was sick in the mind; perhaps it might be a good idea to send She Who Knows off on a little pilgrimage of her own to clear her troubled soul of such disturbed imaginings. Child sacrifice! It was unthinkable.

She forgot about it. And the weeks went by; and the People marched westward, back through the thinning warmth of summer toward the Place of Three Rivers.

And now at last they were on a sloping hillside overlooking the Three Rivers themselves. The long rearward march was almost over. The trail wound gradually downward through one level of hillside after another, and down below, in the misty valley, they could see the shining glint that the water of the Three Rivers made.

It was late in the day, and the People were starting to consider making camp for the evening. And then a strange thing happened.

Goddess Woman was near the front of the file, with Tree Of Wolves on one side of her and Blazing Eye on the other, to help her carry the packets of Goddess-things. Suddenly the air turned intensely bright just beside the path. There was a sparkling. Goddess Woman saw brilliant red and green flashes, glossy loops, a fiery whiteness at the core. The white light moved. It went up and down in the air, whirling as it traveled.

Looking at it was painful. She flung up one hand to shield her eyes. People were crying out in fear all around her.

Then it vanished—as abruptly as it had come. The air beside the path seemed empty. Goddess Woman stood blinking, her eyes aching, her mind aswirl with confusions.

"What was it?" someone asked.

"What will happen next?"

"Save us, Silver Cloud!"

"Goddess Woman? Goddess Woman, tell us what that thing was!"

Goddess Woman moistened her lips. "It was—the Goddess passing by," she improvised desperately. "The edge of Her robe; that was what it was."

"Yes," they said. "The Goddess. The Goddess, it was. It must have been."

Everyone was quiet for a time, wary, motionless, waiting to see if She intended to return. But nothing out of the ordinary happened.

Then She Who Knows cried out, "It was the Goddess, yes, and She has taken Skyfire Face!"

"What?"

"He was right here, just behind me, when the light appeared. Now he's gone."

"Gone? Where? How?"

"Look for him!" someone screamed. "Find him! Skyfire Face! Skyfire Face!"

There was a tremendous hubbub. People were scrabbling about, moving without purpose in every direction, movement just for the sake of movement. Goddess Woman heard Silver Cloud calling out for quiet, for calmness. The Mothers were the most excited: their shrill cries rose above everything else, and they ran about weeping and flailing their arms in the air.

For a moment Goddess Woman wasn't able to remember who the actual mother of Skyfire Face was; then she recalled that it was Red Smoke At Sunrise who had given birth to the little boy with the jagged lightning-bolt birthmark, four summers back. But the Mothers raised all the children of the tribe in common, and it made very little difference to them which one of them had brought a particular child into the world; Milky Fountain and Beautiful Snow and Lake Of Green Ice were just as troubled by his bewildering disappearance as was Red Smoke At Sunrise.

"He must have wandered off the path," Broken Mountain said. "I'll go look for him."

"He was right here," said She Who Knows acidly. "That light swallowed him up."

"You saw it, did you?"

"He was behind me when it happened. But not so far behind that he could have strayed. It was the light that took him. It was the light."

All the same, Broken Mountain insisted on going back to look for him. But it was useless. There was no sign of the boy anywhere. An hour's search produced nothing, not even a footprint; and now it was growing very dark.

"We have to move on," Silver Cloud said. "There's no place here for camping."

"But Skyfire Face—"

"Gone," Silver Cloud said inexorably. "Vanished into the Goddess-light."

"The Goddess-light! The Goddess-light!"

They moved along. Goddess Woman felt numb. She had looked right into the shimmering light, and there was still an ache behind her eyes, and when she closed them she saw patterns of floating purple spots. But had it been the Goddess? She couldn't say. She had never seen anything like that light before. She hoped she never saw it again.

"So the Goddess wanted one of our children after all," She Who Knows said. "Well, well, well."

"You know nothing about these matters!" Goddess Woman told her furiously. "Nothing!"

But what if she was right? Goddess Woman wondered. It was altogether possible that she was. Likely, even. So powerful a light could only have been a manifestation of the Goddess.

The Goddess had claimed a child? Why? What sense did that make?

We can never understand Her, Goddess Woman decided, after wrestling with the strange event far into the night. She is the Goddess, and we are only Her creatures. And Skyfire Face is gone. It is beyond all comprehension, but so be it. She remembered now the rumor there had been that Silver Cloud had been planning to sacrifice a child when they reached the Place of the Three Rivers. Well, at least there would be no more talk of such things. They were almost at their destination, and the Goddess had claimed a child without their having had to give it to her. Goddess Woman hoped that She would be content with that. There were not so many children in the tribe that they could afford to let Her have another one just now.

# CHAPTER THREE

---

# Discovering

[12]

A NEANDERTHAL? A sub-human Neanderthal? Miss Fellowes thought in disbelief and bewilderment, with anger and a keen sense of betrayal rising right afterward. Was that really what the child was? If what Deveney had said was true, her worst fear had been confirmed.

She turned on Hoskins, glaring at him with a kind of controlled ferocity.

"You might have told me, doctor."

"Why? What difference does it make?"

"You said a child, not an animal."

"This is a child, Miss Fellowes. Don't you think so?"

"A *Neanderthal* child."

Hoskins looked puzzled. "Yes, yes, of course. You know what sort of experimentation Stasis Technologies has been involved in. Certainly you aren't going to tell me that you didn't realize the child would be drawn from a prehistoric era. We discussed all that with you."

"Prehistoric, yes. But Neanderthal? I expected to be looking after a human child."

"Neanderthals were human," Hoskins said, showing some signs of annoyance now. "More or less."

"Were they? Is that true?"

She looked toward Candide Deveney in appeal.

Deveney said, "Well, according to the thinking of most paleoan-thropologists over the past sixty or seventy years, the Neanderthals certainly must be considered to be a form of *Homo sapiens*, Miss Fellowes—an archaic branch of the species, perhaps, or a subspecies, a kind of backwoods cousin, so to speak, but definitely close kin, definitely to be considered human—"

Impatiently Hoskins cut in. "Let that point go for a moment, Deveney. There's another issue to address here. —Miss Fellowes, have you ever had a puppy or a kitten?"

"When I was a young girl, yes. But what does that have to do with—"

"Back when you had this puppy of yours, this kitten, did you care for it? Did you love it?"

"Of course. But—"

"Was it human, Miss Fellowes?"

"It was a *pet*, doctor. We're not talking about pets now. This is a professional matter. You're asking a highly trained nurse with a considerable background in advanced pediatric medicine to take care of—of—"

"Suppose this child here were a baby chimpanzee," Hoskins asked. "Would you be repelled? If I asked you to care for it, would you do so or would you turn away in disgust? And this isn't a chimpanzee. It isn't any sort of anthropoid ape. It's a young human being."

"A Neanderthal child."

"Just as I said. A young human being. Strange-looking and wild, precisely as I told you it would be. A difficult case. You're an experienced nurse, Miss Fellowes, with a superb record of achievement. Do you shy away from difficult cases? Have you ever refused to take care of a deformed infant?"

Miss Fellowes felt her argument slipping away. She said, with much less vehemence, "You might have told me."

"And you would have refused the position, is that it?"

"Well—"

"You knew we were dealing with a range of thousands of years here."

" 'Thousands' could mean three thousand. It wasn't until this evening, when you and Mr. Deveney were discussing the project and the phrase 'forty thousand years' suddenly entered it, that I began to realize what was really going on here. And even then I didn't fully understand that a Neanderthal would be involved. I'm no expert in— in— What was it you said, paleoanthropology, Mr. Deveney? I'm not familiar with the time-scale of human evolution the way you people are."

"You haven't answered my question," said Hoskins. "If you had known all the data ahead of time, would you have refused the position or wouldn't you?"

"I'm not sure."

"Do you want to refuse it now? There were other qualified candidates, you know. Is this a resignation?"

Hoskins gazed at her coolly, while Deveney watched from the other side of the room, and the Neanderthal child, having finished the milk and licked the plate dry, looked up at her with a wet face and wide longing eyes.

She stared at the boy. The ugly little boy. She heard her own voice saying, *But Neanderthal? I expected to be looking after a human child.*

The boy pointed to the milk, and to the plate. And suddenly he burst out in a short series of brusque, harsh sounds repeated over and over: sounds made up of weirdly strangled gutturals and elaborate tongue-clickings.

Miss Fellowes said in surprise, "Why, he talks!"

"Apparently he does," said Hoskins. "Or at least he can make a *feed me again* sound. —Which any cat is capable of doing, of course."

"No—no, he was talking," said Miss Fellowes.

"That's yet to be determined. There's plenty of controversy over whether Neanderthals were capable of true speech. That's one of the things we hope we're going to be able to settle during the span of this experiment."

The child made the clicking, gargling sounds again. Looked at Miss Fellowes. Looked at the milk, and at the empty plate.

"There's your answer," she said. "He's definitely talking!"

"If that's so, then he's human, wouldn't you say, Miss Fellowes?"

She let the question pass without responding. The issue was too complex to consider just now. A hungry child was calling to her. She reached for the milk.

Hoskins caught her by the wrist and pulled her upward so that she was facing him. "Wait a moment, Miss Fellowes. Before we go any further, I have to know whether you're planning to stay on the job."

She shook free of him in annoyance. "Will you starve him if I don't? He's asking for more milk, and you're preventing me from giving it to him."

"Go ahead. But I need to know your answer."

"I'll stay with him—for a while."

She poured the milk. The boy crouched down and plunged his face into it, lapping and slurping as if he hadn't had anything to drink or eat in days. He made little crooning noises deep in his throat as he licked the plate.

He's nothing but a little beast, Miss Fellowes thought. A little beast!

She came close to shuddering. She repressed it with a struggle.

## [13]

Hoskins said, "We're going to leave you with the boy, Miss Fellowes. He's been through a considerable ordeal and it's best to clear everyone out of here and allow you to try to settle him down for some rest."

"I agree."

He gestured toward the oval metal doorway, much like the hatch of a submarine, that stood open at the entrance to the dollhouse. "This is the only door to Stasis Section One, and it's going to be elaborately locked and guarded at all times. We'll seal it when we leave here. Tomorrow I'll want you to learn the details of operating the lock, which will, of course, be keyed to your fingerprints as they are already to keyed to mine. The spaces overhead"—he looked upward toward the open ceilings of the dollhouse—"are also guarded by a network of sensors, and we'll be warned immediately if anything untoward takes place in here."

"Untoward?"

"An intrusion."

"Why should there be—"

"We have a Neanderthal child from the year 40,000 B.C. in these chambers," Hoskins said, with barely concealed impatience. "It may sound unlikely to you, but there are all sorts of possibilities for intrusion here, anyone ranging from Hollywood producers to rival scientific groups to one of those self-styled advocates for children's rights that you and I were discussing at our first meeting."

Bruce Mannheim, Miss Fellowes thought. He really is worried about trouble with Mannheim. It wasn't just a hypothetical question, wanting to know if I had ever had any run-ins with Mannheim in my career.

"Well, of course," she said. "The child needs to be protected."

Then something occurred to her. She glanced up toward the topless ceiling, remembering how she had been able to see into the little rooms of the dollhouse from the balcony. —"You mean I'll be in full view of any observers who might be looking down from up there?" she asked indignantly.

"No, no," said Hoskins. He smiled. A benign smile, perhaps a little condescending, she thought. *The prudish spinster lady is worried about Peeping Toms. But there was no reason why she should have to dress and undress under the scrutiny of strangers.* "Your privacy will be respected completely, Miss Fellowes. I assure you of that. Trust me, Miss Fellowes."

There he went. *Trust me* again. He liked to use that phrase; he probably used it all the time, with everyone he dealt with. It wasn't a phrase that inspired much trust. The more often he used it, the less she trusted him.

"If anybody at all can walk onto that balcony and look down into these rooms, I fail to see how—"

"Access to the balcony is going to be strictly restricted—*strictly*," Hoskins said. "The only ones going up there will be technicians who may have to work on the power core, and you'll be given ample notice if they do. The sensors that I spoke about will be conducting purely electronic surveillance, which only a computer will deal with. We won't be spying on you. —You'll stay with him tonight, Miss Fellowes, is that understood? And every night thereafter, until further notice."

"Very well."

"You'll be relieved during the day according to whatever schedule you find convenient. We'll arrange that with you tomorrow. Mortenson, Elliott, and Ms. Stratford will make themselves available on a rotating schedule to fill in for you whenever you're away from the boy. He'll have to be guarded by one of you at all times. It's absolutely essential that he remain within the Stasis area and that you be constantly aware of his whereabouts."

Miss Fellowes peered about the dollhouse with a puzzled expression. "But why is all that necessary, Dr. Hoskins? Is the boy so dangerous?"

"It's a matter of energy, Miss Fellowes. There are conservation laws involved that I can explain to you if you like, but I think you have more important things to deal with just now. The point to bear in mind is simply that he must never be allowed to leave these rooms.

*Never.* Not for an instant. Not for any reason. Not to save his life. Not even to save *your* life, Miss Fellowes. —Is that clear?"

Miss Fellowes raised her chin in something of a theatrical way. "I'm not sure what you mean by a conservation law, but I do understand the orders, Dr. Hoskins. The boy stays in his rooms, if there's some good and sufficient reason for it, and evidently there is. Even if my own life is at stake, melodramatic as that sounds, I'm prepared to abide by that. —The nursing profession is accustomed to placing its duties ahead of self-preservation."

"Good. You can always signal via the intercom system if you need anyone. Good night, Miss Fellowes."

And the two men left. Everyone else had already gone out. The hatch swung shut and Miss Fellowes thought she heard the sound of electronic devices clicking into place.

She was locked in. With a wild child from the year 40,000 B.C.

She turned to the boy. He was watching her warily and there was still milk in the saucer. Laboriously Miss Fellowes tried to show him in pantomimed gestures how to lift the saucer and place it to his lips. The pantomime had no effect. He simply stared but made no attempt to imitate her. She acted it out instead, as she had before, lifting the saucer to her own face and pretending to lick the milk from it.

"Now you," she said. "Try it."

Still he stared. He was trembling.

"It isn't hard," she said. "I'll show you how to do it. Here. Let me have your hands."

Gently—very gently—she put her hands to his wrists.

He growled, a terrifying sound coming out of a child so small, and pulled his arms away from her with startling force. His face blazed with rage and fear. The lightning-bolt birthmark stood out fiercely against his newly cleansed skin.

Dr. Hoskins had seized him by the wrists only a little while ago. And had pulled his arms together across his body and dangled him in mid-air. No doubt the boy still could remember the sensation of those big male hands roughly grasping his wrists.

"No," Miss Fellowes said, in her softest tone. "I'm not trying to hurt you. I just want to show you how to hold your milk saucer."

His frightened eyes were on her, watching, watching for any false move. Slowly she reached for his wrists again, but he shook his head and jerked them out of her reach.

"All right," she said. "I'll hold the saucer. You just lick from it. But at least you won't be crouching on the floor like a little animal."

She poured a little more milk into the plate, lifted it, held it out to him at his own level. And waited.

Waited.

He made the clicking sounds and the guttural gargles that meant hunger. But he didn't move toward the plate.

He looked up at her, big-eyed.

He made a sound, one which she didn't think that she had heard him make before.

What did this one mean? *Put the plate down, you stupid old creature, so I can lick some milk!* Was that it?

"Come on, child. Drink it without going down on the floor, the way a decent little human child should."

He stared. Clicked again, a little mournfully.

"Do it like this," Miss Fellowes said. Practically bending double, she thrust her face forward—it was hard; she didn't have a jutting muzzle-like mouth like his—and lapped a little milk from her side of the saucer as she held it in front of him. He peered solemnly at her from the other side, just a short distance away.

How huge his eyes are, she thought.

"Like this—"

She lapped a little more of the milk.

He moved forward. Kept his hands at his sides, so that she had to continue to hold the plate; but he let his tongue flicker out tentatively, then with more enthusiasm, and began to drink, still standing.

Miss Fellowes started to lower the plate toward the floor.

He grunted in displeasure as it descended and brought his own hands up to maintain it at his level. She took hers quickly away. Now the boy was holding the saucer all by himself. Lapping eagerly.

(Well done, child. Magnificent!)

The plate was empty. Now that he was through drinking, he casually let it drop to the floor, and it smashed into half a dozen pieces. The boy looked up at her in what seemed almost certainly an expression registering dismay, chagrin, maybe even fear. Something like a whimper came from him.

Miss Fellowes smiled.

"It's only a plate, boy. Plates are of no importance. There are plenty more where that one came from. And plenty more milk, too."

She shoved the broken pieces aside with her foot—it would be important to get them picked up in a moment, because they were sharp, but let that wait for now—and drew another plate, identical to the first, from the cabinet at the base of the food cart. She held it up to him.

The whimpering stopped. He smiled at her.

An unmistakable smile, the first one she had seen from him since his arrival. It was astonishingly broad—how wide his mouth was, truly ear to ear!—and wonderfully brilliant, like sudden sunlight breaking through dark clouds.

Miss Fellowes returned the smile. Gingerly she reached out to touch him, to stroke his hair, moving her hand very slowly, letting him follow it with his eyes every inch of the way, making sure that he could see that there was no harm in it.

He trembled. But he remained where he was, looking up at her. For a moment she succeeded in stroking his hair; and then he pulled back, bucking timidly away, she thought, like some frightened little—

—*beast*.

Miss Fellowes' face flamed at the thought.

(Stop it. You mustn't think of him that way. He's not an animal, no matter how he may look. He's a boy, a little boy, a frightened little boy, a frightened little *human* boy.)

But his hair—how coarse it had felt, in that one moment when he had allowed her to touch it! How tangled, how rough, how thick!

What strange hair it was. What very, very, very strange hair indeed.

## [14]

She said, "I'm going to have to show you how to use the bathroom. Do you think you can learn?"

She spoke quietly, kindly, knowing quite well that he wouldn't understand her words, but hoping that he would respond to the calmness of the tone.

The boy launched into a clicking phrase again. More milk, was that was what he wanted? Or was this something new he was saying? Miss Fellowes hoped that they were recording every sound he made. Very likely they were, but she meant to mention it to Hoskins the next day anyway. She wanted to study the child's way of speech, to learn his language if there were some way she could manage it. Assuming it *was* a language, and not just some kind of instinctive animal sounds. Miss Fellowes intended to try to teach him English, if she could, but that might not be possible, and in that case she would at least attempt to learn how to communicate with him in his own fashion.

A strange concept: learning how to speak Neanderthal. But she had done a few things almost as odd in her time, for the sake of making contact with difficult children.

"May I take your hand?" she said.

Miss Fellowes held hers out and the boy looked at it as though he had never seen a hand before. She left it outstretched and waited. The boy frowned. After a moment his own hand rose uncertainly and crept forward, quivering a little, toward hers.

"That's right," she said. "Take my hand."

The trembling hand approached within an inch of hers and then the boy's courage failed him. He snatched it back as though fire were coming from her fingertips.

"Well," said Miss Fellowes calmly, "we'll try again later. Would you like to sit down here?"

She patted the mattress of the bed.

No response.

She pantomimed sitting down.

Nothing. A blank stare.

She sat down herself—not easy, on a small bed so close to the ground—and patted the space beside her.

"Here," she said, giving him her warmest, most reassuring smile. "Sit down next to me, won't you?"

Silence. A stare. Then a barrage of clicking sounds again, and some deep grunting noises—new ones, she was sure of it this time. He seemed to have a considerable vocabulary of clicks and grunts and gargles. It *had* to be a language. A major scientific breakthrough already: Dr. Hoskins had said that no one knew whether the Neanderthals had a language or not, and she had proved right at the outset that they had.

(No, not proved, Miss Fellowes told herself sternly. Merely hypothesized. But it was a plausible hypothesis.)

"Sit down? No?"

Clicks. She listened and tried to imitate them, but they came clumsily off her tongue, with none of his rapid-fire crispness of delivery. He looked at her in—wonder? Amusement? His expressions were so hard to read. But he seemed fascinated by the idea that she was making clicks at him. For all she knew, she was saying something vile and dreadful in his language. Speaking the unspeakable. But it was much more likely that the sounds she was making were just so much incomprehensible gibberish to him. Perhaps he thought she was deranged.

He clicked and growled, in a low, quiet, almost reflective way.

She clicked back at him. She mimicked his growls. They were easier to imitate than the clicks. He stared again. His expression was grave, pensive, very much the way a child who has been confronted by a crazy adult might look.

This is completely ridiculous, Miss Fellowes told herself. I need to stick to English. He'll never learn anything if I make idiotic mumbo-jumbo noises at him in what I imagine is his own language.

"Sit," she said, the way she would have said it to a puppy. "Sit! —No? Well, no, then. Bathroom? Take my hand and I'll show you how to use the bathroom. —No again, is it? You can't just go on the floor, you know. This isn't 40,000 B.C., and even if you're accustomed to digging a hole in the ground after yourself, boy, you aren't going to be able to do that here. Especially with a wooden floor. Take my hand and let's go inside, all right? —No? A little later?"

Miss Fellowes realized that she was starting to babble.

The problem was, she began to see, that she was exhausted. It was getting late, now, and she had been under a bizarre strain since early evening. There was something very dreamlike about sitting here in this dollhouse room trying to explain to a little ape-child with bulging brows and great goggling eyes how to drink milk from a saucer, how to go to the bathroom, how to sit down on a little bed.

No, she thought severely. Not an ape-child.

Never call him that—not even to yourself!

"Take my hand?" Miss Fellowes said again.

He almost did. Almost.

The hours were crawling slowly along, and there had been scarcely any progress. She wasn't going to succeed either with the bathroom or with the bed, that was obvious. And now he too was showing signs of fatigue. He yawned. His eyes looked glazed; his lids were drooping. Suddenly he folded himself up and lay down on the bare floor and then, with a quick movement, rolled beneath the bed.

Miss Fellowes, on her knees, stared down underneath at him. His eyes gleamed out at her and he chattered at her in tongue-clicks.

"All right," she told him. "If you feel safer there, you sleep there."

She waited a little while, until she heard the sound of steady, regular breathing. How tired he must be! Forty thousand years from home, thrust into a baffling alien place full of bright lights and hard floors and strange people who looked nothing at all like anyone he had ever known, and even so he was capable of curling up and falling asleep. Miss Fellowes envied him that wonderful adaptability. Children were so resilient, so capable of accommodating to the most terrible disruptions—

She turned out the light and closed the door to the boy's bedroom, and retired to the cot that had been left for her use in the largest room.

Overhead there was nothing but darkness. She scrutinized it, wondering whether someone might be lurking about on the balcony, observing her. It was impossible to tell. Miss Fellowes knew that she was being absurd, that it was late and there was no one up there. The only eyes that would be watching her were those of a bunch of electronic sensors. But still—to have no privacy at all—

They were filming everything, very likely. Making a complete visual record of all that took place in the Stasis zone. She should never have taken on this job without insisting that Hoskins let her inspect the sort of place where she was going to have to live.

*Trust me,* he had said.

Right. Certainly.

Well, she'd make do for tonight. But tomorrow they were going to have to put a roof over her living quarters, at least. And also, she thought, those stupid men will have to place a mirror in this room and a larger chest of drawers and a separate washroom if they expect me to spend my nights in here.

### [15]

It was difficult to sleep. Tired as she was, she lay with her eyes open, in the kind of absolute wakefulness that one reaches only in a state of the most extreme fatigue. She strained to hear any sounds that might come from the next room.

He couldn't get out, could he? *Could* he?

The walls were sheer and impossibly high, but suppose the child could climb like a monkey?

Up a vertical wall with no hand-holds? And there you go again, thinking of him as a monkey!

He couldn't climb up and over, no. She was certain of that. And in any case, there were Hoskins' ever-watchful sensors up there in the balcony. Surely they'd notice and give an alarm, if the boy started climbing around from room to room in the middle of the night.

Surely.

(There's so much that I didn't take the trouble to find out, Miss Fellowes thought.)

And then suddenly she found herself asking herself: Can he be dangerous? Physically dangerous?

She considered how much trouble it had been to give him his bath. She had watched first Hoskins and then Elliott battling to hold him in place. Just a little child, and how strong he was! The scratch he had given Elliott!

What if he came in here and—

No, Miss Fellowes told herself. He won't hurt me.

Beyond any doubt Hoskins wouldn't have left her in here alone, overhead sensors or no overhead sensors, if he felt there was any risk that—

She tried to laugh at her own fears. He was only a three-year-old child, perhaps four at most. Still, she hadn't managed to get his nails trimmed yet. If he should attack her with nails and teeth while she slept—

Her breath came quickly. Oh, how ridiculous, how completely ridiculous, and yet—

She was endlessly going back and forth, she knew, unable to take a consistent position and hold it for long. Was he a dangerous nasty little ape, or was he a miserably frightened little child far from his loved ones? One or the other, she told herself. But why not some of both? Even a frightened little child can hurt you if he strikes out with enough force. She could remember a few nasty episodes at the hospital—children driven to such desperation that they had attacked staff people with real vehemence and done some real damage.

Miss Fellowes didn't dare let herself fall asleep. Didn't dare.

She lay staring upward, listening with painful attentiveness. And now she heard a sound.

The boy was crying.

Not shrieking in fear or anger; not yelling or screaming. It was crying softly, and the cry was the heartbroken sobbing of a lonely, lonely child.

All her ambivalence dissolved at once. For the first time, Miss Fellowes thought with a pang: Poor thing! Poor terrified child!

Of *course* it was a child. What did the shape of its head matter, or the texture of its hair? It was a child that had been orphaned as no child had ever been orphaned before. Hoskins had said it, and said it accurately, at their first meeting: *"This will be the most lonely child in the history of the world."* Not just its mother and father were gone, but all its species, every last one. Snatched callously out of its proper time, it was now the only creature of its kind in the world.

The last. The only.

She felt her pity for it strengthen and deepen, and with that came shame at her own callousness: the repugnance she had allowed herself to feel for the child, the irritation she had let herself show at its wild ways. How, she wondered, could she have been so cruel? So *unprofessional*. Bad enough to be kidnapped like this; worse to be looked upon with disdain by the very person who was supposed to care for you and teach you to find your way in your bewildering new life.

Tucking her nightgown carefully about her calves—the overhead sensors, she couldn't stop worrying about those idiotic sensors!—Miss Fellowes got out of bed and tiptoed into the boy's room.

"Little boy," she called in a whisper. "Little boy."

She knelt and started to reach under the bed. But then the thought came—shameful but prudent, born of long experience with troubled children—that he might try to bite her, and she pulled back her hand. Instead she turned on the night light and moved the bed away from the wall.

The poor thing was huddled miserably in the corner, knees up against his chin, looking up at her with blurred and apprehensive eyes.

In the dim light she was able to ignore his repulsiveness, the thick blunt features, the big misshapen head.

"Poor little boy," she murmured. "Poor frightened little boy."

Miss Fellowes stroked his hair, that harsh tangled bristly hair that had felt so disagreeable to her a few hours before. Now it merely seemed unusual. He stiffened at the first touch of her hand, but then she saw him relax.

"Poor child," she said. "Let me hold you."

He made a soft clicking sound. Then a little low growl, a kind of gentle unhappy rumbling.

She sat down on the floor next to him and stroked his hair again, slowly, rhythmically. The tension was visibly going from his body. Perhaps no one had ever stroked his hair before, back in whatever ferocious prehistoric life it was that he had left behind. He seemed to like it. Gently, tenderly, she played with his hair, smoothing it, straightening it, picking a few burrs out of it, but mainly just running her hand along the top of his head, slowly, slowly, almost hypnotically.

She stroked his cheek, his arm. He allowed it.

Softly she began to sing a slow and gentle song, a wordless repetitive one, a tune that she had known since childhood, one that she had sung to many disturbed children to soothe them, to calm them.

He lifted his head at that, staring at her mouth in the dimness, as though wondering at the sound.

She maneuvered him closer, gathering him in while he listened to her. He offered no resistance. Slowly she pressed her hand against the side of his head, gently guiding it toward her until it rested on her shoulder. She put her arm under his thighs and with a smooth and unhurried motion lifted him into her lap.

She continued singing, the same quiet, sinuous musical phrase over and over, while she rocked back and forth, back and forth, back and forth.

He had stopped crying, somewhere along the way.

After a while the smooth, even purr of his breathing told Miss Fellowes that he was asleep.

With infinite care she nudged his bed back against the wall, pushing it into place with her knee, and laid him down on it. She pulled the covers over him—had he ever known a coverlet before? Certainly not a bed!—and tucked them in and stood over him for a time, staring down at him. His face looked wondrously peaceful as he slept.

Somehow it didn't matter so much now that it was so ugly. Really.

She made her way out of the room on tiptoes. But as she reached the door she paused and halted, thinking: What if he wakes up!

He might be even more troubled than before, expecting to find her comforting presence close at hand and not knowing where she had gone. He might panic; he might run amok.

Miss Fellowes hesitated, battling irresolutely with herself. She stood above the bed again, studying him as he slept. Then she sighed. There was only one thing to do. Slowly she lowered herself to the bed and lay down beside him.

The bed was much too small for her. She had to draw her legs up close against her chest, and her left elbow pressed against the wall, and to avoid disturbing the boy she had to twist herself around into an intricate uncomfortable curve. She lay there wide awake, cramped and bent, feeling like Alice after she had sampled the "Drink Me" bottle in Wonderland. Very well: so she'd get no sleep this night. This was only the first night. Things would be easier later on. Sometimes there were higher priorities than sleep.

She felt a touch against her hand. The child's fingers, grazing her palm. He was reaching for her in his sleep. The rough little hand crept into hers.

Miss Fellowes smiled.

### [16]

She awoke with a start, wondering where she was, why she felt so stiff and sore. There was the unfamiliar smell of another person in her nostrils and the unfamiliar sense of someone's body pressing against hers.

She had to fight back a wild impulse to scream. She was able just barely to suppress it into a gurgle.

The boy was sitting up, looking at her wide-eyed. The ugly little boy, the child snatched from time. The little Neanderthal child.

It took a long moment for Miss Fellowes to remember getting into bed with him. Then it all came back. She realized that she had managed somehow to fall asleep, despite everything. And now it was morning.

Slowly, without unfixing her eyes from his, she stretched one leg carefully and let it touch the floor, and then the other. Her muscles were tensed for quick disengagement in case the boy should go into a panic.

She cast a quick and apprehensive glance toward the open ceiling. Were they watching, up there? Cameras grinding away as she made her bleary-eyed entry into the new day?

Then the boy's stubby fingers reached out and touched her lips. He said something: two quick clicks and a growl.

Miss Fellowes shrank involuntarily away from him at the touch. She glanced down at him. A little shiver ran through her. She hated herself for it, but there was no preventing it. He was terribly ugly in the light of day.

The boy spoke again. He opened his own mouth and gestured with his hand as though something were coming out.

The meaning wasn't hard to decode. Tremulously Miss Fellowes said, "Do you want me to sing again? Is that it?"

The boy said nothing, but he was staring at her mouth.

In a voice that was quavering and slightly off-key with tension, Miss Fellowes began the little song that she had sung the night before. The ugly little boy smiled. He seemed to recognize the melody, and he swayed clumsily in rough time to it, waving his arms about. He made a little gurgly sound that might have been the beginnings of a laugh.

Miss Fellowes sighed inwardly. Music hath charms to soothe the savage breast. Well, whatever would help—

She said, "You wait. Let me get myself fixed up. It'll just take a minute. Then I'll make breakfast for you."

She rinsed her face and brushed out her hair, maddeningly conscious the whole time of the lack of ceiling covering, the invisible staring electronic eyes. Perhaps not only electronic ones, she thought.

The boy remained in bed, looking toward her. He seemed calm. The fierce frenzied wildness of his first few hours in the twenty-first century seemed long ago, now. Whenever she turned his way, Miss Fellowes waved at him. Eventually he waved back, an awkward but charming gesture that sent a little chill of surprise and delight down her spine.

When she was done she said, "You could use something solid, I suspect. What about some oatmeal with your milk?"

He smiled, almost as though he had understood her. Almost.

It took only a moment to prepare the cereal in the microwave oven. Then she beckoned to the boy.

Whether he understood the gesture or was simply following the aroma, Miss Fellowes had no way of knowing; but he got out of bed and came stumping over to her. His legs were very short in proportion to his stocky trunk, which made them look more bowed than in fact they were.

He glanced down at the floor, plainly in the expectation that she was going to set the bowl of oatmeal in front of him down there for him to lick.

"No," she said. "You're a civilized little boy now. Or at least you're going to be one. Civilized little boys don't eat on the floor."

Clicks. Growls.

"I know you don't understand anything I'm saying. But you will, sooner or later. I don't think I can learn your language, but I'm pretty certain you're capable of learning mine."

She took a spoon from the drawer and showed it to him.

"Spoon."

He looked at it stolidly, without interest.

"To eat with. *Spoon*."

She dipped it into the oatmeal and carried it to her mouth. His eyes widened and his broad nostrils flared even wider and he made a strange uneasy drawn-out noise, like a very quiet howl: the sound, Miss Fellowes suspected, of a hungry creature that thinks some other creature is going to steal its breakfast.

She pantomimed putting the spoon into her mouth, swallowing the oatmeal, licking her lips in pleasure. Round-eyed, unhappy-looking, he watched the process, all too obviously failing to comprehend.

"Now you try it," Miss Fellowes said. She dumped the oatmeal back into the bowl, turning the empty spoon toward him to show him that she hadn't eaten any of it. Then she scooped more onto the spoon and held it out to him.

He drew back, eyes wide with alarm as though the spoon were a weapon. His tawny little face puckered in fright and he uttered a sound that was not quite a sob, not quite a growl.

"Look," she said. "Spoon. Oatmeal. Mouth."

No. Hungry as he was, he didn't want to know anything about the spoon. Well, time enough for that, Miss Fellowes thought. She put the spoon away.

"But you're going to have to hold the bowl in your hands. You know how to do that. There's going to be no crouching on the floor to eat around here."

She offered him the bowl. He glanced at it and looked down at the floor.

"Hold it in your hands."

Clicks. She thought she recognized them as a familiar pattern, but she couldn't be certain. By God, Hoskins would have to tape those sounds! If he wasn't already doing so.

"In your hands," Miss Fellowes said again, firmly. "Here."

He understood. He took the bowl into his hands, with his thumbs sticking into the oatmeal, and lifted it to his face. He did it clumsily enough and it was incredibly messy but most of it did get into him.

So he was a quick learner—when he wasn't numbed by fear. Miss Fellowes doubted that there'd be much more animal-like lapping of food on the floor.

She watched him closely as he ate. He seemed to be in good health, sturdy and strong. His eyes were bright, his color was high, there were no outward signs of fever or illness. So far he appeared to be withstanding the rigors of his extraordinary journey very well indeed.

Although she knew no more than anybody else about the growth patterns of Neanderthal children, Miss Fellowes started to think now that he probably was older than she had originally thought, definitely closer to four years of age than three. He was small, yes, but his physiological development was beyond the modern child's three-year-old level. Of course, some of that might just be the result of the conditions under which he had lived, back there in the Stone Age world. (Stone Age? Yes, of course, Neanderthals must be Stone Age. She was reasonably certain of that. There was so much that she needed to learn, when she had the chance.)

She tried having him drink his milk in a glass this time. He seemed to catch on swiftly to the idea of holding the glass in his hands—he needed both hands to do it, but that was the way most children his age held glasses, and at least he didn't find the glass as threatening as the spoon appeared to have been. But he had trouble with the opening, which was too small for him to get his face into conveniently, and he began to whine, a high-pitched keening sound of frustration that was starting to edge upward into anger. Miss Fellowes put her own hand over the little boy's, making him tip the glass, forcing his mouth to the rim.

Again a mess, but again most went into him. And she was used to messes.

The washroom, to her surprise and immense relief, was a less difficult matter. At first he appeared to think that the toilet bowl was some sort of fountain that might be fun to splash around in, and she was afraid that he was going to climb into it. But Miss Fellowes held him back and stood him in front of it and opened his robe, and he understood right away what it was she expected him to do.

She found herself patting his head, saying, "Good boy. Smart boy."

And to Miss Fellowes' exceeding pleasure, the boy smiled up at her.

It was going to be a morning of discoveries, Miss Fellowes realized pleasantly. For him and for her as well. He was learning about spoons and milk glasses and toilet bowls. She was learning about him. Discovering the essential humanity that lay behind that strange and ugly—oh, so ugly!—face of his.

She replied to his smile with one of her own. He smiled again. It was a very normal smile, the smile of a child who has seen that his smile has brought a pleasing response.

He wasn't at all a normal child, she reminded herself. It would be a serious mistake to allow herself any illusions about that.

But when he smiles, she thought, he's quite bearable. Really.

# CHAPTER FOUR

---

# Studying

[17]

MID-MORNING. She had bathed him again—far less of a battle than it had been yesterday—and given him a fairly close physical inspection—he showed some bruises and scratches of the sort you would expect a boy who had been living under primitive conditions to have, but no obvious signs of disease or serious injury—and had even succeeded, with a great deal of patience and an endless amount of singing to lull him into a peaceful mood, in trimming his fingernails. The toenails would have to wait until later. Neither she nor the boy had sufficient endurance to tackle any further manicure chores today.

Without her noticing it, the door to the Stasis bubble had opened while Miss Fellowes was going about her chores, and Hoskins was standing before her, silent, his arms folded. He might have been there for minutes.

He said, "May I come in?"

Miss Fellowes nodded curtly. "You seem already to have done that, haven't you?"

"I mean into the working area. —You didn't answer when I spoke to you on the intercom from outside."

"I was busy. You may need to speak louder. But come in, come in!"

The boy drew back as Hoskins entered. He gave Hoskins an uneasy look and seemed about to bolt into the rear room. Miss Fellowes smiled and beckoned to him and he came forward instead and clung to her, curling his little bandy legs—so thin, so very thin—about her.

A look of something close to awe blossomed on Hoskins' face. "You've made great progress, Miss Fellowes!"

"A little warm oatmeal can work wonders."

"He seems very attached to you already."

"I know how to do the things I'm supposed to do, Dr. Hoskins. Is that so astonishing?"

He reddened. "I didn't mean to imply—"

"No, of course not. I understand. He was a wild little animal when you last saw him yesterday, and now—"

"Not an animal at all."

"No," Miss Fellowes said. "Not an animal at all." She hesitated just a moment. Then she said, "I had some doubts about that at first."

"How could I forget it? You were quite indignant."

"But no longer. I over-reacted. At first glance I suppose I really did think he was an ape-boy, and I wasn't prepared to be taking on anything like that. But he's settling down amazingly. He's no ape, Dr. Hoskins. He's actually quite intelligent. We're getting along very well."

"I'm glad to hear it. Does that mean you've decided to keep the job, then?"

She gave him a steely glance. "That was never in doubt, was it, Dr. Hoskins?"

"Well—" Hoskins shrugged. "I suppose not. —You know, Miss Fellowes, you aren't the only one who's been a little on edge here. I think you can appreciate what a tremendous effort has gone into this project, and how much we've had riding on its success. And now that it *is* a success, an overwhelming success, we can't help but feel somewhat stunned. Like a man who has gathered up all his strength to go charging through a door that's barring his way. Suddenly he makes his mighty charge, and the door gives way under the onslaught with hardly any of the resistance he'd expected, and he bursts into the place that he's been wanting so hard to reach; and now that he's there, he stops and looks around, a little confused, and says to himself, *All right, I'm finally here, and now what?*"

"A good question, Dr. Hoskins. Now what? You'll be bringing all sorts of experts in to examine the boy, won't you? Specialists in prehistoric life, and people like that?"

"Of course."

"You'll have someone here soon to give him a thorough medical exam, I assume."

"Yes, naturally. —He's all right, though, wouldn't you say? Basically?"

"Basically, yes. He's a rugged little fellow. But I'm not a doctor and he hasn't had any sort of internal examination whatever. There's a difference between *seeming* healthy and *being* healthy. He could be carrying a load of parasites around: amoebas, protozoan infestations, all kinds of things. Probably is. Maybe they're harmless to him, maybe not. Even if they don't seriously threaten his welfare, they might threaten ours."

"We've already thought of that. Dr. Jacobs will be coming in at noon, to run a group of preliminary tests. He's the doctor you'll be working with as long as the project continues. If Dr. Jacobs doesn't upset the boy too much, Dr. McIntyre of the Smithsonian will be seeing him after that for the first anthropological examination. —And then the media will be coming here, too, of course."

That caught her short. "The media? What media? Who? When?"

"Why—they'll want to see the boy as soon as they can, Miss Fellowes. Candide Deveney's already broken the story. We'll have every newspaper and television network in the world banging on our doors by the end of the day."

Miss Fellowes looked down at the child and put her arm protectively to his shoulder. He quivered, just the tiniest of flinches, but made no move to escape her touch.

"You're going to fill this little place with journalists and cameras? On his first full day here?"

"Well, we hadn't thought about—"

"No," she said, "you hadn't thought. That much is obvious. Listen, Dr. Hoskins, he's your little Neanderthal and you can do whatever you want with him. But there'll be no media people in here until he's had his medical checkup and come out with a clean bill of health, at the very minimum. And preferably not until he's had more time to adapt to being here. You do understand what I'm saying, don't you?"

"Miss Fellowes, surely you know that publicity is an essential part of—"

"Yes. Publicity is an essential part of everything, these days. Imagine the publicity you'll get if this child dies of a panic attack right on camera!"

"Miss Fellowes!"

"Or if he catches a cold from one of your precious reporters. I tried to point out to you, when I was asking for a sterile environment, that he's probably got zero resistance to contemporary infectious microorganisms. *Zero.* No antibodies, no inherent resistance, nothing to ward off—"

"Please, Miss Fellowes. Please."

"And what if he gives them all some nice little Stone Age plague that *we* have no immunity to?"

"All right, Miss Fellowes. You've made your point."

"I want to be completely sure that I have. Let your media wait, is what I'm saying. He needs all sorts of protective inoculation first. It's bad enough that he's been exposed to as many people as he was last night; but I'm not going to let a whole mob of reporters in here, not today and not tomorrow, either. If they like, they can photograph him from upstairs, for the time being, outside the Stasis zone entirely, just as though we had a newborn infant in here, and I want them to be quiet about it, too. We can work out a video schedule later in the day. —Oh, and speaking of upstairs. I'm still not happy about the degree of exposure here. I want my quarters roofed over—a tarpaulin of some sort will do for the moment; I don't want workmen clattering around here with construction equipment just yet—and I think the rest of the dollhouse could safely be given a ceiling, too."

Hoskins smiled. "You mince no words. You're a very forceful woman, Miss Fellowes." His tone seemed to have as much admiration as annoyance in it.

"Forceful?" she said. "I suppose I am. At least where my children are concerned."

## [18]

Jacobs was a burly, blunt-faced man of about sixty, with thick white hair cropped close to his skull, military-fashion. He had an efficient, no-nonsense manner, a little on the brusque side, which some might say would be more suitable for an army doctor than for a pediatrician. But Miss Fellowes knew from long experience that children weren't troubled by that sort of brusqueness, so long as it was tempered by a fundamental kindliness. They expected a doctor to be an authority-figure. They wanted him to be one. They looked elsewhere for gentleness, tenderness, comfort. The doctor was supposed to be god-like, the solver of problems, the dispenser of cures.

Miss Fellowes wondered what kind of doctors had ministered to the needs of the little boy's tribe back there in 40,000 B.C. Witch-doctors, no doubt. Terrifying figures with bones through their noses and painted red circles around their eyes, who performed their diagnoses by leaping and cavorting around campfires that burned blue and green and scarlet. How would Dr. Jacobs look with a bone through his nose? she wondered. With a bear-skin around his shoulders instead of that prosaic white coat?

He offered her a quick, uncondescending handshake. "I've heard good things about you, Fellowes."

"So I would hope."

"You worked under Gallagher at Valley General, didn't you? Or so Hoskins said. Fine man, Gallagher. Dogmatic son of a bitch, but at least he swore by the right dogmas. How long were you in his department?"

"Three and a half years."

"You like him?"

Miss Fellowes shrugged. "Not particularly. I heard him say some things once to a young nurse that I thought were out of line. But he and I worked well together. I learned a great deal from him."

"A shrewd man, yes." Jacobs shook his head. "Pity about the way he handled his nurses. In more than one sense of the word. —You didn't happen to have any sort of run-in with him yourself, did you?"

"Me? No. No, nothing of the kind!"

"No, I guess he wouldn't have tried anything with you," Jacobs said.

Miss Fellowes wondered what he had meant by that. Not Gallagher's type, maybe? She wasn't anyone's type, and that was the way she had preferred things to be for many years. She let the remark pass.

Jacobs seemed to have memorized her entire résumé. He mentioned this hospital and that, this doctor and that one, spoke with easy familiarity of heads of nursing and boards of directors. Plainly he had been around. All she knew of Dr. Jacobs, on the other hand, was that he was something big at the state medical institute and had a considerable private practice on the side. Their paths had never crossed professionally. If Hoskins had seen fit to let him see her résumé, he might have thought of letting her see his. But Miss Fellowes let that point pass, too.

"And I suppose that now it's about time that we had a look at this little Neanderthal of yours," Jacobs said. "Where's he hiding?"

She gestured toward the other room. The boy was lurking uneasily in there, now and again peeping out, with a lock of his matted hair showing behind the barrier of the door and, occasionally, the corner of an eye.

"Shy, is he? That's not what I heard from the orderlies. They said he's as wild as a little ape."

"Not any more. His initial terror has worn off, and now he simply feels lost and frightened."

"As well he should, poor little critter. But we've got to get down to this. Call him out here, please. Or will you have to go in there and get him?"

"Maybe I can call him," Miss Fellowes said.

She turned to face the boy. "You can come out, Timmie. This is Dr. Jacobs. He won't hurt you."

*Timmie?*

Where had that come from? She had no idea.

The name had just surged up out of the well of her unconscious that moment. She had never known a Timmie in her life. But the boy had to be called something, didn't he? And it seemed that she had named him, now. Timothy. Timmie for short. So be it. A real name, a human name. Timmie.

"Timmie?" she said again, liking the sound of it, enjoying being able to call him by name. She could stop thinking of him as "the child," "the Neanderthal," "the ugly little boy." He was Timmie. He was a person. He had a name.

And as she approached the other room Timmie slipped back behind the door, out of sight.

"All right," Jacobs said, with some impatience. "We can't spend all day at this. Go in there and bring him out, will you, Fellowes?"

He slipped a surgical mask over his face—as much for his protection, Miss Fellowes guessed, as for Timmie's.

But the mask was a mistake. Timmie peeked out and saw it and let out a shrill piercing howl as though he had seen some demon out of his Stone Age nightmares. As Miss Fellowes reached the door, he flung himself violently against the wall on the far side of the room, like a caged creature fleeing its keeper, and pressed up against it, shivering fearfully.

"Timmie— Timmie—"

No use. He wouldn't let her near him, not with Jacobs anywhere about. The boy had tolerated Hoskins' presence well enough, but Jacobs seemed to scare the daylights out of him. So much for her theory that children wanted their doctors to be brusque no-nonsense military types. Not *this* child, at any rate.

She rang the bell and summoned Mortenson and Elliot.

"We're going to need a little help, I think," Miss Fellowes told them.

The two husky orderlies looked at each other uncertainly. There was a visible bulge along Elliot's left arm, under his uniform jacket—a bandage, no doubt, covering the scratch that Timmie had inflicted yesterday.

"Oh, come *on,*" Miss Fellowes said. "He's only a small child, you know."

But the boy, in his terror, had reverted completely to his original feral mode. Flanked by Mortenson and Elliott, Miss Fellowes entered his room and attempted to take hold of him, but he went scrambling wildly around the room with truly anthropoid agility, and they were hard put to get a grip on him. Finally Mortenson, with a lunge, caught him by the midsection and spun him up off the ground. Elliott cautiously took hold of him by the ankles and tried to prevent him from kicking.

Miss Fellowes went over to him. Softly she said, "It's all right, Timmie—no one will hurt you—"

She might just as well have said, "Trust me." The boy struggled furiously, with nearly as much enterprise as he had shown the day before when they were trying to give him a bath.

Feeling preposterous, Miss Fellowes tried crooning the little tune of the night before at him in an attempt to lull him into cooperating. That was useless, too.

Dr. Jacobs leaned close. "We'll have to sedate him, I guess. —God, he's an ugly little thing!"

Miss Fellowes felt a sharp stab of fury, almost as though Timmie were her own child. How *dare* he say anything like that! How dare he!

Crisply she retorted, "It's a classic Neanderthal face. He's very handsome, by Neanderthal standards." She wondered where she had gotten that from. She knew practically nothing about what a classic Neanderthal face was supposed to be like, and nothing whatever about Neanderthal standards of handsomeness. "—I don't much like the idea of sedating him. But if there's no other alternative—"

"I don't think there is," said the doctor. "We aren't going to get anywhere holding him down by brute force while I try to take my readings."

No, Miss Fellowes thought. The boy wasn't going to have any enthusiasm for having a tongue depressor pushed into his mouth or lights shined into his eyes, no tolerance at all for surrendering a sample of his blood, no willingness to have his temperature taken, even by a remote-control thermocouple relay. Reluctantly she nodded.

Jacobs produced an ultrasonic tranquilizer ampoule from his kit and started to activate it.

"You don't know anything about the appropriate dose," Miss Fellowes said.

The doctor looked at her in surprise. "These doses are calibrated for a body weight of up to thirty kilograms. This should be well within tolerance."

"Calibrated for a *human* body weight of up to thirty kilograms, doctor. This is a Neanderthal child. We don't have any data on their circulatory systems at all."

Her own line of reasoning startled her. In some chagrin she realized that she had drawn a distinction between Neanderthals and humans once again. She didn't seem able to maintain a consistent philosophy about the boy. He *is* human, she told herself vehemently. Human, human, human. He's Timmie and he's human.

But to Jacobs it was an issue not even worth discussing, apparently.

"Even if he were a young gorilla or orangutan, Fellowes, I'd regard this as an appropriate dose. Human, Neanderthal, what does his circulatory system have to do with it? It's body mass that matters. —All right, a half dose this time. Just to take no risks with Hoskins' precious little creature."

Not only Hoskins', Miss Fellowes found herself thinking, to her own astonishment.

Jacobs stepped the dosage down and touched the ampoule to Timmie's forearm. There was a little buzz and the tranquilizer instantly began to do its work.

"Well, now," the doctor said. "Let's get a little of that paleolithic blood of his, and a little prehistoric urine. —Do you have a stool sample for me, Fellowes?"

"He hasn't moved his bowels since he's been here, Dr. Jacobs. The dislocation of the trip through time—"

"Well, when he does, suppose you scrape some up off the floor and let me know, will you?"

"He uses the *toilet*, doctor," Miss Fellowes said in a tone of ringing indignation.

Jacobs looked up at her. Surprise and what could have been anger were evident in his expression; but then he laughed. "You're very quick to defend him, I see."

"Yes. Yes, I am. Is there anything wrong with that?"

"I suppose there isn't. —All right, when the boy next uses the toilet, I want that sample if he happens to move his bowels. I take it he doesn't flush afterward yet, eh, Fellowes?"

This time both Elliott and Mortenson laughed also. Miss Fellowes didn't share in the general amusement.

Timmie seemed asleep—passive, at any rate, quiescent, tolerant. Jacobs had no difficulty opening his mouth to study his dentition. Miss Fellowes, who hadn't had an opportunity of seeing Timmie's teeth before, stared over Jacobs' shoulder, afraid that she was going to behold fierce, savage, ape-like fangs. But no, no: his teeth were nothing like that. They were somewhat large, larger than a modern child's, and they looked strong, but they were nicely shaped, evenly arranged, a very fine set of teeth indeed. And human, definitely human, no terrifying jutting incisors, no great projecting canine teeth. Miss Fellowes let out her breath slowly in a deep sigh of relief.

Jacobs closed the boy's mouth, peered into his ears, rolled back his eyelids. Looked at the palms of his hands, the soles of his feet, tapped his chest, palpated his abdomen, flexed his arms and his legs, dug his fingers lightly into the musculature of his forearms and thighs.

"A little powerhouse is what he is. As you've already had reason to discover. Small for his age and slightly on the thin side but there's no indication of malnutrition. Once we get that stool sample I'll have some idea of what sorts of things he'd been eating, but the most probable guess is a high-protein low-starch diet, pretty much what you'd expect among hunters and gatherers living in a time of adverse climate."

"Adverse?" Miss Fellowes asked.

"An ice age," Jacobs said, a little patronizingly. "That's what was going on most of the time during the Neanderthal era—a glacial period."

How would *you* know? she thought belligerently. Were you there? Are you an anthropologist?

But she held her tongue. Dr. Jacobs was doing everything possible to rub her the wrong way; but nevertheless he was her colleague now, and they would have to maintain a civil relationship. For Timmie's sake, if for no other reason.

[19]

Timmie stirred and became restless by the time the medical exam was half over, and a little while later it was obvious that the tranquilizer had all but worn off. Which meant that a normal dose for an ordinary child of his size would have been the correct one, as Jacobs had insisted, and that Miss Fellowes had erred on the side of over-protectiveness. However else he might differ from a modern child, Timmie had reacted to the sedative just about the same way a modern child would have done. He was coming to seem more and more human as she got to know things about him.

But Jacobs had accomplished all that he could by then anyway, and he packed up and left, saying that he'd return in a day or so to follow up on anything that looked unusual in the preliminary analysis.

"Do you want us to stay?" Mortenson asked.

"No need. Leave me with the boy."

Timmie grew calm as soon as they were gone. Evidently he had already adapted to Miss Fellowes' company; it was others who still made him nervous. But time would take care of that, Miss Fellowes thought.

"That wasn't so bad, was it, Timmie? A little poking, a little prodding—but we have to find out a lot of things about you, don't you see?"

He gazed solemnly at her, saying nothing.

"You do see, don't you, Timmie?"

He made a little growling sound, two syllables. To her astounded ears, it sounded like *Timmie*.

Could it be? Did he know his own name already?

"Say it again! Timmie. Timmie."

He uttered the two muffled syllables again. This time she wasn't so sure that he was saying *Timmie* at all. That could have been her own over-eager imagination. But the possibility was worth following up.

She pointed at him. "Timmie—that's you. Timmie. Timmie. Timmie."

He was staring in silence again.

"And I am—" She pointed to herself, momentarily stymied. *Miss Fellowes* seemed like too much of a mouthful. But *Edith* didn't sound right. *Nurse?* No, not right, either. *Miss Fellowes* it would have to be. "I—Miss Fellowes. You—Timmie." She pointed. "I—Miss Fellowes. You—Timmie." She went through the routine three or four more times. He didn't respond at all. —"You think I'm crazy, don't you?" she asked him, laughing at her own foolishness. "Making all these incomprehensible noises at you, pointing, chanting. And I think all that's on your mind just now is your lunch, right? Am I right, Timmie? Lunch? Food? Hungry?"

He uttered the two growled syllables again, and a few clicks for good measure.

"Hungry, yes. Time for some high-protein low-starch food. The Ice Age special, right, Timmie? Well, let's see what we have here, now—"

[20]

Dr. McIntyre of the Smithsonian's Department of Anthropology arrived in early afternoon. Hoskins took the precaution of calling in on the intercom to ask Miss Fellowes if she thought the boy would be able to handle another visitor so soon after the last one. She looked across the room. Timmie had eaten ravenously—an entire flask of some synthetic vitamin drink that Dr. Jacobs had recommended, plus another bowl of oatmeal and a small piece of toast, the first solid food she had risked letting him have. Now he was sitting on the edge of his bed, looking relaxed and contented, kicking his heels rhythmically back against the underside of the mattress, seeming for all the world like an ordinary little boy amusing himself after lunch.

"What do you say, Timmie? You think you can stand another examination?"

She didn't seriously expect a reply from him, and the clicking sounds that he made didn't seem to constitute one. The boy wasn't looking in her direction and went on kicking his heels. Just talking to himself, no doubt. But he definitely appeared to be in a good mood.

"I think we can risk it," she said to Hoskins.

"Good. —What was that I heard you call him? 'Timmie?' What does that mean?"

"It's his name."

"He told you his *name?*" Hoskins said, sounding thunderstruck.

"Of course not. 'Timmie' is simply what I call him."

There was a short uncomfortable pause.

"Ah," said Hoskins finally. "You call him 'Timmie.' "

"I have to call him something, Dr. Hoskins."

"Ah. Yes. Yes. 'Timmie.' "

" 'Timmie,' " Miss Fellowes said firmly.

" 'Timmie.' Yes. Very well. —I'll send Dr. McIntyre in now, if that's all right, Miss Fellowes. To see Timmie."

Dr. McIntyre turned out to be slender and dapper and very much younger than Miss Fellowes had been expecting—no more than thirty or thirty-five, she guessed. He was a small man, delicately built, with fine gleaming golden hair and eyebrows so pale and soft that they were virtually invisible, who moved in a precise, fastidious, elaborately mannered way, as if following some mysterious inner choreography. Miss Fellowes was taken aback by his elegance and daintiness: that wasn't at all how she had expected a paleoanthropologist to look. Even Timmie seemed mystified by his appearance, so very different from that of any of the other men he had encountered since his arrival. Eyes wide with wonder, he stared at McIntyre as though he were some glittering godlike creature from another star.

As for McIntyre, he appeared so overwhelmed by the sight of Timmie that he was barely able to speak. For a long moment he stood frozen just within the door, staring at the boy just as intently as Timmie was staring at him; then he took a few steps to his left, halted, stared again; and then he moved back past the door to the other side of the room, stopped there, stared some more.

A trifle acidly Miss Fellowes said, "Dr. McIntyre, this is Timmie. Timmie—Dr. McIntyre. Dr. McIntyre has come here to study you. And I suppose you can study him also, if you want to."

McIntyre's pallid cheeks reddened. "I don't believe it," he said in a light voice husky with emotion. "I absolutely can't bring myself to believe it. The child is a pure Neanderthal! Alive, right before my eyes, an actual Neanderthal! —Forgive me, Miss Fellowes. You have to understand—this is something completely staggering for me, so utterly phenomenal, so totally astounding—"

He was virtually in tears. It was an embarrassing display, all this effusiveness. Miss Fellowes found it a little irksome. But then, abruptly, her annoyance dissolved and empathy took its place. She imagined how a historian would feel if he were to walk into a room and find himself offered a chance to hold a conversation with Abraham Lincoln or Julius Caesar or Alexander the Great: or how a Biblical scholar would react if confronted with the authentic stone tablets of the Law that Moses had carried down from the summit of Mount Sinai. Of *course* he'd be overwhelmed. Of course. To have spent years studying something that was known only from the sketchiest of ancient relics, trying to understand it, painstakingly recreating the lost reality of it in your mind, and then unexpectedly to encounter the thing itself, the actual genuine item—

But McIntyre made a swift recovery. In that deft graceful manner of his he moved quickly across the room and knelt just in front of Timmie, his face just a short distance from the boy's. Timmie showed no sign of fear. It was the first time he had reacted so calmly to anyone new. The boy was smiling and humming tunelessly and rocking lightly from side to side as though enjoying a visit from a favorite uncle. That bright glow of wonder still was gleaming in his eyes. He seemed altogether fascinated by the paleoanthropologist.

"How beautiful he is, Miss Fellowes!" McIntyre said, after a long moment of silence.

"Beautiful? I haven't heard many people say that about him so far."

"But he is, he is! What a perfect little Neanderthal face! The supraorbital ridges—they've only just begun to develop, yet already they're unmistakable. The platycephalic skull. The elongated occipital region. —May I touch his face, Miss Fellowes? I'll be gentle. I don't want to frighten him, but I'd like to check a few points of the bony structure—"

"It looks as though he'd like to touch yours," Miss Fellowes said.

Indeed, Timmie's hand was outstretched toward McIntyre's forehead. The man from the Smithsonian leaned a little closer and Timmie's fingers began to explore McIntyre's brilliant golden hair. The boy stroked it as though he had never seen anything so wondrous in his life. Then, suddenly, he twined a few strands of it around his middle finger and tugged. It was a good hard tug.

McIntyre yelped and backed away, his face reddening.

"I think he wants some of it," Miss Fellowes said.

"Not *that* way. —Here, let me have a scissors." McIntyre, grinning now, snipped a bit of hair from his forehead and passed the shining strands to Timmie, who beamed and gurgled with pleasure. —"Tell me, Miss Fellowes, has anyone else who's been in here had blond hair?"

She thought a moment. Hoskins—Deveney—Elliott—Mortenson—Stratford—Dr. Jacobs—all of them had brown hair or black or gray. Her own was brown shading into gray.

"No. Not that I recall. You must be the first."

"The first ever, I wonder? We have no idea, of course, what color Neanderthal hair might have been. In the popular reconstructions it's almost always shown as dark, I suppose because Neanderthals are commonly thought of as brutal apish creatures, and most of the modern great apes have dark hair. But dark hair is more common among warm-weather peoples than it is in northern climates, and the Neanderthals certainly were well adapted to extreme cold. So they might have been as blond as your average Russian or Swede or Finn, for all we know."

"And yet his reaction to your hair, Dr. McIntyre—"

"Yes. No doubt about it, the sight of it does something special for him. —Well, maybe the tribe he came from was entirely dark-haired, or perhaps the entire population in his part of the world. Certainly there's nothing very Nordic about this dusky skin of his. But we can't draw much that's conclusive from a sample consisting of just one child. At least we have that one child, though! And how wonderful that is, Miss Fellowes! I can't believe— I absolutely can't believe—"

For an instant she feared that McIntyre was going to allow himself to be overcome by awe all over again. But he seemed to be keeping himself under control. With great delicacy he pressed the tips of his fingers to Timmie's cheeks, his sloping forehead, his little receding chin. As he worked he muttered things under his breath, technical comments, apparently, words plainly meant for himself alone.

Timmie endured the examination with great patience.

Then, after a time, the boy launched into an extended monolog of clicks and growls, the first time he had spoken since the paleoanthropologist had entered the room.

McIntyre looked up at Miss Fellowes, his face crimsoning with excitement.

"Did you hear those sounds? Has he made any sounds like that before?"

"Of course he has. He talks all the time."

"Talks?"

"What do you think he's doing, if not talking? He's saying something to us."

"You mean you *assume* that he's saying something to us."

"No," Miss Fellowes said, beginning to grow annoyed. "He's speaking, Dr. McIntyre. In the Neanderthal language. There are definite patterns in the things he says. I've been trying to make them out, even to imitate them, but so far no luck."

"What kind of patterns, Miss Fellowes?"

"Patterns of clicks and growls. I'm starting to recognize them.

There's one set of sounds to tell me that he's hungry. Another to show impatience or restlessness. One that indicates fear. —I know these are only my own interpretations, and not very scientific. But I've been in here with this boy around the clock since the moment of his arrival, and I've had some experience in dealing with speech-impaired children, Dr. McIntyre. I listen to them very carefully."

"Yes, I'm sure you do." McIntyre gave her a skeptical glance. "This is important, Miss Fellowes. Has anyone been taping these clicks and growls of his?"

"I hope so. I don't know." (She realized that she had been going to ask Dr. Hoskins about that. But she had forgotten all about it.)

Timmie said something again, this time with a different intonation, more melodic, almost plaintive.

"You see, Dr. McIntyre? That was nothing like what he said before. —I think he wants to play with your hair again."

"You're only guessing about that, aren't you?"

"Of course I am. I don't speak Neanderthal very fluently yet. But look—look, he's reaching out for you the way he did just before."

McIntyre didn't seem to care for having his hair yanked again. He smiled and extended a finger to Timmie instead, but the boy had no interest in that. He said so, with an extended series of clicks punctuated by three unfamiliar high-pitched sounds that were midway between a growl and a whine.

"I think you're right, Miss Fellowes!" said McIntyre, his own voice rising. He looked flustered. "It does sound like formal speech! Definite formal speech. —How old do you think this child is?"

"Somewhere between three and four. Closer to four, is my guess. There's no reason to be so surprised that he can speak so well. Four-year-olds are quite articulate, Dr. McIntyre. If you have any children yourself—"

"I do, as a matter of fact. She's almost three and she has quite a lot to say. But this is a *Neanderthal* child."

"Why should that matter? Wouldn't you expect a Neanderthal child of his age to know how to speak?"

"At this point we have no real reason, Miss Fellowes, to assume that *any* Neanderthals of any age were capable of speech as we understand the concept. That's why the sounds this child is making are of such immense importance to our knowledge of prehistoric man. If they represent speech, actual organized patterns of sound with distinct grammatical structure—"

"But of course that's what they represent!" Miss Fellowes burst out. "Speech is the one thing that distinguishes human beings from animals, isn't it? And if you think that you can get me to believe for one moment that this little boy isn't a human being, you—"

"Certainly the Neanderthals were human, Miss Fellowes. I'd be the last person to dispute that. But that doesn't mean they had a spoken language."

"What? How could they have been human and not be able to speak?"

McIntyre drew a deep breath, the kind of exaggerated gesture of carefully hoarded patience that Miss Fellowes recognized all too well. She had spent her whole working life around people who assumed that she knew less than they did, because she was "only" a nurse. Most of the time that wasn't so, at least in the hospital. But this wasn't the hospital; and when it came to Neanderthals, she knew virtually nothing at all, and this fair-haired young man was an expert. She compelled herself to maintain an expression of studious interest.

"Miss Fellowes," McIntyre began, in an unmistakable here-comes-the-lecture tone, "in order for a creature to be able to speak, it needs not only a certain degree of intelligence but also the physical capacity to produce complex sounds. Dogs are quite intelligent, and have considerable vocabularies—but there's a difference between knowing what 'sit' and 'fetch' mean and being able to say 'sit' and 'fetch' yourself, and no dog since time began has ever been able to manage anything better than 'woof.' And surely you know that chimpanzees and gorillas can be taught to communicate quite well, through signs and gestures—but they can't shape words any more than dogs can. They simply don't have the anatomical equipment for it."

"I wasn't aware of that."

"Human speech is a very complicated thing," said McIntyre. He tapped his throat. "The key to it is a tiny U-shaped bone called the hyoid, at the base of the tongue. It controls eleven small muscles that move the tongue and the lower jaw and also are capable of lifting and depressing the larynx to bring forth the vowels and consonants that make up speech. The hyoid bone isn't present in apes. Therefore all they can do is grunt and hiss."

"What about parrots and myna birds? They can speak actual words. Are you telling me that the hyoid bone evolved in them, and not in chimpanzees?"

"Birds like parrots and mynas simply mimic the sounds humans make, using entirely different anatomical structures. But what they do can't be regarded as speech. There isn't any verbal understanding there. They don't have any idea of what they're saying. It's just a playback of the sounds they hear."

"All right. And Neanderthals—don't they have hyoid bones? If they're considered human beings, they must."

"We haven't been sure that they do," McIntyre said. "You need to bear in mind, first, that the total number of Neanderthal skeletons ever discovered, since the first one came to light in 1856, is not quite two hundred, and a lot of those are fragmentary or otherwise badly damaged. And, second, that the hyoid bone is very small and isn't connected to any other bones of the body, only to the muscles of the larynx. When a body decays, the hyoid falls away and can easily be separated from the rest of the skeleton. Of all the Neanderthal fossils we've examined, Miss Fellowes, a total of one—*one*—still had a hyoid bone in place."

"But if one of them had it, all of them must have!"

McIntyre nodded. "Very likely so. But we've never seen a Neanderthal larynx. Soft tissues don't survive, of course. And so we don't know what function the hyoid served in the Neanderthal. Hyoid or not, we've had no way of being certain that the Neanderthals actually were capable of speech. All we can say is that the anatomy of the vocal apparatus was probably the same in Neanderthals as it is in modern humans. *Probably.* But whether it was developed sufficiently to allow them to articulate understandable words—or whether their brains were advanced enough to handle the concept of speech—"

Timmie was clicking and growling again.

"Listen to him," Miss Fellowes said triumphantly. "There's your answer! He's got a fine language and he speaks it perfectly well. And before he's been here much longer, he'll be speaking English, too, Dr. McIntyre. I'm certain of that. And then you won't need to speculate any longer about whether the Neanderthals were capable of speech."

[21]

McIntyre seemed to want to solve all the Neanderthal riddles at once. He made clicking sounds at Timmie in the hope of eliciting clicks in return; he produced colored plastic blocks from his briefcase, some sort of intelligence test, no doubt, and tried to get Timmie to arrange them in sequences of size and color; he offered the boy crayons and paper and stood back waiting for him to draw something, which Timmie seemed to have no interest in doing; he had Miss Fellowes lead Timmie around the room by the hand, and photographed him as he moved. There were other tests he wanted to carry out on Timmie, too; but Timmie had his own thoughts about that. Just as McIntyre began to set up some arrangement of spools and spindles, which looked like a toy but was actually a device to measure the boy's coordination, Timmie sat down in the middle of the floor and began to cry. Loudly.

It was the first time he had really *cried*—as opposed to sobbing or whimpering or moaning—since the night he had arrived. It was the very familiar cranky bawling of a very tired child who had been pushed too far. Miss Fellowes was glad to hear it, though she was astonished at how wide his mouth could get when he opened it to its full extent, how his nose suddenly seemed even bigger than it already was, how far those strange heavy ridges of bone over his eyes protruded when he scrunched his eyes closed the way he was doing now. With his face distorted like this in anguish, he looked almost terrifyingly alien.

And yet, and yet—that wailing sound, that ululating outpouring of emotion—if she didn't look at him, she could easily believe that the child who was thumping his heels against the floor and screaming his heart out was simply any ordinary four-year-old having a severe attack of impatience.

"What did I do that upset him like that?" McIntyre asked.

"You outlasted his attention span, I imagine," said Miss Fellowes. "You wore out your welcome. He's only a little boy, Dr. McIntyre. He can't be expected to put up with an endless amount of chivvying and probing. —A little boy who's very recently been through a highly traumatic separation from anything and everything that he can understand, I ought to remind you."

"But I wasn't chivvying and—well, perhaps I was. I'm sorry about that. —Here, Timmie—here, see the hair? See the bright hair? Do you want to play with my hair? Do you want to *pull* my hair?"

McIntyre was dangling his golden forelock practically in Timmie's face. Timmie took no notice. His screaming grew even louder.

Disgustedly Miss Fellowes said, "He doesn't want to play with your hair right now, Dr. McIntyre. And if he does decide to pull it, I think you'll regret it. Best to let him be. There'll be plenty of other opportunities to examine him."

"Yes. So there will." The paleoanthropologist stood up, looking abashed. "You understand, Miss Fellowes, this is like being handed a sealed book containing the answers to all the mysteries of the ages. I want to open it and read it right away. Every page of it."

"I understand. But I'm afraid that your book is hungry and cranky and I think he'd like to go to the bathroom, besides."

"Yes. Yes, of course."

McIntyre hastily began to gather up all of his testing equipment. As he started to put the spools and spindles away, Miss Fellowes said, "Can you leave one of those here?"

"You want to test his intelligence yourself?"

"I have no need to test his intelligence, doctor. He seems quite intelligent to me. But I think he could use a few toys, and this one already happens to be here."

Color came to McIntyre's cheeks once again. He seemed to blush very readily, Miss Fellowes thought.

"Of course. Here."

"And—speaking of open books, Dr. McIntyre, do you think you could arrange to get me some material about Neanderthal Man? Two or three basic texts, something that might provide me with a little of the fundamental information that nobody has bothered to supply me with up till now? —They can be fairly technical. I'm quite capable of reading scientific prose. I need to know things about the Neanderthal anatomy, their way of life, the sort of foods they ate, whatever has been discovered up to this point. Could you do that for me?"

"I'll have everything you'll need sent over first thing tomorrow. Though I warn you, Miss Fellowes, that what we know about Neanderthals now is next to nothing, compared with what we're going to find out from Timmie as this project unfolds."

"All in due course." She grinned. "You *are* eager to get at him, aren't you?"

"Obviously."

"Well, you'll have to be patient about it, I'm afraid. I won't let you wear the boy out. We've subjected him to too much intrusion today, and that isn't going to happen again."

McIntyre looked uncomfortable. He managed a rigid little smile and headed for the door.

"And when you pick out the books for me, doctor—"

"Yes?" McIntyre said.

"I particularly would like to have one that discusses Neanderthals in terms of their relationship to humans. To modern humans, I mean to say. How they differed from us, how they're similar. The evolutionary scheme as we understand it. That's the information I want most of all." She looked at him fiercely. —"They *are* humans, aren't they, Dr. McIntyre? A little different from us, but not all that much. Isn't that so?"

"That's essentially so, yes. But of course—"

"No," she said. "No 'but of courses.' We're not dealing with some sort of ape, here, that much I already know. Timmie's not any kind of missing link. He's a little boy, a little *human* boy. —Just get me some books, Dr. McIntyre, and thank you very much. I'll see you again soon."

The paleontologist went out. The moment he was gone, Timmie's wailing tapered off into a querulous uncertain sobbing, and then, swiftly, to silence.

Miss Fellowes scooped him into her arms. He clung tightly to her, shivering.

"Yes," she said soothingly. "Yes, yes, yes, it's been a busy day. Much too busy. And you *are* just a little boy. A little lost boy."

Far from home, far from anything you ever knew.

"Did you have brothers and sisters?" she asked him, speaking more to herself than to him. Not expecting an answer; simply offering the comfort of a soft voice close to his ear. "What was your mother like? Your father? And your friends, your playmates. All gone. All gone. They must already seem like something out of a dream to you. How long will you remember anything about them at all, I wonder?"

Little lost boy. *My* little lost boy.

"How about some nice warm milk?" she suggested. "And then, I think, a nap."

# INTERCHAPTER THREE

# *The Place of Three Rivers*

IN THE NIGHT Silver Cloud dreamed of the sea.

He was young again, in his dream. He dreamed that was only a boy, just a summer or two older than the boy Skyfire Face who had been taken by the Goddess in a whirl of light. He stood by the edge of the sea, feeling the strange wet wind blowing against his lips. His father and mother were with him, Tall Tree and Sweet As A Flower, and they were holding his hands and leading him gently toward the water.

"No," he said. "It's cold. I'm afraid to go into it."

"It can't hurt you," Tall Tree said.

But that wasn't true. No one went into the sea, *no one*, not ever. Every child learned that as soon as he was old enough to learn anything. The sea killed. The sea would drain your life away in an instant, and cast you back up on the shore, empty and still. Only last year the warrior Speared Five Mammoths had slipped on a snowy cliff and fallen into the sea, and when he washed ashore a little while later he was dead, and they had had to bury him in a little cavern in the rock near the place where he fell, chanting all night and burning a strange-colored fire. Now here were his own father and mother urging him toward the sea. Did they want him to die the way Speared Five Mammoths had died? Were they tired of him? What kind of betrayal was this?

"The sea will make you strong," Sweet As A Flower told him. "The sea will make you a man."

"But Speared Five Mammoths died in it!"

"It was his time to die. The sea called to him and took him. But your time to die is far away, boy. You have no reason to be afraid."

Was it true? Could he trust them?

They were his mother and his father. Why would they want him to die?

He held their hands tightly and stepped forward with them, toward the brink of the sea.

He had never been this close to it before, although his tribe had always lived in the coastal plain, wandering up and down along the shore following the game animals. Now he stared at the water in wonder and fear. It was like a great powerful flat beast lying before him, dark and shining. A roaring sound came from it, and along its edges a part of it was rippling and surging with white foam. Here and there a piece of the sea would rise up high into the air and come crashing down against the rocks along the edge. Sometimes, standing on cliffs much like the one where Speared Five Mammoths had fallen to his death, Silver Cloud had looked far out into the sea and had seen graceful animals moving about in it, moving among the floating blocks of ice. They were different animals from the mammoths and musk oxen and rhinos of the land—slim, sleek, shining things that moved through the sea as though they were flying through air.

Last spring one of those sea animals had come ashore, and the Hunting Society had fallen on it and killed it, and the tribe had enjoyed a great feast. How tender its meat had been! How strange! And its thick beautiful fur—how soft, how wonderfully soft. Tall Tree had made a mantle for Sweet As A Flower from the sea-creature's dark rich fur, and she wore it proudly on the special days of the year.

Were they going to give him to the sea in return for the fur of the sea-creature? Was that it?

"Take another step, boy," Tall Tree urged. "There's nothing to be afraid of."

Silver Cloud looked up. But his father was smiling.

He had to trust his father. He stepped forward, clinging tightly to their hands. The edge of the sea came up around his ankles. He had expected it to be cold, but no, no, it was warm, it was hot, it burned like fire. Yet after a moment he no longer felt the burning. The sea pulled back from him, and then it returned, higher than before, up to his knees, his thighs, his belly. Tall Tree and Sweet As A Flower walked farther out into it, taking him with them. The ground on the floor of the sea was very soft, as soft as the sea animal's fur, and it seemed to move about under his feet as he walked.

He was chest-deep in the sea, now. It wrapped itself around him like a warm blanket.

"Are your feet still touching the bottom?" Tall Tree asked him.

"Yes. Yes."

"Good. Bend forward. Put your head in the sea. Cover your face with the sea."

He did as he was told. The sea swept up and over him, and it was like being covered by a blanket made of snow. Snow too ceased to be cold, when you got deep down into it. It became warm, like fire, and if you stayed in it long enough you would fall asleep as if you were wrapped in a rug. That was what an older girl had told him: she had watched, once, as an old woman of the tribe whose bones were bent and whose eyes were dim was taken out and put into the snow; she had closed her eyes and gone to sleep, very peacefully indeed.

So now I will go to sleep in the sea, Silver Cloud thought, and that will be the end of me. And somehow dying no longer seemed to matter. He raised his head to see whether his father and mother had their faces covered with the sea also, but to his surprise they were no longer beside him, nowhere to be seen at all. He was entirely alone.

He could hear his father's voice coming to him from far away, telling him, "Come out of the sea, now, boy. Turn around and walk out."

Yes. He would do that.

But as he walked toward the shore he felt his body changing with every step he took, stretching, growing taller and thicker, and he realized that he was turning into a man, getting older moment by moment. His shoulders were becoming broad, his chest was deepening, his thighs had become thick and strong. By the time he stepped out onto the rocky shore he was a warrior in the prime of his life. He looked down at his naked body and it was a man's body, dark and hairy. He laughed. He rubbed his chest and slapped his hands against his thighs. In the distance he saw the fires of the encampment, and he began to sprint toward it to tell everyone of the strange thing that had happened to him.

As he ran, though, another strangeness overtook him: for he realized that he was continuing to grow older every moment. Age had him in its grip and would not release him. He had left his childhood in the sea. Then, coming out of the sea, he had been full of the jubilant strength of young manhood. But now he was panting a little, then gasping for breath, slowing down from a sprint to a trot, and then to a walk. And then he was limping along, hobbling, for something had happened to his left thigh and his whole leg was stiff and sore. He looked down at it. There was blood all over it, as though an animal had raked it with its claws. And he remembered, yes, yes, he had been hunting with the Hunting Society, and the snow-leopard had come down suddenly on him from above—

How difficult it was to walk, now. How old and tired I am, he thought. I can no longer stand straight. Look, my hair is turning silver all over my body.

There was pain in him everywhere. He felt his strength going from him. What a strange, troublesome dream this was! First a boy entering the sea, and then coming forth and rapidly growing old, and now he was dying, dying, in some unfamiliar inland place far from the sea, where the earth was cold and hard and the wind was dry, and there were only strangers all about him. Where was Tall Tree, where was Sweet As A Flower—where was Silver Cloud?

"Help me," he called, sitting up in his sleep. "The sea has killed me! The sea—the sea—"

"Silver Cloud?"

Someone was at his side. He blinked and peered. She Who Knows, it was, kneeling next to him, staring at him anxiously. He struggled to regain control of himself. He was trembling like a sick old woman and his chest was heaving wildly. No one must see him like this—no one. He fumbled about for his staff, caught its end, levered himself awkwardly to a standing position.

"A dream," he muttered. "Bad omens. I'll need to make a sacrifice right away. Where's Goddess Woman? Get me Goddess Woman!"

"She's gone down there," She Who Knows said. "She's cleansing the shrine."

"Shrine? What? Where?"

"At the Three Rivers. —What's wrong with you, Silver Cloud? You seem all confused!"

"The dream," he said. "Very bad."

He stomped forward, leaning on his staff. His mind was beginning to grow clear again. He knew where he was. There were three rivers meeting in the valley beyond.

Yes. The long pilgrimage backward along the trail had come to its end. They were camped on the high sloping plateau that looked down into the flat place where the three rivers flowed together. By the misty light of dawn Silver Cloud saw the rivers below, the largest one coming sluggishly in from the north carrying with it a rich cargo of blocks of ice, the two smaller and swifter ones merging at sharp angles out of the east and west.

Last year—it seemed like ages ago—they had paused in this very place for many weeks, hungry weeks at that, until the Goddess had miraculously sent them a herd of reindeer, so dazed with hunger themselves that the Hunting Society was easily able to drive a dozen of the bewildered beasts over the edge of a cliff. What a fine harvest of meat that had been! In gratitude they had built a wonderful shrine to the Goddess at the place where the rivers met, using the heaviest blocks of stone they could lift, and decorating them with a curious shining rock that they had been able to pry out of the side of the cliff in thin glittering sheets; and then they had moved onward, continuing their long eastward migration.

And now they had returned.

"I don't see Goddess Woman down there," Silver Cloud said to She Who Knows.

"She should be at the shrine."

"I see the shrine. I don't see Goddess Woman."

"Your eyes are no good any more, Silver Cloud. Here, let me look."

She stepped in front of him and looked into the misty valley. After a moment she said, sounding perplexed, "No, you're right, she's not there. She must be on her way back already. But she said she was going to stay down there all morning, saying the prayers and purifying the shrine—"

"Silver Cloud! Silver Cloud!"

"Goddess Woman? What are you—"

The priestess came rushing up the side path that led from the valley. Her face was flushed and her robes hung askew and she was sucking in breath as though she had run all the way.

"What is it? *What is it,* Goddess Woman?"

"Other Ones!"

"What? Where?"

"All around the shrine. I didn't see them, but their footprints were everywhere. The long feet—I know those feet. The prints everywhere in the wet ground. Fresh prints, Silver Cloud. They're all over the place, down there. We've walked right into their midst!"

# CHAPTER FIVE

# Misjudging

[22]

HOSKINS SAID, "And how's our boy doing this morning, Miss Fellowes?"

"Why don't you see for yourself, doctor?"

Hoskins' face registered a mixture of amusement and annoyance. "Why do you call me 'doctor' all the time?" he asked.

"Because you are one, or so I believe," she said, thinking of that "Ph.D." label so proudly engraved on the name-plate in his office.

"A doctorate in physics; that's all."

"A doctorate is a doctorate."

"And you've been accustomed for a long time to calling people in positions of authority 'doctor,' is that it? Especially if they happen to be men?"

His words startled her. They were right on the mark, of course: throughout her career the senior figures at the hospitals where she had worked had all had medical degrees. Most of them, by no means all, had been men. She fell easily and automatically into the habit of tacking the word "doctor" to every other sentence when addressing someone she regarded as her superior.

Her husband had been a doctor, too—with a Ph.D. in physics, like Hoskins. Miss Fellowes wondered strangely whether she would be calling him "doctor" too, as she did Hoskins, if they had managed to stay married all these years. A curious thought. She rarely thought of him at all any more; the whole notion of being married, of having a husband, had come to seem remote and implausible to her. She had been married for such a short time, such a long time ago.

"What would you prefer?" she asked. "Should I call you '*Mr.* Hoskins,' then?"

"Most people around here call me 'Jerry.' "

Miss Fellowes looked at him strangely. "I couldn't do that!"

"You couldn't?"

"It—wouldn't feel right."

"Wouldn't feel right," Hoskins repeated, musingly. "To call me 'Jerry.' He studied her closely, as though seeing her for the first time. His wide, fleshy face broke into a warm smile. "You really are a very formal person. I hadn't realized quite *how* formal, I guess. All right, then: you can go on calling me 'Dr. Hoskins,' if that's what you're most comfortable with. And I'll go on calling you 'Miss Fellowes.' "

What did he mean by that? she wondered.

Had he been thinking of calling her 'Edith'?

*Nobody* did that. Hardly anyone, at any rate: maybe six people in all the world. Most of the time she was 'Miss Fellowes' even to herself, whenever she thought of herself in the third person, which wasn't often. It was just a habit: she never gave it any thought at all. But how odd, she told herself now, to think of yourself that way. How austere, how stiff. I have really become someone quite peculiar now that I'm middle-aged, Miss Fellowes thought. And I've never even noticed it.

Hoskins was still looking steadily at her, still smiling.

There was something very warm about the man, she realized suddenly, very likable. That too was a fact she hadn't noticed before. In their earlier meetings he had struck her mainly as someone who presented himself to the world as taut, guarded, inflexible, with only occasional moments when a little humanity showed through. But possibly the tensions of the final days before the Stasis experiment had made him seem that way; and now that the time-scoop had done its work and the success of the project was confirmed, he was more relaxed, more human, more himself. And quite a nice man indeed.

Miss Fellowes found herself wondering for an idle moment if Hoskins was married.

The speculation astonished and embarrassed her. He had told her a couple of weeks back that he had a son, hadn't he? A small son, barely old enough to know how to walk. Of course he was married. Of *course.* What could she be thinking of? She thrust the whole line of inquiry aside in horror.

"Timmie!" she called. "Come here, Timmie!"

Like Hoskins, the boy also appeared to be in a cheerful, outgoing mood this morning. He had slept well; he had eaten well; now he came hustling out of his bedroom, showing no uneasiness whatever at Hoskins' presence. He walked boldly up to Hoskins and uttered a stream of clicks.

"Do you think he's saying something, Miss Fellowes? Not just making sounds for the fun of hearing his own voice?"

"What else can he be doing but saying something, doctor? Dr. McIntyre asked me the same thing yesterday when he heard Timmie speaking. How can anybody doubt that the boy's using a language—and a very elaborate one at that?"

"Dr. McIntyre's extremely conservative. He doesn't believe in jumping to conclusions."

"Well, neither do I. But that's a genuine language or I'm not speaking one myself."

"Let's hope so, Miss Fellowes. Let's certainly hope so. If we can't develop any way of communicating with Timmie, then much of the value of having brought him here will be lost. Naturally we want him to tell us things about the world he came from. All manner of things."

"He will, doctor. Either in his language or in ours. And my guess is that he'll learn to speak ours long before we've found out anything about his."

"You may be right, Miss Fellowes. Time will tell, won't it? Time will tell."

Hoskins crouched down so that his face was on the same level as Timmie's and let his hands rest lightly on the boy's rib-cage, fingers outspread. Timmie remained calm. Miss Fellowes realized after a moment that Hoskins was ever so gently tickling the boy, working his fingertips lightly around in an easy, playful way that bespoke more than a little knowledge of how to handle small boys. And Timmie liked being tickled.

"What a sturdy little fellow," Hoskins said. "Tough as they come. —So you're going to learn English, are you, Timmie? And then you'll dictate a book to us all about life in the Paleolithic Era, and everybody will want to read it and it'll be a big bestseller, and we'll start to see a little return on our investment in you, eh, Timmie? Eh?" He glanced up at Miss Fellowes. —"We've got a tremendous amount riding on this boy, you know. I hardly need tell you. Not simply money, but our entire professional futures."

"Yes. I imagine you do."

Hoskins tousled Timmie's thick unruly hair, patted the boy, and stood up. "We've been working on a shoestring budget for years, scrounging funds a dime at a time wherever we could. You can't believe the energy costs involved in maintaining Stasis, even for a moment—enough to power up a whole city for days—and the energy's only one part of the overhead we run here. We've been right on the edge of going under at least half a dozen times. We had to shoot the works on one big show to save ourselves. It was everything—or nothing. And when I say the works, I mean it. But Timmie here has saved us. He's going to put Stasis Technologies, Ltd. on the map. We're in, Miss Fellowes, we're in!"

"I would have thought bringing back a live dinosaur would have sufficed to achieve that, Dr. Hoskins."

"We thought so, too. But somehow that never captured the public's imagination."

"A *dinosaur* didn't?"

Hoskins laughed. "Oh, if we had brought back a full-grown brontosaurus, I suppose, or a rip-snorting tyrannosaur, something on that order. But we had our mass limitations to deal with, you know, and they tied our hands considerably. Not that we would have known how to keep a tyrannosaur under control, even if we'd been able to bring one back. —I should take you across the way one of these days and let you see our dinosaur, I guess."

"You should, yes."

"He's very cute."

"*Cute?* A dinosaur?"

"You'll see. Yes. A cute little dinosaur. Unfortunately, people don't seem to be very excited by cute little dinosaurs. 'How interesting,' they said, 'these scientists have brought a live dinosaur back from prehistoric times.' But then they got a look at the dinosaur on television and they didn't find it very interesting at all, because it wasn't twice as high as a house and breathing fire, I guess. A Neanderthal boy, now—an actual prehistoric human being, quite strange-looking but nevertheless something everyone can identify with and care deeply about—that'll be our salvation. —Do you hear that, Timmie? You're our salvation." To Miss Fellowes again Hoskins said, "If this hadn't worked out, I'd have been through. No doubt about it. This whole corporation would have been through."

"I see."

"But we're all right now. We'll have plenty of money soon. Funds have been promised from every source. This is all wonderful, Miss Fellowes. So long as we can keep Timmie healthy and happy, and maybe get him to speak a few words of English—'Hello, everybody out there, this is Timmie from the Stone Age'—"

"Or some such thing," Miss Fellowes said drily.

"Yes. Some such thing. —Healthy and happy, that's the key to it all. If anything happens to him, our name is mud, and worse than mud, Miss Fellowes. Which makes you the central figure in our whole operation, do you realize that? We depend on you to provide a supportive, nourishing environment for our boy. Your word will be law: whatever Timmie needs, Timmie gets. You were absolutely right yesterday when you refused to let the media have a whack at him so soon."

"Thank you."

"Naturally, you understand that we *do* want to have a press conference just as soon as possible—that it's vital to everybody's interests that we maximize the publicity value of the Timmie project as quickly as we can—"

Suddenly Hoskins seemed less genial and likable again, more the driven executive who said things like "Trust me" when he was at his least trustworthy.

Coolly Miss Fellowes said, "Does that mean you want to bring them in here this afternoon?"

"Well, if you thought he was ready for—"

"I don't. Not yet."

Hoskins moistened his lips. "Your word is law. Just tell us when."

"I will."

"I mean, can you give us an estimate now? What about our having the press conference tomorrow? —The day after tomorrow?"

"Let's just put it on hold, doctor. All right? I simply don't want to commit Timmie to anything as stressful as a press conference at this point. He's still catching his breath, so to speak, still getting his feet on the ground—whatever metaphor you want to use. He's made fine progress after those first terrified moments. But he could revert in a second to the wild, frightened child you saw that night. Even Dr. McIntyre yesterday managed to get him upset, after a while."

Hoskins looked troubled. "We can't keep the press out indefinitely, Miss Fellowes."

"I'm not talking about indefinitely. I'm talking about a few days.

Two, three, four—let me be the judge of it, yes, Dr. Hoskins? My word is law?"

"Your word is law," Hoskins said, not sounding terribly pleased. He was silent for a moment. Then he said, "You haven't been out of the Stasis zone since the night of the experiment, have you, Miss Fellowes? Not even for a moment."

"No!" she said indignantly. "I know my responsibilities, Dr. Hoskins, and if you think—"

"Please, Miss Fellowes." He smiled and held up his hand. "I'm not implying anything. I'm just working my way around to pointing out that we really don't intend to cage you up in here with the boy twenty-four hours a day, seven days a week. I'm aware that in the critical first few couple of days it was best that you be on hand round the clock, and that in fact I told you at our first interview that you'd be on duty constantly in the beginning, at least. But Timmie seems to be stabilizing very nicely now. You'll need to work out a schedule of time off for recreation and relaxation. Ms. Stratford can fill in for you for an hour or so at first, and then perhaps you can have whole afternoons off, later on."

"Whatever you say."

"You don't sound very enthusiastic. I didn't realize you were such a workaholic, Miss Fellowes."

"That's not quite the right word. It's simply that—well, Timmie's in such a frighteningly vulnerable position. Disoriented, isolated, far from home—so much in need of love and protection as he comes to terms with what's happened to him. I haven't wanted to leave him even for a short while."

"Very commendable of you. But now that the worst of the transition is over, you've got to start coming out of here, if only for short breaks."

"If that's what you want, doctor."

"I think it's best. For your own good, Miss Fellowes. You're entitled to a little respite from your work. And I wouldn't want Timmie to become totally dependent on having you right here at hand, either. There's no telling what sort of intense bonding might develop if this full-time nursing goes on very much longer. And then, if for some reason you *have* to leave the Stasis zone, Timmie might not be able to handle that. The situation wouldn't be entirely healthy. Do you follow me?"

Miss Fellowes nodded. "You have a point there."

"Good. Do you want to try a little experiment, then? We'll call Ms. Stratford in and let her look after Timmie for an hour or two, and you come out with me this very day and I'll take you on a tour of the rest of the laboratory."

"Well—"

"You don't like it, do you? —Look, we'll put a beeper on you. If Ms. Stratford starts running into the slightest problem with Timmie, we'll have you back inside here in five minutes, okay? Trust me."

"All right," Miss Fellowes said, less grudgingly than before. She had to admit the validity of Hoskins' reasoning. Now that she had eased Timmie through the first two days, it probably would be wise to test the boy's ability to withstand her absence for a short while. "I'm willing to give it a try. Take me to see your dinosaur."

"I'll show you everything," said Hoskins. "Animal, vegetable, and mineral in equal parts." He looked at his watch. "Suppose I give you —ah—ninety minutes to finish up whatever you were doing when I arrived this morning, and to brief Ms. Stratford on what she needs to watch out for. Then I'll come back here and pick you up for a personal tour."

Miss Fellowes thought for a moment. "Make it two hours, I think."

"Two hours? Fine. I'll be back at eleven sharp. See you then. —You don't have any problems about this, do you?"

She smiled happily. "Actually, I'm looking forward to it. —You can spare me for a little while, can't you, Timmie?"

The boy made clicking sounds.

"You see, doctor? He knows when I'm asking him a question, and he responds, even if he doesn't know what I'm actually saying to him. There's a real intelligence inside that head of his."

"I'm sure there is," Hoskins said. He nodded and smiled and left.

Miss Fellowes found herself humming as she went through her morning chores. She had told the truth when she said she was looking forward to getting out of the Stasis bubble for a while. Much as she loved caring for Timmie, even she needed to take a break.

Or was it just the thought of spending some time in Hoskins' company?

Really—to think so was ridiculous, she knew—but really, it was almost like—like making a date.

He has a young son, she told herself again, very sternly. Which means he's almost certainly got a wife. A young and pretty wife.

Even so, Miss Fellowes had changed from her nurse's uniform into

a dress when Hoskins returned at eleven to get her. A dress of conservative cut, to be sure—she had no other kind—but she hadn't felt
so feminine in years.

He complimented her on her appearance with staid formality and
she accepted with equally formal grace. It was really a perfect prelude,
she thought. And then the next thought came inexorably. *Prelude to
what?*

### [23]

She said goodbye to Timmie and assured him that she'd be coming
back soon. She made sure Ms. Stratford knew what to give him for
lunch, and when. The young orderly seemed a little uneasy about
taking on the responsibility of being alone with Timmie, Miss Fellowes thought. But then Ms. Stratford remarked that Mortenson
would be nearby in case Timmie turned difficult, and Miss Fellowes
realized that the woman was more worried about finding herself with
a wild battle on her hands than she was about any harm that might
come to Timmie while he was in her care. Perhaps she needs to be
transferred to some other duties, Miss Fellowes thought. But there
was no choice other than to turn Timmie over to her for now. The
beeper in her purse would summon her quickly enough, if need
should develop.

They went out. From Timmie came one little whimper of—surprise? Despair?

"Don't worry, Timmie! I'll be coming back! I'll be coming back!"

The break had to be made, she thought. The sooner the better—for
the boy, for her.

Hoskins led her upward through the maze of harshly lit hallways
and echoing vaults and gloomy metal staircases that they had traversed
on the night of Timmie's arrival, a night which to Miss Fellowes now
seemed so long ago that it felt more like the memory of a dream than
an actual event. For a brief while they were outside the building entirely, blinking into the midday brilliance of a clear, golden day; and
then they plunged into another bleak, barn-like building very much
like the one where Timmie's Stasis bubble had been formed.

"This is the old Stasis lab," Hoskins told her. "Where it all began."

Again, security checks; again, clattering staircases and musty passageways and dismal cavernous vaults. At last they were in the heart of
a bustling research zone, far busier than the other. Men and women in

laboratory coats were going this way and that, carrying stacks of reports, files, computer cubes. Hoskins greeted many of them by first name, and they hailed him the same way. Miss Fellowes found the informality jarring.

But this is not a hospital, she told herself. These people simply *work* here. There's a difference.

"Animal, vegetable, mineral," Hoskins said. "Just as I promised. Animal right down there: our most spectacular exhibits. Before Timmie, I mean."

The space was divided into many rooms, each a separate Stasis bubble somewhat smaller than the one Timmie was housed in. Hoskins led her to the view-glass of one and she looked inside.

What she saw impressed her at first as a scaled, tailed chicken. It ran back and forth from one wall to the other in a nervous, frenzied way, skittering on two thin legs, looking this way and that. But there had never been a chicken that looked anything like this one: a wingless chicken with two small dangling arms terminating in handlike paws, which clenched and unclenched constantly. Its narrow head was delicate and birdlike, with weirdly glittering scarlet eyes. Its skull was surmounted by a bony keel a little like the comb of a rooster, but bright blue in color. Its body was green with darker stripes, and there was a gleaming reptilian sheen to it. The thin serpentine tail lashed nervously from side to side.

Hoskins said, "There's our dinosaur. Our pride and joy—until Timmie came here."

"Dinosaur? *That?*"

"I told you it was small. You want it to be a giant, don't you, Miss Fellowes?"

She dimpled. "I do, I suppose. It's only natural. The first thing anyone thinks of when dinosaurs are mentioned is their enormous size. And this one is, well, so *tiny*."

"A small one is all we aimed for, believe me. You can imagine what would happen here if a full-grown stegosaurus, say, suddenly came thundering into Stasis and started lumbering around the laboratory. But of course there isn't enough electrical energy in six counties to create a Stasis field big enough to handle something that size. And the technology itself isn't developed enough yet to allow for significant mass transfer, even if we could get the power we'd need to do it."

Miss Fellowes stared. She felt a chill. A living dinosaur, yes! How fantastic!

But so tiny—more like a bird without feathers, it was, or some peculiar kind of lizard—

"If it isn't big, why is it a dinosaur?"

"Size isn't the determining factor, Miss Fellowes. What causes an animal to be classed as a dinosaur is its bony structure. The pelvic anatomy, primarily. Modern reptiles have limbs that go out sideways, like *this*. Think of the way a crocodile walks, or a lizard. More of a waddle than a stride, wouldn't you say? There aren't any upright crocodiles walking around on their hind legs. But the dinosaurs had birdlike pelvises. As everyone knows, many of them were able to walk upright as modern two-legged creatures do. Think of an ostrich; think of long-legged wading birds; think of the way our own legs are attached. Even the dinosaurs who stayed closer to the ground on all four legs had the sort of pelvis that allowed the legs to descend straight instead of sticking out to the sides the way a lizard's do. It's an entirely different evolutionary model, a line one which led down from dinosaurian reptiles through birds to mammals. And the saurian end of it died out. The only reptiles that survived the Great Extinction at the end of the Mesozoic were the ones with the other kind of pelvic arrangement."

"I see. And there were small dinosaurs as well as big ones. It just happens that the big ones are the ones that captured our imaginations."

"Right. Those are the famous ones that everybody goggles at in the museums. But plenty of species were only a few feet high. This one, for instance."

"I can understand now why people lost interest in it so fast. It isn't scary. It isn't awesome."

"Laymen may have lost interest, Miss Fellowes. But I assure you that this little fellow has been a revelation to scientists. It's being studied day and night, and some very interesting things have been discovered. For instance, we've been able to determine that it's not entirely cold-blooded. Which confirms one of the most controversial theories about dinosaurs ever set forth. Unlike any modern species of reptile, it has a method of maintaining internal temperatures higher than that of its environment. Not a perfect method, not by any means —but the fact that it has one at all backs up the skeletal evidence putting dinosaurs on the direct line of evolution leading toward birds and mammals. The creature that you're looking at is one of our own most distant ancestors, Miss Fellowes."

"If it is, aren't you messing up evolutionary history by pulling it out of its own era? Suppose this one dinosaur was the key link in the whole evolutionary chain?"

Hoskins laughed. "I'm afraid evolution doesn't work as simply as that. No, there's no risk here of changing evolutionary history. The fact that we're all still here, after this fellow has been transported a hundred million years across time, should be proof enough of that."

"I suppose so. —Is it a male or a female dinosaur?"

"Male," said Hoskins. "Unfortunately. Ever since we brought it in, we've been trying to get a fix on another of the same species that might be female. But doing that makes looking for a needle in a haystack seem like a cinch."

"Why get a female?"

He looked at her quizzically. "So that we might have a fighting chance to obtain some fertile eggs, and breed a line of baby dinosaurs here in the laboratory."

She felt foolish. "Of course."

"Come over here," Hoskins said. "The trilobite section. You know what trilobites are, Miss Fellowes?"

She didn't answer. She was watching the little dinosaur pathetically skittering around in its confinement area, bewilderedly running from one wall to the other. It would run right into the wall and bounce off before turning back. The stupid creature didn't seem to be able to comprehend the reason why it couldn't just keep going, out into the open, off into the dank swamps and torrid forests of its prehistoric home.

She thought of Timmie, penned up across the way in his own little set of rooms.

"I said, Miss Fellowes, do you know what trilobites are?"

"What? Oh—yes. Yes. Some sort of extinct kind of lobster, isn't that so?"

"Well, not exactly. A crustacean and extinct, but not at all like a lobster. Not much like anything now living, as a matter of fact. Once they were the dominant life-form of the Earth, the crown of creation. That was half a billion years ago. There were trilobites wherever you looked, then. Crawling around on the floor of every ocean by the millions. And then they all died out: we can't yet say why. Leaving no descendants, no genetic heritage whatever. They were here, they were fruitful and multiplied, and then they vanished as though they had never been. Leaving fossils of themselves behind in enormous quantities."

Miss Fellowes peered into the trilobite tank. She saw six or seven sluggish gray-green creatures three or four inches long, sitting on a bed of gray ooze. They looked like something you might see at the seashore in a tide-pool. Their narrow, oval, hard-looking bodies were divided the long way into three ridged sections, a raised central one and two smaller side lobes fringed with little spikes. Huge dark eyes were visible at one end, faceted like the eyes of insects. As Miss Fellowes watched, one of the trilobites pushed an array of tiny jointed legs outward from its sides and began to crawl—slowly, *very* slowly—across the bottom of the tank.

The crown of creation. The dominant life-form of its time.

A man in a lab coat appeared, wheeling a tray on which some complex, unfamiliar device was mounted. He greeted Hoskins amiably and gave Miss Fellowes an impersonal grin.

"This is Tom Dwayne of Washington University," Hoskins said. "He's one of our trilobite people. Tom's a nuclear chemist. —Tom, I want you to meet Edith Fellowes, R.N. She's the wonderful woman who's taking care of our new little Neanderthal."

The newcomer smiled again, considerably less impersonally this time. "A great honor to meet you, Dr. Fellowes. You've got a tremendous job on your hands."

"*Miss* Fellowes will do," she said, trying not to sound too stuffy about it. —"What does a nuclear chemist have to do with trilobites, if you don't mind my asking?"

"Well, actually I'm not studying the trilobites per se," Dwayne said. "I'm studying the chemistry of the water that came here with them."

"Tom's taking isotope ratios on the oxygen contained in the water," said Hoskins.

"And why is that?"

Dwayne replied, "What we have here is primeval water, at least half a billion years old, maybe as much as six hundred million. The isotope ratio gives us the prevailing temperature of the ocean at that time—I could explain in detail, if you like—and when we know the ocean temperature, we can work out all sorts of other things about the ancient planetary climate. The world was mostly ocean at the time the trilobites flourished."

"So you see, Miss Fellowes, Tom doesn't really care about the trilobites at all. They're just ugly little annoyances, crawling around in his precious primeval water. The ones who study the trilobites themselves have a much easier time of it, because all they have to do is dissect the critters, and they don't need anything but a scalpel and a microscope for that. Whereas poor Tom has to set up a mass spectrograph in here each time he conducts an experiment."

"Why's that? Can't he—"

"No, he can't. He can't take anything out of its Stasis bubble and there's no way around that. It's a matter of maintaining the balance of temporal potential."

"The balance of temporal potential," Miss Fellowes repeated, as though Hoskins had said something in Latin.

"An energy-conservation problem. What comes across time is traveling across lines of temporal force. It builds up potential as it moves. We've got that neutralized inside Stasis and we need to keep it that way."

"Ah," said Miss Fellowes. Her scientific training had never included much physics. Its concepts were largely lost on her. It was a reaction, perhaps, to the unhappy memories of her marriage. Her former husband had liked to go on and on about the "poetry" inherent in physics, the mystery and magic and beauty of it. Maybe it actually had some. But anything that could be associated with her former husband was something that Miss Fellowes didn't care to think about very deeply.

Hoskins said, "Shall we move along and leave Tom here to his trilobites?"

There were samples of primordial plant life in sealed chambers— odd scaly little plants, eerie and unbeautiful—and chunks of rock formations, looking no different from twenty-first-century rocks so far as Miss Fellowes could see. Those were the vegetable and mineral parts of the collection. Animal, vegetable, mineral, yes, just as Hoskins had said—a comprehensive raid on the natural history of the past had been carried out here. And every specimen had its investigator. The place was like a museum: a museum that had been brought to life and was serving as a superactive center of research.

"And you have to supervise all of this, Dr. Hoskins?"

"Only indirectly, Miss Fellowes. I have subordinates, thank heaven. The general administrative work of running the corporation is enough to keep me busy three times over."

"But you aren't a businessman, really," she said, thinking of that vaunted Ph.D. in physics. "You're basically a scientist who has gradually drifted across into being a corporate executive, isn't that so?"

He nodded, looking wistful. " 'Drifted' is the right word. I began on the theoretical side. My doctorate dealt with the nature of time, the technique of mesonic intertemporal detection, and so on. When we formed the company, I didn't have the slightest idea that I'd be anything other than head of theoretical research. But then there were —well, problems. I don't mean technical ones. I mean the bankers came in and gave us a good talking-to about the way we were going about our business. After that there were personnel changes at the highest levels of the corporation and one thing led to another and next thing I knew they were turning to me and saying, 'You have to be C.E.O., Jerry, you're the only one who can steady the place down,' and I was fool enough to believe them, and then, well—well—" He grinned. "There I am with a fine mahogany desk and all. Shuffling papers, initialling reports, holding meetings. Telling people what to do. With maybe ten minutes left here and there in the day to think about anything like my own actual scientific research."

Miss Fellowes felt an unexpectedly powerful burst of sympathy. At last she understood why there was that "Ph.D." tag on the nameplate on Hoskins' desk. He wasn't boasting. He had it there simply to remind himself of who and what he really was.

How sad, she thought.

"If you could step aside from the business end of things," she said, "what sort of research do you think you'd want to do?"

"Short-range temporal transfer problems. No question of it. I'd want to work on a method of detecting objects that lie closer to us in time than the present limit of 10,000 years. We've done some promising preliminary studies, but we haven't been able to get further than that. A matter of available resources—financial, technical—of priorities, of accepting the limitations of the moment. If we could manage to reach our scoop into historical times, Miss Fellowes—if we could make contact with the living Egypt of the pharaohs, or the people of Babylonia or ancient Rome or Greece or—"

He broke off in mid-sentence. Miss Fellowes could hear a commotion coming from one of the distant booths, a thin voice raised querulously. Hoskins frowned, muttered a hasty "Excuse me," and went rushing off.

Miss Fellowes followed as best she could without actually running.

She didn't feel much like being left here by herself in the midst of all this hubbub of bygone ages.

An elderly man in street clothes with a thin gray beard and an angry, reddened face was arguing with a much younger uniformed technician who wore the red and gold Stasis Technologies, Ltd. monogram on his lab coat. The irate older man was saying, "I had vital aspects of my investigations to complete. Don't you understand that?"

"What's going on?" Hoskins asked, hastily coming between them.

The technician said, "Attempted removal of a specimen, Dr. Hoskins."

"Removal from Stasis?" Hoskins said, eyebrows rising. "Are you serious?" He turned to the older man. —"I can't believe this is true, Dr. Adamewski."

The older man pointed into the nearest Stasis bubble. Miss Fellowes followed his pointing hand. All she saw was a small gray lab table on which a totally undistinguished sample of rock was sitting, along with some vials of what she supposed were testing reagents.

Adamewski said, "I still have extensive work to do in order to ascertain—"

The technician cut him off. "Dr. Hoskins, Professor Adamewski knew from the start that his chalcopyrite specimen could only stay here for a two-week period. And the time's up today."

"Two weeks!" Adamewski erupted. "Who can say in advance how long a research task is going to take? Did Roentgen work out the principles of X rays in two weeks? Did Rutherford solve the problem of the atomic nucleus in two weeks? Did—"

"But two weeks was the limitation imposed for this experiment," said the technician. "He knew that."

"What of it? I wasn't able to guarantee I'd be able to finish my work in so short a time. I can't see the future, Dr. Hoskins. Two weeks, three weeks, four—what matters is solving the problem, is it not?"

"The problem, professor," Hoskins said, "is that our facilities are limited here. We've got only so many Stasis bubbles and there's an infinite amount of work to be done. So we have to keep specimens rotating. That piece of chalcopyrite has to go back where it came from. There's a long list of people waiting to use this bubble."

"So let them use it," said Adamewski heatedly. "And I'll take the specimen out of there and finish working on it at my university. You can have it back whenever I'm done."

"You know that isn't possible."

"A piece of chalcopyrite! A miserable three-kilogram chunk of rock with no commercial value! Why not?"

"We can't afford the energy expense!" Hoskins said. "You know that. None of this comes as any news to you, and please don't try to pretend otherwise."

The technician said, "The point is, Dr. Hoskins, that he tried to remove the rock against the rules and while he was in there I almost punctured Stasis, not realizing he was still inside the bubble."

There was an icy silence.

After a moment Hoskins turned to the scientist and said in a coldly formal way, "Is that so, professor?"

Adamewski looked uncomfortable. "I saw no harm in—"

"No harm? No *harm?*" Hoskins shook his head. He seemed to be penning up real anger with a considerable effort.

There was a red-handled pull-lever dangling just within reach outside the Stasis chamber that contained Professor Adamewski's mineral specimen. A nylon cord ran from the end of it, through the wall, into the chamber. Hoskins reached up unhesitatingly and jerked down on the lever.

Miss Fellowes, looking into the Stasis bubble, drew in her breath sharply as a quick burst of brilliant light flickered around the chunk of rock, surrounding it for the briefest of moments with a dazzling halo of red and green. Before she even had time to close her eyes against the brightness of the flare the light was gone. And so, too, was the chunk of rock. Its existence had flickered out. The gray lab table was bare.

Adamewski stood gasping in outrage and frustration. "What have you—"

Hoskins cut him off brusquely. "You can clear out your cubicle, professor. Your permit to investigate material in Stasis is permanently voided, as of this moment."

"Wait. You can't—"

"I'm sorry. I can, professor. And I have. You've violated one of our most stringent rules."

"I will appeal this to the International Association of—"

"Appeal away," Hoskins said. "In a case like this, you'll find I can't be overruled."

He turned away deliberately, leaving the professor still protesting, and swung around toward Miss Fellowes. She had watched the entire episode with mounting discomfort, hoping that her beeper would go off and give her some excuse to get away from this disagreeable scene.

Hoskins' face was white with anger.

"I regret that we've had to interrupt this tour with such unpleasantness, Miss Fellowes. But occasionally things like this are necessary. If there's anything else you'd like to see in here—any further questions—"

"If it's all right with you, doctor, I think I've seen enough. Perhaps I ought to be getting back to Timmie now."

"But you've only been out of your chamber for—"

"Perhaps I should, anyway."

Hoskins' lips moved silently for a moment. He seemed to be framing some sort of appeal. At length he said, "Suppose you check with Ms. Stratford and see how Timmie's doing. And if everything's all right with the boy, maybe you can allow yourself a little more free time. I'd like to invite you to have lunch with me, Miss Fellowes."

## [24]

They went into the small executive alcove of the company cafeteria. Hoskins greeted people on all sides and introduced Miss Fellowes with complete ease, although she herself felt painfully self-conscious.

What must they think, seeing us together? she wondered, and tried desperately to look businesslike. She wished now that she hadn't changed out of her nurse's uniform. The uniform served as a kind of armor for her. It allowed her to face the world in the guise of a function rather than as a person.

There was nothing fancy about the cafeteria fare. Salads, sandwiches, fruit plates, rolls—that was about it. Just as well: she had never been much for elaborate dining, especially in the middle of the day. And her years of hospital life had left her not only accustomed to cafeteria food but actually with a preference for it. She picked out a few simple things to put on her tray: a salad of lettuce and strawberries and orange slices, a couple of pieces of rye bread, a small flask of buttermilk.

When they were seated, Miss Fellowes said, "Do you have that kind of trouble often, Dr. Hoskins? The sort you just had with the professor, I mean."

"That was a new one," he said. "Of course, I'm always having to argue people out of removing specimens when their experimental time is up. But this is the first time one actually has tried to *do* it."

"Which would have created some terrible problem with—ah—the balance of temporal potential?"

"Exactly," said Hoskins, looking pleased at her use of the phrase. "Of course, we've tried to take such possibilities into account. Accidents will happen and so we've got special power sources designed to compensate for the drain of accidental removals from Stasis. But that doesn't mean we want to see a year's supply of energy gone in half a second. We couldn't afford any such thing, not without having to cut back on our operations for months to come in order to make up the costs. —And on top of everything else, there's the angle that the professor would have been in the room at the moment Stasis was being punctured."

"What would have happened to him if he had been?"

"Well, we've experimented with inanimate objects—and with mice, for that matter—and whatever we've had in the bubble at the time of puncture has disappeared."

"Gone back in time, you mean?"

"Presumably. Carried along, so to speak, by the pull of the object that's simultaneously snapping back into its natural time. That's the theory, anyway, and we don't have any reason to doubt it: an object returning to its place in the space-time matrix generates such powerful forces in its immediate vicinity that it takes with it anything that's nearby. The mass limitations seem to apply only in the forward direction. If there had been an elephant in the bubble with the rock sample, it would have been swept back in time when the rock went back. I don't even want to think about the conservation-law violations involved in *that.*"

"The lab table didn't go," Miss Fellowes pointed out.

Hoskins grinned. "No, it didn't. Or the floor, or the windows. The force has *some* limitations. It can't take the whole building with it, obviously. And it doesn't seem to be strong enough to sweep objects backward in time that are fixed in place. It just scoops up the loose things nearby. And so we anchor anything within Stasis that's in proximity to the transit object that we don't want to move, which is a fairly complicated procedure."

"But the professor wouldn't have been anchored."

"No," Hoskins said. "The idiot would have gone right along with

the rock, straight back to the place where it came from in the Pliocene."

"How dreadful it would have been for him."

"I suppose it would. Not that I'd weep a lot, I assure you. If he was
fool enough to break the rules, and as a result he happened to be in
the wrong place at the wrong time and something nasty happened to
him, it would have served him right. But ultimately *we'd* have been
the ones to suffer. Can you imagine the lawsuit we'd be hit with?"

"But if he died as a result of his own negligence—"

"Don't be naïve, Miss Fellowes. For decades now all sorts of
damned idiots in this country have been doing negligent things and
the lawyers for their estates have been nailing the responsibility to
other people's hides. The drunk who falls in front of the subway train
—the burglar who drops through a skylight and cracks his skull—the
schoolboy who climbs on the back of the bus and falls off—don't you
think they've all been able to come away with huge payments in dam-
ages? Adamewski's heirs would say that *we* were the negligent ones,
because we didn't check the bubble before we punctured Stasis to
make sure that it was empty. And the courts would agree, regardless
of the fact that the man had no business creeping inside the bubble to
try to steal the specimen. —Even if we won the case, Miss Fellowes,
can you imagine the effect it would have on the public if the story ever
came out? Gentle old scientist killed in Stasis accident! The terrible
dangers of the time travel process! Unknown risks to the public! Who
knows, perhaps Stasis can be used to generate some kind of death-ray
field! What kind of deadly experiments are actually going on behind
those gates? Shut them down! Shut them down! —Do you see? Overnight we'd be turned into some sort of monsters and funds would be
choked off like that," Hoskins said, snapping his fingers. He scowled,
looked down into his plate, played moodily with his food.

Miss Fellowes said, "Couldn't you get him back? The way you got
the rock in the first place?"

"No, because once an object is returned, the original fix will be lost
unless we take steps ahead of time to retain it—and we wouldn't have
done that in this case. As a matter of fact, we never take such steps in
any case. There's no reason for it. Finding the professor again would
mean relocating a specific fix across five million years or thereabouts
and that would be like dropping a line into the oceanic abyss for the
purpose of dredging up one particular fish. —My God, when I think
of the precautions we take to prevent accidents, it makes me furious.

We have every individual Stasis unit set up with its own puncturing device—we have to, since each unit has its own separate fix and needs to be independently collapsible. The point is, though, none of the puncturing devices is ever activated until the last minute. And then we deliberately make activation impossible except by—you saw me do it, didn't you?—by the pull of a lever whose handle is carefully placed outside Stasis. The pull is gross mechanical motion that requires a strong effort, not something that's likely to be done accidentally."

"So you'd simply have to leave Professor Adamewski back there in —what did you say?—the Pliocene?"

"There'd be no alternative."

"And the Pliocene was five million years ago?"

"It began about ten million years ago, as a matter of fact. And lasted for something like eight million years. But that particular rock came from five million years back."

"Would the professor have been able to survive there very long, do you think?"

Hoskins turned his hands upward in a gesture of uncertainty. "Well, the climate probably wouldn't be as rough as it would get later on in the glacial period your Timmie comes from, and the atmosphere he'd find himself in would be more or less identical to the stuff we breathe today—minus a lot of the garbage that we've pumped into it in the past couple of hundred years, of course. So if Adamewski knew anything about hunting and finding edible plants, which I would say is highly doubtful, he'd have been able to cope for a while. Anywhere between two weeks and two months, is my guess."

"Well, what if he met some Pliocene woman during that time, and she took a liking to him and taught him how to gather food?" Then an even wilder idea occurred to Miss Fellowes. —"And he might even mate with her back there and they would have children, a whole new genetic line, a modern man's genes combining with those of a prehistoric woman. Wouldn't that change all of history to come? That would be the biggest risk of having the professor go back in time, wouldn't it?"

Hoskins was trying to smother an attack of giggles.

Miss Fellowes felt her face turning a hot red. "Have I said something very stupid, doctor?"

It was another moment before he was able to reply. "Stupid? Well, that's too harsh a word. —Naïve, is what I'd prefer to say. Miss Fellowes, there weren't any women conveniently waiting back there in the Pliocene for our Dr. Adamewski to set up housekeeping with. Not anybody that he'd regard as an eligible mate, anyway."

"I see."

"I forget most of the details of what I once knew about hominid ancestry, but I can tell you quite confidently that Adamewski wouldn't have found anything that looked like *Homo sapiens* back there. The best he could hope for would be some primitive form of australopithecine, maybe four feet tall and covered with hair from head to toe. The human race as we understand it simply hadn't evolved at such an early date. And I doubt that even a passionate man like Dr. Adamewski"—Hoskins smothered another burst of giggles— "would find himself so enamored of your average Pliocene hominid female that he'd want to have sexual relations with her. Of course, if he ran into the Pliocene equivalent of Helen of Troy—the ape that launched a thousand ships, so to speak—"

"I think I get the point," Miss Fellowes said primly, regretting now that she had led the discussion in this direction in the first place. "But I asked you before, when you showed me the dinosaur, why it was that moving something in and out of time doesn't change history. I understand now that the professor wouldn't have been able to start a family in the Pliocene, but if you sent someone back in time to an era when there were actual human beings—say, twenty thousand years ago—"

Hoskins looked thoughtful. "Well, then, there'd be some minor disruption of the time-line, I suppose. But I don't think there'd be anything big."

"So you simply can't change history using Stasis?"

"Theoretically, yes, you can, I suppose. Actually, except in really unusual cases, no. We move objects out of Stasis all the time. Air molecules. Bacteria. Dust. About ten per cent of our energy consumption goes to make up micro-losses of that sort. But even moving large objects in time sets up changes that damp out. Consider Adamewski's chunk of chalcopyrite from the Pliocene. During the two weeks it was up here in our time, let's say, some insect that might have taken shelter under it couldn't find it, and was killed. That could initiate a whole series of changes along the time-line, I imagine. But the mathematics of Stasis indicates that it would be a converging series. The amount of change tends to diminish with time and eventually things return to the track they would have followed all along."

"You mean, reality heals itself?"

"In a manner of speaking. Yank a human being out of the past, or send one back, and you make a larger wound. If the individual is an ordinary one, that wound would still heal itself—that's what the calculations show. Naturally there are a great many people who write to us every day and want us to bring Abraham Lincoln into the present, or Mohammed, or Alexander the Great. Well, we don't have the technical ability to do that just yet, not that we'd be likely to if we could. But even if we could cast our net such a short distance into the past, and were able to locate a specific human being such as the three I named, the change in reality involved in moving one of the great molders of history would be too huge to be healed. There are ways of calculating when a change is likely to be too great, and we make sure that we don't come anywhere near that limit."

Miss Fellowes said, "Then Timmie—"

"No, he doesn't present any problems of that sort. One small boy who belonged to a human subspecies that was destined to die out in another five or ten thousand years is hardly going to be a history-changer because we've brought him forward to our era. Reality is safe." Hoskins gave her a quick, sharp glance. "You don't need to worry about it."

"I'm not. I'm just trying to understand how things work around here."

"Which I applaud."

Miss Fellowes took a long deep sip of her buttermilk. "If there wasn't any historical risk in bringing one Neanderthal child into our time, then it would be possible to bring another one eventually, wouldn't it?"

"Of course. But one is all we'll need, I imagine. If Timmie helps us learn everything that we want to—"

"I don't mean to bring another one here for purposes of research. I mean as a playmate for Timmie."

"What?"

It was a concept that had burst into her mind as suddenly and unexpectedly as the name "Timmie" itself had—an impulse, a spontaneous thing. Miss Fellowes was astonished at herself for having brought it up.

But she pursued it, now that it was here.

"He's a normal, healthy child in every way, so far as I can see. A child of his time, of course. But in his own way I think he's outstanding."

"I certainly think so too, Miss Fellowes."

"His development from here on, though, may not continue normally."

"Why not?" Hoskins asked.

"Any child needs stimulation and this one lives a life of solitary confinement. I intend to do what I can, but I can't replace an entire cultural matrix. What I'm saying, Dr. Hoskins, is that he needs another boy to play with."

Hoskins nodded slowly. "Unfortunately, there's only one of him, isn't there? Poor child."

Miss Fellowes watched him shrewdly, hoping that she had picked the right moment for this.

"If you could bring a *second* Neanderthal forward to share his quarters with him—"

"Yes. That would be ideal, Miss Fellowes. —But of course it can't be done."

"It can't?" said Miss Fellowes, with sudden dismay.

"Not with the best will in the world, which I like to think is what we have. We couldn't possibly expect to find another Neanderthal close to his age without incredible luck—it was a very sparsely populated era, Miss Fellowes; we can't just dip casually into the Neanderthal equivalent of a big city and snatch a child—and even if we could, it wouldn't be fair to multiply risks by having another human being in Stasis."

Miss Fellowes put down her spoon. Heady new ideas were flooding into her mind. She said energetically, "In that case, Dr. Hoskins, let me take a different tack. If it's impossible to bring another Neanderthal child into the present, so be it. I'm not even sure I could cope with a second one, anyway. But what if—a little later, once Timmie is better adapted to modern life—what if we were to bring another child in from the outside to play with him?"

Hoskins stared at her in concern. "A *human* child?"

"*Another* child," said Miss Fellowes, with an angry glare. "Timmie is human."

"Of course. You know what I meant. —But I couldn't dream of such a thing."

"Why not? Why couldn't you? I don't see anything wrong with the idea. You pulled that child out of time and made him an eternal prisoner. Don't you owe him something? Dr. Hoskins, if there is any man who, in this present-day world, can be considered that child's father—

in every sense but the biological—it's you. Why can't you do this little thing for him?"

Hoskins said, "His *father?*" He rose, somewhat unsteadily, to his feet. "Miss Fellowes, I think I'll take you back now, if you don't mind."

They returned to the dollhouse that was Stasis Section One in a bleak silence that neither broke.

[25]

As he had promised, McIntyre sent over a stack of reference works that dealt with Neanderthals. Miss Fellowes plunged into them as if she were back at nursing school and a critical exam was coming up in a couple of days.

She learned that the first Neanderthal fossils had been discovered in the middle of the nineteenth century by workmen digging in a limestone quarry near Düsseldorf, Germany, at a place called the Neander Valley—*Neanderthal*, in German. While cleaning away the mud that covered a limestone deposit in a grotto sixty feet above the valley floor, they came across a human skull embedded in the grotto floor, and other bones not far away.

The workmen gave the skull and a few of the other bones to a local high school teacher, who took them to Dr. Hermann Schaafhausen of Bonn, a well-known anatomist. Schaafhausen was startled by their strangeness. The skull had many human features, but it was curiously primitive in appearance, long and narrow, with a sloping forehead and an enormous bony ridge bulging above the brows. The thighbones that accompanied the skull were so thick and heavy that they scarcely looked human at all.

But Schaafhausen *did* think the Neanderthal bones were human relics—extremely ancient ones. In a paper he read at a scientific meeting early in 1857, he termed the unusual fossils "the most ancient memorial of the early inhabitants of Europe."

Miss Fellowes looked up at Timmie, who was playing with some toy on the far side of the room.

"Listen to that," she said. " 'The most ancient memorial of the early inhabitants of Europe.' That's one of your relatives he's talking about, Timmie."

Timmie didn't seem impressed. He uttered a few indifferent clicks and went back to his game.

Miss Fellowes read on. And quickly the book confirmed what she already vaguely knew: that the Neanderthal people, while certainly ancient inhabitants of Europe, were far from being the *most* ancient ones.

The discovery of the original Neanderthal fossils had been followed, later in the nineteenth century, by similar discoveries in many other parts of Europe—more fossilized bones of prehistoric human-like creatures with sloping foreheads, huge beetling brows, and—another typical characteristic—receding chins. Scientists debated the meaning of these fossils, and, as Darwin's theories of evolution came to gain wide acceptance, general agreement developed that the Neanderthal-type specimens were the remains of a brutish-looking prehistoric kind of human being, ancestral to modern humanity, perhaps midway on the evolutionary scale between apes and humans.

" 'Brutish-looking.' " Miss Fellowes sniffed. "All in the eye of the beholder, eh, Timmie?"

But then had come the discovery of other types of fossil humans—in Java, in China, elsewhere in Europe—that seemed even more primitive in form than the Neanderthals. And in the twentieth century, when reliable methods of dating ancient sites were developed, it became clear that the Neanderthal people must have lived relatively recently on the time-scale of human evolution. The Javan and Chinese forms of primitive human being were at least half a million years old, perhaps even more, whereas the Neanderthals had not appeared on the scene until something like 150,000 years ago. They had occupied much of Europe and the Near East, apparently, for over a hundred thousand years, flourishing until about 35,000 years ago. Then they had disappeared—replaced at all locations by the modern form of the human race, which evidently had already come into existence at the time the first Neanderthals emerged. It appeared that humans of the modern type had lived alongside the Neanderthals, peacefully or otherwise, for thousands of years before undergoing a sudden population explosion and completely displacing the other human form.

There seemed to be several different theories to explain why the Neanderthals had suddenly become extinct. But one thing all the experts agreed on was that they had vanished from the Earth late in the period of the ice ages.

The Neanderthals, then, hadn't been some brutish ape-like ancestor of modern man. They weren't ancestral at all. They were simply humans of another form, different in various ways from their contemporaries, who were the kind of human that had survived into modern times. Distant cousins, perhaps. The two races had had a parallel existence in Ice Age times, an uneasy coexistence. But only one of the two forms had lasted beyond the time when the great glaciers had covered Europe.

"So you *are* human, Timmie. I never really doubted it—" (though she had, for a bad moment right at the beginning, for which she still felt shame) "—but here it is in black and white. You're just a little unusual-looking, that's all. But you're as human as I am. As human as anybody here."

Clicks and murmurs came from Timmie.

"Yes," Miss Fellowes said. "You think so, too, don't you?"

And yet, the differences, the differences—

Miss Fellowes' eyes raced over the pages. What had the Neanderthals really looked like? At first there had been hot debates over that, because so few fossil specimens of Neanderthals had been found, and one of the earliest skeletons to be discovered turned out to be that of a man whose bones had been crippled by osteoarthritis, creating a distorted impression of how a normal man of his people would have appeared. But gradually, as more skeletal evidence was uncovered, a generally accepted picture of the Neanderthal people had emerged.

They had been shorter than modern humans—the tallest of the men were probably no more than about five-feet-four in height—and very stocky, with wide shoulders and deep barrel-chests. Their foreheads sloped backward, their brow ridges were enormous, they had rounded lower jaws instead of chins. Their noses were big and broad and low-bridged, and their mouths jutted forward like muzzles. Their feet were flat and very wide, with short stubby toes. Their bones were heavy, thick, and large-jointed and their muscles probably were extremely well developed. Their legs were short in proportion to their torsos and possibly were naturally bowed, with permanently flexed knees, so that they might have walked in a sort of shuffle.

Not pretty, no. Not by modern standards.

But human. Unquestionably human. Give a Neanderthal man a shave and a haircut and put him into a shirt and a pair of jeans and he could probably walk down a street in any city of the world without attracting anyone's attention.

"And listen to this part, Timmie!" Miss Fellowes ran her finger across the page and read out loud to him. *" 'He had a big brain. The brains of skeletons are measured by cranial capacities—that is, how much volume, in cubic centimeters, the skull cavity has. Among modern* Homo sapiens, *the average cranial capacity is something like 1,400 or 1,500 c.c. Some men have brain capacities of 1,100–1,200 c.c. The average brain capacity of Neanderthal man was about 1,600 c.c. for male skulls, and about 1,350 c.c. for female skulls. This is higher than the average figure for* Homo sapiens.' " She chortled. "What do you think of that, Timmie? 'Higher than the average figure for *Homo sapiens*'!"

Timmie smiled at her. Almost as if he had understood! But Miss Fellowes knew there was no chance of that.

"Of course," she said, "it isn't really the size of the skull that counts, it's the quality of the brain inside it. Elephants have bigger skulls than just about anybody, but they can't do algebra. Nor can I, for that matter, but I can read a book and drive a car, and show me the elephant that can do those things! —Do you think I'm silly, Timmie? Talking to you this way?" The boy's face was solemn; he offered her a click or two. "But you need someone to talk to in here. And so do I. Come over here for a moment, will you?" Miss Fellowes beckoned to him. He stared blankly but stayed where he was. "Come over here to me, Timmie. I want to show you something."

But he didn't budge. It was a pretty fantasy, imagining that he was beginning to understand her words; but she knew very well that there was no substance to it.

She went to him instead, sitting down beside him and holding out the book she had been reading. There was a painting on the left-hand side of the page, an artist's reconstruction of a Neanderthal man's face, massive and grizzled, with the typical jutting mouth and great flattened nose and fierce tangled beard. His head was thrust forward from his shoulders. His lips were drawn back a little, baring his teeth. A savage countenance, yes. Brutish, one might even say: there was no getting away from that.

But yet there was the indisputable light of intelligence in his eyes, and a look of something else, something—what? Tragic? A look of anguish, a look of pain?

He was staring off into the distance as though looking across thousands of years of time. Looking into a world where none of his kind existed any longer, except for one small boy who had no proper business being there.

"How does he look, Timmie? Do you recognize him at all? Does he seem anything like the way your people actually were?"

Timmie made a few clicks. He glanced at the book without apparent interest.

Miss Fellowes tapped the picture a couple of times. Then she took his hand and put it on the page to direct his attention toward the plate.

He just didn't understand. The image on the page seemed to mean nothing to him at all.

He ran his hand over the page in a remote, uninterested way, as though the smooth texture of the paper was the only aspect of the book that had caught his attention. Then the boy turned the lower corner of the page upward and began idly to pull on it, so that the page started to rip from the binding.

"No!" Miss Fellowes cried, and in a quick reflexive gesture she pulled his hand away and slapped it, all at once—a light slap, but an unmistakable reprimand.

Timmie glared at her. His eyes were bright with fury. He made a ghastly snarling sound and his hand became a claw; and he reached for the book again.

She pulled it out of his reach.

He dropped down on his knees and growled at her. A terrifying growl, a deep eerie rumbling, eyes turned upward, lips drawn back, teeth bared in a frightful grimace of rage.

"Oh, Timmie, Timmie—" Tears welled up in Miss Fellowes' eyes, and she felt a vast sense of despair, of defeat—of horror, even—rising within her.

Groveling on the floor and growling like a little wild beast, she thought, appalled. Snarling at her as if he'd like to jump at her and rip her throat out just as he had clawed at that book, wanting to tear out a page.

*Oh, Timmie—*

But then Miss Fellowes forced herself back to calmness. This was no way to react to the child's little outburst. What had she expected? He was four years old at most and came out of some primitive tribal culture and he had never seen a book before in his life. Was he supposed to look at it with respect and awe, and thank her politely for having made this valuable source of information available to his eager young mind?

Even modern four-year-olds from nice educated households, she reminded herself, have been known to tear pages out of books. And also sometimes to growl and snarl and look angry when you slap their hands for doing it. Nobody thinks that they're little savage beasts, just because they do things like that. Not at that age. And Timmie isn't a beast either, just a small boy, a small wild boy who finds himself a prisoner in a world he can't begin to understand.

Carefully Miss Fellowes put the books McIntyre had given her away in one of her lockers. When she returned to the other room she found Timmie calm again, playing with his toy as though nothing unusual had taken place.

Her heart flooded with love for the boy. She yearned to beg his forgiveness for having seemed once again to give up on him so quickly. But what good would that do? He couldn't begin to understand.

Well, there was another way.

"I think it's time for some oatmeal, Timmie. Don't you?"

# CHAPTER SIX

# Disclosing

## [26]

LATER IN THE DAY Dr. McIntyre arrived at the dollhouse for
his second visit with Timmie. Miss Fellowes said, as he came in,
"Thank you for the books, doctor. I want to assure you that I've been
doing my homework very thoroughly."

McIntyre smiled his small, precise, not very radiant smile. "I'm
pleased to have been of some help, Miss Fellowes."

"But there's still more I'd like to know. I mean to keep reading,
but since you're here, I thought I'd ask you—"

The paleoanthropologist smiled again, even less glowingly. He was
all too evidently eager to get down to his session with the Neanderthal
child, and not at all enthusiastic about stopping to answer a nurse's
unimportant questions. But after the fiasco of the last visit, Miss Fellowes was determined not to allow McIntyre to drive Timmie into
tears with the intensity of his scientific curiosity. The session would
proceed slowly, at the pace Miss Fellowes intended to set, or it
wouldn't proceed at all. Her word was going to be law: that was
Hoskins' phrase, but she had adopted it as her own.

"If I can help you, Miss Fellowes—something you weren't able to
discover in the books—"

"It's the one central question that has troubled me since I came to
work with Timmie. We all agree that Neanderthals were human. What
I'm trying to find out is *how* human they were. How close they are to
us—where the similarities are, and where the differences. I don't
mean the physical differences, particularly—those are obvious enough

and I've studied the texts you sent over. I mean the cultural differences. The differences in intelligence. The things that really determine humanity."

"Well, Miss Fellowes, those are exactly the things I'm here to try to learn. The purpose of the tests I'm going to give Timmie is precisely to determine—"

"I understand that. Tell me first what's *already* known."

McIntyre's lips quirked irritably. He ran his hand through his fine, shining golden hair.

"What in particular?"

"I learned today that the two different races, the Neanderthal race and the modern human one—is that correct, calling them races?— lived side by side in Europe and the Near East for perhaps a hundred thousand years during the glacial periods."

" 'Races' isn't quite the proper word, Miss Fellowes. The various 'races' of mankind, as we employ the term nowadays, are much more closely related to each other than we are to the Neanderthals. 'Subspecies' might be more accurate when talking about ourselves and the Neanderthals. They belonged to the subspecies *Homo sapiens neanderthalensis* and we're classed as *Homo sapiens sapiens.*"

"All right. But they did live side by side."

"Apparently they did, at least in some areas. In the warmer places, that is—the Neanderthals probably had the colder regions all to themselves, because they were better adapted to deal with the conditions there. Of course, we're talking about very small populations, widely scattered bands. It's altogether possible that an individual Neanderthal tribe could have persisted for centuries without ever once encountering *Homo sapiens sapiens.* On the other hand, they might have been next-door neighbors in some places, especially as the last glacial period started to draw to its close and more of Europe became habitable by our ancestors."

"You don't think there's any chance that the Neanderthals were our ancestors at all, then."

"Oh, no. They're a separate group, off on an evolutionary branch of their own, or so nearly every scientist believes today. Close enough to us so that they could interbreed with *Homo sapiens sapiens*—we have some fossil evidence that they did—but mainly they must have kept to themselves, conserved their own gene pool, contributed very little if anything at all to the modern-day human genetic mix."

"Backwoodsmen. Country cousins."

"That's not a bad description," McIntyre said.

"Thank you. —And were they less intelligent than *Homo sapiens sapiens?*"

He looked impatient again. "That's something I really can't say, Miss Fellowes, until you let me get down to some serious testing of Timmie's mental capacity and ability to—"

"What's your guess, as of this afternoon?"

"Less intelligent."

"Based on what, Dr. McIntyre? Pro-*sapiens* prejudice?"

McIntyre's delicate complexion flooded with color. "You asked me to offer an opinion before I've had a chance to examine the only real evidence that's ever been available to science. What else can my answer be except an expression of prejudice? By definition that's what it is."

"Yes, yes, I understand that. But it must be based on something concrete. What?"

Controlling himself, McIntyre said, "The Mousterian cultural level —that's our technical term for Neanderthal culture, *Mousterian*— wasn't very sophisticated and didn't show much sign of progress over the hundreds of centuries that it lasted. What we find at Neanderthal sites are simple flint tools, scarcely ever changing with time. Whereas the *sapiens* line made steady improvements in its technology all during the Paleolithic, and has continued to do so until the present day, which is why it is *sapiens* humans who have brought a Neanderthal child out of the depths of time and not vice versa." McIntyre paused for breath. —"Also, there's no Neanderthal art that we know about: no sculptures, no cave paintings, no sign of any decoration that we could consider to be religious in nature. We assume that they must have had a religion of some sort, because we've found Neanderthal graves, and a species that buries its dead almost certainly has to have some kind of belief in an afterlife, and therefore in higher spiritual entities. But those few Neanderthal dwelling sites that we've examined don't give us evidence of anything but the simplest, most basic sort of hunting-and-gathering tribal life. And as I mentioned the other day, we haven't even been altogether certain they were physiologically capable of using language. Or that they had the intellectual capacity to do so even if their larynxes and tongues were able to shape sounds."

Miss Fellowes felt herself bogging down in gloom. She looked over at Timmie, glad that he could understand nothing of what McIntyre was telling her.

"So you think that they were an intellectually inferior race, then? Compared to *Homo sapiens sapiens*, I mean?"

"Certainly we have to think so on the basis of what we know as of now," McIntyre said. "On the other hand, that's not being entirely fair to them. The Neanderthals may not have *needed* the sorts of cultural frills and fol-de-rols that the *sapiens sapiens* subspecies thought were important. Mousterian tools, simple as they were, were perfectly well suited for the tasks they had to perform—killing small game, chopping up meat, scraping hides, felling trees, things like that. And if the Neanderthals didn't go in for painting and sculpture, well, they may simply have felt that such things were blasphemous. We can't say that they didn't. More recent cultures than theirs have had prohibitions dealing with making graven images, you know."

"But even so you think the Neanderthals were an inferior race. —An inferior subspecies, I should say."

"I do. It's prejudice, Miss Fellowes, sheer prejudice, and I admit it freely. I can't help it that I'm a member of *Homo sapiens sapiens*. I can make a case out for the Neanderthals, but the fact remains that I basically see them as a slow-witted unprogressive form of humanity that was outmaneuvered and eventually obliterated by our own people. —Of course, when we talk about *physical* superiority, that's a different matter. In terms of the living conditions that existed in their time, the Neanderthals could well be considered the superior form. The very features that make us think of them as ugly brutes may have been marks of that superiority."

"Give me an example."

"The nose," McIntyre said. He pointed toward Timmie. "His nose is a lot larger than a modern child's."

"Yes. It is."

"And some might say it's ugly, because it's so wide and thick and protrudes so much."

"Some might say so," Miss Fellowes agreed coolly.

"But then consider the climate that Paleolithic man had to deal with. Much of Europe was covered by permafrost. A constant cold, dry wind blew across the central plains. Snow might fall in any season of the year. You know what it feels like to breathe really cold air. But one purpose that the human nose serves is the warming and moistening of inhaled air on its way to the lungs. The bigger the nose, the more effective the warming capacity."

"Serving as a kind of radiator, you mean?"

"Exactly. The whole Neanderthal facial structure seems designed to keep cold air from reaching the lungs—and the brain, too; don't forget that the arteries that feed blood to the brain are located just back of the nasal passages. But the big Neanderthal nose, its forward location, the extremely large maxillary sinuses, the large diameter of the blood vessels serving the face—they may all have been adaptations to the glacial environment, making it far easier for the Neanderthals to deal with the cold than were our own ancestors. The heavy musculature as well, the sturdy body structure—"

"So the so-called 'brutish' look of the Neanderthals may have been nothing more than natural selection at work, a specialized evolutionary response to the harsh conditions with which man had to cope in ice-age Europe."

"Quite so."

"If they were so well designed to survive," Miss Fellowes said, "then why did they become extinct? A change in the climate making their specializations no longer advantageous?"

McIntyre sighed heavily. "The question of Neanderthal extinction, Miss Fellowes, is such a vexed one, so fraught with controversy—"

"Well, what's *your* view? Were they simply exterminated, because they were as slow-witted as you seem to think? Did their special genetic characteristics disappear through intermarriage with the other line? Or was it some combination of—"

"May I remind you, Miss Fellowes, that I have work to do here today?" McIntyre said. Exasperation was beginning to show in his eyes. "Much as I'd like to discuss Neanderthals with you, the fact remains that we have an actual living Neanderthal right in this room awaiting study, and I have only a limited amount of time in which to—"

"Then go ahead, Dr. McIntyre," said Miss Fellowes in resignation. "Examine Timmie as much as you'd like. You and I can talk some other time. Just make sure you don't upset the boy the way you did before."

## [27]

And now the time had arrived for the first press conference—the public unveiling of Timmie. Miss Fellowes had delayed it as long as possible. But Hoskins was insistent. Publicity, he had been saying all along, was essential to the financing of the project. Now that it was undeniably clear that the boy was in good physical shape, that he apparently wasn't going to come down with any twenty-first-century bacterial infection, that he was capable of withstanding the stress of a meeting with the media, it simply had to happen. Miss Fellowes' word might be law, but it was clear that there was one word she didn't have the leeway to utter. This time Hoskins wasn't going to take "no" for an answer.

"I want to limit the public viewing to five minutes, then," she said.

"They've asked for fifteen."

"They could ask for a day and a half, Dr. Hoskins. But five minutes is all that I consider to be acceptable."

"Ten, Miss Fellowes."

She could see the determination in his face.

"Ten at the absolute limit. Less if the boy shows any sign of distress."

"You know he'll show signs of distress," said Hoskins. "I can't simply let a little whimpering be the signal to throw the reporters out."

"I'm not talking about a little whimpering, doctor. I'm talking about hysteria, profound psychosomatic reactions, potentially life-threatening responses to a massive invasion of his living space. You remember how wild the boy was the night he arrived here."

"He was frightened out of his wits that night."

"And you think a bunch of television cameras poked into his face won't upset him all over again? Bright hot lights? A lot of loud-mouthed strangers yelling things at him?"

"Miss Fellowes—"

"How many reporters are you planning to let in here, anyway?"

Hoskins paused and counted up mentally. "About a dozen, most likely."

"Three."

"Miss *Fellowes!*"

"The Stasis bubble is small. It's Timmie's sanctuary. If you let it be invaded by a vast pack of—baboons—"

"They'll be science reporters like Candide Deveney."

"Fine. Three reporters."

"You really are determined to be difficult, aren't you?"

"I have a child to care for. That's what you're paying me for and what I intend to do. If I'm too difficult to work with, you can always give me notice, you know."

The words slipped out unexpectedly. Miss Fellowes felt a sudden stab of alarm. What if Hoskins decided to call her bluff? Sent her away, called in one of the rejected applicants—there must surely have been rejected applicants—to take charge of Timmie?

But the idea of dismissing her seemed to alarm Hoskins as much as it did her.

"I don't want to do that, Miss Fellowes. You know that very well."

"Then listen to me. The concept of a press pool isn't unknown around here, is it? Let your precious media people choose three representatives to come in here and inspect Timmie. Or, rather, to stand outside the Stasis bubble's door while I show him to them. They can share the information with the others. Tell them that any more than three would endanger the boy's health and mental stability."

"Four, Miss Fellowes?"

"Three."

"They're going to give me hell if I tell them—"

"Three."

Hoskins stared at her. Then he began to laugh. "All right, Miss Fellowes. You win. Three media people. But they can see him for ten minutes altogether. I'll let them know that if they have any complaints they should direct them to Timmie's nurse, not to me."

[28]

Later in the day the gentlemen of the press arrived. Two gentlemen and a lady, more accurately: John Underhill of the *Times,* Stan Washington of Globe-Net Cable News, Margaret Anne Crawford of Reuters.

Miss Fellowes held Timmie in her arms just at the perimeter of Stasis and he clung to her wildly while they set their cameras to work and called requests to her through the open door from their places just outside the bubble. She did her best to cope, turning Timmie this way and that so they could see his face and head from various angles.

"Is it a boy or a girl?" the Reuters woman asked.

"Boy," said Miss Fellowes brusquely.

"He looks almost human," said Underhill of the *Times*.

"He *is* human."

"We were told he was a Neanderthal. If you tell us now that he's human—"

"I assure you," said Hoskins' voice suddenly, from behind her, "that no deception has been practiced here. That child is authentic *Homo sapiens neanderthalensis*."

"And *Homo sapiens neanderthalensis*," Miss Fellowes said in a crisp tone, "is a form of *Homo sapiens*. This boy is as human as you and I."

"With an ape's face, though," said Washington of Globe-Net Cable News. "An ape-boy; that's what we've got here. How does he act, nurse? Like an ape?"

"He acts exactly the way a little boy acts," snapped Miss Fellowes, moving deeper into her mode of belligerent defensiveness with every moment. Timmie squirmed madly against her shoulder. She could hear him uttering soft little clicks of fear. "He is not an ape-boy in any sense. His facial features are those of the Neanderthal branch of the human race. His behavior is that of a completely normal human child. He's intelligent and responsive when he isn't being terrified by a bunch of noisy strangers. His name is—is Timothy—Timmie—and it's an absolute error to regard him as—"

"Timothy?" said the man from the *Times*. "What's the significance of calling him that?"

Miss Fellowes colored. "There's no particular significance. It's simply his name."

"Tied to his sleeve when he got here?" asked Globe-Net Cable News.

"I gave him the name."

"Timmie the ape-boy," Globe-Net said.

The three reporters laughed. Miss Fellowes felt her anger rising to the point where she feared she was going to have trouble holding it in check.

"Put it down, can't you?" the woman from Reuters called. "Let's see how it walks."

"The child's too frightened for that," Miss Fellowes replied, wondering if they expected Timmie to walk about the room with his knuckles dragging against the floor. "Much too frightened. Can't you see? Isn't that obvious?"

Indeed, Timmie's breath had been coming in ever-deeper sighs as he gradually gathered momentum for an outburst of wailing. And now it began—piercing agonized screams mixed with a cascade of growls and clicks. They went on and on. She could feel him quivering against her. The laughter, the hot lights, the barrage of questions— the boy was completely terrified.

"Miss Fellowes—Miss Fellowes—"

"No more questions!" she shot back. "This press conference is over."

She spun around, holding Timmie tightly, and headed back into the inner room. On the way she strode past Hoskins, whose face was tight with consternation but who gave her a quick, tense nod and a small smile of approval.

It took her a couple of minutes to calm the boy down. Gradually the tension left his small quivering body; gradually the fear ebbed from his face.

A press conference! Miss Fellowes thought bitterly. For a four-year-old. The poor suffering child! What will they do to him next?

After a time she went out of the room again, flushed with indignation, closing Timmie's door behind her. The three reporters were still there, huddling in the space just outside the bubble. She stepped through the Stasis boundary and confronted them out there.

"Haven't you had enough?" she demanded. "It's going to take me all afternoon to repair the damage to the boy's peace of mind that you've done here today. Why don't you go away?"

"We have just a few more questions, Miss Fellowes. If you don't mind—"

She looked toward Hoskins in appeal. He shrugged and gave her a weak smile as though to counsel patience.

"If we could know a little about your own background, Miss Fellowes—" said the woman from Reuters.

Hoskins said quickly, "We can provide you with a copy of Miss Fellowes' professional credentials, if you wish, Ms. Crawford."

"Yes. Please do."

"Is she a time-travel scientist?"

"Miss Fellowes is a highly experienced nurse," said Hoskins. "She was brought to Stasis Technologies, Ltd., specifically for the purpose of caring for Timmie."

"And what do you expect to do with—Timmie," asked the man from the *Times*, "now that you have him?"

"Well," Hoskins said, "from my point of view the chief purpose of the Neanderthal project was simply to find out whether we could aim our scoop at the relatively short-range target of the Paleolithic era with sufficient accuracy to bring back a living organism. Our previous successes, as you know, have all involved a target zone in the millions of years, rather than a mere forty thousand. That has now been accomplished, and we are continuing to work on ever narrower refinements of our process with the goal of even shorter-range targeting. —But of course we also now have a live Neanderthal child in our midst, a creature which is at the edge of being human or indeed must actually be considered to be human. The anthropologists and the physiologists are naturally very much interested in him and he'll be the subject of intensive study."

"How long will you keep him?"

"Until such a time as we need the space more than we need him. Quite a while, perhaps."

The man from Globe-Net Cable said, "Can you bring him out into the open so we can set up a sub-etheric transmission and give our viewers a real show?"

Miss Fellowes cleared her throat loudly.

But Hoskins was a step ahead of her. "I'm sorry, but the child can't be removed from Stasis."

"And what is Stasis again, actually?" asked Ms. Crawford of Reuters.

"Ah." Hoskins permitted himself one of his short smiles. "That would take a great deal of explanation—more, I think, than your readers would care about at this point. But I can give you a brief summary. —In Stasis, time as we know it doesn't exist. Those rooms are inside an invisible bubble that is not exactly part of our universe. A self-contained inviolable environment, one might say. That's why the child could be plucked out of time the way it was."

"Wait a minute, now," Underhill of the *Times* objected. "Self-contained? Inviolable? The nurse goes into the room and out of it."

"And so could any of you," said Hoskins matter-of-factly. "You would be moving parallel to the lines of temporal force and no great energy gain or loss would be involved. The child, however, was taken from the far past. It moved across the time lines and gained temporal potential. To move it into the universe—*our* universe, and into our own time—would absorb enough energy to burn out every line in the place and probably to knock out power in the entire city. When he arrived, all sorts of trash came with him—dirt and twigs and pebbles and things—and we've got every crumb of it all stored out back of this area. When we get a chance we'll ship it back where it came from. But we don't dare let it out of the Stasis zone."

The media people were busily jotting down notes as Hoskins spoke to them. Miss Fellowes suspected that they didn't understand very much and that they were sure that their audience wouldn't either. But it sounded scientific and that was what counted.

The Globe-Net man said, "Would you be available for an all-circuit interview tonight, Dr. Hoskins?"

"I think we can manage that," said Hoskins at once.

"But not the boy," said Miss Fellowes.

"No," said Hoskins. "Not the boy. But I'll be happy to answer any further questions you might have. And now, please, if we can clear the area—"

Miss Fellowes watched them go with no regret.

She closed the door and heard the electronic locks kicking in and stood there for a moment, reflecting on all that had just been said.

Once again, this business of the build-up of temporal potential, of power surges, of the fear of removing anything from Stasis that had come forward in time, had come up. She remembered how agitated Dr. Hoskins had been when Professor Adamewski was caught trying to sneak a rock sample out of his research area, and the explanations he had given her then. Much of that had quickly become hazy to her; but, reminded of it now, Miss Fellowes saw one thing with terrible clarity, a conclusion to which she had given no serious thought when she had brushed against it earlier.

Timmie was doomed never to see anything of the world into which he had—without his comprehension or consent—been thrust. The bubble would be his entire universe so long as he remained in modern time.

He was a prisoner and always would be. Not by the arbitrary fiat of Dr. Hoskins, but by the inexorable laws of the process by which he had been snatched out of his own time. It wasn't that Hoskins *would* not ever let him out of the Stasis bubble. Hoskins *could* not let him out.

Words came back to her from her conversation with Hoskins on the night of Timmie's arrival.

*The point to bear in mind is simply that he must never be allowed to leave these rooms.* Never. *Not for an instant. Not for any reason. Not to save his life. Not even to save* your *life, Miss Fellowes.*

Miss Fellowes hadn't really paid much attention then to the perfunctory explanation Hoskins had offered. *A matter of energy,* he had said. *There are conservation laws involved.* She had had other things to think about then, much more urgent things. But it was all as clear to her now as it needed to be. The few little rooms of this dollhouse were forever to be the boundaries of Timmie's world.

Poor child. Poor child.

She became suddenly aware that he was crying and she hastened into the bedroom to console him.

[29]

Hoskins was getting ready to call the meeting of the board of directors to order when his telephone rang. He stared at it in irritation. What now?

It went on ringing.

"Excuse me, will you?" he said, looking around the room. He switched it to audio-only and said, "Hoskins."

"Dr. Hoskins, this is Bruce Mannheim. Of the Children's Advocacy Council, as I think you know."

Hoskins choked back a cough.

"Yes, Mr. Mannheim. What can I do for you?"

"I saw your telecast last night, of course. The little Neanderthal boy. Fascinating, fascinating, an absolutely miraculous scientific achievement!"

"Why, thank you. And—"

"But of course, the situation raises some moral and ethical problems. As I think you know. To have taken a child of an alien culture from his own nurturing family situation, and to bring him into our own era—" Mannheim paused. "I think we need to talk about this, Dr. Hoskins."

"Perhaps we do. But right at this moment—"

"Oh, not at this moment," Mannheim said airily. "I didn't intend that at all. I simply want to propose that we set up a time for a more extended discussion of the issues which—"

"Yes," Hoskins said, rolling his eyes toward the ceiling. "Of course. Of course, Mr. Mannheim. If you'll leave your number with my secretary, she'll get back to you just as soon as possible, and we can organize an appointment."

"Very good, Dr. Hoskins. Thank you very much."

Hoskins put the telephone down. He stared bleakly around the room.

"Bruce Mannheim," he said dolefully. "The famous children's advocate. Wants to talk to me about the boy. —My God, my God! It was inevitable, wasn't it? And now here it all comes."

## [30]

In the weeks that followed, Miss Fellowes felt herself grow to be an integral part of Stasis Technologies, Ltd. She was given a small office of her own with her name on the door, an office quite close to the dollhouse (as she never stopped calling Timmie's Stasis bubble). Her original contract was torn up and Hoskins offered her a new one providing for a substantial raise. She and Hoskins might be destined to be adversaries now and again but she had clearly won his respect. The dollhouse was covered with the ceiling she had requested at the outset; its furnishings were elaborated and improved; a second washroom was added, and better storage facilities for Miss Fellowes' belongings.

Hoskins told her that an apartment of her own could be made available on the company grounds, so she could get away from having to be on duty twenty-four hours a day. But she refused. "I want to stay close to Timmie while he's sleeping," she explained. "He wakes up crying almost every night. He seems to have very vivid dreams— terrifying ones, I'd guess. I can comfort him. I don't think anyone else would be able to."

Miss Fellowes did leave the premises occasionally, more because she felt that she should than because she wanted to. She would go into town to carry out little chores—making a bank deposit, perhaps some shopping for clothing or toys for Timmie, even seeing a movie once. But she was uneasy about Timmie all the time, eager to get back. Timmie was all that mattered to her. She had never really noticed, in the years when she had worked at the hospital, how totally her life was centered around her work, how sparse were her connections to the world outside. Now that she actually lived at the place where she worked, it was exceedingly clear. She desired little contact with the outside, not even to see her few friends, most of them nurses like herself. It was sufficient to speak with them by telephone; she felt little impulse to visit them.

It was on one of these forays into the city that Miss Fellowes began to realize just how thoroughly accustomed to Timmie she had become. One day she found herself staring at an ordinary boy in the street and finding something bulgy and unattractive about his high domed forehead and jutting chin, his flat brows, his insignificant little nub of a nose. She had to shake herself to break the spell.

Just as she had come to accept Timmie as he was, and no longer saw anything especially strange or unusual about him, Timmie, too, seemed to be settling fairly quickly into his new life. He was becoming less timid with strangers; his dreams appeared not to be as harrowing as they had been; he was as comfortable with Miss Fellowes now as though she were his actual mother. He dressed and undressed himself, now, climbing in and out of the overalls that he usually wore with distinct signs of pleasure in the accomplishment. He had learned to drink from a glass and to use—however clumsily—a plastic fork to convey his food to his mouth.

He even seemed to be trying to learn how to speak English.

Miss Fellowes had not managed to get anywhere in decoding Timmie's own language of clicks and growls. Though Hoskins had indeed recorded everything, and she had listened over and over to the playbacks of Timmie's statements, there didn't seem to be any intelligible verbal pattern behind them. They were just clicks, just growls. He made certain sounds when he was hungry, certain sounds when he was tired, certain sounds when he was frightened. But, as Hoskins had pointed out long ago, even cats and dogs made recognizable sorts of sounds in response to particular situations, but no one had ever identified specific "words" in any cat or dog "language."

Perhaps she was just failing to hear the linguistic patterns. Perhaps they all were. She still was sure that there was a language there—one so remote in its structure from modern tongues that no one alive today could begin to comprehend how it was organized. But in darker moments Miss Fellowes feared that Timmie simply wasn't going to turn out to be capable of learning true language at all—either because Neanderthals were too far back along the evolutionary path to have the intellectual capacity for speech, or else because, having passed his formative years among people who spoke only the simplest, most primitive of languages, it was too late now for Timmie to master anything more complex.

She did some research on the subject of feral children—children who had spent prolonged periods living wild, virtually animal lives, on their own in primitive regions—and discovered that even after these children had been found and brought back into civilization, they usually never did develop the knack of uttering more than a few crude grunts. It appeared that even where the physiological and intellectual capability for speech existed, the right learning stimuli needed to be provided in the early years of life, or else the child would never learn how to speak.

Miss Fellowes desperately wanted Timmie to prove her—and Dr. McIntyre—wrong about that, so that no one could doubt that he was human. And what trait was there that more clearly distinguished human beings from beasts than that of being able to speak?

"Milk," she said, pointing. "A glass of milk."

Timmie made what she took to be the hunger-clicks.

"Yes. Hungry. Do you want some milk?"

No response.

She tried a different tack.

"Timmie—you. You—Timmie." Pointing.

He stared at her finger but said nothing.

"Walk."

"Eat."

"Laugh."

"Me—Miss Fellowes. You—Timmie."

Nothing each time.

Hopeless, Miss Fellowes thought bitterly. Hopeless, hopeless, hopeless!

"Talk?"

"Drink?"

"Eat?"

"Laugh?"

"Eat," Timmie said suddenly.

She was so astounded that she nearly dropped the plate of food she had just prepared for him.

"Say that again!"

"Eat."

The same sound. Not really clear. More like "Eeeh." She hadn't been able to detect the final consonant either time. But it was the *right* sound for the context.

She held the plate toward him, too high for him to be able to reach it.

"Eeeh!" he said again, more insistently.

"Eat?" she asked. "You want to eat?"

"*Eeeeh!*" Real impatience now.

"Here," Miss Fellowes said. "Eat, yes, Timmie. Eat! Eat your food!"

"Eeeh," he said in satisfaction, and seized his fork and fell to vigorously.

"Was it good?" she asked him afterward. "Did you like your lunch?"

But that was expecting too much of him. Even so, she wasn't going to give up now. Where there was one word there might be others. *Had* to be others.

She pointed to him. "Timmie."

"Mmm-mmm," he said.

Was that his way of saying "Timmie"?

"Does Timmie want to eat some more? Eat?"

She pointed to him, then to her mouth, and made eating motions. He looked at her and said nothing. Well, why should he? He wasn't hungry any longer.

But he knew that he was Timmie. Didn't he?

"Timmie," she said again, and pointed to him.

"Mmm-mmm," he said, and tapped his chest.

There could be no mistake about that. A stunning surge of —was it pride? Joy? Astonishment?—ran through her. All three. Miss Fellowes thought for a moment that she was going to burst into tears.

Then she ran for the intercom. "Dr. Hoskins! Will you come in here, please? And you'd better send for Dr. McIntyre, too!"

## [31]

"It's Bruce Mannheim again, Dr. Hoskins."

Hoskins stared at the telephone in his hand as though it had turned into a serpent. This was the third call from Mannheim in less than two weeks. But he tried to sound jovial.

"Yes, Mr. Mannheim! Good to hear from you!"

"I just wanted to let you know that I've discussed the results of my very amiable conversation with you last week with my board of advisers."

"Yes?" Hoskins said, not so jovially. He hadn't found the last conversation quite as amiable as Mannheim apparently had. He had found it prying and intrusive and generally outrageous.

"I told them that you had answered my preliminary queries very satisfactorily."

"I'm glad to hear that."

"And the general feeling around here is that we don't intend to take action at this time concerning the Neanderthal boy, but that we'll need to monitor the situation closely while we complete our studies of the entire question. I'll be calling you next week with a further list of points that need to be satisfied. I thought you'd like to know that."

"Ah—yes," Hoskins said. "Thank you very much for telling me, Mr. Mannheim."

He closed his eyes and forced himself to breathe slowly in and out. *Thank you very much, Mr. Mannheim. How kind of you to allow us to continue our work for the time being. While you complete your studies of the entire question, that is. Thank you. Very much. Very, very, very, much.*

[32]

The day Timmie spoke his first words of English was a wondrous one for Miss Fellowes. But other days followed soon afterward that were much less wondrous.

The problem was that Timmie wasn't just a little boy who happened to have been placed in her care. He was an extraordinary scientific specimen, and scientists from all over the world were jostling with one another for the privilege of studying him. Dr. Jacobs and Dr. McIntyre had been only the tip of the wave, the first indications of the deluge to follow.

Jacobs and McIntyre were still very much in evidence, of course. They had been lucky enough to have first shot at Timmie, and they still had the inside track with him because of their priority status. But they were aware that they could not have a monopoly on him. A horde of anthropologists, physiologists, cultural historians, and specialists of a dozen other sorts was at the door, knocking to get in. And each one had his own agenda for the little Neanderthal boy.

The fact that Timmie could speak English now made them all the more eager. Some of them acted as if they could simply sit down with the boy and start asking him questions about life in the Paleolithic Era as he remembered it:

"What species of animals did your tribe hunt?"

"What were your people's religious beliefs like?"

"Did you migrate with the seasons?"

"Was there warfare between tribes?"

"What about warfare between your subspecies and the other one?"

He was the only possible source. Their minds bubbled with queries that Timmie alone could answer. Tell us, tell us, tell us, tell us! We want to know all that there is to know about your people's—

kinship structures—

totemic animals—

linguistic groups—

astronomical concepts—

technological skills—

But of course no one got to ask Timmie any of these fascinating and important questions, because Timmie's command of English, though it was growing stronger day by day, was still confined at the moment to phrases like "Timmie eat now" and "Man go away now."

Besides which, Miss Fellowes was the only one who could understand Timmie's words with any degree of reliability. To the others, even those who saw the boy virtually every day, his thick, strangled attempts at pronunciation were only barely recognizable as carrying meaning. Evidently the original speculations about Neanderthal linguistic ability were correct, at least in part: though the Neanderthals obviously did have the intellectual capacity for speech, and the anatomical ability to produce intelligible words, their tongues and larynxes were apparently unable to create sounds with the degree of articulation required by modern-day languages. At least, Timmie couldn't manage it. Even Miss Fellowes had to strain much of the time to figure out what he was trying to say.

It was a frustrating business for everyone—for Timmie, for Miss Fellowes, and especially for the scientists who were so anxious to question the boy. And it reinforced the poignancy of Timmie's isolation. Even now that he was beginning to learn how to communicate with his captors—and that's what we are, Miss Fellowes found herself thinking again and again, his *captors*—it was a terrible struggle for him to get even the simplest of concepts across to the one person who could at least partially understand him.

How lonely he must be! she thought.

And how baffled and frightened by all the hubbub that went on constantly around him!

She did her best to protect him. She could not and would not allow herself to accept the fact that what she was engaged in was simply a scientific experiment. It certainly was that; but there was a small unhappy child at the center of it; and she would not let him be treated *only* as an experimental subject.

The physiologists put him on special diets. She purchased toys for him. They plagued her with requests for blood samples, X-ray pictures, even clippings of Timmie's hair. She taught him songs and nursery rhymes. They put Timmie through exhaustive and exhausting tests of his coordination and reflexes, his visual acuity, his hearing, his intuitive intelligence. Miss Fellowes comforted him afterward, holding him and stroking him until he was calm again.

They demanded more and more of his time.

She insisted on strict limits to the daily inquisitions. Most of the time her wishes prevailed, though not always. The visiting scientists undoubtedly thought she was an ogre, an impediment to knowledge, a stubborn and irrational woman. Miss Fellowes didn't care. Let them think whatever they wanted; it was Timmie's interests that concerned her, not theirs.

The closest thing to an ally she had was Hoskins. He came to visit the dollhouse virtually every day. It was obvious to Miss Fellowes that Hoskins welcomed any chance to escape from his increasingly difficult role as head of Stasis Technologies, Ltd., and that he took a sentimental interest in the child who had caused all this furor; but it seemed to her also that he enjoyed talking to her.

(She had learned a few things about him by this time. He had invented the method of analyzing the reflections cast by the past-penetrating mesonic beam; he had been one of the inventors of the method of establishing Stasis; his often chilly, exceedingly businesslike manner was only an effort to hide a kindly nature that was sometimes too easy for others to take advantage of; and, oh yes, he *was* married, very definitely and happily so.)

One day Hoskins walked in on her just in time to catch her in the process of erupting.

It had been a bad day, very bad. A new team of physiologists from California had showed up with a whole new series of tests they wanted to put Timmie through—right *now*—something having to do with his posture and pelvic structure. The tests involved an intricate arrangement of cold metal rods and a lot of pushing and pressing. Timmie wasn't much in the mood just then to be pushed and pressed against cold metal rods. Miss Fellowes, watching them manipulating him as though he were some sort of laboratory animal, found herself being swept by the hot urge to kill.

"Enough!" she cried, finally. "Out! Out!"

They gaped and gawped at her.

"I said, Out! Session's over! The boy is tired. You're twisting his legs and straining his back. Don't you see that he's crying? Out! *Out!*"

"But, Miss Fellowes—"

She began to gather up their instruments. They snatched them hastily from her. She pointed to the door. Muttering among themselves, they scuttled out.

She was staring after them in a blind fury, looking out the open door and wondering what kind of intolerable intrusion was next on the schedule, while Timmie stood sobbing behind her. And then she realized that Hoskins was there.

He said, "Is there a problem?"

She glowered at him. "I'll say there is!"

Turning to Timmie, she gestured and he came running to her, clinging to her, twining his legs around her. She heard the boy murmur something, very low, words she couldn't quite make out. She held him close.

Hoskins said gravely, "He doesn't seem happy."

"Would you be, in his place? They're at him every day now with their blood samples and their probings and their tests. You should have seen what they were doing to him just now—trying to find out which way his legs were fastened to his body, is what it looked like. And now his food's been changed too. The synthetic diet that Jacobs has had him on since Monday is stuff that I wouldn't feed a pig."

"Dr. Jacobs says that it'll build up his strength, that it'll make him better able to withstand—"

"Withstand *what*? Even more testing?"

"You have to bear in mind, Miss Fellowes, that the primary purpose of this experiment is to learn as much as can be learned about—"

"I *do* bear that in mind, doctor. And *you* bear in mind that what we have here isn't a hamster or a guinea pig or even a chimpanzee—but an actual human being."

"No one denies that," Hoskins said. "But—"

She cut him off yet again. "But you're all ignoring the fact that that's what he is: a human being, a human *child*. I suppose you see him as nothing more than some kind of little ape wearing overalls, and you think that you can—"

"We do *not* see him as—"

"You do! You do! Dr. Hoskins, I insist. You told me it was Timmie's coming that put your company on the map. If you have any gratitude for that at all, you've *got* to keep them away from the poor child at least until he's old enough to understand a little more of what's being asked of him. After he's had a bad session with them, he has nightmares, he can't sleep, he screams for hours sometimes. Now I warn you" (and she reached a sudden peak of fury) "I'm not letting them in here any more. Not!"

(She realized that her voice had been grow louder and louder as she spoke and now she was screaming. But she couldn't help it.)

Hoskins was looking at her in deep chagrin.

"I'm sorry," she said after a moment, in a much more temperate tone. "I didn't mean to yell that way."

"I understand that you're upset. I understand *why* you're upset."

"Thank you."

"Dr. Jacobs assures me that the boy's health is fine, that he's not in any way impaired by the program of research to which he's being—subjected."

"Then Dr. Jacobs ought to spend a night sleeping in here and he might have a different view," Miss Fellowes said. She saw a startled look come into Hoskins' eyes and her face blossomed with embarrassment at the unintended, implausible other meaning of what she had just said. —"To listen to him crying in the dark. To watch me have to go into his bedroom and hold him and sing lullabies to him. Not impaired, Dr. Hoskins? If he hasn't been impaired by all this, it's because he spent the first few years of his life under the most dreadful conditions imaginable and somehow survived them. If a child can survive an ice-age winter, he can probably survive a lot of poking and testing by a pack of people in white coats. But that doesn't mean it's good for him."

"We'll need to discuss the research schedule at the next staff meeting."

"Yes. We will. Everyone is to be reminded that Timmie has a right to humane treatment. To *human* treatment."

Hoskins smiled. She gave him an interrogative look.

He said, "I was just thinking how you've changed since the first day, when you were so angry because I had foisted a Neanderthal on you. You were ready to quit, do you remember?"

"I would never have quit," Miss Fellowes said softly.

" 'I'll stay with him—for a while,' you said. Those were your exact words. You seemed quite distraught. I had to convince you that you really would be taking care of a child and not some sort of little primate that belonged in a zoo."

Miss Fellowes lowered her eyes. She said in a low voice, "I suppose that at first glance I didn't quite understand—" and trailed off.

She glanced down at Timmie, who still clung to her. He was very much calmer now. She patted the little boy gently on his rump and sent him off toward his playroom. Hoskins looked in as Timmie opened the door, and smiled briefly at the display of toys that could be seen in there.

"Quite an array," he said.

"The poor child deserves them. They're all that he has and he earns them with what he goes through."

"Of course. Of course. We ought to get him even more. I'll send you a requisition form. Anything that you think he'd like to have—"

Miss Fellowes smiled warmly. "You do like Timmie, don't you?"

"How could I not like him? He's such a sturdy little fellow! He's so brave."

"Brave, yes."

"And so are you, Miss Fellowes."

She didn't know what to make of that. They stood facing each other in silence for a moment. Hoskins seemed to have his guard down: Miss Fellowes could see deep weariness in his eyes.

She said, with real concern, "You look worn out, Dr. Hoskins."

"Do I, Miss Fellowes?" He laughed, not very convincingly. "I'll have to practice looking more lifelike, then."

"Has some problem come up that I ought to know about?"

"Problem?" He seemed surprised. "No, no problem! Why would you think that? —I have a demanding job; that's all. Not because it's so complex, you understand. I don't mind complexity. But it's not the thing I'd be happiest doing. If I could simply get back into the laboratory end of things again—" He shook his head. "Well, that's neither here nor there. I've taken note of your complaint, Miss Fellowes. We'll see what we can do about easing up a little on Timmie's schedule of research interviews. In so far as we legitimately can, that is, considering the great importance of what we can learn from him. I'm sure you take my meaning."

"I'm sure that I do," said Miss Fellowes, in a tone of voice that was perhaps a shade too dry.

# The War Society

IT WAS DAWN, and the sky was a dead-looking gray, with a hard wind blowing from two directions at once. A little white piece of the moon was still showing, like a bone knife hanging in the sky. The men of the War Society were getting themselves ready to go down the sloping hill to the shrine of the shining rocks at the place where the three rivers met.

She Who Knows stood apart, watching them from a distance, wishing she could go down there with them.

It was always the men who got to do everything interesting, and always the same ones, the young ones full of juice. The old men like Silver Cloud and Stinking Musk Ox and Fights Like A Lion made the pronouncements and issued the orders, but it was the young ones, Tree Of Wolves and Broken Mountain and Blazing Eye and Caught Bird In Bush and three or four others, who actually *did* things. They were the ones who were truly alive, She Who Knows thought, envying them fiercely.

When there was game in the plains, they were the Hunting Society. They sharpened the tips of their spears and wrapped dark strips of wolf fur around their ankles to give them speed and ferocity, and they went out and stampeded the mammoths over cliffs, or gathered around some hapless stray rhinoceros and stabbed it until it fell, or threw the rocks-with-strings at the swift reindeer in the hope of entangling their legs and bringing them down. And afterward they carried or dragged their kill back to the camp, singing and dancing triumphantly, and everyone came out to praise them and chant their names, and they were given the first pick of the newly cooked meat: the heart and the brains and the other good parts.

And when someone had transgressed, or a chieftain had come to the end of his days and had to be sent to the next world, they became the Killing Society and donned the masks made of bearskin and brought forth the ivory club of death, and they went off with their victim out of the sight of the tribe and did what had to be done. And then solemnly returned, walking in line one by one and singing the Song of the Next World, which only the men of the Killing Society were permitted to sing.

And when there were enemies lurking nearby, it was time for the men, these very same men, to become the War Society and paint themselves with the blue stripes across their shoulders and the red stripes around their loins, and wrap the yellow lion-mantles around their shoulders. That was what they were doing now, and She Who Knows was bitterly envious. The men were standing naked in a circle, edgily joking and laughing, while the old craftsman Mammoth Rider finished mixing the pigments. War was the only occasion on which the men of the tribe ever painted their bodies; and it had been a long time now since the last such occasion, so the pigments had to be mixed fresh. That took time. But Mammoth Rider knew how to grind the rocks and how to mix the antelope fat with the powder so that it would stick to the skin. He sat crosslegged, bending over his work. And the men of the Killing Society waited for him to be done. He had brought forth the tubes of bone in which the pigments were stored and he was stirring the fat into the powder in a stone bowl. And now at last the colors were ready. Mammoth Rider handed the bowl of red color to Broken Mountain and the bowl of blue color to Young Antelope, and the other men lined up to be painted.

The laughing and joking grew even louder now. The men were frightened of what was to come: that was why they were laughing so much. The two painters used foxtail brushes to apply the color, and that in itself made them all laugh, because the brushes tickled so much. The shoulder-stripes were easy, one narrow blue one across the back, one wide one across the chest, and then a blue Goddess-dab right on the throat in the place where the hard part of the throat sticks out, and another one over the heart. It was painting the lower parts that caused all the amusement. First came a thick red stripe across the base of the belly just above the place where the man-parts are, going all the way around back and across the top of the buttocks; then a thin stripe encircling each thigh just below the man-parts; and then, what always made them laugh, the Goddess-stripe running the length of the man-organ and two more dots of red on the round parts that dangled below it. Broken Mountain put the paint down there on with a great flourish and the men made a pretense of finding it unendurably ticklish. Or perhaps they weren't pretending.

Go on, She Who Knows thought. Paint me also! I have no man-parts but you can put the red stripes around my loins and on the tips of my breasts, and it will be just as good when the time of battle comes. Because I am every bit as much of a warrior as any of you. Every bit as much.

They were almost finished now. All the men were done except the two painters themselves. Now Broken Mountain put the lower stripes on Young Antelope and Young Antelope put the upper stripes on Broken Mountain; and then they exchanged paint-bowls, and Young Antelope put the red on Broken Mountain, and Broken Mountain put the blue on Young Antelope. And they all tied their loincloths around their waists and their lion-mantles over their shoulders and picked up their spears and they were ready to make war.

Or almost ready. Goddess Woman had to say the war-words over them first, in front of the three bear-skulls. But even now She Who Knows could see the two younger Goddess Women setting out the skulls across the way, and Goddess Woman herself putting on the special robes that she had to wear when she administered the war-blessing.

She Who Knows looked down the hill, toward the shrine of shining rocks at the place where the rivers met. There was no one down there.

All this would be for nothing if the Other Ones had gone off somewhere else. Goddess Woman had reported that the footprints of the Other Ones around the shrine were fresh ones, but what did Goddess Woman know? She was no hunter. The footprints she had seen could have been three days old. The Other Ones might be far from here by now.

All that needed to be done was to go quickly down to the shrine and perform the rites that Silver Cloud seemed to think were necessary; and then the People could turn east again—getting away from this place and heading back into the flat cold empty country where the Other Ones rarely went—and go on with their lives. If there was in fact no need of sending the War Society down there first to sniff out the territory and make sure no Other Ones were skulking near the shrine, then Silver Cloud was wasting valuable time. The year was moving along. The days were shorter now. It would be snowing every day, soon. The People needed quickly to finish what they had come here to do, and find some safe place where they could settle in during the bad months that were coming.

But most likely Goddess Woman was right, and Other Ones *were* someplace nearby. And there would be war; and men would die, and perhaps not only men.

Keeps The Past, coming up behind her, said practically into her ear, "The Goddess is being very hard on us these days. We came here to worship Her; but first She takes the little boy, and then She brings us right into the midst of the Other Ones."

She Who Knows shrugged. "I see no Other Ones. We've been here two days and nobody has seen any Other Ones."

"But they're there. Waiting for us, hidden below, ready to attack. I know that."

"How do you know?"

"I dreamed it," said Keeps The Past. "They were invisible, like creatures of mist, and then they became half-solid like shadows, and then they were springing up out of the earth all around us and they began to kill us."

She Who Knows laughed harshly. "Another dark dream."

"Another?"

"The night before last, Silver Cloud dreamed that he was a boy again and he went into the sea and when he came out of it he began to grow older with every step he took, until within a few moments he was withered and crooked and feeble. A dream of death, is what that was. And now you dream Other Ones waiting for us at the shrine."

Keeps the Past nodded. "And the Goddess has taken the boy Skyfire Face without giving us any sign of Her pleasure in return. We should leave this place, I think, without staying to perform any cere-monies at that shrine down there."

"But Silver Cloud says we must."

"Silver Cloud grows timid and weak with age," said Keeps The Past.

She Who Knows turned furiously to the chronicler. "Would you like to be chieftain in his place?"

"Me?" Keeps The Past smiled. "Not I, She Who Knows. I want no part of being chieftain. If there's any woman in the world who yearns in her heart to be a chieftain, She Who Knows, I think it's you. But I have no appetite for such burdens. —Even so, I think the time may have come for Silver Cloud to put down his wand and cap and mantle."

"No."

"He's old and getting feeble. You can see the weariness in his eyes."

"He's strong and wise," said She Who Knows, without much conviction.

"You know that you are saying that which isn't true."

"Am I, Keeps The Past? Am I?"

"Go easy, woman. If you hit me, I'll have you thrown down the hill."

"You called me a liar."

"I told you that you said that which isn't true."

"It's the same thing."

"A liar who lies even to herself is no true liar, but a fool. You know and I know and Goddess Woman knows that Silver Cloud is no longer fit to be chieftain. Each of us has thought it and said it in her own way. —And when the men begin to realize that too, the Killing Society will have to do its work."

"Perhaps so," said She Who Knows uneasily.

"Then why do you defend him?"

"I feel sorry for him. I don't want him to have to die."

"How tender of you. But the chieftain knows how things are done. Do you remember the days when Black Snow was chieftain, and he fell sick with the green bile and nothing could heal him, and he stood up before us all and said his time had come? Did he hesitate even a moment? And it was the same with Tall Tree before him, Silver Cloud's father, when I was a girl. You weren't born then. Tall Tree was a great chieftain; but one day he said, I am too old, I can no longer be chieftain, and by nightfall he was dead. As must happen to Silver Cloud."

"Not yet. Not yet."

Coolly, Keeps The Past said, "Even if he leads us into disaster? Which perhaps he is doing right now. It was a mistake to come to this place: I see that now, though at first I didn't. Why are you so strong in his defense? He means nothing to you. I didn't think you even liked him."

"If Silver Cloud dies, who will be chieftain in his place, do you think?"

"Blazing Eye, I suppose."

"Exactly. Blazing Eye!" She Who Knows grinned vindictively. "I tell you, Keeps The Past, I'd rather stay with bumbling old Silver Cloud and die beneath the spears of the Other Ones than have to live another ten years with Blazing Eye as chieftain of this tribe!"

"Ah," said Keeps The Past. "Aha! Now I understand. You put your own little personal resentments ahead of common sense—even ahead of life itself, She Who Knows. How absurd you are! How foolish!"

"You're going to make me hit you, after all."

"But don't you see—"

"No," said She Who Knows. "No, I don't see at all. —But enough of this. Look, look, down there!"

While the two women had been talking, Goddess Woman had finished performing the War Society blessing and the men of the War Society, properly painted and outfitted, had descended the hill to take up positions around the shrine of the shining rocks. There they stood now in front of it, shoulder to shoulder, brandishing their spears and glaring defiantly in all directions.

And there were the Other Ones, materializing out of nowhere like the creatures of mist who had turned solid in Keeps The Past's dream.

Where had they come from? They must have been crouching in the dense bushes alongside one of the three rivers, down out of sight, perhaps hiding themselves in some magical way so that they had looked like bushes themselves until the time came for them to emerge.

There were eight or ten of them. No, more than ten. She Who Knows tried to count them, but she used up both her hands and there were still more of them to count. There might be at least another full hand of them besides. Whereas the War Society numbered only nine warriors.

It was going to be a massacre. Silver Cloud had sent all the young men of the tribe to their deaths.

"How hideous they are!" Keeps The Past whispered harshly, clutching She Who Knows' forearm so hard that her grip was painful. "Like monsters! Like nightmare things! When I saw them in my dream they were nothing as disgusting as this!"

"They look just like themselves," said She Who Knows. "That is how the Other Ones look."

"You've seen them before. I haven't. Foh, the flat faces of them! Their skinny necks. Their arms, their legs—so long. Like spider legs!"

"Like spiders, yes."

"Look. Look."

Everyone in the tribe was clustering together now at the little over-look point above the shrine of the three rivers. All eyes were on the scene below. She Who Knows heard Silver Cloud's rough, heavy breathing nearby. A child was crying. A couple of the Mothers seemed to be crying too.

A strange thing was happening down below. It was almost like a dance.

The men of the War Society were still standing shoulder-to-shoulder, in a straight line in front of the shrine. They looked uneasy, but they were holding their ground, however eager they might be inside to bolt and run.

The Other Ones had formed a line facing them, perhaps twenty paces away. They too stood shoulder to shoulder: tall strange-looking flat-faced men, holding long spears.

But there was no attack.

The two groups of warriors simply stood there, glaring at each other across the area of no-man's-land that separated them. Nobody moved. The men didn't even seem to be breathing. They were as still as rocks. Could it be that the Other Ones were just as frightened as the men of the War Society must be? They were supposed to be such ruthless killers, the Other Ones were. And they outnumbered the War Society men by at least one hand's worth. But nothing was happening. No one was willing to make a move.

It was Blazing Eye who made the first attempt to break the impasse. He stepped forward one pace. A moment later everyone in the War Society line stepped forward one pace also.

Blazing Eye shook his spear menacingly and glared across toward the Other Ones and uttered a sound, long and low, that came floating up the hill to the watchers above:

*"Hoooo."*

The Other Ones exchanged glances and frowns. They looked con-fused, uncertain, troubled.

One of their men stepped forward also; and *his* whole line followed him. He too shook his spear.

*"Hooooo."*

*"Hoooooo."*

*"Hoooooooo."*

She Who Knows and Keeps The Past looked at each other in won-der. All they were doing on both sides was making foolish noises at each other down there! Was this how a battle was supposed to begin? Perhaps it was: she couldn't be sure. But it was a silly way to go about things, if it was.

Maybe the men down there weren't sure of what they were supposed to do, either. These warriors, She Who Knows realized, had never fought against the Other Ones before, had never even encountered them until this moment. She was the only one of the tribe who had, that time when she had met the lone Other One by the icy pool. And that one time, so long ago, the Other One had turned and run from her.

Now these Other Ones were simply standing there looking worried, and mimicking the silly noises that the men of the War Society were making. Even though the Other Ones outnumbered the men of the Killing Society and seemed to have better weapons.

Why? Were the dreaded Other Ones a race of cowards?

"*Hooooo.*"

"*Hooooo.*"

"*Hooooo.*"

"*Hooooo.*"

"Listen to them," She Who Knows said, snickering. "Like owls, they sound."

Just then there was a little movement down below. The entire line of War Society men had turned ever so slightly, so that it was now at a little angle from the front of the shrine. And the Other Ones had turned also at the same angle, still staying in formation, continuing to face the War Society men.

There was more hooting. The lines moved a little more, without actually going anywhere. Then they moved back. Spears were raised and shaken, but were not thrown.

"They're afraid of each other!" Keeps The Past said, in astonishment.

"*Hoooo.*"

"*Hoooo.*"

"We should just charge at them," She Who Knows muttered. "They'd turn and run in a moment!"

"*Hoooo.*"

"*Hoooo.*"

"Like owls," said Keeps The Past.

It was maddening. The stalemate could go on forever. She Who Knows was unable to take it any longer. She went across to the place where Mammoth Rider was sitting, with the two bowls of warpaint on the ground in front of him, and stripped away her robe. Mammoth Rider looked up at her, puzzled.

"Give me the paint," She Who Knows said.

"But you can't—"

"I can."

She bent and quickly snatched up the bowl of blue pigment, and splattered some carelessly on each of her breasts. Then she took up the red, and drew a big triangle on her middle, across the base of her belly and up both her thighs, and one splash on the dark hair at her loins. Everyone was staring at her now. She didn't bother asking Mammoth Rider to put stripes of warpaint on her back; she doubted that he would do it, and she didn't want to waste time discussing it with him. It didn't matter. She wasn't planning to turn her back on any of the enemy down there.

Other Ones! she thought fiercely. Cowards, all of them!

Silver Cloud was coming toward her now, moving hesitantly, favoring his sore leg.

"What are you doing, She Who Knows?"

"Getting ready to fight your war for you," she said. And put her robe back on and started down the hill toward the place of the shrine of the shining rocks.

# CHAPTER SEVEN

# Resisting

## [33]

S AM AICKMAN said, "Play the bastard's call one more time, will you, Jerry?"

Hoskins slipped the transcript cube into the access slot. On the screen at the front end of the boardroom Bruce Mannheim's face appeared, reproduced just as it had been on the screen of Hoskins' own telephone at the time of the call. An insistently blinking green rosette at the lower right-hand corner of the screen signaled that the call had been recorded with the knowledge and permission of the caller.

Mannheim was a youngish, full-faced man with dense waves of thick red hair clinging close to his scalp and a ruddy, florid complexion. Though beards had been out of fashion for some years except among extremely young men and very old ones, he wore a short, neatly trimmed goatee and a bushy little mustache.

The well-known advocate for the rights of children looked very sincere, very earnest, very serious.

To Hoskins he also looked very annoying.

On-screen, Mannheim said, "The situation is, Dr. Hoskins, that our most recent discussion was not at all fruitful, and I simply can't take your word any longer that the boy is being held under acceptable conditions."

"Why?" the Hoskins on the screen replied. "Has my word suddenly become untrustworthy?"

"That's not the point, doctor. We have no reason to doubt your word. But we have no reason to take it at face value, either, and some members of my advisory board have begun to feel that I've been too willing up to now to accept your own evaluations of the boy's status. The point is that there's been no on-site inspection."

"You speak of the child as though he's some kind of hidden weapon, Mr. Mannheim."

Mannheim smiled, but there wasn't much amusement visible in his pale gray eyes. "Please understand my position. I'm under considerable pressure from the sector of public opinion that I represent, Dr. Hoskins. Despite all your publicity releases, many people continue to feel that a child who was brought here as this one was and who is kept in what amounts to solitary confinement for an indefinite period is a child who is being subjected to cruel and inhuman punishment."

"You and I have been through all this more than once," said Hoskins. "The child is receiving the best care in the world, and you know it. He has twenty-four-hour-a-day nursing attention and daily medical checkups and he's on a perfectly balanced diet that has already done wonders for his physical condition. We'd be crazy to do things any other way, and whatever else we may be, we aren't crazy."

"I grant you that you've told me all that. But you still aren't allowing any outside confirmation of the things you claim. And the letters and calls that I'm receiving daily—the outcries, the pressure from concerned individuals—"

"If you're under pressure, Mr. Mannheim," said Hoskins unceremoniously, "may I suggest that it's because you've stirred this matter up by yourself in the first place, and now your own people are turning on you a little of the heat that you singlehandedly chose to generate?"

"That's the way to talk to him, Jerry-boy!" said Charlie McDermott, the comptroller.

"Maybe a bit on the blunt side, seems to me," Ned Cassiday said. He was the head of Legal: it was his job to err on the side of prudence.

The recorded conversation was proceeding on the screen.

"—neither here nor there, Dr. Hoskins. We have to keep returning to one basic point here, which is that a child has been ripped away from his parents and his home—"

"A *Neanderthal* child, Mr. Mannheim. Neanderthal Man was a primitive, savage, nomadic form of humanity. It's anybody's guess whether or not Neanderthals had homes of any real sort, or even that they understood the concept of the parent-child relationship as we know it. For all we know we may have pulled this child out of an absolutely brutish, hostile, miserable existence—much more likely, I'd say, than the picture you offer of our callously yanking him out of his idyllic little Christmas-card family life back there in the Pleistocene."

"Are you telling me that Neanderthals are no more than animals?" Mannheim asked. "That the child you've brought back from the Pleistocene is actually just some kind of ape that walks on his hind legs?"

"Certainly not. We aren't trying to pretend anything of the sort. Neanderthals were primitive but they were unquestionably human."

"—Because if you're going to try to claim that your captive has no human rights because he isn't human, Dr. Hoskins, then I must point out that scientists are completely unanimous in their belief that *Homo neanderthalensis* is in fact simply a subspecies of our own race, *Homo sapiens,* and therefore—"

"Jesus Suffering Christ," Hoskins exploded, "aren't you listening to me at all? I just got through saying that we concede the point that Timmie is human."

"Timmie?" Mannheim said.

"The child has been nicknamed Timmie around here, yes. It's been in all the news reports."

From the sidelines Ned Cassiday murmured, "Which was probably a mistake. Creates too much identification with the child as child per se. You give them names, you start making them seem too real in the eyes of the public, and then if there happens to be any sort of trouble—"

"The child *is* real, Ned," Hoskins said. "And there's not going to be any trouble."

On screen Mannheim was saying, "Very well, doctor. We both agree that we're talking about a human child. And we have no real disagreement on another basic point, which as I said a few moments back is that you've taken custody of this child by your own decision and you have no legal claim to him. You've essentially *kidnapped* this child, I could quite accurately say."

"Legal claim? What legality? Where? Tell me what laws I've broken. Show me the Pleistocene court where I can be brought to justice!"

"The fact that Pleistocene people have no courts doesn't mean that they have no rights," said Mannheim smoothly. "You'll notice that I use the present tense to refer to these extinct people. Now that time travel has become a working reality, *everything* is present tense. If we are capable of intruding on the lives of people who lived 40,000 years ago, then we must of necessity extend to those people the same human rights and courtesies that we regard as inalienable in our own society. You certainly wouldn't try to tell me that Stasis Technologies, Ltd. would have the right to reach into some village in contemporary Brazil or Zaire or Indonesia and simply seize any child it felt like seizing, purely for the sake of—"

"This is a unique experiment of immense scientific importance, Mr. Mannheim!" Hoskins sputtered.

"Now I think you're failing to listen to me, Dr. Hoskins. I'm not discussing motive; I'm discussing simple legalities. Even for the sake of scientific research, would you feel justified in swooping down on some child in his native village in some present-day tribal culture and bringing him here so that anthropologists could study him, regardless of the feelings of the child's parents or other guardians?"

"Of course not."

"But tribal cultures of the past are fair game?"

Hoskins said, "There's no analogy. The past is a closed book. The child now in our custody *has been dead*, Mr. Mannheim, for 40,000 years."

Ned Cassiday let out a gasp and began to shake his head violently. It struck Hoskins that Cassiday must see novel and disturbing legal ramifications here that probably should never have been allowed into the discussion.

Mannheim said, "I see. The child is dead, but he receives round-the-clock nursing care? Come off it, Dr. Hoskins. Your reasoning's absurd. In the era of time travel the old distinctions between 'dead' and 'alive' no longer have the same validity. You've opened the closed book that you just spoke of, and you can't just close it again by your own say-so. Like it or not, we live in an age of paradox now. The child's as alive as you and I, now that you've moved him from his proper era to our own, and we both agree that he's human and deserving of the sort of treatment that any child is entitled to. And that brings us right back to the question of the care he's receiving while he's here among us. Call him a kidnap victim, call him the subject of a unique scientific experiment, call him an involuntary guest in our era, whatever semantic spin you want to put on things—all that really matters is that you've arbitrarily removed a child from his native environment without the consent of anybody concerned and you're keeping him locked up in some kind of containment unit. Must we continue to go around in circles? There's only one issue here. You know what it is. I represent a large body of concerned opinion and I've been asked to ascertain that the human rights of this unfortunate child are being properly respected."

"I object to your use of the word 'unfortunate.' I've made it clear again and again that the child is—"

"All right. I retract the word if it bothers you so much. The rest of my statement stands as is."

Hoskins said, making no attempt to conceal his thinning patience, "What is it specifically that you want from us, Mr. Mannheim?"

"I've told you. On-site inspection, so that we can see the child's condition and attitude for ourselves."

The on-screen Hoskins closed his eyes a moment. "You're very persistent, aren't you? Nothing will please you short of coming in here and checking things out in person?"

"You know the answer to that."

"Well, I'll have to get back to you, Mr. Mannheim. We've been allowing only qualified scientific investigators to see Timmie up till this point, and I'm not sure you fit that category. I'll need to convene a meeting of *my* advisory board to discuss all this. Thank you very much for calling, Mr. Mannheim. It's been a pleasure speaking with you."

The screen went dark.

Hoskins looked around the room.

"Well? There it is. You see the problem. He's like a bulldog who's got his teeth in the cuff of my pants. He won't let go no matter how I try to shake him off."

Ned Cassiday said, "And if you do manage somehow to shake the bulldog off, he'll come right at you again, and this time the teeth very likely will clamp onto your leg, Jerry, not just your pants cuff."

"What are you telling me, Ned?"

"That we ought to let him have his on-site inspection. As a gesture of good will."

"That's your considered legal opinion?"

Cassiday nodded. "You've been stonewalling this guy for weeks now, right? He calls, you give him a runaround, he calls again, you find some new way of deflecting his arguments, and so on and so on and so on. But you can't keep it up forever. He's just as stubborn as you are, and the difference is that in his case stubbornness looks like dedication to a worthy cause, and in your case it looks like willful obstructionism. —This is the first time he's actually asked to set foot on the premises, isn't it?"

"Right," Hoskins said.

"You see? He can always keep coming up with new maneuvers. And you can't counter this one with more press releases, or another interview with Candide Deveney on the sub-etheric. Mannheim'll go public right away with claims that there's a cover-up going on here, that we have something terrible to hide. —Let him come and see the little boy. It might just shut him up long enough for us to get our work on this project finished."

Sam Aickman shook his head. "I don't think there's a reason in the world why we need to cave in to that colossal pain in the neck, Ned. If we were keeping the kid chained up in a closet, maybe—if he was just a miserable sickly bag of bones with pimples and scurvy, who cries bloody murder all day and all night—but the kid is flourishing, according to Jerry. He's putting on a little weight, I hear that he's even learning to speak some English—he's never had it so good and that ought to be obvious, even to Bruce Mannheim."

"Exactly," Cassiday said. "We *don't* have anything to hide. So why should we give Mannheim the chance to make it seem as though we do?"

"Good point," said Hoskins. He glanced around the room. "I'd like a show of opinion on this. Do we invite Mannheim here to see Timmie or don't we?"

"I say to hell with him," Sam Aickman said. "He's nothing more than a pest. No reason in the world why we should cave in to him."

"I'm with Ned Cassiday," said Frank Bruton. "Let him come in so we can get this over with."

"It's risky," said Charlie McDermott. "Once he's in the door, there's no telling what further issues he'll raise. As Ned says, there's always some new maneuver. Allowing him to visit the boy won't get him off our backs and might just make the situation worse for us. I say no."

"What about you, Elena?" Hoskins said, turning toward Elena Saddler, who ran materiels procurement.

"I vote for letting him come. As Ned says, we've got nothing to hide. We can't let this man go on smearing us the way he's done. Once he's been here, it's simply his word against ours, and we've got our televised glimpses of Timmie to show the world that we're right and he's wrong."

Hoskins nodded glumly. "Two for it, two against. So I get to cast the deciding vote. —Okay. So be it. I'll tell Mannheim he can come."

Aickman said, "Jerry, are you sure you want to—"

"Yes," said Hoskins. "I don't like him any more than you do, Sam. Or want him sniffing around this place for so much as two minutes. He's a pest, just as you say. And it's precisely because he *is* such a pest that I've come around to thinking we'd better give him his way. Let him see Timmie, thriving and flourishing. Let him meet Miss Fellowes and find out for himself whether there's any sort of child abuse going on around here. I agree with Ned that the visit might just shut him up. If it doesn't, well, we're no worse off than we are now: he'll continue to agitate and howl, and we'll continue to deny all his accusations. But if we simply refuse his request to visit, he'll wrap all sorts of bizarre new charges around our necks, and God only knows what we'll have to do to counter them. So my vote is for tossing the bulldog a bone. That way we stand a chance against him; the other way, we're sunk. Mannheim gets an invitation to come here, and so be it. —Meeting adjourned."

## [34]

Miss Fellowes was giving Timmie his bath when the intercom sounded in the next room. The interruption drew a scowl from her. She looked at the boy in the tub. Bath-time was no longer an ordeal for him. It was more like sport: he looked forward to it every day. The sensation of lying half submerged in warm water no longer was threatening to him. Plainly it was a wondrous luxurious treat for him, not only the feel of the warm water itself, but the delight of coming forth pink, clean, sweet-smelling. And of course there was the fun of doing a little splashing around. The longer he lived here, the more like an ordinary little boy Timmie was coming to seem, Miss Fellowes thought.

But she didn't like the idea of leaving him in the tub for long, unattended. Not that she worried much about his drowning. Little boys his age didn't generally drown in their tubs, and this one seemed to have a healthy enough sense of self-preservation. But if he decided to get out on his own, and somehow slipped and fell—

She said, "I'll be right back, Timmie. You stay in the tub by yourself, all right?"

He nodded.

"Stay *in* the tub. In the tub. You understand?"

"Yes, Miss Fellowes."

Nobody in the world would have recognized the sounds Timmie had uttered as being *Yes, Miss Fellowes*. Nobody but Miss Fellowes.

Still a little uneasy, she hurried into the other room and said to the intercom vent, "Who's calling?"

"It's Dr. Hoskins, Miss Fellowes. I'd like to know if Timmie can stand another visitor this afternoon."

"He's supposed to have free time this afternoon. I'm already giving him his bath. He never has visitors after he's had his bath."

"Yes, I know. This is a special case."

Miss Fellowes listened for sounds from the bathroom. Timmie was splashing around vociferously, and obviously having a wonderful time. She heard the boy's pealing laughter.

She said reproachfully, "They're *all* special cases, aren't they, Dr. Hoskins? If I let everybody in here who was some sort of special case, the boy would be on display to special cases all day and all night too."

"This one is *really* special, Miss Fellowes."

"I'd still rather not. Timmie's entitled to some time off, just like anyone else. And if you don't mind, Dr. Hoskins, I'd like to get back to his bath before—"

"This visitor is Bruce Mannheim, Miss Fellowes."

"What?"

"You're aware that Mannheim's been plaguing us with his standard sort of trumped-up charges and inflammatory nonsense practically from the moment we announced that Timmie was here, aren't you?"

"I suppose so," Miss Fellowes said. She hadn't actually been paying much attention.

"Well, he's been calling here about every third day to register this or that expression of outrage. And finally I asked him what he wants from us and he said he insists on on-site inspection. That was the term he used: 'on-site inspection.' Of Timmie. As if we had some sort of missile emplacement here. We aren't enthusiastic about it, but we had a board meeting and decided finally that it would do more harm than good to refuse. I'm afraid there's no choice, Miss Fellowes. We have to let him come in."

"Today?"

"About two hours from now. He's a *very* insistent man."

"You could have given me a little more notice."

"I would have if I could, Miss Fellowes. But Mannheim caught me

by surprise when I called him to say we'd let him in. He told me he'd
be right over; and when I said I wasn't sure that was workable, he
started in again on all his suspicions and accusations. I think he was
implying that we were playing for time so we'd be able to cover up all
of the bruises Timmie has from the whippings we give him, or some
such crazy thing. In any case, he also said that he'd be going before
the monthly meeting of his board of directors tomorrow, and that this
would be a fine chance for him to report to them on Timmie's condition, and therefore—" Hoskins let his voice trail off. "I know it's
short notice, Miss Fellowes. *Please* don't put up a fuss, all right?
*Please.*"

She felt a burst of pity for him. Caught between the tireless political
agitator on the one hand and the ill-tempered gorgon of a nurse on
the other—the poor weary man.

"All right, Dr. Hoskins," she said. "Just this once. —I'll see what I
can do about having all the bruises covered over with makeup before
he gets here."

She went back to the bathroom while Hoskins' gratitude was still
coming out of the intercom. Timmie was busy conducting a naval
battle between a green plastic duck and a purple plastic sea monster.
The duck seemed to be winning.

"You're going to have company this afternoon," Miss Fellowes told
the boy. She was bubbling over with fury. "A man's coming here to
check up on us. To see whether we've been mistreating you, if you can
believe that. Mistreating!"

Timmie gave her a blank look. His fledgling vocabulary didn't
stretch anywhere nearly that far. Miss Fellowes hadn't really expected
it to.

"Who coming?" he asked.

"A man," she said. "A visitor."

Timmie nodded. "Nice visitor?"

"Let's hope so. —Come on, now, it's time to get you out of the
tub and dry you off."

"More bath! More bath!"

"More bath tomorrow. Come on, now, Timmie!"

Reluctantly he clambered out of the tub. Miss Fellowes toweled
him off and gave him a quick inspection. No, no whip marks showing.
No sign of damage at all. The boy was in fine shape. Especially when
she compared him with the filthy, scruffy, bruised and scratched child
who had tumbled out of the Stasis scoop amidst a mass of dirt and

pebbles and ants and chunks of grass on that first strange, frightening night. Timmie was glowing with good health. He had gained several pounds since then; his scratches had healed and his assortment of bruises had vanished long ago. His hair was neatly cut; his fingernails were trimmed. Let Bruce Mannheim try to find something to complain about. Let him try!

Ordinarily she would have put Timmie into his pajamas after the bath; but everything was changed now, because of the visitor who was coming, the very special visitor. That called for formal dress: the purple overalls with the red buttons, Miss Fellowes thought.

Timmie grinned when he saw them. They were his favorite overalls, too.

"And now, I think, a nice little snack, before the company gets here. What do you say to that, Timmie?"

She was still shaking with anger.

*Bruce Mannheim,* she thought icily. That busybody. That troublemaker. A children's advocate, he called himself! Who had ever asked him to advocate anything? A professional agitator; that was all he was. A public nuisance.

"Miss Fellowes?"

Hoskins' voice was coming through on the intercom again.

"What is it, doctor? Mr. Mannheim isn't due here for another half an hour, I thought."

"He's early," Hoskins said. "That's the sort of person he is, I'm afraid." There was something strangely sheepish about his voice. —"And I'm afraid that he's brought someone with him, too, without telling us he was going to."

"Two visitors is too many," Miss Fellowes said adamantly.

"I know. I know. *Please,* Miss Fellowes. I had no idea he was bringing someone else. But Mannheim's pretty insistent on having her see Timmie with him. And now that we've gone this far—the risk of offending him—you see? You see?"

So he was begging again. This Mannheim really had him terrified. Where was the strong and indomitable Dr. Gerald Hoskins she once had known?

"And who's this other person?" she asked, after a moment. "This unexpected guest?"

"An associate of his, a consultant to his organization. You may even know her. You probably do. She's an expert on troubled children, someone mixed up with all sorts of governmental commissions and

institutions, a very high-profile individual. She was even under consideration for a while, I should tell you, for the very job you have today,
although we felt—*I* felt—that she didn't quite have the kind of
warmth and sympathy we were looking for. Her name's Marianne
Levien. I think she might be a little dangerous. The last thing we can
risk is to turn her away at the entrance, now that she's here."

Miss Fellowes put her hand over her mouth in horror.

Marianne Levien! she thought, aghast. God preserve me. God preserve us all!

### [35]

The oval door to the dollhouse opened and Hoskins came in, with
two figures close behind him. Hoskins looked dreadful. His fleshy face
seemed to be sagging, so that he appeared to have aged ten years in a
day. His skin was leaden. His eyes had an oddly defeated, almost
*cowed* expression that Miss Fellowes found strange and frightening.

She scarcely recognized him. What was going on?

He said, in a low, uneasy tone, "This is Edith Fellowes, Timmie's
nurse. —Bruce Mannheim, Miss Fellowes. Marianne Levien."

"And this is Timmie?" Mannheim asked.

"Yes," Miss Fellowes said, booming the word out to make up for
Hoskins' sudden diffidence. "This is Timmie!"

The boy had been in the back room, his bedroom and playroom,
but he had tentatively poked forward when he had heard the visitors
entering. Now he came toward them in a steady, bouncy, outgoing
stride that drew a silent cheer from Miss Fellowes.

*You show them, Timmie! Are we mistreating you? Are you hiding
under your bed, quivering with fear and misery?*

Resplendent in his finest overalls, the boy marched up to the newcomers and stared up at them in frank curiosity.

*Good for you,* Miss Fellowes thought. *And good for all of us!*

"Well," Mannheim said. "So you're Timmie."

"Timmie," said Timmie, though Miss Fellowes was the only one in
the room who realized that that was what he was saying.

The boy reached upward toward Mannheim. Mannheim evidently
thought he wanted to shake hands, and offered his own. But Timmie
didn't know anything about handshakes. He avoided Mannheim's
outstretched hand and waggled his own in an impatient little side-to-

side gesture, while continuing to strain upward as far as he could. Mannheim seemed puzzled.

"Your hair," Miss Fellowes said. "I suspect he's never seen anyone with red hair before. They must not have had it in Neanderthal times and no redheads have visited him here. Fair hair of any sort appears to fascinate him tremendously."

"Ah," Mannheim said. "So that's it."

He grinned and knelt and Timmie immediately dug his fingers into Mannheim's thick, springy crop of hair. Not only the color but also the coiling texture of it must have been new to him, and he explored it thoughtfully.

Mannheim tolerated it with great good humor. He was, Miss Fellowes found herself conceding, not at all what she had imagined. She had expected him to be some sort of wild-eyed fire-breathing radical who would immediately begin issuing denunciations, manifestos, and uncompromising demands for reform. But he was turning out in fact to be rather pleasant and gentle, a thoughtful and serious-looking man, younger than she had expected, who seemed to be losing no time making friends with Timmie.

Marianne Levien, though, was a very different sort of item. Even Timmie, when he had grown tired of examining Bruce Mannheim's hair and had turned to get a look at the other visitor, seemed hard-pressed to know what to make of her.

Miss Fellowes had already formed her opinion: she disliked Levien on sight. And she suspected that it was Levien's unexpected arrival, rather than the presence of Bruce Mannheim, that was causing Dr. Hoskins such obvious distress.

What is she doing here? Miss Fellowes wondered. What kind of trouble is she planning to make for us?

Levien was known far and wide through the child-care profession as an ambitious, aggressive, controversial woman, highly skilled at self-promotion and the steady advancement of her career. Miss Fellowes had never actually come face to face with her before; but, as the nurse looked at her now, Levien appeared every bit as formidable and disagreeable as her reputation suggested.

She seemed more like an actress—or a businesswoman—or like an actress playing the role of a businesswoman—than any sort of child-care specialist. She was wearing some slinky shimmering dress made from close-woven strands of metallic fabric, with a huge blazing golden pendant in the form of a sun on her breast and a band of intricately woven gold around her broad forehead. Her hair was dark and shining, pulled back tight to make her look all the more dramatic. Her lips were bright red, her eyes were flamboyantly encircled with makeup. An invisible cloud of perfume surrounded her.

Miss Fellowes stared at her in distaste. It was hard to imagine how Dr. Hoskins could have considered this woman even for a fraction of a second as a potential nurse for Timmie. She was Miss Fellowes' antithesis in every respect. And why, Miss Fellowes wondered, had Marianne Levien been interested in the job in the first place? It required seclusion and total dedication. Whereas Levien, Miss Fellowes knew, was forever on the go, constantly buzzing all around the world to scientific meetings, standing up and offering firmly held opinions that other people of greater experience tended to find controversial and troublesome. She was full of startling ideas about how to use advanced technology to rehabilitate difficult children—substituting wondrous glittering futuristic machinery for the down-to-earth love and devotion that had usually managed to do the job throughout most of humanity's existence.

And she was an adept politician, too—always turning up on this committee or that, consultant to one or another influential task force, popping up everywhere in all manner of significant capacities. A highly visible person, rising like a rocket in her profession. If she had wanted the job here that Miss Fellowes ultimately had gained, it must only have been because she saw it, somehow, as the springboard to very much bigger things.

I must be very old fashioned, Miss Fellowes thought. All I saw was a chance to do some good for an unusual little boy who needed an unusual amount of loving care.

Timmie put his hand out toward Marianne Levien's shimmering metallic dress. His eyes were glowing with delight.

"Pretty," he said.

Levien stepped back quickly, out of his reach. "What did he say?"

"He admires your dress," Miss Fellowes said. "He just wants to touch it."

"I'd rather he didn't. It's easily damaged."

"You'd better watch out, then. He's very quick."

"Pretty," Timmie said again. "Want!"

"No, Timmie. No. Mustn't touch."

*"Want!"*

"I'm sorry. No. N—O."

Timmie gave her an unhappy look. But he made no second move toward Marianne Levien.

"Does he understand you?" Mannheim asked.

"Well, he isn't touching the dress, is he?" said Miss Fellowes, smiling.

"And you can understand him?"

"Some of the time. Much of the time."

"Those grunts of his," said Marianne Levien. "What do you think they could have meant?"

"He said, 'pretty.' Your dress. Then he said, 'want!' To touch, he meant."

"He was speaking English?" Mannheim asked in surprise. "I wouldn't have guessed."

"His articulation isn't good, probably for some physiological reason. But I can understand him. He's got a vocabulary of—oh, about a hundred English words, I'd say, maybe a little more. He learns a few every day. He picks them up on his own by this time. He's probably about four years old, you realize. Even though he's getting such a late start, he's got the normal linguistic ability that you'd expect in a child of his age, and he's catching up in a hurry."

"You say that a Neanderthal child has the same linguistic ability as a human child?" Marianne Levien asked.

"He *is* a human child."

"Yes. Yes, of course. But different. A separate subspecies, isn't that so? And therefore it would be reasonable to expect differences in mental aptitude that could be as considerable as the differences in physical appearance. His extremely primitive facial structure—"

Miss Fellowes said sharply, "It's not all that primitive, Ms. Levien. Go look at a chimpanzee sometime if you want to see what a truly subhuman face is like. Timmie has some unusual anatomical features, but—"

"You used the word subhuman, not me," Levien said.

"But you were thinking it."

"Miss Fellowes! Dr. Levien! Please! There's no need for such rancor!"

*Doctor* Levien? Miss Fellowes thought, with a quick glance at Hoskins. Well, yes, yes, probably so.

Mannheim said, glancing around, "These little rooms here—this is the boy's entire living environment?"

"That's correct," Miss Fellowes replied. "That's his bedroom and playroom back there. He takes his meals here, and that's his bathroom. I have my own living area over here, and these are the storage facilities."

"He never goes beyond this enclosed area?"

"No," Miss Fellowes said. "This is the Stasis bubble. He doesn't leave the bubble, not ever."

"A very confining sort of life, wouldn't you agree?"

Hoskins said quickly, too quickly, "It's an absolutely necessary confinement. There are technical reasons for it, having to do with the buildup of temporal potential involved in bringing the boy across time, that I could explain in detail if you wanted the full background. But what it comes down to is that the energy cost of allowing the boy to cross the Stasis boundary would be prohibitive."

"So to save a little money, you plan to keep him cooped up in these few small rooms indefinitely?" Levien asked.

"Not just a little money, Dr. Levien," Hoskins said, looking more harried than ever. "I said that the cost would be prohibitive. It goes even beyond cost. The available metropolitan energy supply would have to be diverted in a way that I think would cause insuperable problems for the entire utility district. There's no problem when you or I or Miss Fellowes cross the Stasis line, but for Timmie to do it would be, well, simply not possible. Simply not possible."

"If science can find a way to bring a child across forty thousand years of time," Marianne Levien said grandly, "science can find a way to make it possible for him to walk down that hallway if he wanted to."

"I wish that were true, Dr. Levien," Hoskins said.

"So the child is permanently restricted to these rooms," said Mannheim, "and if I understand you rightly, no research is currently under way to find a way around that problem?"

"That's correct. As I've tried to explain, it can't be done, not within the real-world considerations that we have to put up with. We want the boy to be comfortable, but we simply can't divert our resources into trying to solve insoluble problems. —As I told you, I can provide you later on with the full technical analysis, if you want to check it over."

Mannheim nodded. He seemed to be checking something off on some list he kept in his mind.

Levien said, "What sort of diet is the boy on?"

"Would you like to examine the pantry?" Miss Fellowes asked, in no very friendly way.

"Yes, as a matter of fact. Yes, I would."

Miss Fellowes made a sweeping gesture toward the refrigeration cabinets.

Take a good look, she thought. I think you'll be happy when you do.

Indeed Levien seemed pleased by what she found—a bunch of vials and ampoules and drip-globes and mixation pods. The entire inhuman assortment of synthetic diets, so remote from anything that Miss Fellowes thought of as wholesome food, that Dr. Jacobs and his associates had insisted Timmie had to eat against Miss Fellowes' vehement objections. Levien prowled through the racks of high-tech foodstuffs with evident approval. It was just the kind of superfuturistic stuff she'd be likely to go for, Miss Fellowes thought angrily. She probably ate nothing but synthetics herself. If she ate anything at all.

"No complaints there," Levien said after a time. "Your nutrition people seem to know what they're doing."

"The boy does appear healthy," said Mannheim. "But I'm concerned about this enforced solitude of his."

"Yes," Marianne Levien chimed in. "So am I. Very much so."

Mannheim said, "It's bad enough that he's being deprived of the supportive tribal structures into which he was born—but the fact that Timmie has to do without companionship of any sort does indeed seem extremely troublesome to me."

"Don't I count as companionship, Mr. Mannheim?" Miss Fellowes asked, with some asperity. "I'm with him virtually all the time, you know."

"I was referring to the need for someone close to his own age. A playmate. This experiment is planned to run for a considerable length of time, Dr. Hoskins, is it not?"

"There's a great deal we hope to learn from Timmie about the era from which he comes. As his command of English improves—and Miss Fellowes assures me that he's becoming quite fluent, even though it's not easy for some of us to make out exactly what he's saying—"

"In other words, you intend to keep him here for a period of some years, Dr. Hoskins?" Marianne Levien said.

"That could be, yes."

Mannheim said, "Perpetually penned up in a few small rooms? And never being exposed to contact with children of his own age? Is that any kind of life for a healthy young boy like Timmie, do you think?"

Hoskins' eyes moved quickly from one to the other. He looked outnumbered and beleaguered.

He said, "Miss Fellowes has already brought up the issue of getting a playmate for Timmie. I assure you that we've got no desire whatever to cripple the boy's emotional development or any other aspect of his existence."

Miss Fellowes glanced at him in surprise. She had brought the issue up, yes. But nothing had come of it. Since that one inconclusive conversation in the company cafeteria, Hoskins hadn't said the slightest thing to her in response to her request that Timmie be given a child to keep him company. He had brushed the idea off then as unworkable, and he had seemed so taken aback by the whole notion, in fact, that Miss Fellowes had hesitated to bring it up with him a second time. For the moment Timmie had been getting along quite satisfactorily on his own. But lately she had begun to look ahead, thinking that Timmie's adaptation to modern life was proceeding so quickly that the moment to raise the point again with Hoskins was approaching.

And now Mannheim was raising it first, for which Miss Fellowes was immensely grateful. The children's advocate was absolutely right. Timmie couldn't be kept in here all by himself like an ape in a cage. Timmie wasn't an ape. And even a gorilla or a chimpanzee wouldn't do well cut off indefinitely from the society of his peers.

Mannheim said, "Well, then, if you've already been working on getting a companion for him, I'd like to know what progress has been made along those lines."

Suddenly his tone was no longer so amiable.

Sounding flustered, Hoskins said, "So far as bringing a second Neanderthal back to the present time to put in here with Timmie goes, which was Miss Fellowes' original suggestion, I have to tell you that we simply don't intend—"

"A second Neanderthal? Oh, no, Dr. Hoskins," said Mannheim. "We wouldn't want that at all."

"It's a serious enough matter that there's one already incarcerated here," Marianne Levien said. "To capture a second one would only compound the problem."

Hoskins shot her a venomous glare. Sweat was streaming down his face.

"I *said* that we don't intend to bring a second Neanderthal here," he replied, virtually between clenched teeth. "That's never been under consideration. Never! There are a dozen different reasons why. When Miss Fellowes brought it up the first time, I told her—"

Mannheim and Levien exchanged glances. They appeared bothered by Hoskins' sudden vehemence. Even Timmie began to seem a little alarmed, and moved up close against Miss Fellowes' side as though seeking protection.

Smoothly Mannheim said, "We're all agreed, Dr. Hoskins, that a second Neanderthal would be a bad idea. That's not the point at all. What we want to know is whether it would be possible for Timmie to be given a—well, what word do I want? Not human, because Timmie *is* human. But modern. A modern playmate. A child of this era."

"A child who could visit Timmie on a regular basis," said Marianne Levien, "and provide him with the kind of developmental stimuli that would tend to further the healthy sociocultural assimilation which we all agree is necessary."

"Just a minute," Hoskins snapped. "*What* assimilation? Are you imagining a pleasant future life in some cozy little suburb for Timmie? Applying for American citizenship, joining a church, settling down and getting married? May I remind you that what we have here is a prehistoric child from an era so remote that we can't even call it barbaric—a Stone Age child, a visitor from what you yourself, Dr. Levien, once described with some accuracy as an alien society. And you think he's going to become—"

Levien cut in coolly. "Timmie's hypothetical citizenship application and church membership aren't the issue, Dr. Hoskins, or any other such reductio ad absurdum. Timmie is still a child, and it's the quality of the childhood that he experiences that Mr. Mannheim and I are primarily concerned with. The conditions under which he's being held as of now are unacceptable. They would, I'm sure, have been unacceptable in Timmie's own society, however alien from ours in some respects it must surely have been. Every human society we know, no matter how remote its paradigms and parameters may be from ours, assures its children the right to a nurturing integration into its social matrix. There's no way that we can regard Timmie's present living conditions as providing him with that sort of adequately nurturant social matrix."

Acidly Hoskins said, "Which means in words of one syllable comprehensible by a mere physicist like myself, Dr. Levien, that you think Timmie ought to have a playmate."

"Not merely 'ought to,' " Levien said. *"Must."*

"I'm afraid we're going to take the position that companionship for the child is essential," said Mannheim in a less belligerent tone than Levien's.

"Essential," Hoskins repeated bleakly.

"A minimum first step," Levien said. "This is not to say that we are prepared to regard the boy's incarceration in our era for a prolonged period as acceptable or permissible. But for the moment, at least, we think we can waive our other outstanding objections and therefore the experiment can be permitted to continue—is that not so, Mr. Mannheim?"

*"Permitted!"* Hoskins cried.

"Provided," Marianne Levien continued serenely, "that Timmie be allowed the opportunity to enjoy regular and emotionally nourishing contact with other children of his chronological peer group."

Hoskins looked toward Miss Fellowes for some sort of support under this onslaught. But she could offer him no help.

"I have to agree, Dr. Hoskins," said Miss Fellowes, feeling like a traitor. "I've felt this way all along, and it's becoming more urgent now. The boy's coming along very nicely, indeed. But the point is close at hand where continuing to live in this kind of social vacuum will be very bad for him. And since there aren't going to be any other children of Timmie's own subspecies available to him—"

Hoskins turned to her as if to say, *You're against me too?*

There was silence for a moment in the room. Timmie, who seemed increasingly disturbed by the vociferousness of the discussion, clung ever tighter to Miss Fellowes.

At length Hoskins said, "Those are your terms, Mr. Mannheim? Dr. Levien? A playmate for Timmie or you'll bring your hordes of protesters down on my head?"

Mannheim said, "No threats are being made, Dr. Hoskins. But even your own Miss Fellowes sees the need for implementing our recommendation."

"Right. And you think it'll be easy to find people who'll cheerfully let their young children come in here and play with a little Neanderthal? With all those fantastic notions circulating out there about how savage and ferocious and primitive Neanderthal Man must have been?"

"It should be no harder," Mannheim said, "than being able to bring a little Neanderthal child into the twenty-first century in the first place. A good deal easier, I'd like to think."

"I can imagine what our counsel would have to say about that. The cost of liability insurance alone—assuming we can find anyone crazy enough to allow their child inside the Stasis bubble with Timmie—"

"Timmie doesn't seem all that ferocious to me," said Mannheim. "He seems quite gentle, as a matter of fact. Wouldn't you say so, Miss Fellowes?"

"And as Miss Fellowes pointed out earlier," Marianne Levien said with icy sweetness, "we must not regard Timmie as being in any way subhuman, merely as unusual in certain physical aspects."

"So of course you'd be delighted to let your own small child come in and play with him," said Hoskins. "Except you don't happen to have any children, do you, Dr. Levien? No, of course you don't. —What about you, Mannheim? Do you have a little boy you'd like to volunteer for us?"

Mannheim looked stung. Stiffly he said, "That's neither here nor there, Dr. Hoskins. I assure you that if I had been fortunate enough to have children, I wouldn't hesitate to offer to help. —I understand your resentment at what you see as outside interference, doctor. But by transporting Timmie to our era, you've taken the law into your own hands. It's time now to consider the full implications of what you've done. You can't keep the boy in solitary confinement simply because there's a scientific experiment going on here. You can't, Dr. Hoskins."

Hoskins closed his eyes and took several deep breaths.

"All right," he said finally. "Enough of this. I concede the point. We'll get a playmate for Timmie. Somewhere. Somehow." His eyes blazed with sudden fury. "Unlike either of you, I *do* have a child. And if necessary, I'll bring *him* in to be Timmie's friend. My own son, if I have to. Is that enough of a guarantee for you? Timmie won't be left lonely and miserable any longer. All right? All right?" Hoskins glowered at them. —"Now that that's settled, do you have any further requests to make? Or can we be permitted to continue with our scientific work in peace?"

# INTERCHAPTER FIVE

# *The Other Ones*

SHE WHO KNOWS could feel the warpaint glowing like fire on her body beneath her robe as she descended the hill. If she dared, she would have gone down the hill naked, and let them all see how she was painted, both the Other Ones and the men of her own tribe. *Especially* the men of her own tribe. Let them know that a woman could wear the paint as well as a man; and that if they did not choose to strike a blow against the enemy, she was capable of doing it for them.

But of course she couldn't go down the hill that way. A woman covered her lower parts except when she was offering herself in the coupling-rites: that was the rule. If she were wearing a loincloth the way the men did, she could at least go bare-chested to the battle, as they did, and let the enemy see the paint that was on her breasts. But she had no loincloth. All she had was a robe, and that covered everything. Well, she would open it in front when she came before the Other Ones, and they would know from the color that was on her skin that they were facing a warrior, even if she was a warrior who had breasts.

She heard Silver Cloud shouting at her, far behind her on the path into the valley. She ignored him.

And now the men of the War Society could see her approaching them. They were still locked in their absurd stalemate, face-to-face with the row of the Other Ones; but they turned their heads and stared at her in amazement as they drew near.

"Go back, She Who Knows," Blazing Eye called to her. "This is no place for a woman."

"You call me a woman, Blazing Eye? Woman yourself! Women, all of you! I see no warriors here. *You* go back, if you're afraid to fight."

"What is she doing here?" Tree Of Wolves asked, speaking to the air.

"She's crazy." That was Young Antelope. "She always has been."

"Go back!" the men called. "Get away from us! This is war, She Who Knows! This is war!"

But no one was going to make her go back now. Their angry shouts were like the buzzing of harmless insects in her ears.

She Who Knows reached the bottom of the path and strode toward the shrine. The ground was spongy here, because of the three rivers. There must be water running under the earth, she thought. With every step her bare toes dug deep into the cold, moist, yielding soil.

Behind her the sun was getting higher, rising now over the crest of the hill on which the People were camped. The little white sliver of the moon that had been showing before was no longer visible. The wind was in her face, brisk and hard, like a slap. She came forward until she was close to the line of War Society men.

Nobody was moving. The Other Ones warriors were frozen like statues.

Caught Bird In Bush was standing at the end of the row nearest to her. "Give me your spear," She Who Knows said to him.

"Go away," said Caught Bird In Bush, sounding as if he was being strangled.

"I need a spear. Do you want me to face the Other Ones warriors without a spear?"

*"Go—away."*

"Look! I have the war paint on!" She opened her robe in front and let her breasts show through, boldly splattered with the blue pigment. "I'm a warrior today. A warrior needs to have a spear!"

"Make one yourself, then."

She Who Knows spat and stepped past him. "You, Young Antelope! Let me have yours. You don't have any need of it."

"You are a crazy woman."

Tree Of Wolves reached out across Young Antelope and caught She Who Knows by the elbow. "Look," he said, "you can't be here. There's going to be a war."

"A war? When? You just stand here and make stupid noises at them.

And they do the same thing. They're just as cowardly as you are. Why don't you attack?"

"You don't understand these things," said Tree Of Wolves disgustedly.

"No. No, I suppose that I don't."

But it was pointless to ask any of them for a spear. They didn't intend to let her have one; and they were all holding tight to their weapons, no doubt remembering how she once had grabbed up Blazing Eye's spear and threatened him with it. That had been a defilement. Blazing Eye had had to make a new spear afterward. Stinking Musk Ox had told him that he couldn't go into battle carrying a spear that had been handled by a woman, and he had burned the old one and carved another, cursing and muttering all the while. But what good was the new one, She Who Knows asked herself, if Blazing Eye was too timid to use it?

"Very well. I'll do without one."

She swung around and stepped forward, taking two or three steps toward the line of Other Ones, who were watching her as though she were a demon with three heads and six tusks.

"You! You Other Ones! Look here, look at me!"

They gaped at her. She opened her robe again and let them see her painted breasts.

"I'm the warrior of the Goddess," she told them. "That's what this paint means. And the Goddess orders you to leave this place. This is Her shrine. We built it for Her. You have no business being here."

They were still staring, astounded.

She Who Knows let her eyes rove up and down the line of them. They were all tall and pale, with rank black hair dangling down past their shoulders, but cut short across their foreheads, as if they deliberately wanted to expose the hideous flat high-rising domes of their skulls.

Their arms were long and narrow and so were their legs. Their mouths were small and their little noses were absurd and their chins stuck out in a repellent way. Their jaws seemed feeble and their eyes looked colorless. The sight of them stirred old memories in her, and she saw once again the thin, lanky Other One whom she had encountered beside that little rock-rimmed pool, long ago when she had been a girl. These men looked just like him. She couldn't tell one from another, or any of them from the one she had once met. For all she knew, he was here today, that one from the pool. And then she realized it was impossible, for these men all looked young, and he would have to be old by now, nearly as old as she was herself.

"How ugly you are," she told them. "What pale simpering monstrosities you are! Why are you sniffing around at a shrine of the Goddess? The Goddess never made you! You were made out of rhinoceros dung by some passing hyena!"

The Other Ones continued to look at her in a blankfaced bewildered way.

She Who Knows took another step forward. She gestured at them, making a chopping movement with her hand, as though to sweep them away from the vicinity of the shrine.

One of the Other Ones spoke.

At least she assumed that that was what he was doing. He uttered a long series of thick, furry sounds that came out of his mouth as though his tongue were attached the wrong way around. It was mere noise. None of it made the slightest sense.

"Can't you speak right?" She Who Knows asked. "It's impossible to understand a thing you're saying. Let somebody else speak, if you aren't good at it."

He spoke again, just as incomprehensibly as before.

"No," she said. "I don't know what you're trying to say."

She walked closer and swung herself about so that she was facing toward the far end of the line of Other Ones.

"You," she said to a man down there. "Can you speak any better than that one?"

She pointed at him and clapped her hands. His eyes went wide and he made a kind of dull mumbling sound.

"Use words!" She Who Knows ordered him. "Don't just make idiotic noises! —Pah! Are all of you foolish in the head?" She pointed to the man again. "Speak! With words! Didn't any of you ever learn how to speak words?"

The Other One made the same sound again.

"Stupid as well as ugly," said She Who Knows, shaking her head. "The work of hyenas, is what you are! Made out of rhinoceros dung."

The men were baffled by her. No one moved.

She walked past them, to the shrine itself. The waters of the three rivers came pouring in from all sides, splashing high. The People had built the shrine right at the meeting place of the rivers, against an outcropping of rock that rose above the water. Goddess Woman had gone crawling out amidst the icy spray to place the rocks in the proper pattern and to pile the sheets of the special shining rock between them. Approaching now, She Who Knows saw the Goddess-lines that the priestesses had scratched in the stone: five this way, three that, three the other way. But something had been done to them. Someone not of the People had drawn a circle around each group of the Goddess-lines, digging deep into the rock, and had added other figures above them, strange disagreeable-looking symbols, painted ones that curled and twisted around like something you might see in a bad dream. They had painted some animal pictures there, too: a mammoth with a big humped head, a wolf, and a creature She Who Knows could not recognize. That had to be the work of the Other Ones, She Who Knows thought. The People used paint to color themselves, when the need arose; but they never drew painted symbols on rocks. Never. And to paint pictures of animals was simply foolish. It could anger the spirits of the animals you were painting, and you would never have success at hunting such animals again.

"What have you done, you filthy beasts? This is a shrine of the Goddess that you've defiled. A shrine of the *Goddess.*" And she said again, louder, since they showed no sign of having understood: "A shrine of the Goddess."

Blank looks. Shrugs.

She Who Knows pointed to the earth, and to the sky: the universal signs of the Goddess. She touched her own breasts, her womb, her loins; she was made in the image of the Goddess, and surely they would understand the gesture. Surely.

But they just went on staring.

"You don't have any intelligence at all, do you?" she cried. "Stupid! Stupid! You're a bunch of stupid animals!"

She clambered up onto the rocks, slipping and sliding on the wet surface, nearly falling at one point into the rushing river. That would be the end of her, falling in the river; but she caught a jutting fang of the rock and steadied herself. When she came close to the shrine she reached out and tapped her finger against the painting of the mammoth.

"Wrong!" she shouted. "Evil! Sacrilege!"

She wet her finger and rubbed it against the painted image. It smeared and became blurry.

The Other Ones looked perturbed, now. They were turning to each other, muttering, shuffling their feet back and forth in place where they stood.

"Your paintings don't belong here!" She Who Knows cried. "This is our shrine! We built it for Her! And we came here to worship Her and ask Her guidance." Diligently she scrubbed at the painted image until it was a messy ruin. She reached for the others then, but she wasn't able to reach them: her arms were too short. Only the spider-like arms of Other Ones could reach that far up the rock.

But she was satisfied that she had made her point. She scrambled down from the rocks and walked back to the place where the two groups of warriors still faced each other.

"You understand?" she asked the Other Ones. "This is our shrine! Ours!" She went toward them, right up to them, fearlessly. They stirred uneasily, but none lifted his spear. They were afraid of her, she knew. A holy woman, a woman with the Goddess within her: they didn't dare offer any resistance.

She glared up into their faces. They towered above her, tall as trees, tall as mountains. She pointed toward the west.

"Go back there, to your own country," she said. "Leave us alone. Let us make our offering in peace, you ugly bad-smelling animals! You blockheads! You stupid beasts!"

She caught hold of the Other One closest to her and pushed him in the direction she had been pointing. He drew back from her touch, taking a few steps away. She made a shooing gesture at him.

"Keep going! All of you, get moving!"

She Who Knows moved among them like a whirlwind, shouting, pushing. They edged nervously away from her as though she were carrying a plague. She followed after, waving her arms, yelling at them, single-handedly driving them out of the immediate vicinity of the shrine.

Then she halted and watched them go. They drew off perhaps a hundred and fifty paces, to a place where one of the two smaller rivers emerged around a bend and shot forth between a double wall of rocks. There they halted; and now, for the first time, She Who Knows saw that there was an encampment of Other Ones back there, a cluster of women and children and old people, hidden away in a bushy gully.

All right, She Who Knows thought. They have been driven away from the shrine; that was as much as she could hope to accomplish. But it was no small thing, and she had done it all by herself—though the fire of the Goddess had been burning within her all the while, or she never would have succeeded.

She went back to the men of the War Society.

"Without even a spear," she said to them triumphantly.

Young Antelope shook his head. "What a crazy woman you are!" But his eyes were shining with admiration.

# CHAPTER EIGHT

# Dreaming

## [36]

LATE IN THE AFTERNOON, long after Bruce Mannheim and Marianne Levien had left, Hoskins returned to the dollhouse. He looked haggard and grim.

"Is Timmie sleeping?" he asked.

Miss Fellowes nodded. "Finally. He needed plenty of calming down." She put down the book she had been reading and regarded Hoskins without warmth. It had been a tense, disturbing afternoon, and she would just as soon have been left alone now.

Hoskins said, "I'm sorry things got so testy."

"There was a lot of shouting, yes. More than the boy really needed. Don't you think that discussion could have taken place someplace else?"

"I'm sorry," Hoskins said again. "I flew off the handle, I guess. —That man is going to drive me crazy."

"Actually, he didn't seem as awful as I had expected. I think he's genuinely got Timmie's welfare at heart."

"No doubt he does. But to come butting in here uninvited, telling us what to do—"

"The boy does need a playmate."

Hoskins gave her a despondent look, as though he thought the debate was going to get started all over again. But he managed to master himself in time.

"Yes," he said quietly. "So he does. I won't argue with you about that. But where are we going to get one? The problems are enormous."

"You weren't serious about bringing your own son in here if all else failed, then?"

Hoskins seemed startled. Perhaps she might be pushing him too far. But she hadn't asked him to come back here a second time today.

"Serious? —Yes, yes, of course I was serious. If we can't find anybody else. Do you think I'm afraid my boy would come to some harm at Timmie's hands? But my wife would have some objections, I suspect. She'd see risks. A lot of people on the outside seem to think Timmie's some kind of wild ape-boy. A savage creature that lived in caves and ate raw meat."

"What if we had an interview with him go out on the subetheric?" Miss Fellowes suggested. She was surprised to hear herself proposing more media incursions on Timmie's privacy; but if it would help overcome popular prejudices about the boy, it would be worth the strain on him. "Now that he speaks English—if people knew that he does—"

"I don't think that would be likely to improve things, Miss Fellowes."

"Why not?"

"His English really isn't very good, you know."

She was indignant at once. "What do you mean? He's got an amazing vocabulary, considering the point that he started from. And learning more words every day."

Hoskins' eyes seemed very weary. "You're the only one who can understand him. To the rest of us the things he says might just as well be Neanderthal words. They're practically unintelligible."

"You aren't listening carefully to him, then."

"No," Hoskins said without much vigor. "Perhaps not."

He shrugged and looked away and seemed to sink into some sort of reverie. Miss Fellowes picked up her book again and opened it to the page she had been on, without looking down at it, hoping that he would take the hint. But Hoskins sat where he was.

"—If only that miserable woman hadn't become involved in this thing!" he burst out suddenly, after a time.

"Marianne Levien?"

"That robot, yes."

"Surely she isn't!"

"No, not really," Hoskins said, with a tired little smile. "She just seems like one to me. Here we have a boy out of the past in the next room, and a woman who seems like something out of the future comes around to make trouble for me. I wish I'd never met her in the first place. Mannheim by himself isn't so bad—just one of those fuzzy-brained socially conscious guys, full of all sorts of lofty ideals, who goes running around all over the place determined to make the world a better place according to his own lights; that sort of thing. Your basic high-minded do-gooder. But Levien—that chrome-plated bitch —excuse my language, Miss Fellowes—"

"But that's exactly what she is."

"Yes. Yes, she is, isn't she?"

Miss Fellowes nodded. "I have trouble believing that a woman like that was once actually being considered for the job of looking after Timmie."

"One of the first to apply. Eager for the job. Hungry for it, as a matter of fact."

"She seems so—unsuitable."

"Her credentials were terrific. It was her personality that turned me off. She was very surprised not to be hired. —Well, somehow she's gotten herself entangled with Mannheim's crowd now, more's the pity. Probably deliberately, by way of paying me back for not giving her the job. Her way of getting revenge. Hell hath no fury, and so forth. She'll stir him up and stir him up and stir him up—she'll fill his head with her silly jargon, as though he doesn't have enough goofy psychobabble of his own stirring around in there—she'll keep him coming after me, fire him up to persecute me steadily—"

His voice was starting to rise.

Firmly Miss Fellowes said, "I don't think you can call it persecution when someone suggests that Timmie is a very lonely child and that something needs to be done about it."

"Something *will* be done about it."

"But why do you think she's being vengeful, when it seems to me she's simply pointing out—"

"Because she *is* vengeful!" Hoskins said, more loudly than before. "Because she wanted to come in here and take charge of this project when it was just getting under way, but she didn't get the opportunity, and now she intends to bring it all down around our ears. She'll have no mercy. Mannheim's a pushover compared with her. He can be manipulated, if you know the right buttons to push. He'll settle for constant statements of good intentions, polite reassurances that I'm going to follow his party line. But she'll be demanding on-site inspections every other Tuesday, now that she's calling the tune for him, and she'll want results. Changes. Things that'll keep us in turmoil all the time. She'll want Timmie to have psychotherapy next, or orthodontia, or plastic surgery to give him a nice cheerful *Homo sapiens* face—she'll meddle and meddle and meddle, one damned intrusion after another, making use of Mannheim's publicity machine to smear us, to make us look like evil mad scientists cold-bloodedly tormenting an innocent child—" He turned away and stared at Timmie's closed bedroom door. Morosely Hoskins said, "Mannheim's helpless in the power of a woman like that. She's probably sleeping with him, too. She must own him by now. He doesn't stand a chance against her."

Miss Fellowes' eyes widened. "What a thing to say!"

"Which?"

"That she and he—that she would use her— You have no proof of that. The whole suggestion's out of line, Dr. Hoskins. Absolutely out of line."

"Is it?" Hoskins' anger seemed to dissolve in an instant. He looked toward her and grinned shamefacedly. "—Yes, I suppose it is. You're right. I don't know anything about who Mannheim may be sleeping with, if anybody, and I don't care. Or Levien. I just want them to get out of our hair so we can do our research, Miss Fellowes. You know that. You also know that I've taken every step possible to make Timmie happy here. But I'm so tired, now—so damned tired—"

Impulsively Miss Fellowes went to him and seized his hands in hers. They were cold. She held them for a moment, wishing she could pump life and energy into them.

"When was the last time you had a vacation, Dr. Hoskins?"

"A vacation?" He chuckled hollowly. "I don't think I know what the word means."

"Maybe that's the problem."

"I can't. I simply can't. I turn my back for a minute, Miss Fellowes, and anything will happen here. A dozen different Adamewskis trying to steal scientific specimens out of Stasis. People running strange new experiments without authorization, doing God knows what at God knows what cost. Equipment that we can't afford purchased to set up projects that don't have a chance of working. We've got a lot of wild characters around this place, and I'm the only policeman. Until we've finished this phase of our work I don't dare take time off."

"A long weekend, at least? You need some rest."

"I know that. God, do I know that! —Thank you for caring so much, Miss Fellowes. Thank you for everything. In this whole madhouse of a research institute you've been one of the few pillars of sanity and dependability."

"And *will* you try to get a little rest?"

"I'll try, yes."

"Starting now?" she asked. "It's getting toward six o'clock. Your wife's expecting you at home. Your little boy."

"Yes," Hoskins said. "I'd better be heading out of here. And once again: thank you for everything, Miss Fellowes. Thank you. Thank you."

## [37]

In the night she was awakened by the sound of sobbing coming from Timmie's room. It was the first time she had heard that in a long while.

She got quickly out of bed and went to him. She had long ago mastered the skill of waking up in a hurry when a troubled child was calling out.

"Timmie?" she called.

She turned the night-light on. He was sitting up in bed, staring straight forward, with his eyes wide open, making the eerie high-pitched sound that was his kind of sobbing. But he didn't seem to see her. He took no notice of her at all as she entered the room, and the sobbing went on and on.

"Timmie, it's me. Miss Fellowes." She sat down beside him and slipped her arm around his shoulders. "It's all right, Timmie. It's all right!"

Slowly the sobbing stopped.

He looked at her as though he had never seen her before in his life. His eyes had a weirdly glassy look and his lips were drawn back in a bizarre way. In the half-darkness the lightning-bolt birthmark stood out fiercely on his cheek. She had virtually stopped noticing it but his face seemed pallid, almost bloodless, just now and the birthmark looked brighter than it had ever been before.

He's still asleep, she thought.

"Timmie?"

He made clicking sounds at her, Neanderthal speech. He seemed to be talking not so much *to* her as *through* her, to some invisible entity standing behind her.

Miss Fellowes hugged him and rocked him lightly from side to side, murmuring his name, crooning to him. His small body was rigid. He might almost have been under some kind of a spell. The clicking went on and on, interspersed with the sort of feral growls he had uttered in the early weeks of his stay. It was frightening to hear him revert like that to his prehistoric self.

"There, there, Timmie—little boy—Miss Fellowes' little boy—it's all right, everything's all right, there's nothing to worry about. —Would you like some milk, Timmie?"

She felt him grow less stiff. He was waking up now.

"Miss—Fellowes," he said haltingly.

"Milk? A little warm milk, Timmie?"

"Milk. Yes. Want milk."

"Come," she said, and swooped him up out of the bed, carrying him into the kitchen. It didn't strike her as a good idea to leave him alone just now. She perched him on the stool next to the refrigeration unit, got out a flask of milk, popped it in the heater for a moment.

"What was it?" she asked him, as he drank. "A dream? A bad dream, Timmie?"

He nodded, busy with the milk. Miss Fellowes waited for him to finish.

"Dream," he said. It was one of his newest words. "Bad. Bad dream."

"Dreams aren't real." Did he understand that? "You don't have to be afraid of dreams, Timmie."

"Bad—dream—"

His face was solemn. He seemed to be shivering, though the dollhouse was as warm as ever.

"Come back to bed now," she told him, scooping him up again. She tucked him in. —"What did you dream, Timmie? Can you tell me what it was?"

He made clicks again, a long series of them, interrupted by two short, soft growls.

Reverting to the old ways in the stress of the night? Or was it simply that he lacked the vocabulary to describe the dream in English?

Then he said, "Out—side."

His enunciation was so poor she wasn't certain that she heard him right.

"Outside? Is that what you said?"

"Out—side," he said again.

Yes, she was fairly sure of it. "Outside the bubble?" Miss Fellowes pointed toward the wall. "Out there?"

He nodded. "Out—side."

"You dreamed that you were outside there?"

Vigorous nodding. "Yes."

"And what did you see out there?"

He made clicks.

"I can't understand you."

The clicks became more insistent.

"No, Timmie. It's no good. You have to speak my kind of words. I don't understand yours. When you dreamed you were outside—what did you see?"

"Nothing," he said. "Empty."

Empty, yes. No wonder. He had no idea what was out there. The dollhouse's single window showed him only a little grassy patch, a fence, a meaningless sign.

"Big—empty," he said.

"You didn't see anything at all out there?"

Clicks.

Perhaps in his sleep he had been back in his Neanderthal world, and he had seen Ice Age scenes, drifts of snow, great shambling hairy animals wandering across the land, people clad in robes made of fur. But he had no words in English to describe any of that to her; and so he used the only sounds he did know.

"Outside," he said again. "Big—empty—"

"Scary?" Miss Fellowes prompted.

"Empty," he said. "Timmie alone."

Yes, she thought. Timmie alone. You poor, poor child.

She hugged him and tucked him in a second time, for he had pulled the coverlet free, and she gave him one of his favorite toys, a shapeless green floppy-limbed animal that was supposed to be a dinosaur. Dr. McIntyre had scowled when he saw it, and had given her one of his little paleoanthropological lectures about how it was a mistake to think that prehistoric man had been in any way a contemporary of the dinosaurs—a common popular error, he said, but in fact the Mesozoic Era had ended many millions of years before the appearance on the evolutionary scene of the first manlike primates. Yes, Miss Fellowes said, I know all that. But Timmie doesn't, and he loves his dinosaur very much. The boy hugged it now; and Miss Fellowes stood beside his bed until he had fallen asleep again.

No more bad dreams, she told him silently. No dreams of the great empty place outside where Timmie is all alone.

She went back to her own bed. A glance at the clock on the dresser told her that the time was a quarter to five. Too close to morning; she doubted that she would get back to sleep. More likely she'd simply lie awake, vigilantly listening for sounds from Timmie's room, and before long it would be dawn.

But she was wrong. Sleep took her quickly; and this time she was the one who dreamed.

She was in her bed, not here in the dollhouse but in her little apartment on the other side of town, which she hadn't seen in so many months. Someone was knocking on her door: eagerly, urgently, impatiently. She rose, slipping on a bathrobe, and activated the security screen. A man stood in the hall: a youngish man with close-clinging red hair, and a reddish beard, too.

Bruce Mannheim.

"Edith?" he said. "Edith, I have to see you."

He was smiling. Her hands shook a little as she undid the safeties on the door. He loomed before her in the dark, shadowy hallway, taller than she remembered, broad-shouldered, a sturdy virile figure. "Edith," he said. "Oh, Edith, it's been such a long time—"

And then she was in his arms. Right there in the hall, heedless of the staring neighbors, who stood in their doorways, pointing and murmuring. He swept her up as she had swept Timmie up not long before—carried her into her own apartment—whispering her name all the while—

"Bruce," she said. And realized that she had spoken the name aloud. She was awake. She sat up quickly and pressed both her hands over her mouth. Her cheeks were hot and stinging with embarrassment. Fragments of the dream whirled in her astounded mind. The absurdity of it—and its blatant schoolgirlish eroticism—stunned and dismayed her. She couldn't remember when she had last had any such sort of dream.

And to pick Bruce Mannheim as her dashing romantic hero—of all people—!

She began to laugh.

Dr. Hoskins would be appalled, if he knew! His reliable, dependable

Miss Fellowes—consorting intimately with the enemy, even if only in her dreams!

How ridiculous—how preposterous—

*How pathetic,* she told herself abruptly.

The aura of the dream still hovered about her. Some of the details were already gone from her mind. Others burned as vividly as though she were still asleep. His ardent embrace, his steamy passionate whispering. *Edith—Edith—it's been such a long time, Edith—*

A spinster's pitiful little fantasy. Sick. Sick. Miss Fellowes began to tremble, and had to struggle to fight off tears. The dream no longer seemed in any way funny to her. She felt soiled by it. An intrusion into her mind; an invasion of her neat enclosed life: where had it come from? Why? She had shut off all such yearnings years ago—or so she wanted to think. She had opted for a life without the disturbances that desire brought. A maidenly life; a spinster's life. Strictly speaking, she was neither, for she had been married, after all—if only for a handful of months. But that chapter was closed. She had lived as an island, entire of herself, for years—for decades. Devoted to her work, to her children. And now *this*—

It was only a dream, she told herself. And dreams aren't real. She had told Timmie the same thing just a little while before.

Only a dream. *Only.* The sleeping mind is capable of liberating any kind of thought at all. Strange things drift around randomly in there, floating on the tides of the unconscious. It meant nothing, nothing at all, other than that Bruce Mannheim had come here today and he had left some kind of impression on her that her sleeping mind had rearranged into a startling and improbable little scenario. But Mannheim was at least ten years younger than she was. And, pleasant-looking though he was, she didn't find him particularly attractive—not even in fantasy. He was just a man: someone she had met that day. Sometimes, despite everything, she did feel attracted to men. She had felt attracted to Hoskins, after all—a pointless, useless, meaningless attraction to a happily married man with whom she happened to work. There was some slight reality to the feeling she had for Hoskins, at least. There was none here. Only a dream, Miss Fellowes told herself again, only a dream, only a dream.

The thing to do now was to go back to sleep, she decided. By the time morning came she would probably have forgotten the whole thing.

Miss Fellowes closed her eyes again. After a while, she slept. The shadow of the dream was still with her, though, the vague outline and humiliating essence of it, when she woke once again a little past six as Timmie began to move about in his room: the urgent knocking at her door, the breathless greeting, the passionate embrace. But the whole thing simply seemed absurd to her now.

## [38]

After all the talk of the need to get a playmate for Timmie, Miss Fellowes expected that Hoskins would produce one almost immediately, if only to pacify the powerful political forces that Mannheim and Marianne Levien represented. But to her surprise weeks went by and nothing seemed to happen. Evidently Hoskins was having just as much difficulty arranging for someone's child to be brought into the Stasis bubble as he had anticipated. How he was managing to stall Mannheim off, Miss Fellowes didn't know.

Indeed she saw almost nothing of Hoskins in this period. Evidently he was preoccupied with other activities of Stasis Technologies, Ltd., and she caught no more than an occasional glimpse of him in passing. Running the company was obviously a full time job for him, and then some. Miss Fellowes had already gotten the impression, from little bits and snatches of comment that she had picked up from other people, that Hoskins was constantly struggling to cope with a staff of talented but high strung prima donnas hungry for Nobel prizes while he presided in his harried way over one of the most complex scientific ventures in history.

Be that as it may. He had his problems; she had hers.

Timmie's increasing loneliness was one of the worst of them. She tried to be everything the boy needed, nurse and teacher and surrogate mother; but she couldn't be enough. He dreamed again and again, always the same dream—not every night but often enough so that Miss Fellowes began keeping a record of the frequency of the dream—of that big, empty place outside the dollhouse where he could never be allowed to go. Sometimes he was alone out there; sometimes there were shadowy, mysterious figures with him. Because his English was still so rudimentary, she still wasn't able to tell whether the big empty place represented the lost Ice Age world to him or his imagined fantasy of the strange new era into which he had been brought. Either way, it was a frightening place to him, and he often awoke in tears. It wasn't necessary to have a degree in psychiatry to know that the dream was a powerful symptom of Timmie's isolation, his deepening sadness.

During the daytime he went through long woebegone periods when he was aimless and withdrawn, or when he spent silent hours at the dollhouse window with its prospect of little more than nothing—staring out into the big empty of his dream, perhaps thinking nostalgically of the bleak ice-swept plateaus of his now distant childhood, perhaps simply wondering what lay beyond the walls of the rooms in which his existence was confined. And she thought furiously: Why don't they bring someone here to keep him company? Why?

Miss Fellowes wondered if she ought to get in touch with Mannheim herself and tell him that nothing was being done, urge him to bring more pressure on Hoskins. But that seemed too much like treachery to her. Devoted as she was to Timmie, she still couldn't bring herself to go behind Hoskins' back that way. Yet her anger mounted.

The physiologists by now had learned about all they could from the boy, short of dissecting him, and that didn't appear to be part of the research program. So their visits became less frequent; someone came in once a week to measure Timmie's growth and ask a few routine questions and take some photographs, but that was all. The needles were gone, the injections and withdrawals of fluid; the special diets were deemed no longer necessary; the elaborate and taxing studies of how Timmie's joints and ligaments and bones were articulated became much less frequent.

So much to the good. But if the physiologists were growing less interested in the boy, the psychologists were only just beginning to turn up the heat. Miss Fellowes found the new group just as bothersome as the first, sometimes a good deal more so. Now Timmie was made to overcome barriers to reach food and water. He had to lift panels, move bars, reach for cords. And the mild electric shocks made him whimper with surprise and fear—or else to snarl in a highly primordial way. All of it drove Miss Fellowes to distraction.

She didn't want to appeal to Hoskins, though. She didn't wish to go to Hoskins at all. He was keeping his distance, for whatever reason; and Miss Fellowes was afraid that if she carried new demands to him now, she'd lose her temper at the slightest sign of resistance, might even quit altogether. That was a step she didn't want to find herself taking. For Timmie's sake she had to stay here.

Why had the man backed off from the Timmie project, though?

Why this indifference? Was this his way of insulating himself from Bruce Mannheim's complaints and requests? It was stupid, she thought. Timmie was the only victim of his remoteness. Stupid, stupid, stupid.

She did what she could to limit access to Timmie by the scientists. But she couldn't seal the boy off from them entirely. This *was* a scientific experiment, after all. So the probing and the poking and the mild electrical shocks went on.

And there were the anthropologists, too, armies of them, eager to interrogate Timmie about life as it had been lived in the Paleolithic. But even though Timmie now had a surprisingly good command of English—his kind of English—they still were doomed to frustration. They could ask all they wanted; but he could answer only if he understood the questions, and if his mind still retained any information about those aspects of his now remote days in the Stone Age world.

As the weeks of his sojourn in the modern era turned into months Timmie's speech had grown constantly better and more precise. It never entirely lost a certain soft slurriness that Miss Fellowes found rather endearing, but his comprehension of English was now practically the equal of that of a modern child of his age. In times of excitement, he did tend to fall back into bursts of tongue-clicking and occasional primordial growling, but those times were becoming fewer. He must be forgetting the life he had known in the days before he came into the twenty-first century—except in his private world of dreams, where Miss Fellowes could not enter. Who knew what huge shambling mammoths and mastodons cavorted there, what dark scenes of prehistoric mystery were enacted on the screen of the Neanderthal boy's mind?

But to Miss Fellowes' surprise, she was still the only one who could understand Timmie's words with any degree of assurance. Some of the others who worked frequently inside the Stasis bubble—her assistants Mortenson, Elliott, and Stratford, Dr. McIntyre, Dr. Jacobs—seemed able to pick out a phrase or two, but it was always a great effort and they usually misconstrued at least half of what Timmie was saying. Miss Fellowes was puzzled by that. In the beginning, yes, the boy had had a little difficulty in shaping words intelligibly; but time had gone by and he was quite fluent now. Or so it seemed to her. But gradually she had to admit that it was only her constant day-and-night proximity to Timmie that had made her so readily capable of understanding him. Her ear automatically compensated for the differences between what he said and the way the words really should be pronounced. He *was* different from a modern child, at least so far as his capacity to speak was concerned. He understood much of what was said to him; he was able to reply now in complex sentences—but his tongue and lips and larynx and, Miss Fellowes supposed, his little hyoid bone simply didn't appear to be properly adapted to the niceties of the twenty-first-century English language, and what came out was thick with distortions.

She defended him to the others. "Have you ever heard a Frenchman trying to say a simple word like 'the'? Or an Englishman trying to speak French? And there are letters in the Russian alphabet that we have to break our jaws to pronounce. Each linguistic group gets a different sort of training of the linguistic muscles from birth and for most people it's just about impossible to change. That's why there's such a thing as accents. Well, Timmie has a very pronounced Neanderthal accent. But it'll diminish with time."

Until that happened, Miss Fellowes realized, her own position would be one of unanticipated power and authority. She was not only Timmie's nurse, she was also his interpreter: the conduit through which his memories of the prehistoric world were transmitted to the anthropologists who came to interrogate him. Without her as an intermediary, they would find it impossible to get coherent answers to the questions they wanted to put to the boy. Her help was necessary if the project was to achieve its full scientific value. And so Miss Fellowes became essential, in a way that no one including herself had expected, to the ongoing work of exploring the nature of human life in the remote past.

Unfortunately, Timmie's interrogators almost always went away dissatisfied with the boy's revelations. It wasn't that he was unwilling to cooperate. But he had spent only three or four years in the world of the Neanderthals—the *first* three or four years, at that. There weren't many children of his age in any era who were prepared to offer a comprehensive verbal account of the workings of the society they lived in.

Most of what he did manage to convey were things that the anthropologists already suspected, and which, perhaps, they themselves planted in the boy's mind by the very nature of the questions which they had Miss Fellowes put to him.

"Ask him how big his tribe was," they would say.

"I don't think he has any word for tribe."

"How many people there were in the group that he lived with, then."

She asked him. She had begun teaching him recently how to count. He looked confused.

"Many," he said.

"Many," in Timmie's vocabulary, could be anything more than about three. It all seemed to be the same to him, beyond that point.

"*How* many?" she asked. She lifted his hand and ran her finger across the tips of his. "This many?"

"More."

"How many more?"

He made an effort. He closed his eyes for a moment as if staring into another world, and held out his hands, wriggling his fingers at her in rapid in-out gestures.

"Is he indicating numbers, Miss Fellowes?"

"I think so. Each hand movement is probably a five."

"I counted three movements of each hand. So the tribe was thirty people?"

"Forty, I think."

"Ask him again."

"Timmie, tell me again: how many people were there in your group?"

"Group, Miss Fellowes?"

"The people around you. Your friends and relatives. How many were there?"

"Friends. Relatives." He considered those concepts. Vague unreal words to him, very likely.

Then after a time he stared at his hands, and thrust his fingers out again, the same quick fluttery gesture, which might have been counting or might have been something else entirely. It was impossible to tell how many times he did it: perhaps eight, perhaps ten.

"Did you see?" Miss Fellowes asked. "Eighty, ninety, a hundred people, I think he's saying this time. If he's really answering the question at all."

"The number was smaller before."

"I know. This is what he's saying now."

"It's impossible. A tribe that primitive couldn't have more than thirty! At most."

Miss Fellowes shrugged. If they wanted to taint the evidence with their own preconceptions, that wasn't her problem. "Then put down thirty. You're asking a child who was only around three years old to give you a census report. He's only guessing, and the amazing thing is that he can even guess what we're trying to get him to tell us. And he may not be. What makes you think he knows how to count? That he even understands the concept of number?"

"But he does understand it, doesn't he?"

"About as well as any five-year-old does. Ask the next five-year-old how many people he thinks live on his street, and see what he tells you."

"Well—"

The other questions produced results nearly as uncertain. Tribal structure? Miss Fellowes managed to extract from Timmie, after a lot of verbal gyration, that there the tribe had had a "big man," by which he evidently meant a chief. No surprise there. Primitive tribes of historic times always had chiefs; it was reasonable to expect that Neanderthal tribes had had them, too. She asked if he knew the big man's name, and Timmie answered with clicks. Whatever the chief's name might be, the boy couldn't translate it into English words or even render a phonetic equivalent: he had to fall back on Neanderthal sounds. —Did the chief have a wife? the scientists wanted to know. Timmie didn't know what a wife was. —How was the chief chosen? Timmie couldn't understand the question. —What about religious beliefs and practices? Miss Fellowes was able, by dint of giving Timmie all sorts of scientifically dubious prompting, to get some sort of description from the boy of a holy place made of rocks, which he had been forbidden to go near, and a cult which might or might not have been run by a high priestess. She was sure it was a priestess, not a priest, because he kept pointing to her as he spoke; but whether he really understood what she was trying to learn from him was something not at all certain to her.

"If only they had managed to bring a child who was older than this across time!" the anthropologists kept lamenting. "Or a full-grown Neanderthal, for God's sake! If only! If only! How maddening, to have nothing but an ignorant little boy as our one source of information."

"I'm sure it is," Miss Fellowes agreed, without much compassion in her tone of voice. "But that ignorant little boy is one more Neanderthal than any of you ever expected to have a chance to interrogate. Never in your wildest dreams did you think you'd have any Neanderthals at all to talk to."

"Even so! If only! If only!"

"If only, yes," said Miss Fellowes, and told them that their time for interviewing Timmie was over for that day.

## [39]

Then Hoskins reappeared, arriving at the dollhouse without advance word one morning.

"Miss Fellowes? May I speak with you?"

He was using that sheepish tone of his again, the one that conveyed extreme embarrassment. As well he might, Miss Fellowes thought.

She came out coldly, smoothing her nurse's uniform. Then she halted in confusion. Hoskins wasn't alone. A pale woman, slender and of middle height, was with him, hovering at the threshold of the Stasis zone. Her fair hair and complexion gave her an appearance of fragility. Her eyes, a very light blue in color, were searching worriedly over Miss Fellowes' shoulders, looking diligently for something, flickering uneasily around the room as though she expected a savage gorilla to jump out from behind the door to Timmie's playroom.

Hoskins said, "Miss Fellowes, this is my wife, Annette. Dear, you can step inside. It's perfectly safe. You'll feel a trifling discomfort at the threshold, but it passes. —I want you to meet Miss Fellowes, who has been in charge of the boy since the night he came here."

(So this was his wife? She wasn't much like what Miss Fellowes would have expected Hoskins' wife to be; but then, she considered, she had never really had any clear expectations of what Hoskins' wife ought to be like. Someone more substantial, a little less fidgety, than this all too obviously ill-at-ease woman, at any rate. But, then, why? A strong-willed man like Hoskins might have preferred to choose a weak thing as his foil. Well, if that was what he wanted, so be it. On the other hand, Miss Fellowes had imagined Hoskins' wife would be young, young and sleek and glamorous, the usual sort of second wife that she had been told successful businessmen of Hoskins' age liked to acquire. Annette Hoskins didn't quite fall into that category. She was a good deal younger than Hoskins, yes, and younger than Miss Fellowes, too, for that matter. But she wasn't really young: forty, perhaps. Or close to it.)

Miss Fellowes forced a matter-of-fact greeting. "Good morning, Mrs. Hoskins. I'm pleased to meet you."

"Annette."

"I beg your pardon?"

"Call me Annette, Miss Fellowes. Everyone does. And your name is—"

Hoskins cut in quickly. "What's Timmie doing, Miss Fellowes? Taking a nap? I'd like my wife to meet him."

"He's in his room," Miss Fellowes said. "Reading."

Annette Hoskins gave a short, sharp, almost derisive-sounding laugh. "He can *read*?"

"Simple picture books, Mrs. Hoskins. With short captions. He's not quite ready for real reading yet. But he does like to look at books. This one's about life in the far north. Eskimos, walrus-hunting, igloos, that sort of thing. He reads it at least once a day."

(*Reading* wasn't exactly the most accurate description of what Timmie did, Miss Fellowes knew. In fact it was something of a fib. Timmie wasn't reading at all. As far as she could tell, Timmie only looked at the pictures; the words printed under them seemed to have no more than a decorative value to him, mere strange little marks. He had showed no curiosity about them at any time thus far. Perhaps he never would. But he was *looking* at books, and apparently understanding their content. That was the next best thing to actual reading. For the purpose of this conversation it might just be a good idea to let Hoskins' wife jump to the conclusion that Timmie really could read, though surely Hoskins himself was aware of the truth.)

Hoskins said in a robust, curiously pumped-up tone, "Isn't that amazing, Miss Fellowes? Do you remember what he was like the night we brought him in? That wild, screaming, dirty, frantic little prehistoric creature?"

(As though I could ever forget, Miss Fellowes thought.)

"And now—sitting quietly in there, reading a book—learning about Eskimos and igloos—" Hoskins beamed with what seemed almost like paternal pride. "How marvelous that is! How absolutely splendid, isn't it! What wonderful progress the boy has been making in your care!"

Miss Fellowes studied Hoskins suspiciously. There was something odd and unreal about this suddenly grandiose oratorical tone of his. What was he up to? He knew Timmie wasn't really able to read. And why bring his wife here after all this time, why be making all this insincere-sounding noise about Timmie's wonderful progress?

And then she understood.

In a more normal voice Hoskins said, "I have to apologize for stopping by so infrequently of late, Miss Fellowes. But as you can guess I've been tied up having to deal with all manner of peripheral distractions. Not the least of which is our friend Mr. Bruce Mannheim."

"I imagine you have been."

"He's called me just about every week since the day he was here. Asking me this, asking me that, fretting about Timmie as if the boy was his own son and I was the headmaster of some school he had sent him away to. —Some ghastly school out of a novel by Charles Dickens, one would think."

"Asking you particularly about what you've been doing to get Timmie a companion?" Miss Fellowes said.

"Especially that."

"And what actually have you been doing along those lines, Dr. Hoskins?"

Hoskins winced. "Having a very difficult time. We've interviewed at least half a dozen children, perhaps more, as potential playmates for Timmie. And interviewed their parents as well, naturally."

That was news to Miss Fellowes. "And?"

"What it comes down to is that there were two little boys who seemed suitable, but their parents raised all sorts of special conditions and objections that we were in no position to deal with. There was another boy who might have worked out, and we were just about ready to bring him in here for a trial visit with Timmie, but at the last moment it was conditions and objections again; the parents brought in a lawyer who wanted us to post bond, tie ourselves up in some very elaborate contractual guarantees, and commit ourselves to various other things that *our* lawyers thought were unwise. As for the rest of the children we saw, the question of liability didn't arise, because their parents seemed only interested in the fee we were offering. But the kids all struck us as wild little roughnecks who'd do Timmie more harm than good. Naturally we turned them down."

"So you don't have anyone, is what you're saying."

Hoskins moistened his lips. "We decided finally that we'd stay in-house for this—that we'd use the child of a staff member. This particular staff member standing here in front of you. Me."

"Your own son?" Miss Fellowes asked.

"You recall, don't you, that when Mannheim and Dr. Levien were here I said, more in anger than otherwise, that if necessary I'd make my own boy available? Well, it's come down to that. I'm a man of my word, Miss Fellowes, as I think you realize. I'm not going to ask anyone else in the company to do something that I'm not prepared to do. I've decided to put my boy Jerry forth as the playmate that Timmie needs so badly. —But of course that can't be my unilateral decision alone."

"So you brought Mrs. Hoskins here so that she could satisfy herself that your son wouldn't be in any danger at Timmie's hands," Miss Fellowes said.

Hoskins looked overwhelmed with gratitude. "Yes, Miss Fellowes. Yes, exactly so!"

Miss Fellowes glanced again at Hoskins' wife. The woman was chewing her lip and staring once more at the door behind which the terrifying Neanderthal lurked.

She must believe that Timmie's an ape, Miss Fellowes thought. A gorilla. A chimpanzee. Who will instantly leap on her precious little baby and rend him limb from limb.

Icily Miss Fellowes said, "Well, shall I bring him out and show him to her now?"

Mrs. Hoskins tensed visibly, and she had been tense to begin with. "I suppose you should—Miss Fellowes."

The nurse nodded.

"Timmie?" she called. "Timmie, will you come out here for a moment? We have visitors."

Timmie peered shyly around the edge of the door.

"It's all right, Timmie. It's Dr. Hoskins and his wife. Come on out."

The boy stepped forward. He looked quite presentable, Miss Fellowes thought, uttering a little prayer of gratitude. He was wearing the blue overalls with the big green circles on them, his second-favorite pair, and his hair, which Miss Fellowes had brushed out thoroughly an hour ago, was still relatively unmussed and unsnarled. The slender book he had been looking at dangled from his left hand.

He peered up expectantly at the visitors. His eyes were very wide. Plainly Timmie recognized Hoskins, even after all this time, but he didn't seem sure what to make of Hoskins' wife. No doubt something in her body language, something tightly strung and wary about her, had put the boy on guard. Primitive reflexes—instincts, you could almost say—coming to the fore in him, perhaps?

There was a long awkward silence.

Then Timmie smiled.

It was a warm, wonderful smile, Timmie's extraspecial ear-to-ear smile. Miss Fellowes loved him for it. She could have gathered him up and hugged him. How delicious he looked when he did that! How sweet, how trusting, how childlike. Yes. A little boy coming out of his nursery to greet the company. How could Annette Hoskins possibly resist that smile?

"Oh," the woman said, as though she had just found a beetle in her soup. "I didn't realize he'd look so—strange."

Miss Fellowes gave her a baleful scowl.

Hoskins said, "It's mostly his facial features, you know. From the neck down he just looks like a very muscular little boy. More or less."

"But his face, Gerald—that huge mouth—that enormous nose—the eyebrows bulging like that—the chin—he's so *ugly*, Gerald. So weird."

"He can understand much of what you're saying," Miss Fellowes warned in a low, frosty voice.

Mrs. Hoskins nodded. But she still wasn't able to stop herself. "He looks very different in person from the way he looks on television. He definitely seems much more human when you see him on—"

"He *is* human, Mrs. Hoskins," Miss Fellowes said curtly. She was very tired of having to tell people that. "He's simply from a different branch of the human race, that's all. One that happens to be extinct."

Hoskins, as though sensing the barely suppressed rage in Miss Fellowes' tone, turned to his wife and said with some urgency, "Why don't you talk to Timmie, dear? Get to know him a little. That's why you came here today, after all."

"Yes. Yes."

She seemed to be working up her courage.

"Timmie?" the woman said, in a thin, tense voice. "Hello, Timmie. I'm Mrs. Hoskins."

"Hello," Timmie said.

He put out his hand to her. That was what Miss Fellowes had taught him to do.

Annette Hoskins glanced quickly at her husband. He rolled his eyes toward the ceiling and nodded.

She reached out uncertainly and took Timmie's hand as though she were shaking hands with a trained chimpanzee at the circus. She gave it a quick unenthusiastic shake and let go of it in a hurry.

Timmie said, "Hello, Mrs. Hoskins. Pleased to meet you."

"What did he say?" Annette Hoskins asked. "Was he saying something to me?"

"He said hello," Miss Fellowes told her. "He said he was pleased to meet you."

"He *speaks*? English?"

"He speaks, yes. He can understand easy books. He eats with a knife and a fork. He can dress and undress himself. It shouldn't be any surprise that he can do all those things. He's a normal little boy, Mrs. Hoskins, and he's something more than five years old. Maybe five and a half."

"You don't know?"

"We can only guess," Miss Fellowes said. "He didn't have his birth certificate in his pocket when he came here."

Mrs. Hoskins looked at her husband again. "Gerald, I'm not so sure about this. Jerry isn't quite five yet."

"I know how old our son is, dear," Hoskins said stonily. "He's big and sturdy for his age, though. Bigger than Timmie is. —Look, Annette, if I thought there was any risk at all—the slightest possibility of—"

"I don't know. I just don't know. How can we be certain that it's safe?"

Miss Fellowes said at once, "If you mean is Timmie safe to be with your son, Mrs. Hoskins, the answer is yes, of course he is. Timmie's a gentle little boy."

"But he's a sav—savage."

(The ape-boy label from the media, again! Didn't people ever think for themselves?)

Miss Fellowes said emphatically, "He is not a savage, not in the slightest. Does a savage come out of his room carrying his book, and put out his hand for a handshake? Does a savage smile like that and say hello and tell you that he's pleased to meet you? You see him right in front of you. What does he really look like to you, Mrs. Hoskins?"

"I can't get used to his face. It's not a human face."

Miss Fellowes would not let herself explode in wrath. Tautly she said, "As I've already explained, he's as human as any of us. And not a savage at all. He is just as quiet and reasonable as you can possibly expect a five-and-some-months-year-old boy to be. It's very generous of you, Mrs. Hoskins, to agree to allow your son to come here to play with Timmie, but please don't have any fears about it."

"I haven't said that I've agreed," Mrs. Hoskins replied with some mild heat in her voice.

Hoskins gave her a desperate glare. "Annette—"

"I haven't!"

(Then why don't you get out of here and let Timmie go back to his book?)

Miss Fellowes struggled to keep her temper.

(Let Dr. Hoskins handle this. She's his wife.)

Hoskins said, "Talk to the boy, Annette. Get to know him a little. You did agree to do that much."

"Yes. Yes, I suppose." She approached the boy again. "Timmie?" she said tentatively. Timmie looked up. He wasn't doing the ear-to-ear smile this time. He had already learned, strictly from the verbal intonations he was picking up, that this woman was no friend of his.

Mrs. Hoskins did smile, but it wasn't a very convincing one. —"How old are you, Timmie?"

"He's not very good at counting," Miss Fellowes said quietly.

But to her astonishment Timmie held up the five fingers of his left hand, splayed out distinctly.

"Five!" the boy cried.

"He put up five fingers and he said five," Miss Fellowes said, amazed. "You heard him, didn't you?"

"I heard it," said Hoskins. —"I think."

"Five," Mrs. Hoskins said, grimly continuing. She was working at making contact with Timmie now. "That's a very nice age. My boy Jerry is almost five himself. If I bring Jerry here, will you be nice to him?"

"Nice," Timmie said.

*"Nice,"* Miss Fellowes translated. "He understood you. He promised to be nice."

Mrs. Hoskins nodded. Under her breath she said, "He's small, but he looks so *strong.*"

"He's never tried to hurt anyone," Miss Fellowes said, conveniently allowing herself to overlook the frantic battles of the long-ago first night. "He's extremely gentle. Extremely. You've got to believe that, Mrs. Hoskins." To Timmie she said, "Take Mrs. Hoskins into your room. Show her your toys and your books. And your clothes closet." *Make her see that you're a real little boy, Timmie. Make her look past your brow ridges and your chinless chin.*

Timmie held out his hand. Mrs. Hoskins, after only a moment of hesitation, took it. For the first time since she had entered the Stasis bubble something like a genuine smile appeared on her face.

She and Timmie went into Timmie's room. The door closed behind them.

"I think it's going to work," Hoskins said in a low voice to Miss Fellowes, the moment his wife was gone. "He's winning her over."

"Of course he is."

"She's not an unreasonable woman. Trust me on that. Or an irrational one. But Jerry's very precious to her."

"Naturally so."

"Our only child. We'd been married for several years, and there were fertility problems in the beginning, and then we managed—we were finally able—"

"Yes," Miss Fellowes said. "I understand." She wasn't enormously interested in hearing about the fertility problems of Dr. and Mrs. Hoskins. Or how they had finally been able to overcome them.

"So you see—even though I've been over this thoroughly with her, even though she understands the problems that Mannheim and his crowd has been making for me and the importance of ending Timmie's isolation, she's still somewhat hesitant about exposing Jerry to the risk that—"

"There is no risk, Dr. Hoskins."

"I know that. You know that. But until *Annette* knows that, too—"

The door of Timmie's playroom opened. Mrs. Hoskins emerged. Miss Fellowes saw Timmie hanging back, peering out in that wary way he sometimes adopted. Her breath stopped. Something must have gone wrong in there, she thought.

But no. Annette Hoskins was smiling.

"It's a very cute little room," she said. "He can fold his own clothes. He showed me. I wish Jerry could do it half as well. And he keeps his toys so neatly—"

Miss Fellowes let her breath out.

"So we can give it a try?" Hoskins asked his wife.

"Yes. I think we can give it a try."

# INTERCHAPTER SIX

# *Stalemate*

SMOKE WAS RISING above the camp of the Other Ones by the bank of the smallest river, off to the west of the Goddess-shrine. When Silver Cloud looked the other way he saw the white smoke of his own people's fire rising from their campfire, back against the gently sloping hill that they had descended when they emerged out of the mountains of the east. There was no one in front of the shrine itself. During this interminable time of stalemate a tacit agreement had sprung up between the two tribes: the shrine was neutral territory. Nobody from either party could go close to it. Each side kept sentries posted day and night at the edge of the shrine area to make sure there were no transgressions.

Silver Cloud stood by himself, leaning on his spear. Darkness was falling already, though it seemed to him that the day had only just begun. The year was gliding quickly along. Night came sooner and sooner all the time. Morning arrived later and later. The daylight hours were being squeezed from both sides. Soon it would be the season of the long snows, when only a fool would go outside: time to hunker down in some sheltered place, living on the autumn's stored food and waiting for spring.

But we still have not made our peace with the Goddess and received Her guidance, thought Silver Cloud disconsolately. And how can we, when the Other Ones hover constantly near the shrine, keeping us away from it?

"Silver Cloud! Is it going to snow again?"

The voice of She Who Knows came drifting to him on the wind. She was standing across the way, near the riverbank, with Goddess Woman and Keeps The Past. The three women had been talking for a long while. Silver Cloud frowned. They were nothing but trouble, those three. Three powerful women, full of Goddess-strength. They made him uneasy. And yet he knew how important they were, each in her own way, to the life of the tribe.

"Will it snow, Silver Cloud? Tell us!"

He shrugged. Then he tapped his knee and nodded.

The old wound in his leg was aching fiercely. It always did, when a snowy time was coming on. But now it was throbbing worse than ever.

Yesterday snow had fallen for nearly an hour, and there had been snow the day before yesterday also, for just a little while. Now it would do it again. That was bad, when the snow started to come every day. Much of yesterday's snow was still on the ground. The wind—it was blowing from the north, the demon-wind—scooped it up and whipped it around, throwing it in Silver Cloud's face.

We should leave here, he thought. We should be finding our winter camp.

She Who Knows had turned away from Keeps The Past now, and was coming over to talk with him. That meant trouble, most likely. Since her bold exploit before the shrine, She Who Knows had moved with such self-assurance and majesty that it almost seemed as though she were chieftain in his place. No one dared jeer at her, no one dared so much as look at her the wrong way, since that remarkable day when she had covered her body with war-paint and gone forth to defy the entire group of Other Ones warriors. She had always been strange; she had always been fierce; but now she had moved on into some new kind of ferocious strangeness that made her seem to walk in realms of her own.

She said, "This goes on and on, Silver Cloud, and nothing ever changes. And the snowy time is coming."

"I know that."

"We should attack and be done with it."

"They are too many for us," Silver Cloud told her. "You know that." This was not the first time that they had had this discussion.

"Not that many. We could handle them. But instead we simply sit here. They're afraid of us and we're afraid of them and nobody budges. How much longer will you keep us here?"

"Until we've gone before the Goddess at Her shrine and learned Her will."

"Then we have to attack," She Who Knows said.

Silver Cloud stared steadily at her. Her eyes were frightening, not a woman's eyes at all, not even a warrior's eyes. They were like eyes of polished stone.

"You were down there with the men," Silver Cloud said. "You saw that the men would not attack. Do you want to fight the Other Ones all alone, She Who Knows?"

"You're the chieftain. Order them to fight. I'll fight alongside them."

"Everyone will die."

"And if we stay here and wait for winter? Everyone will die in that case too, Silver Cloud."

He nodded gloomily. True enough: they couldn't stay here much longer. He realized that as well as she did.

It was probably a mistake to have come here at all, Silver Cloud knew. But that was something he could never admit to anyone else.

He said, "We can't go, She Who Knows. Not until we've been to the shrine."

"We can't go and we can't stay. And we can't get to the shrine. This is very bad trouble, Silver Cloud."

"Perhaps."

"I said that we should never come here. Right at the beginning, when you announced that the Summer Festival was going to be canceled, I told you that."

"I remember that, She Who Knows. But we *are* here. And here we stay, until we perform the rite that we have come here for. We can't simply walk away without having heard the voice of the Goddess."

"No," She Who Knows said. "I agree with you about that. I didn't want to come here; but now that we're here, we must go before the Goddess, just as you say. I have no quarrel with you on that point."

He was grateful for that much.

"But if we can't stay here much longer because of the snow, and we can't go without performing the rite, and the Other Ones prevent us from performing the rite because they are here and defile the shrine by their presence, then we have to drive them away," said She Who Knows. "It's as simple as that."

"They'll kill us if we attack them."

"Winter will kill us if we don't."

"This goes in circles," Silver Cloud said. "This brings us to no place at all."

He looked at her somberly. Her face was inexorable. But She Who Knows was offering him no answers except the answer of certain death at the hands of the enemy.

Around and around in circles, yes. We cannot leave and we cannot stay. He had canceled the Summer Festival for the sake of the rite that he believed it was necessary to perform here. If he canceled that rite, too, because of the presence of Other Ones close by the shrine, then there would have been no rite at all either in summer or autumn, which surely would bring the anger of the Goddess down upon the People in full measure. The People would starve; and they would blame the chieftain for that. Silver Cloud knew that he was in danger of being removed from office if he didn't repair matters soon. And there was no such thing as a living ex-chieftain, among the People. The custom was very clearly understood by all. To give up the chieftainship meant saying goodbye to life itself.

There was hot fire running along the wounded part of his leg. Perhaps it wouldn't be such a bad thing, Silver Cloud thought, to step aside and let someone else bear the burden. And make an end to this pain and weariness forever.

Goddess Woman joined them now. "Has She Who Knows convinced you that we should attack?"

"No."

"Are you so much afraid to die?"

Silver Cloud laughed. "The question is more foolish than you realize, Goddess Woman. What I'm afraid of is that *you* will die, and Milky Fountain and Fights Like A Lion and Beautiful Snow and everyone else. My task is to keep the People alive, not to lead them into certain death."

"The snowy time is coming. That will kill us also, if we stay out here in the open."

With a sigh he said, "Yes, yes, I know that, too."

"I didn't want to make this pilgrimage," Goddess Woman said. "Do you remember? I said there was no need to come all the way back here to learn the will of the Goddess. But Keeps The Past talked me into letting you have your way."

"I remember," said Silver Cloud patiently. "It makes no difference now. We are here. Can we leave, do you think, without speaking with the Goddess?"

"Perhaps the Goddess has already spoken," said Goddess Woman, "and what She has said is that we are fools led by a fool, and therefore we deserve to die. Better to die fighting against the enemy, in that case, than to die standing here, endlessly talking to one another while the snow piles up around us. Or perhaps you think—"

"Look," She Who Knows broke in. "One of the Other Ones is coming to talk to us!"

Silver Cloud swung around, startled. Yes, it was so: a tall young warrior carrying a spear that had a strip of red fur tied around its point had left the other camp and was heading toward them. As the envoy passed the area in front of the shrine, Broken Mountain, who was on sentry duty, bristled at him and presented his weapon. The Other One made an Other One sound at Broken Mountain and kept on going, striding past him without pausing.

Blazing Eye and Tree Of Wolves came out of the encampment and pointed to the Other One as if they thought Silver Cloud had not noticed him. They brandished their spears and indicated that they were ready to jump forward and attack. Silver Cloud angrily gestured at them to get back. What did they think, that this was a one-man war party? Obviously the man was coming here to talk. Obviously.

But how am I supposed to talk with an Other One? Silver Cloud wondered.

The envoy took a zigzag path over the snowy ground, going around the places where underground water made the surface marshy, and came across to the place along the riverbank where Silver Cloud was standing with She Who Knows and Goddess Woman. He elevated his spear in what could only have been some sort of gesture of greeting and waved it solemnly from side to side.

Silver Cloud lifted his own spear a little way from the ground by way of acknowledgment and lowered it again, and waited to see what would happen next.

The Other One made Other One sounds. To Silver Cloud they were like the groaning of an animal in pain.

"Do you think there's something wrong with him?" he asked She Who Knows.

"He's saying something. That's how they speak."

"That? Speaking? It's just noise."

"It's the way they speak," She Who Knows said. "I'm certain of that."

"All right," said Silver Cloud. "Tell me what he's trying to say, then."

"Ah. Ah. How can I do that?"

"You are She Who Knows. You say so yourself."

"I only know what I know. The language of the Other Ones is not something I know."

"Ah," said Silver Cloud. "So there's something you don't know! I've never heard you say a thing like that before, She Who Knows."

She gave him a sour smile and did not reply.

The Other One was speaking again. His voice was pitched very high, and he seemed to be straining as he spoke, pushing the sounds out, working hard to make his meaning clear, as though he were speaking to children. But there was no meaning. Silver Cloud stared intently, watching the man's mouth, and he could not make out a single intelligible word. The sounds that the Other One was making were not the sounds of speech.

Silver Cloud said, "Can't you speak properly? I can't understand you if you moan like that."

The Other One leaned forward and thrust his head outward to bring it closer to Silver Cloud and put one hand behind his ear, the way a deaf man does, although Silver Cloud had been speaking very loudly indeed. It was a strange pose. The Other One was very tall, unbelievably tall, head halfway to the sky, and when he leaned forward he looked like some long-legged bird of the marsh country. Silver Cloud stared at him with utter fascination. How did he keep his balance? How was it that he didn't fall over, standing on legs so thin and long? Or break in half when he moved? And the ugliness of him—that pale skin, like a ghost's—the way his face jutted out below his mouth, and the weird tininess of his features—

"I said, can't you speak properly? Speak in words if you want to talk to me!"

"Those are his words," She Who Knows said suddenly. "He has his own words." She had an odd look on her face, the look of one who has been struck by a strange new truth. "The Other Ones have a language of their own, different from ours."

"What?" Silver Cloud said, mystified. "What does that mean? There's only one language, She Who Knows. There are words that can be understood, and there are noises that can't. We can't understand what he's saying, and therefore his sounds are only noises. How can there be more than one language? The sky is the sky. A mountain is a mountain. Water is water, snow is snow. Everybody knows that. How can anyone call them by other names?"

"Two peoples—two languages. One language for us—a different one for them—"

The thought made Silver Cloud's head ache. There might actually be some sense to it, he had to admit—two peoples, two languages, why not? —but it was very difficult to think about such a thing now. Ideas like that needed careful contemplation at a quiet time. He pushed the problem aside and looked back toward the Other One.

He was speaking again, as unintelligibly as before. This time he was making gestures too, perhaps trying to act out the message he had come here to deliver, seeing that speech was not turning out to be very useful. He pointed with his fur-wrapped spear at the shrine; he pointed at the hill country to the east out of which the People had come; he pointed westward, to the lands that ran toward the sea, which now belonged entirely to the Other Ones. He pointed to the shrine again. He pointed to Silver Cloud; he pointed to himself. He pointed to the shrine.

"Goddess Woman?" Silver Cloud said. "Do you make any sense of this?"

"He wants us to leave, so they can have the shrine," Goddess Woman said immediately.

Silver Cloud wasn't so sure of that. There was too much back-and-forth pointing. If he were the one who had gone to the Other Ones to tell them to leave, he would simply have pointed to the shrine and to the Other Ones, and then to the western lands, and made a flicking gesture with his hand to tell them that they should go back where they had come. Anyone with any intelligence ought to be able to understand that.

In fact, why not try it now? And he did.

The Other One watched him with the sort of look on his face that one might give a child who was stammering through some long-winded interruption of a perfectly sensible adult conversation. When Silver Cloud was done, the Other One responded by going through his whole point-at-this-point-at-that routine all over again.

She Who Knows said, "I think he's trying to tell us that we can share the shrine, his people and ours worshipping at it together."

"Share a shrine with filth?" Goddess Woman cried. "The shrine is ours!"

"Is that what you're telling me?" Silver Cloud asked the Other

One, speaking as slowly and loudly as he could. "You think that we both can use the shrine? But you can't be serious. It's a shrine of the Goddess. You aren't people of the Goddess. —Or are you? Are you?"

He waited, hoping for an answer he could understand.

But the Other One said incomprehensible Other One things again. He did the pointing-with-the-spear one more time.

"Hopeless," Silver Cloud said. "Hopeless, hopeless, hopeless. I don't understand you and you don't understand me. No question about that. She Who Knows and Goddess Woman think they understand you, but they don't, not really. They're both just hearing the things they want to think you're saying."

"I could sit down with him and try to teach him our language," She Who Knows offered. "Or maybe I could learn how to speak his."

"Keep away from him," Goddess Woman said. "He's unclean, and this is holy land."

"But if we were able to speak with—"

"It's no use," said Silver Cloud. "Even if those noises of his are a language, you'd never learn it. How could you? It's like sitting down with a bear and trying to learn bear-noises. Or to teach a bear to speak. It can't be done."

"Old men always say that things can't be done," She Who Knows retorted.

"Old? Old?" Silver Cloud cried.

But now the Other One was gesturing again with his spear, and making his sounds again. One last attempt, perhaps, to get his message across to Silver Cloud. It was as incomprehensible, though, as it had been before. Silver Cloud felt a great sadness coming over him, and not only because She Who Knows had called him old, or because there was fiery pain in his leg, or because the snowy time was coming and the People had not yet made provision for winter camp. No, it was because this strange stork-like man had come to him with what might have been a message of peace, but he could not understand it and could not make himself understood, and so the stalemate would continue. It was like a wall of stone between them, cutting off communication.

The Other One finished his speech and waited.

"I'm sorry," Silver Cloud said. "I just don't understand. The problem is that I don't speak your language. And I guess you don't speak mine."

"So you agree it's a language, then!" She Who Knows said in triumph.

"Yes," said Silver Cloud glumly. "For whatever good that does."

The parley was over. The Other One, looking irritated and morose, swung around and walked quickly away, back toward his own encampment. Silver Cloud watched, astonished by the loose-jointed free-wheeling stride of the man. It seemed a wonder that his arms and legs didn't fall off as he walked, so poorly strung together was he, so badly designed. Or that his head didn't roll right off his flimsy neck. Silver Cloud felt grateful for his own sturdy, compact body, weary and aching though it had become of late. It had served him well for a great many years. It was the work of the Goddess, that body. He pitied the Other Ones for their fragility and their ugliness.

As the envoy of the Other Ones passed the sentry zone again, Broken Mountain once more shook his spear at him and made a hissing sound of defiance. The Other One took no notice. Broken Mountain looked to Silver Cloud for instruction, but Silver Cloud shook his head and told him to hold his peace. The Other One disappeared into the distant encampment of his people.

So that was that. Nothing accomplished.

Silver Cloud felt racked by doubts. Whatever he did these days led only to muddle. The Goddess had gone unworshipped, a little boy had vanished into thin air, the shrine they had come all this way to venerate was inaccessible to them, and the season was quickly turning against them; and now he had failed to achieve anything at all by way of parley. No doubt She Who Knows was right, as she usually was, much as he hated to admit that to himself: he was too old for the job. Time to step aside, to let the Killing Society do its work, and lie down in the sleep that never ends.

Blazing Eye would be chieftain in his place. Let Blazing Eye worry about what to do next.

But even as the thought crossed his mind, Silver Cloud was angered by it. Blazing Eye? A fool. He would do foolish things, as fools can be expected to do. It would be a sin to hand the tribe over to Blazing Eye.

Who, then? Broken Mountain? Tree Of Wolves? Young Antelope?

All fools. He couldn't give the tribe to any one of them. Maybe they would outgrow their foolishness someday; but he wasn't very confident of that.

Then who will be chieftain after me?

Let the Goddess decide, Silver Cloud told himself. After I'm gone. It'll be Her problem then, not mine.

He would not resign. He would wait for death to claim him. He knew that he was a fool, too—or else they would not be here in this useless deadlock now—but at least he was less foolish than the younger men, and he might just as well keep his chieftainship a little while longer.

"What are you going to do now, Silver Cloud?" She Who Knows asked.

"Nothing," he said. "What is there to do?"

He went back to the camp and sat down by the fire. Some child came over to him—he couldn't remember her name—and he drew her close against his side, and they sat there staring at the leaping flames for a long while. The presence of the child lifted a little of the sadness that had come over him. From this little girl the People of tomorrow someday would come forth, long after he was gone. That was a comforting thought: that chieftains might die, that warriors died, that everyone died sooner or later, but the People would go on and on, into time immemorial, world without end. Yes. Yes. A good thing to bear in mind.

Shortly it began to snow, and the snow went on falling late into the night.

# CHAPTER NINE

# Becoming

[40]

THREE DAYS LATER Hoskins stopped by to see Miss Fellowes and said, "It's all been worked out. My wife has no further problem about letting Jerry come here to play with Timmie, and Ned Cassiday has drafted a liability agreement that he thinks will stand legal muster."

"Liability? Liability for what, Dr. Hoskins?"

"Why, any sort of injury that might be inflicted."

"By Timmie on Jerry, you mean."

"Yes," Hoskins said, in that sheepish voice of his once again.

Miss Fellowes instantly began to bristle. "Tell me: do you seriously think there's any chance of that happening? Does your wife?"

"If we were really worried about that, we wouldn't be volunteering Jerry to be Timmie's playmate. My wife had her doubts at first, as you know, but it didn't take long for Timmie to win her over. Still, there's always the chance, when you bring two small boys together who don't know each other, that one of them will take a swing at the other, Miss Fellowes. I surely don't have to remind you of that."

"Of course. But parents don't usually insist on liability agreements before they'll allow their child to play with other children."

Hoskins laughed. "You don't understand. It's the company that insists on the liability agreement, not us. Annette and I are the ones who are guaranteeing to the company that we won't take any legal action against Stasis Technologies, Ltd., in case something happens. —It's a *waiver* of liability, Miss Fellowes."

"Oh," she said, in a very small voice. —"I see. When will you be bringing Jerry here, then?"

"Tomorrow morning? How would that be?"

## [41]

Miss Fellowes waited until breakfast time to tell him. She hadn't wanted to say anything the night before, thinking that the excitement of anticipation might unsettle Timmie's sleep, making him edgy and unpredictable when Jerry arrived.

"You'll be getting a friend today, Timmie."

"A friend?"

"Another little boy. To play with you."

"A little boy just like me?"

"Just like you, yes." In every way that really mattered, Miss Fellowes told herself fiercely. "His name is Jerry. He's Dr. Hoskins' son."

"Son?" He gave her a puzzled look.

"Dr. Hoskins is his father," she said, as though that would help.

"Father."

"Father—son." She held her hand high in the air, then lower down. "The father is the big man. The son is the little boy."

He still looked baffled. There were so many basic assumptions of life, so many things that everyone took for granted, that were alien to him. It was because he had spent all this time in the isolation of the Stasis bubble. But certainly he knew what parents were. Or had he forgotten even that? Not for the first time Miss Fellowes found herself detesting Gerald Hoskins and everyone else connected with Stasis Technologies, Ltd., for having ripped this little boy out of his own proper time and place. She could almost agree with the Bruce Mannheim crowd that a very sophisticated kind of child abuse had taken place here.

Rummaging in Timmie's pile of storybooks, Miss Fellowes found one of his favorites, a retelling of the story of William Tell. What meaning the story itself had for him was something she couldn't even begin to guess, but the book was boldly and vividly illustrated and he pored over it again and again, lightly rubbing his fingers over the bright pictures. She opened it now to the two-page spread showing William Tell shooting the apple off his son's head with a bolt from his crossbow, and indicated, first the archer in his medieval costume, then his son.

"Father—son—father—son—"

Timmie nodded gravely.

What, she wondered, was he thinking? That Dr. Hoskins was really a handsome man with long blond hair who wore strange clothing and carried a curious machine under his arm? Or that someone was going to come here to shoot apples off his head? Perhaps it had been an error to muddle the moment with abstract concepts like "father" and "son."

Well, all that was really important was that Timmie would have a friend soon.

"He'll be coming after we've finished breakfast," Miss Fellowes told him. "He's a very nice boy." She profoundly hoped that he was. "And you'll show him what a nice boy you are too, won't you?"

"Nice boy. Yes."

"You'll be his friend. He'll be your friend."

"Friend. Nice boy."

His eyes were gleaming. But did he understand? Did he understand any of this at all?

She felt all sorts of unexpected misgivings as the time of Jerry Hoskins' arrival drew near. She saw all sorts of problems that she had not considered before.

Stop it, she told herself.

(You've wanted this for Timmie for months. And now it's happening. There's nothing to worry about. Nothing.)

"Miss Fellowes?"

Hoskins' voice, on the intercom.

"Here they are," she said to Timmie. "Jerry's coming!"

To her surprise, Timmie went scuttling into his playroom and closed the door partway. He peered out uneasily. Not a good sign, she thought.

"Timmie—" she began.

And then the whole Hoskins family was at the threshold of the Stasis bubble.

Hoskins said, "This is my boy Jerry. Say hello to Miss Fellowes, Jerry."

She saw a round-faced, large-eyed child, with pale cheeks and loose, unruly brown hair, clutching at Annette Hoskins' skirt. He looked very much like his father: a five-year-old version of Gerald Hoskins, yes.

"Say hello," Hoskins said to the boy, a little ominously this time.

"Hello." It was barely audible. Jerry receded a bit farther into the folds of the maternal skirt.

Miss Fellowes gave him her warmest, most inviting smile. "Hello, Jerry. Would you like to come in? This is where Timmie lives. —Timmie's going to be your friend."

Jerry stared. He looked as though he would much rather bolt and run.

"Lift him over the threshold," Hoskins said to his wife, not very patiently.

She gathered the boy into her arms—it was a distinct effort; Jerry was big for his age—and stepped over the threshold. Jerry squirmed visibly as the threshold sensations of Stasis passed through him.

"He isn't happy, Gerald," Mrs. Hoskins said.

"I can see that. It'll take a little time for him to feel at ease. Put him down."

Annette Hoskins' eyes searched the room. The muscles in her arms tensed visibly. However much she might have been won over by Timmie on her earlier visit, she seemed more than a little apprehensive now. Her precious little child, turned loose in the cage of this ape-boy—

"Put him down, Annette."

She nodded. The boy backed up against her, staring worriedly at the pair of eyes which were staring back at him from the next room.

"Come out here, Timmie," Miss Fellowes said. "This is your new friend, Jerry. Jerry wants very much to meet you. Don't be afraid."

Slowly Timmie stepped into the room. Jerry squirmed. Hoskins bent to disengage Jerry's fingers from his mother's skirt. In a stage whisper he said, "Step back, Annette. For God's sake, give the children a chance."

The youngsters faced one another, standing virtually nose to nose. Although Jerry was almost certainly some months younger than Timmie, nevertheless he was an inch taller. And in the presence of Jerry's straightness and his high-held well-proportioned head, Timmie's grotesqueries of appearance were suddenly almost as pronounced in Miss Fellowes' eyes as they had been in the earliest days.

Miss Fellowes' lips quivered.

There was a long silent awkward moment of mutual staring. It was the little Neanderthal who spoke first, finally, in childish treble.

"My name is Timmie."

And he thrust his face suddenly forward as though to inspect the other's features more closely.

Startled, Jerry responded with a vigorous shove that sent Timmie tumbling. Both began crying loudly, and Mrs. Hoskins snatched up her child, while Miss Fellowes, flushed with repressed anger, lifted Timmie quickly and comforted him. The little animal! she thought vehemently. The vicious little beast!

But she knew that she was being much too harsh. Timmie had startled Jerry; Jerry had defended himself in the only way he knew. Nothing out of the ordinary had taken place. Something like this was exactly what they should have expected at the outset, Miss Fellowes told herself.

"Well," Hoskins said. "Well!"

Annette Hoskins said, "I knew this wasn't a good idea. They just instinctively don't like each other."

"It isn't instinctive," Miss Fellowes said firmly.

"No," Hoskins said. "It's not instinctive at all. Any more than when any two children dislike each other on first sight. Put Jerry down and let him get used to the situation."

"What if that cave-boy hits Jerry back?"

"It won't be at all amazing if he does," said Hoskins. "But he can take care of himself. And if he can't, it's time he started learning how. We just have to let him get accustomed to this by himself."

Annette Hoskins still looked uncertain.

"In fact," her husband went on, "I think the best thing is for you and me to leave. If there are any problems, Miss Fellowes will know how to handle them. And after an hour or so she can bring Jerry to my office and I'll have him taken home."

## [42]

It was a long hour. Timmie retreated to the far end of the room and glowered malevolently at Jerry as though trying to eradicate him from the universe by the intensity of his glare alone. Evidently he had decided not to take refuge in the back room as he often did when he felt troubled, perhaps thinking that it was unwise to withdraw and thereby concede the front section of his domain to the enemy by default.

As for Jerry, he huddled miserably at the opposite end of the room, crying for his mother. He looked so unhappy that Miss Fellowes, though aware that she risked upsetting Timmie even further, went to him and tried to reassure him that his mother was nearby, that he hadn't been abandoned at all, that he'd be seeing her again in just a short while.

"Want her *now!*" Jerry said.

(You probably think you've been left here to live in this room forever, don't you, child? Just you and Timmie, locked up in this little dollhouse with each other. And you hate the idea. Of course you do. Just as Timmie must.)

"Home!" Jerry said. "Now!"

"You'll be going home soon, Jerry," she told the boy. "This is only a little visit."

He struck out at her with his clenched fists.

"No," Miss Fellowes said, catching him deftly by his belt and holding him at arm's length while he flailed unsuccessfully at her. "No, Jerry! No, don't hit. —How would you like a lollipop, Jerry?"

"No! No! No!"

Miss Fellowes laughed. "I think you would, though. You stay right where you are and I'll get one for you."

She unlocked the hidden lollipop cache—Timmie had already proved he couldn't be trusted to keep away from the supply she kept on hand—and pulled out a huge spherical green one, almost too big to fit in the boy's mouth.

Jerry's eyes went wide and he stopped wailing instantly.

"I thought so," Miss Fellowes said, with a grin. She handed the lollipop to him, and he stuck it into his mouth with no difficulty at all.

From behind her Timmie made a low growling sound.

"Yes, I know, you want one, too. I haven't forgotten about you, Timmie."

She pulled a second one out, orange this time, and held it out toward him. Timmie grabbed at it with the ferocity of a caged animal, pulling it from her hand.

Miss Fellowes gave him a troubled look. She hadn't expected this visit to go serenely; but this was disturbing, these signs of reversion to savagery in Timmie.

Savagery? No, she thought. That was too harsh an interpretation of Timmie's behavior. It had been Jerry who struck the first blow, Miss Fellowes reminded herself. Timmie had come over and introduced himself to Jerry in a polite, civilized way, after all. And Jerry had pushed him. Quite probably Timmie reasoned that savage growls and snarls were the only sensible response to that sort of behavior.

The children glared at each other now over their lollipops across the whole width of the room.

The first hour wasn't going to be a lot of fun for anyone, Miss Fellowes realized.

But this sort of thing was nothing new to her, and not all that intimidating. She had presided over many a pitched battle between angered children—and had seen many a truce come into being eventually, and then friendships. Patience was the answer. In dealing with children, it almost always was. Problems like this had a way of solving themselves, given time.

"What about blocks?" she asked them. "Timmie, would you like to play with your blocks?"

Timmie gave her a dark, sullen look—more or less an acquiescent one, she decided, though she wasn't altogether confident she was right about that.

"Good," she said. She went into the other room and brought the blocks out—state-of-the-art stuff, smoothly machined cubes that clicked together elegantly and made a soft chiming sound when you brought the similarly-colored faces into contact. Miss Fellowes laid them out in the middle of the floor. —"And is it all right if Jerry plays with your blocks too, Timmie?"

Timmie made a grumbling sound.

"It *is* all right," she said. "Good boy! I knew you wouldn't mind. —Come on over here, Jerry. Timmie's going to let you play with his blocks."

Hesitantly Jerry approached. Timmie was down on the floor already, picking through the blocks for the ones he considered his favorites. Jerry watched in a gingerly way from a comfortable distance. Miss Fellowes came up behind him and gently but forcefully nudged him downward toward the blocks.

"Play with the blocks, Jerry. Go ahead. It's all right. Timmie doesn't mind."

He looked back and up at her, very doubtfully.

Then he cautiously selected a block. Timmie made a louder grumbling noise, but stayed where he was when Miss Fellowes shot him a swift warning look. Jerry took another block. Another. Timmie snatched up two of them, and moved them around in back of himself. Jerry took a third block.

In hardly any time at all the pile of blocks had been divided roughly in half, and Timmie was playing with one group of them on one side of the room and Jerry was studiously playing with the others at the opposite end, close to the door. The two children ignored each other as thoroughly as though they had been on two different planets. There was no contact at all between them, not even a furtive glance.

But at least they were playing with the same set of blocks, Miss Fellowes thought. It was a start.

She dropped back out of their way and let them play. From time to time she looked over at them to see whether either of them had begun to think of crossing the invisible wall that they had drawn across the middle of the room. But no: they were still lost in their individual spheres of play. They were working so hard at paying no attention to each other that it must have been tiring for them. Timmie had matched all his blocks and had arranged them in a ragged square, with its ends open at two corners. Jerry had put his blocks together in a much more intricate way, forming them into a perfect pyramid after making some minor trial-and-error adjustments.

Miss Fellowes found herself a little disheartened by the greater complexity of Jerry's arrangement of the blocks. Another example of the superiority of the *Homo sapiens sapiens* mind over that of *Homo sapiens neanderthalensis*? Maybe so. But it was just as plausible to think that Jerry had a set of blocks just like these at home, and that his father—the scientist, the physicist—had taught him all about piling them up in a neat little pyramid like that. Poor fatherless Timmie had had no such advantage; Miss Fellowes had made no attempt to give Timmie instruction in the art of piling up blocks. That had never occurred to her at all. She had been pleased enough that Timmie had been able to figure out how to play with the blocks on his own, almost as if by instinct. Now, feeling abashed by Timmie's relative lack of intellectual prowess, she wanted to think that Dr. Hoskins must have devoted great effort to expanding Jerry's mastery of block-pile construction. She certainly hoped he had.

"Would you boys like some milk?" Miss Fellowes asked, as the hour was coming to its end.

They did; but they were no more social than before when she served it out. Each retreated to his corner of the room to drink it.

Miss Fellowes noted with displeasure how much more dextrous Jerry was in handling his glass than Timmie.

*Stop that,* she ordered herself sternly. *Jerry's had all sorts of opportunities to learn things that Timmie never had. He didn't just drop into this world at age four without knowing how to do anything that modern people do.*

Even so, she couldn't quite succeed in fighting off a mood of mild dejection when she took Jerry back to Hoskins' office at the end of the first hour.

"Well, how did it go?" Hoskins asked.

"We made a beginning," Miss Fellowes said. "Only a beginning, but you have to start somewhere."

"No more hitting?"

"No." She told him about the blocks, leaving out any description of Jerry's apparent superiority as an architect. "They tolerated each other. That's the best way I can put it. Timmie stayed in one zone and Jerry in the other. It's going to take some time for them to warm up to one another."

"Yes, I'm sure that's true," Hoskins said. He sounded utterly indifferent, almost impatient to have her leave. She noted that he hadn't said a word to his own son since the boy had entered the office.

There were papers strewn all over Hoskins' desk: printouts, strips of visual tape, a stack of data wheels.

"A new experiment?" Miss Fellowes ventured.

"Yes, as a matter of fact. Or rather, a breakthrough of sorts in an older one. We're closing in on short-range scooping. We're on the verge of attaining intertemporal detection at extremely close range."

"Intertemp—"

"Narrowing down the limits of our reach. We're well within the ten-thousand-year envelope now, and the way it looks we can achieve a quantitative improvement of several magnitudes on our next pass through."

Miss Fellowes, her mind full of Timmie and Jerry, Jerry and Timmie, looked at him blankly.

Hoskins went blithely on. "By which I mean we anticipate attaining the ability to reach back in time within a thousand years—or even less, Miss Fellowes! And there's more. We're stepping up our mass limitations, too. The old forty-kilogram limit is about to become a thing of the past. We think eighty, even one hundred kilograms is well within possibility now."

"I'm very happy for you, Dr. Hoskins." She said it with no warmth whatsoever in her voice, but Hoskins didn't appear to observe that.

"Yes. Thank you, Miss Fellowes." Hoskins glanced at his son as though noticing him for the first time, and gathered him in against him with a casual sweep of his arm. —"Well, we'll have to bring Jerry back here in another couple of days and see if things work out a little better between them the next time, eh, Miss Fellowes?"

"Yes. Yes, of course."

She hesitated.

"Is there anything else?" Hoskins asked.

Yes, there was. She wanted to tell him how grateful to him she was for having allowed Jerry to come to visit Timmie at all. Even though it hadn't gone particularly well. She knew that the initial tensions would ebb, that fears and uncertainties would vanish over the course of time, that the boys would eventually become friends. Timmie's willingness to share the blocks, however tepid it had been, told her that much. And a friend was what Timmie needed more than anything. As time went along, Jerry's presence would cause wonderful changes in Timmie: opening him up, allowing him to reach out to someone who was his peer, enabling him to become the boy he was meant to be. Yes. At last Timmie would be able to become Timmie. He couldn't do that while living alone, no matter how lovingly she cared for him. Miss Fellowes was grateful indeed to Hoskins, almost maudlinly grateful, for having brought Jerry to him.

But she couldn't bring herself to tell Hoskins that. She searched for ways to thank him, but his very formality, his remoteness, his preoccupation with the printouts and data wheels of this new experiment of his, served as a chilly rebuff. Perhaps he still remembered that time when they had had lunch together—when she had spoken of him as though he were Timmie's father, in every sense but the biological, and said that he was being cruel by denying Timmie a companion, that he *owed* it to the boy. So he had brought in his own real son. Perhaps bringing Jerry here had been an attempt, after all, to prove himself both a kind father to Timmie and, also, not his father at all. Both at the same time! And with all manner of buried resentments involved.

So all she could say was, "I'm very pleased you've allowed your boy to come here. Thank you. Thank you very much, Dr. Hoskins."

And all he could say was, "That's all right. Don't mention it, Miss Fellowes."

[43]

It became a settled routine. Jerry returned three days later, and four days after that. The second visit lasted as long as the first; the third one was extended to two hours, and that remained the rule thereafter.

There was no repetition of the staring and shoving of the first visit. The two boys eyed each other a little fretfully when Jerry—without either of his parents—was brought through the Stasis barrier the second time; but Miss Fellowes quickly said, "Here's your friend Jerry again, Timmie," and Timmie nodded in acknowledgment of Jerry's presence without any show of hostility. He was starting to accept Jerry as a fact of life in the bubble, like the visits of the anthropologists or the tests administered by Dr. Jacobs.

"Say hello, Timmie."

"Hello."

"Jerry?"

"Hello, Timmie."

"Now you say, 'Hello, Jerry,' why don't you, Timmie?"

A pause. "Hello, Jerry."

"Hello, Timmie."

"Hello, Jerry."

"Hello, Timmie."

"Hello, Jerry—"

They wouldn't stop. It had become a game. They were both laughing. Miss Fellowes felt relief flooding her spirit. Children who could be silly together were children who weren't likely to start punching each other the moment she turned her back on them. Children who made each other laugh weren't going to hate each other.

"Hello, Timmie."

"Hello, Jerry."

"Hello—"

And another thing. Jerry didn't seem to be having any trouble understanding what Timmie was saying. Not that "Hello, Jerry" was a particularly complicated series of sounds, but plenty of adult visitors to the dollhouse had failed completely to comprehend even a syllable of Timmie's speech. Jerry didn't have an adult's preconceptions about enunciation and pronunciation, though. Timmie's thick-tongued manner of speaking apparently held no mysteries for him.

"Would you like to play with the blocks again?" Miss Fellowes asked.

Enthusiastic nods. She brought them in from the other room and dumped them on the floor.

Quickly the boys divided them once again into approximately equal heaps. Each went swiftly to work on his own heap. But this time there was no retreating to opposite ends of the room. They worked side by side, in silence, neither one paying any great attention to what the other was doing but having no problem with the other one's proximity.

Good. Good.

What wasn't so good was the fact that the division of the blocks hadn't been quite as equal as Miss Fellowes had thought at first glance. Jerry had appropriated considerably more than half of them— close to two thirds, as a matter of fact. He was rapidly arranging them into the pyramid shape again, carrying out the construction more easily now that he had a greater supply of building material.

As for Timmie, he was working on some kind of X-shaped pattern, but he didn't quite have enough blocks to make his design turn out properly. Miss Fellowes saw him glance thoughtfully at Jerry's pile of blocks, and got herself ready to intervene in case a squabble began. But Timmie didn't actually reach across to help himself to any of Jerry's blocks; he contented himself simply with staring at them.

A laudable sign of self-restraint? The politeness of the well-bred child toward his guest?

Or was there something more worrisome in Timmie's reluctance to take blocks away from Jerry? One thing that Timmie *wasn't* was well-bred. Miss Fellowes had no illusions about that. She had trained him with all her skill and diligence to be courteous and deferential; but nevertheless it was folly to believe that Timmie was any model of deportment. What he was was the child of a primitive society where manners as they were understood today were probably unknown, and after being taken from his own tribe he had been compelled to live in isolation in the Stasis bubble, which had given him no opportunity to develop many of the social traits that ordinary children had picked up by the time they were his age. And ordinary children his age weren't all that polite either.

If Timmie wasn't reaching out to take the blocks from Jerry—*his* blocks, after all—that he wanted, the reason probably wasn't that he was such a nice little boy, but simply that he was intimidated by Jerry. Afraid to reach out and help himself to the blocks the way any boy might be expected to do.

Had that single shove at the first visit so cowed Timmie?

Or was it something else—something deeper, something darker, something lost in the forgotten history of the human race's earliest days?

## [44]

Early one evening after Timmie had gone to his room, the telephone rang and the switchboard voice said, "Miss Fellowes, I have a call for you from Bruce Mannheim."

She raised her eyebrows. Mannheim calling *her*? Nobody called her here, not ever. By her own choice she lived almost completely cut off from the outside world, lest she be bothered by the media, by curious-minded people of all sorts, by crackpots and fanatics, and by people like—Bruce Mannheim. But here he was on the telephone. How had he managed to get through to her behind Hoskins' back? He must be calling with Hoskins' knowledge and permission, she decided.

"Yes, Mr. Mannheim. How are you?"

"Fine, Miss Fellowes, just fine. —Dr. Hoskins tells me that Timmie finally has the playmate he needs."

"So he does. Dr. Hoskins' own son, as a matter of fact."

"Yes. I know that. We all think it was perfectly splendid of Dr. Hoskins to do that. —And how is everything working out, would you say?"

Miss Fellowes hesitated. "Quite well, actually."

"The boys are getting along with each other?"

"Of course they are. There was the usual little edginess at first—more on Jerry's part than Timmie's, I have to say; Timmie took to Jerry very readily, even though he'd never seen a child his own age of our kind before."

"But Jerry? Confronted with a Neanderthal, he didn't react so well?"

"I don't know whether Timmie's being a Neanderthal had anything to do with it, Mr. Mannheim. He was just edgy, that's all. A straight child-child reaction, without any special anthropological undertones, is what I'd call it. Push came to shove—it could have happened between any two. But it's not like that now. They're very peaceful with each other."

"Glad to hear it," Mannheim said. "And Timmie is thriving?"

"He's doing very well, yes."

There was a pause. She hoped the children's advocate wasn't leading up to telling her that he had wangled permission to pay another call on the dollhouse so that he could check up on Timmie's new friendship. Timmie didn't need any more visitors than he already had; and Miss Fellowes was wary of having an outsider like Mannheim on hand while Timmie and Jerry were together. Their developing relationship, while it was just as peaceful as she had told Mannheim it was, had a subtext of potential volatility that was all too likely to turn into something troublesome in the presence of a stranger.

But Mannheim wasn't planning to visit, it seemed. He said, after a moment, "I just want to tell you, Miss Fellows, how pleased we all are that a capable nurse like you is looking after Timmie."

"That's very kind of you."

"The boy's been put through a very frightening experience and he's made a wonderful adaptation—so far. Much of the credit for that must go to you."

(What did he mean, *so far?*)

—"We'd much rather have preferred it, of course, that Timmie had been left to live out his natural life among his own people," Mannheim continued. "But since that option wasn't allowed him, it's good to know that a devoted, dedicated woman like you has been placed in charge of him, that you've been giving him the kind of care you have ever since he came to our era. You've worked wonders. I have no other word for it."

"That's very kind of you," Miss Fellowes said again, more lamely than before. She had never cared much for praise; and Mannheim was laying it on pretty thickly.

"And Dr. Levien feels the same way that I do."

"Ah," said Miss Fellowes. "Yes." And, coolly, stiffly: "That's—very good to hear."

"I'd like to give you my number," Mannheim said.

(Why?)

"I can always reach you through Dr. Hoskins," Miss Fellowes replied.

"Yes, of course. But a time might come when you'd want to reach me more directly."

(Why? Why? What is this all about?)

"Well, perhaps—"

"I feel that you and I are natural allies in this enterprise, Miss Fellowes. The one thing we have at heart, above all else, is Timmie's welfare. However we may feel about child-care techniques, about politics, about anything in the world, we both are concerned with Timmie. Deeply so. And therefore if you need to talk to me about Timmie's welfare, if any changes take place in the setup at Stasis Technologies that might have an unfavorable impact on Timmie's existence there—"

(Ah. You want me to be a spy for you.)

"I'm sure that everything's going to keep on going very smoothly, Mr. Mannheim."

"Of course it will. Of course. But all the same—"

He gave her the number. She wrote it down, not knowing why.

Just in case, Miss Fellowes told herself.

In case of what?

## [45]

"Is Jerry coming again today, Miss Fellowes?" Timmie asked.

"Tomorrow."

The boy's disappointment was all too obvious. His round face dissolved into wrinkles, his jutting brow knotted in a frown. "Why not today?"

"Today isn't Jerry's day, Timmie. Jerry has—a place to go today."

"What place?"

"A place," she said, being deliberately vague. How could she describe kindergarten to him? What would Timmie think, knowing that other children, many of them, came together to play games, to chase each other in laughter around a schoolyard, to daub pieces of paper with gloriously gooey fingerpaints. "Jerry'll be here tomorrow."

"I wish he could come every day."

"So do I," Miss Fellowes said.

(But do I? Really?)

## [46]

The problem was not that Timmie had a friend, but that the friend was becoming too confident, too aggressive, as time went along. Jerry had overcome his initial timidity entirely by now, and he was very much the dominant member of the pair.

He had been bigger than Timmie to start with, and he seemed to be growing faster now. The height differential was close to an inch and a half by this time, and Jerry was heavier than Timmie as well. And quicker and stronger and—Miss Fellowes had trouble with this aspect of it—quite possibly more intelligent, too. Jerry seemed to figure out new toys much more swiftly than Timmie, and to find interesting things to do with them. And when she gave them paints or crayons or modeling clay to play with, Jerry quickly set to work creating designs and shapes, while Timmie simply made messes. Timmie appeared to have no artistic aptitude at all, not even the minimal skills one would expect from any reasonably intelligent child his age.

Of course, she argued, Jerry goes to kindergarten every day. He's learned all about how to use crayons and paints and clay there.

But Timmie had had them too, long before Jerry had first come here. He had never managed to master them, but that hadn't troubled Miss Fellowes at the time; she hadn't been comparing Timmie with any other children then, and she was making allowances for the blankness of his first few years.

Now she remembered what she had read in the books Dr. McIntyre had given her. About the total absence of any known examples of Neanderthal art. No cave paintings, no statuettes, no designs carved on walls.

*(What if they really were inferior? And that was why they died out when we came along.)*

Miss Fellowes didn't want to think about that.

Yet here was Jerry, swaggering in here now twice a week as if he owned the place. "Let's play with the blocks," he would say to Timmie. Or "let's paint" or "let's watch the whirloscreen." And Timmie would go along with it, never suggesting some preference of his own, always blandly following Jerry's agenda. Jerry had forced Timmie into a completely secondary role. The only thing that reconciled Miss Fellowes to the developing situation was that, despite difficulties, Timmie looked forward with more and more delight to the periodic appearances of his playfellow.

Jerry is all he has, she told herself mournfully.

And once, as she watched then, she thought: Hoskins' two children, one by his wife and one by Stasis.

Whereas she herself—

Heavens, she thought, putting her fists to her temples and feeling ashamed: I'm jealous!

# CHAPTER TEN

# Reaching

[47]

"M ISS FELLOWES," Timmie said, "when will I be starting to go to school?"

The question, coming out of nowhere, hit her with the force of a thunderbolt.

She looked down at those eager brown eyes turned up to hers and passed her hand softly through his thick, coarse hair, automatically picking through the rough tangles of it and trying to straighten them. Timmie's hair was always disheveled. Miss Fellowes cut it herself while he squirmed restlessly under the scissors. The idea of having a barber in here for Timmie displeased her; and in any case the very clumsiness of the cut she gave him served to mask the retreating fore part of his skull and the bulging hinder part.

Carefully Miss Fellowes said, "Where did you hear about school, Timmie?"

"Jerry goes to school."

(Of course. Where else would he have heard of it but from Jerry?)

"Jerry goes to kin-der-gar-ten." Timmie pronounced the long word slowly and with unusual precision. "That's only one of the places he goes. He goes to the store with his mother. He goes to the movies. The zoo. All kinds of places outside. —When can I go out-side, Miss Fellowes?"

A small pain centered in Miss Fellowes' heart.

It was inevitable, she knew, that Jerry would talk about the outside world with Timmie. They communicated freely and easily—two small boys who understood each other without difficulty. And Jerry, the emissary from the mysterious and forbidden world beyond the door of the Stasis bubble, would certainly want to tell Timmie all about it. There was no way of avoiding that.

But it was a world that Timmie could never enter.

Miss Fellowes said, with a studied gaiety that was her best attempt at distracting him from the anguish he must surely feel, "Why, whatever would you do out there, Timmie? Why would you want to go there? Do you know how cold it gets out there in the winter?"

"Cold?"

A blank look. He didn't know the word.

(But why would cold bother him, this boy who had learned how to walk in the snowfields of Ice Age Europe?)

"Cold is like the way it is in the refrigerator. You go outside and in a minute or two your nose begins to hurt from it, and your ears. But that's only in the winter. In the summer, outside gets very hot. It feels like an oven. Everyone sweats and complains about how hot it is outside. And then there's rain, too. Water falling down on you out of the sky, soaking your clothes, getting you all damp and nasty—"

It was a miserably cynical line of reasoning, and she knew it and felt dreadful about what she was trying to do. Telling a boy who could never go outside these few little rooms that the world out there held some minor physical discomforts was like telling a blind child that colors and shapes were boring, annoying distractions, that in fact, there was nothing very interesting worth seeing anyway.

But Timmie ignored her pitiful sophistries as though she hadn't said a thing.

"Jerry says that at school they can play all kinds of games that I don't have here. They have picture tapes and music. He says there are lots of children in the kin-der-gar-ten. He says—he says—" A moment of thought, then a triumphant upholding of both small hands with the fingers splayed apart. "He says this many."

Miss Fellowes said, "You have picture tapes."

"Just a few. Jerry says he sees more picture tapes in a day than I see all the time."

"We can get you more picture tapes. Very nice ones. And music tapes, too."

"Can you?"

"I'll get some this afternoon."

"Will you get me the Forty Thieves?"

"Is that a story Jerry heard in kindergarten?"

"There are these thieves in a cave, and these jars—" He paused. "Big jars. What are thieves?"

"Thieves are—people who take things that belong to other people."

"Oh."

"I can get you the Forty Thieves picture tape," Miss Fellowes told him. "It's a very famous story. And there are others like it. *Sinbad the Sailor*, who traveled everywhere in the world, who saw—everything." Her voice faltered for a moment. But Timmie hadn't picked up any depressing implications. "And *Gulliver's Travels*, I can get you that one. He went to a land of tiny people, and then afterward to a land of giants, and then—" Miss Fellowes faltered again. So many travelers, all these omnivorous devourers of experience! But maybe that was good: satisfy Timmie in his imprisonment with vicarious tales of far voyaging. He wouldn't be the first shut-in to revel in such narratives. "Then there's the story of *Odysseus*, who fought a war and spent ten years afterward trying to find his way home to his family." Again a pang. Her heart went out to the boy. Like *Gulliver*, like *Sinbad*, like *Odysseus*, Timmie too was a stranger in a strange land, and she could never forget that. Were all the great stories of the world about wanderers carried to strange places who were striving to reach their homes?

Timmie's eyes were glowing, though. "Will you get them right now? Will you?"

And so he was temporarily comforted.

## [48]

She ordered all the picture tapes of myth and fable that were in the catalog. They stacked up higher than Timmie in the playroom. On days when Jerry wasn't there he pored over them hour after hour.

How much he actually understood was hard to say. Certainly they were full of concepts, images, locales, that could make very little sense to him. But how much did any child of five or six understand of those stories? There was no way for an adult to enter a child's mind and know for sure. Miss Fellowes had loved those stories herself without fully understanding them when she was a child, though, and so had children before her for hundreds, even thousands of years; and whatever they might have lacked in detail-by-detail comprehension, all those children had made up for by using their own imaginations. So too was it with Timmie, she hoped.

After her early moments of uncertainty over Gulliver and Sinbad and Odysseus, she made no attempts to eliminate from his growing library of picture tapes anything that might stir some disturbing thoughts in him about his own plight. Children, she knew, were less easily disturbed than adults feared they were. And even an occasional nightmare wouldn't do any real harm. No child had ever died of fright while hearing the story of *Goldilocks and the Three Bears,* even though it was, on its most literal level, a horrifying tale. None of the slavering wolves and shambling bogeymen and terrible trolls of childhood fable had left any lasting scars. Children loved to hear about such things.

Was the bogeyman of myth—beetle-browed, shaggy, glowering—a vestige of the racial memory of the time when Neanderthals roamed Europe? Miss Fellowes had seen a reference to that theory in one of the books she had borrowed from Dr. McIntyre. Would Timmie be upset by the thought that he was a member of a tribe that had survived in folk tale as something to fear and loathe? No, no, she thought: it would never occur to him. Only overeducated adults would worry about such contingencies. Timmie would be as fascinated by bogeymen as any child, and would huddle under his coverlet in delicious terror, seeing shapes in the dark—and there wasn't a chance in a billion that he would draw any dire conclusions about his own genetic status from those scary stories.

So the tapes came flooding in, and the boy watched them one after another after another: as though a dam had been breached and the whole glorious river of the human imagination was rushing into Timmie's soul. Theseus and the Minotaur, Perseus and the Gorgon, King Midas and his golden touch, the Pied Piper of Hamelin, the labors of Hercules, Bellerophon and the Chimaera, Alice through the Looking-Glass, Jack and the beanstalk, Aladdin and the magic lamp, the Fisherman and the Genie, Gulliver among the Lilliputians and the Houyhnhnms, the adventures of Odin and Thor, the battle between Osiris and Set, the wanderings of Odysseus, the voyage of Captain Nemo—there was no end of it, and Timmie devoured it all. Did it all get muddled in his mind? Was he able to tell one tale from another, or remember any of them an hour later? Miss Fellowes didn't know, and didn't try to find out. For the moment, she was concerned only with allowing him to immerse himself in this tremendous torrent of story—of filling his mind with it—of reaching out toward the magical world of myth, since the real world of houses and airplanes and highways and people must forever remain beyond his grasp.

When he tired of watching tapes, she read to him out of ordinary books. The tales were the same; but now he created the pictures in his own mind as she read the words.

There had to be some impact. More than once she heard him telling some wildly garbled version of one of his picture tapes to Jerry—Sinbad traveling by submarine, or Hercules tied down by Lilliputians—and Jerry would listen solemnly, enjoying the story as much as Timmie enjoyed telling it.

Miss Fellowes made sure that everything the boy said was being recorded. It was vital evidence of his intelligence. Let anyone who imagined that the Neanderthals had been mere bestial shaggy half-men listen to Timmie retelling the story of Theseus in the Labyrinth! Even if he did seem to think that the Minotaur was the hero of the story.

## [49]

But then there were the dreams. He was having them more often, now that the world outside the bubble was becoming a reality in his mind.

It was always the same dream, so far as she could tell—always about the outside. Timmie tried haltingly to describe it to Miss Fellowes. In his dreams he invariably found himself outside, in that big empty place about which he had told her so often. It was no longer empty in the newer dreams. Now there were children in it, and queer indescribable objects half-digested in his thought out of bookish descriptions half-understood, or out of distant Neanderthal memories half-recalled.

But the children ignored him and the objects eluded him when he tried to touch them. Though he was in the world, he was never part of it. He wandered through the big empty place of his dreams in a solitude just as absolute as that of his own room. And would wake up crying more often than not.

Miss Fellowes wasn't always there to hear him when he cried out in the night. She had begun sleeping three or four nights a week in the apartment elsewhere on the grounds that Hoskins had offered her long ago. It seemed wise to begin weaning Timmie from his dependence on her perpetual presence. The first few nights she tried it, she felt so guilty over abandoning him that she could scarcely sleep; but

Timmie said nothing in the morning about her absence. Perhaps he expected to be left on his own, sooner or later. She allowed herself to feel more comfortable about sleeping away from the dollhouse, after a time. She realized that Timmie wasn't the only one being weaned from a dependence.

She took elaborate notes every morning about his dreams and tried to regard them as nothing more than useful material for the psychological study of Timmie's mind that would ultimately be one of the most valuable products of this experiment. But there were nights when she was alone in her room when she cried, too.

### [50]

One day as Miss Fellowes was reading to him—the book was *Tales from the Arabian Nights,* one of his special favorites—Timmie put his hand under her chin and lifted it gently so that her eyes left the book and met his.

He said, "Every time you read me that story it's exactly the same. How do you always know how to say it the same way, Miss Fellowes?"

"Why, I'm reading it right from this page!"

"Yes, I know. But what does that mean, *reading?*"

"Why—why—" The question was so basic that she scarcely knew at first how to tackle it. Ordinarily, when children learned to read, they seemed somehow intuitively to divine the nature of the process by themselves, and then went on to the next step of learning the meaning of the coded symbols on the page. But Timmie's ignorance seemed to be more deeply rooted than that of the usual four-or-five-year-old who was just beginning to discover that there was such a thing as *reading* which perhaps he or she might actually be able someday to master. The essential concept was foreign to him.

She said, "You know how, in your picture books—not the tapes, the *books*—there are marks along the bottoms of the pages?"

"Yes," he said. "Words."

"The book I'm reading is all words. No pictures, just words. These marks are the words. I look at the marks and I hear words in my mind. That's what reading is—turning the marks on the page into words."

"Let me see."

She handed him the book. He swung it around sideways and then upside down. Miss Fellowes laughed and turned it right side up again.

"The marks only make sense when you look at them this way," she said.

He nodded. He bent low over the page, so low that the words couldn't possibly have been in focus, and stared long and curiously. Then he backed off a few inches, until the text was legible. Experimentally he turned the book sideways again. Miss Fellowes said nothing this time. He turned it back the right way.

"Some of these marks are the same," he said, after a very long time.

"Yes. Yes." She laughed with pleasure at this sign of shrewdness. "So they are, Timmie!"

"But how do you know which marks mean what word?"

"You have to learn."

"There are so many words, though! How could anyone learn all that many marks?"

"Little marks are used to make the big marks. The big marks are the words; the little marks are called letters. And actually there aren't that many little marks," she said. "Only twenty-six." She held up her hand and flashed her fingers five times, and then one finger more. "All the words are made up out of those few little letter-marks, arranged in different ways."

"Show me."

"Here. Look." She pointed to *Sinbad* on the page. "Do you see these six little marks here, between the two blank spaces? Those are the marks that mean *Sinbad*. This one is the 's' sound. This is the 'i' and this is the 'n'." She spoke the letters phonetically instead of pronouncing their names. "You read them one by one and you put all the sounds together—*Ess-ih-nnn-bbb-aaah-ddd. Sinbad.*"

Did the boy even begin to understand?

"Sinbad," Timmie said softly, and traced the name on the page with his fingertip.

"And this word is *ship*. You see, it begins with the same little mark as *Sinbad*? Sssssss. The name of that mark is 's.' This time she pronounced it, "ess". "And this one is 'i,' from *Sinbad*, only here it is in *ship*, over here."

He stared at the page. He looked lost.

"I'll show you all the marks," she offered. "Would you like that?"

"It would be a nice game, yes."

"Then get me a piece of paper, and a crayon. And get one for yourself, too."

He settled down beside her. She drew an *a*, a *b*, a *c*, and right on through the alphabet, in two long columns. Timmie, clutching the crayon clumsily in his fist, drew something that he must have thought was an imitation of her *a,* but it had long wobbly legs that wandered all over the page and left no room for any other letters.

"Now," she said, "let's look at the first mark—"

To her shame, it had never occurred to her before this that it might actually be possible for him to learn to read. For all the boy's vast hunger for picture books and picture tapes, this was the first time that he had shown any real interest in the printed symbols that accompanied them. Something else that Jerry had inspired in him? She made a mental note to ask Jerry, the next time he was here, whether he had begun to learn how to read. But in any event Miss Fellowes had simply dismissed *a priori* the idea that Timmie someday might.

Racial prejudice, she realized. Even now, after having lived with him for so long, having seen his mind grow and flower and develop, she still thought of him on some level as not quite human. Or at least too primitive, too backward, to master so sophisticated a skill as reading.

And while she was showing him the letters, pointing them out on her chart and pronouncing them and teaching him how in his clumsy way to draw them himself, she still did not seriously believe that he could ever put any of that to use.

She went on not believing it until the very moment that he read a book to her.

It was many weeks later. He was sitting in her lap, holding one of his books, turning the pages, looking at the pictures—or so she assumed.

And suddenly he ran his fingertip along a line of type and said aloud, haltingly but with stubborn determination, "The dog began—to chase—the cat."

Miss Fellowes was feeling drowsy and was barely paying attention. "What did you say, Timmie?"

"The cat—ran up—the tree."

"That wasn't what you said before."

"No. Before I said, 'The dog began to chase the cat.' Just like it says here."

"What? What?" Miss Fellowes' eyes were wide open now. She glanced down at the slim book that the child in her lap was holding.

The caption on the left-hand page said: *The dog began to chase the cat.*

And the caption on the facing page was: *The cat ran up the tree.*

He was following the printing in the book, word by word. He was reading to her!

In amazement Miss Fellowes got to her feet so quickly that the boy went tumbling to the floor. He seemed to think it was some new game, and looked up at her, grinning. But she pulled him quickly to his feet and set him upright.

"How long have you been able to read?"

He shrugged. "Always?"

"No—really."

"I don't know. I looked at the marks and heard the words, the way you said."

"Here. Read to me from this one." Miss Fellowes snatched up a book at random from his heap and opened it to its center pages. He took it and studied it, frowning in that intense way that emphasized the great bony shelf that was his brow. His tongue came forth and wandered along his lips.

Slowly, painfully, he said, "Then the—tra-in—blew its—whuh—its whuh—whuh-is—its whuh-is—"

"Its whistle!" she finished for him. "You can read, Timmie! You can actually read!"

Excited nearly to frenzy, she swung him up into her arms and danced him around the room while he stared at her in huge-eyed amazement.

"You can read! You can read!"

(Ape-boy, was he? Cave-boy? Some lesser form of human life? *The cat ran up the tree. The train blew its whistle.* Show me the chimp that can read those lines! Show me the gorilla that can! *The train blew its whistle.* Oh, Timmie, Timmie—)

"Miss Fellowes?" he said, sounding a little startled, as she swung him wildly around.

She laughed and put him down.

This was a breakthrough that she had to share. The answer to Timmie's unhappiness was in her hand. Picture tapes might keep him amused for a time, but he was bound to outgrow them. Now, though, as he grew older, he would have access to the full, rich world of books. If Timmie couldn't leave the Stasis bubble to enter the world, the world could be brought into these three rooms to Timmie—the whole world in books. He must be educated to his full capacity. That much was owed to him.

"You stay here with your books," she told him. "I'll be back in a little while. I have to see Dr. Hoskins."

She made her way along the catwalks and through the tortuous passageways that led out of the Stasis zone, and into the executive area. Hoskins' receptionist looked up in surprise as Miss Fellowes came bursting into the anteroom of Hoskins' office.

"Is Dr. Hoskins here?"

"Miss Fellowes! Dr. Hoskins isn't expecting—"

"Yes, I know that. But I want to see him."

"Is there some problem?"

Miss Fellowes shook her head. "News. Exciting news. Please, just tell him I'm here."

The receptionist pressed a button. "Miss Fellowes to see you, Dr. Hoskins. She has no appointment."

(Since when do I need—?)

There was an uncomfortable pause. Miss Fellowes wondered if she was going to have to make a scene in order to be admitted to Hoskins' presence. Whatever he might be doing in there, it couldn't be as important as what she had to tell him.

Hoskins' voice out of the intercom said, "Tell her to come in."

The door rolled open. Hoskins rose from behind the desk with its GERALD A. HOSKINS, PH.D. nameplate to greet her.

He looked flushed and excited himself, as though his mood was precisely analogous to hers: a kind of triumph and glory. "So you've heard?" he said at once. "No, of course, you couldn't have. We've done it. We've actually done it."

"Done what?"

"We have intertemporal detection at close range."

He was so full of his own success that for a moment Miss Fellowes allowed it to shove her own spectacular news into the background.

"You can reach historical times, you mean?" she said.

"That's exactly what I mean. We have a fix on a fourteenth-century individual right now. Imagine. *Imagine!* We're ready to launch Project Middle Ages. Oh, Miss Fellowes, if you could only know how glad I'll be to shift from the eternal concentration on the Mesozoic—to get away from all these trilobites and rock samples and bits and pieces of ferns and things—to send the paleontologists home and bring some historians in here at last—" He stopped in midflow. —"But there's something you want to tell me, isn't there? And here I am, running on and on, without giving you a chance to speak. Well, go ahead. Go ahead, Miss Fellowes! You find me in a very fine mood, indeed. Anything you want, just ask for it."

Miss Fellowes smiled. "I'm glad to hear it. Because I wonder if we can start bringing in tutors for Timmie."

"Tutors?"

"To give him instruction. I can teach him only so much, and then I ought to step aside in favor of someone who has the proper training for it."

"Instruction? In what?"

"Well, in everything. History, geography, science, arithmetic, grammar, the whole elementary school curriculum. We have to set up a kind of school in here for Timmie. So that he'll be able to learn all that he needs to know."

Hoskins stared at her as though she were speaking some alien language.

"You want to teach him long division? The story of the Pilgrims? The history of the American Revolution?"

"Why not?"

"We can try to teach him, yes. And trigonometry and calculus, too, if you like. But how much can he learn, Miss Fellowes? He's a great little boy, no question of it. But we must never lose sight of the fact that he's only a Neanderthal."

"Only?"

"They were a people of very limited intellectual capacity, according to all the—"

"He already knows how to read, Dr. Hoskins."

Hoskins' jaw sagged open.

"What?"

"*The cat ran up the tree.* He read it to me right off the page. *The train blew its whistle.* I picked the book and showed him the page and he read me the words."

"He can read?" said Hoskins in wonder. "Really?"

"I showed him how the letters were shaped, and how they were put together in words. And he did the rest. He's learned it in an astonishingly short span of time. I can't wait for Dr. McIntyre and the rest of the crew to find out about it. So much for the very limited intellectual capacity of the Neanderthals, eh, Dr. Hoskins? He can read a storybook. And as time goes along you'll see him reading books without any pictures at all, reading newspapers, magazines, textbooks—"

Hoskins sat there, seemingly suddenly depressed. "I don't know, Miss Fellowes."

She said, "You just told me that anything I wanted—"

"I know, and I shouldn't have said that."

"A tutor for Timmie? Is that such a big expense?"

"It isn't the expense I'm concerned with," said Hoskins. "And it's a wonderful thing that Timmie can read. Astonishing. I mean that. I want to see a demonstration of it right away. But you talk about setting up a school for him. You talk about all the things he'll learn as time goes along. —Miss Fellowes, there isn't much more time."

She blinked. "There isn't?"

"I'm sure you must be aware that we aren't able to maintain the Timmie experiment indefinitely."

A surge of horror swept through her. She felt as though the floor had turned to quicksand beneath her feet.

What did he mean? Miss Fellowes wasn't sure that she understood. *We aren't able to maintain the Timmie experiment indefinitely.* What? What?

With an agonizing flash of recollection, she recalled Professor Adamewski and his mineral specimen that was taken away after two weeks because the Stasis facility that contained it had to be cleared for the next experiment.

"You're going to send him back?" she said in a tiny voice.

"I'm afraid so."

"But you're talking about a boy, Dr. Hoskins. Not about a rock."

Uneasily Hoskins said, "Even so. He can't be given undue importance, you know. We've learned just about as much from him as we're likely to. He doesn't remember anything about his life in the Neanderthal era that's of any real scientific value. The anthropologists can't make much sense out of what he says, and the questions they've put to him with you as the interpreter haven't yielded a lot of worthwhile data, and so—"

"I don't believe this," Miss Fellowes said numbly.

"Please, Miss Fellowes. It's not going to happen today, you know. But there's no escaping the necessity of it." He indicated the research materials on his desk. "Now that we expect to be bringing back individuals out of historical time, we'll need Stasis space—all we can get."

She couldn't grasp it.

"But you can't. Timmie—Timmie—"

"Please don't get so upset, Miss Fellowes."

"The world's only living Neanderthal, and you're talking about sending him *back*?"

"As I've said. We've learned all we can. Now we have to move along."

"No."

"Miss Fellowes, please. *Please*. I know you're deeply attached to the boy. And who can blame you? He's a terrific kid. And you've lived with him day and night for a long time now. But you're a professional, Miss Fellowes. You understand that the children under your care constantly come and go, that you can't hope to keep them forever. This is nothing new. —Besides, Timmie isn't going to go right away; perhaps not for months. Meanwhile, if you want a tutor for him, yes, yes, of course, we'll do whatever we can."

She was still staring at him.

"Let me get you something, Miss Fellowes."

"No," she whispered. "I don't need anything."

She was trembling. She rose and stumbled across the room in a kind of nightmare and waited for the door to open, and walked through the antechamber without looking either to the right or to the left.

Send him back?

Send him *back*?

Were they out of their minds? He wasn't a Neanderthal any more, except on the outside. He was a gentle good-natured little boy who wore green overalls and liked to look at picture tapes and books that told tales out of the *Arabian Nights*. A boy who tidied up his room at the end of the day. A boy who could use a knife and a fork and a spoon. A boy who could *read*.

And they were going to send him back to the Ice Age and let him shift for himself in some Godforsaken tundra?

They couldn't mean it. He didn't stand a chance, back in the world he had come from. He was no longer fitted for it. He no longer had any of the skills that a Neanderthal needed to have, and in their place he had acquired a great many new skills that were absolutely worthless in the Neanderthal world.

He would die there, she thought.

No.

Timmie, Miss Fellowes told herself with all the ferocity that there was in her soul, you will *not* die. You will *not*.

[51]

Now she knew why Bruce Mannheim had given her his telephone number. She hadn't understood it at the time, but obviously Mannheim had been thinking ahead. Something was going to come up that would jeopardize Timmie. He had seen it, and she hadn't. She had simply blinded herself to the possibility. She had carefully ignored every obvious clue that pointed to the blunt realities Hoskins had just been explaining to her. She had allowed herself to assume, against all the evidence, against all reason—that Timmie was going to be spending the rest of his life in the twenty-first century.

But Mannheim knew it wasn't so.

And he had been waiting all this time for her to call him.

"I need to see you right away," she told him.

"At the Stasis headquarters?"

"No," she said. "Somewhere else. Anywhere. In the city somewhere. You pick the place."

They met at a small restaurant near the river, where Mannheim said no one would bother them, on a rainy midweek afternoon. Mannheim was waiting for her when she arrived. It all seemed terribly clandestine to Miss Fellowes, vaguely scandalous: lunch with a man who had made all sorts of trouble for her employer. And—for that matter— lunch with a *man*. A man she scarcely knew, a young attractive man. Not like Edith Fellowes at all to be doing things like this, she told herself. Especially when she thought of that dream she had once had, Mannheim knocking at her door, swooping her off her feet when she answered—

But this was no romantic assignation. The dream had only been a dream, a fugitive fantasy of her unconscious mind. She felt not the slightest shred of attraction for Mannheim. This was business. This was a matter of life and death.

She fidgeted with her menu and wondered how to begin.

He said, "How's Timmie doing these days?"

"Fine. Fine. You wouldn't believe the progress he's been making."

"Getting big and strong?"

"Every day. And now he can read."

"Really!" Mannheim's eyes twinkled. He has a very nice smile, Miss Fellowes thought. How could Dr. Hoskins have thought he was such a monster? "That's an amazing step forward, isn't it? I bet the anthropology boys were startled when they found out about it."

She nodded. She turned the pages of the menu as though she had no idea what it was. The rain intensified outside; it drummed against the window of the little restaurant with almost malevolent force. They were practically the only customers.

Mannheim said, "I like the chicken in red wine sauce here, particularly. And they do some fine lasagna. Or maybe you'd like the veal."

"It doesn't matter. I'll have whatever you're having, Mr. Mannheim."

He gave her an odd look. "Call me Bruce. Please. Shall we get a bottle of wine?"

"Wine? I never drink wine, I'm afraid. But if you'd like to get some for yourself—"

He was still looking at her.

Over the drumbeat of the rain he said, "What's the trouble, Edith?"

*(Edith?)*

For a moment she was unable to say anything.

(All right, Edith. Pull yourself together, Edith! He'll think you're a gibbering idiot!)

She said, "They're going to send Timmie back."

"Back? You mean back in time?"

"That's right. To his own era. To Neanderthal times. To the Ice Age."

A broad smile spread across Mannheim's face. His eyes lit up. "Why, that's wonderful! That's absolutely the finest news I've heard all week!"

She was horrified. "No—you don't understand—"

"I understand that that sad little captive child is finally going to be returned to his proper people, to his mother and father and sisters and brothers, to the world he belonged to and loved. That's something to celebrate. Waiter! Waiter! I'd like a bottle of Chianti—make it a half-bottle, I guess, my friend won't be having any—"

Miss Fellowes stared at him in dismay.

Mannheim said, "But you look so troubled, Miss Fellowes. Edith. Don't you *want* Timmie to return to his people?"

"Yes, but—but—" She waved her hands in a helpless gesture.

"I think I see." Mannheim leaned across the table toward her. He glowed with sympathy and concern. "You've cared for him so long that you find it hard to let go of him now. The bond between you and

Timmie has become so strong that it's a real shock to you to hear that he's being sent back. I can certainly understand how you feel."

"That's part of it," Miss Fellowes replied. "But only a very small part."

"What's the real problem, then?"

At that moment the waiter arrived with the wine. He made a great show of displaying its label to Mannheim and of pulling the cork, and poured a little into Mannheim's glass to taste. Mannheim nodded. To Miss Fellowes he said, "Are you sure you don't want any, Edith? On a foul rainy day like this—"

"No. Please," she said, almost in a whisper. "Go ahead. You drink it. It would only be wasted on me."

The waiter filled Mannheim's glass and went away.

"Now," he said. "Timmie."

"He'll die if he's returned. Don't you see that?"

Mannheim set down his glass with such abruptness that the wine brimmed over and splashed the tablecloth. "Are you telling me that a return trip in time is fatal?"

"No, that isn't it. Not as far as I know, and I don't think it would be. But it would be fatal for Timmie. Look, he's *civilized* now. He can tie his shoelaces and cut a piece of meat with a knife and a fork. He brushes his teeth morning and night. He sleeps in a bed and takes a shower every day. He watches picture tapes and now he can read simple little books. What good are any of those skills in the Paleolithic era?"

Suddenly solemn, Mannheim said, "I think I see what you're getting at."

"And meanwhile," she went on, "he's probably forgotten whatever he knew about how to live under Paleolithic conditions—and very likely he didn't know a lot to begin with. He was only a little child when he came to us. His parents, his tribal guardians, whoever, must have still been taking care of him. Even Neanderthals wouldn't have expected a boy of three or four to know how to hunt and forage for himself. And even if he did know a little bit at that age, it's been several years since he was exposed to those conditions. He won't remember a thing."

"But surely if he's returned to his own tribe, they'll take him in, they'll re-educate him in tribal ways—"

"Would they? He can't speak their language very well any more; he doesn't think the way they do; he smells funny because he's so clean. —They might just as readily kill him, wouldn't you say?"

Mannheim gazed thoughtfully into his wineglass.

Miss Fellowes went on, "Besides, what guarantee is there that he'll return to his tribe at all? I don't understand a lot about how time travel works, and I'm not sure the Stasis people really do, either. Will he go back right to the exact moment when he left? In that case he'll be three years older and from their point of view he'll have changed tremendously in a single instant—and they won't know what to make of him. They might think he was a demon of some kind. Or will he return to the same place on Earth, but a time three years after he left? If that's how it works, then his tribe will have moved on to some other region long ago. Surely they were nomads then. When he arrives in the past, there'll be no one around to take him in. He'll be completely on his own in a rugged, hostile, bitterly cold environment. A little boy facing the Ice Age by himself. Do you see, Mr. Mannheim? Do you see?"

"Yes," Mannheim said. "I do."

He was quiet a long while. He seemed to be working out some profound calculation in his mind.

Finally he said, "When is he supposed to be shipped back? Do you know?"

"Perhaps not for months, Dr. Hoskins told me. I can't say whether that means two months or six."

"Not much time, either way. We'd have to organize a campaign, a Save Timmie campaign—letters to the newspapers, demonstrations, an injunction, maybe a Congressional investigation into the whole Stasis Technologies operation. —Of course, it would be useful if you'd take part by testifying to Timmie's essential humanity, by providing us with videos showing how he reads and looks after himself. But you'd probably have to resign your post there if you were to do that, and that would cut you off from Timmie, which you wouldn't want, and which wouldn't be useful to us, either. A problem. On the other hand, suppose—"

"No," Miss Fellowes said. "It's no good."

Mannheim glanced up, surprised. "What?"

"A campaign of the kind you're talking about. It'll backfire. The moment you start with your protests and your talk of demonstrations and injunctions, Dr. Hoskins will simply pull the switch on Timmie. That's all it is—a switch, a handle. You yank it and whatever's in the cubicle goes back where it came from. The Stasis people couldn't afford to let things get to the point where you have them tied up with an injunction. They'd act right away and make the whole thing a moot issue."

"They wouldn't dare."

"Wouldn't they? They've already decided the Timmie experiment is over. They need his Stasis facility for something else. You don't know them. They're not sentimental people, not really. Hoskins is basically a decent man, but if it's a choice between Timmie and the future of Stasis Technologies, Ltd., he wouldn't have any problem choosing at all. And once Timmie's gone, there's no bringing him back. It'll be a *fait accompli*. They could never find him in the past a second time. Your injunction would be worthless. And somebody who lived forty thousand years ago and died before civilization was ever imagined wouldn't have any recourse in our courts."

Mannheim nodded slowly. He took a long, reflective sip of his wine. The waiter came by, hovering with his order pad at the ready, but Mannheim waved him away.

"There's only one thing to do," he said.

"And that is?"

"We have people in Canada who'd be glad to raise Timmie. In England, in New Zealand also. Concerned, loving people. Our organization could provide a grant that would cover the cost of employing you as his full-time nurse. Of course, you'd have to make a total break with your present existence and start all over again in some other country, but my reading of you is that for Timmie's sake you'd have no problem with—"

"No. That wouldn't be possible."

"No?"

"No. Not at all."

Mannheim frowned. "I see." Though it was apparent that he didn't. "—Well, then, Edith, even if you have a problem yourself about leaving the country, and I completely understand that, I think we can count on you at least to help us in smuggling Timmie out of the Stasis facility, can't we?"

"I don't have any problem with leaving the country, if that's what I'd need to do to save Timmie. I'd do whatever I could and go wherever I had to, for Timmie's sake. It's smuggling him out of the Stasis facility that isn't possible."

"Is it as tightly guarded as all that? I assure you, we'd find ways of infiltrating the security staff, of working out a completely foolproof plan for taking Timmie from you and getting him out of that building."

"It can't be done. Scientifically, it can't."

"Scientifically?"

"There's something about temporal potential, an energy build-up, lines of temporal force. If we moved a mass the size of Timmie out of Stasis it would blow out every power line in the city. Hoskins told me that and I don't question the truth of it. They've got a bunch of pebbles and dirt and twigs that they brought here when they scooped Timmie out of the past, and they don't even dare take *that* stuff out and throw it away. It's all stored in the back of the Stasis bubble. —Besides all that, I'm not even sure whether moving Timmie outside of Stasis would be safe for him. I'm not certain about that part, but maybe it could be dangerous for him. I'm only guessing at this part. For all I know, he might undergo some kind of temporal-force effect too if he was brought out of the bubble into our universe. The bubble *isn't* in our universe, you know. It's in some special place of its own. You can feel the change when you pass through the door, remember? So your idea of kidnapping Timmie from Stasis and sending him to people overseas —No, no, the risks are too big. Not for you or for me, really, but maybe for Timmie."

Mannheim's face was bleak.

"I don't know," he said. "I offer to raise a legal firestorm in Timmie's defense and you say it won't work, they'll simply pull the switch on him the moment we make any trouble. Then I come up with the completely illegal resort of *stealing* Timmie from Stasis and putting him beyond Hoskins' jurisdiction and you tell me we can't do that either, because of some problem in the physics of it. All right. I want to help, Edith, but you've got me stymied and right now I don't have any further ideas."

"Neither do I," Miss Fellowes said miserably.

They sat there in silence as the rain hammered at the windows of the restaurant.

# CHAPTER ELEVEN

# Going

[52]

P ROJECT MIDDLE AGES—that was all that anyone was talking
about at Stasis Technologies, Ltd. now. It was the beginning of
an amazing new phase for the time-travel operation, everyone agreed.
The unique process that Stasis Technologies controlled would open
the gateway to the historical past—would bring new and astounding
knowledge of antiquity pouring into the twenty-first century, an incredible intellectual treasure. And perhaps treasure of another kind,
some said: if they could reach back into any century of historic times
and bring people back, why not scoop up works of art, rare books and
manuscripts, valuable objects of all sorts? Overnight the resources of
the museums of the world could be doubled, tripled, quadrupled!
And everything in perfect condition—and at no expense other than
the energy costs.

Everyone in the company prayed that Project Middle Ages would
come off without a hitch. Everyone but Edith Fellowes, who quietly
prayed that it would fail. That Hoskins' theories would be wrong, or
that the equipment would not be equal to the task. It was the only
thing she could cling to, now—the only hope she had that Timmie
would not die. If the attempt to bring a man forward from the four-
teenth century turned out to be a flop, there'd be no need to vacate
the Stasis bubble that Timmie occupied. Then everything could go on
as before.

So she hoped for the failure of the project; but the rest of the world
hoped for its success. And, irrationally, Miss Fellowes hated the world

for it. Project Middle Ages was reaching a climax of white-hot publicity now. The media and the public both were obsessed with it. It was a long time since Stasis Technologies, Ltd. had had anything to catch their attention. A new rock or another ancient fish would hardly stir them. The little dinosaur had caused a ripple in its time, but then they had forgotten about it. As for Timmie the Neanderthal, little Timmie the cave-boy, well, he might have held the public fancy for a while longer if he had been anything like the ferocious ape-child that some people had anticipated. But Stasis Technologies' Neanderthal had turned out not to be an ape-child at all, just an ugly little boy. An ugly little boy who wore overalls and had learned to read picture-books— what was exciting about that? There was nothing very prehistoric about him any longer. Maybe if he bellowed in anger and hammered his fists against his chest, yes, and roared some savage primordial gibberish, that might have held their interest a little longer. But that wasn't Timmie's style.

A historical human, though—a full-grown person stepping out of the past, someone who had looked with his own eyes upon Joan of Arc or Richard the Lion-Hearted or Saladin—someone who could speak a known language, someone who could bring the pages of history to life—

The weeks went by. The time came closer.

And now the day of Zero Hour for Project Middle Ages was at hand.

Hoskins and his associates had learned a good deal about the techniques of public relations since the day of Timmie's arrival three years before. This time it wouldn't be a matter of a handful of onlookers on a balcony. This time the technicians of Stasis Technologies, Ltd., would play out their role before nearly all of mankind.

Miss Fellowes herself was all but savage with anticipation. She wanted the suspense to be over; she wanted to know whether the project would succeed or fail. She meant to be there in the assembly hall as the final switches were being thrown. If only the new relief orderly would show up so that she would be free to go over there— Mandy Terris was her name, she had been taken on last week, a replacement for Ms. Stratford, who had gone on to a better-paying job in another state—

"Miss Fellowes?"

She whirled, hoping it was Mandy Terris at last. But no, it was just Dr. Hoskins' secretary, bringing Jerry Hoskins for his scheduled playtime with Timmie. The woman dropped Jerry off and hurried away. She, too, was rushing for a good place from which to watch the climax of Project Middle Ages.

Jerry sidled toward Miss Fellows, looking embarrassed.

"Miss Fellowes?"

"What is it, Jerry?"

The boy took a ragged news-strip cutting from his pocket and held it out to her.

"This is a picture of Timmie, isn't it?"

Miss Fellows glanced at it quickly. It was Timmie, all right, grinning out from the page. The excitement over Project Middle Ages had brought about a pale revival of interest in Timmie on the part of the press. The news-strip picture was a photo that had been taken not long ago, on the third anniversary of his arrival. Timmie's birthday party, they had called it—celebrating his "birth" into the twenty-first century, a few of the scientists and a few reporters and Jerry and Timmie. Timmie was holding one of his "birthday" presents, a shining robot toy.

"What about it?" Miss Fellowes asked.

Jerry watched her narrowly. "It says Timmie is an ape-boy. They aren't supposed to say that, are they?"

"*What?*"

She snatched the clipping from young Hoskins' hand and stared at it. There was a caption that she had not bothered to read before:

PREHISTORIC APE-BOY

GETS TOY ROBOT

FOR HIS BIRTHDAY

*Ape-boy, Ape-boy, Prehistoric ape-boy.* Miss Fellowes' eyes brimmed with hot tears of rage. With a vicious twist of the wrist, she tore the news-strip into a dozen pieces and threw them on the floor.

"Why'd you do that, Miss Fellowes? Because it said Timmie was an ape-boy? He isn't an ape-boy, is he? Or is he?"

She caught the youngster's wrist and repressed the impulse to shake him. "No, he isn't an ape-boy! And I don't want you ever to say those words again. Never, do you understand? It's a nasty thing to say and you mustn't do it."

Jerry struggled out of her grip, looking frightened.

Her heart was pounding. Miss Fellowes fought to get control of herself.

"Go inside and play with Timmie," she said. "He's got a new book to show you."

"You hurt me."

"I'm sorry. I didn't mean to."

"I'll tell my fa—"

"Go inside! Quick! I told you I was sorry."

The boy scurried away, through the door of the bubble, turning once to look back at her with anger in his eyes. Miss Fellowes heard footsteps from the other direction and turned to see Mandy Terris approaching. About time, she thought.

"You're a little late, aren't you?" she said, trying to keep querulousness out of her voice. "Jerry Hoskins is here already. Inside, playing with Timmie."

"I know, Miss Fellowes. I was trying to hurry, but there are crowds everywhere. There's just so much excitement."

"I know. Now, I want you—"

Mandy said, "I guess you're in a rush to go off and watch, aren't you?" Her thin, vacuously pretty face filled with envy. "Of all times for me to have to be on duty—"

"You can watch it on the evening news," Miss Fellowes said curtly. "Let's go inside, shall we?" It would be the first time she had left Mandy Terris alone with Timmie. "The boys won't give you any trouble. They've got milk handy and all the toys they'll need. In fact, it'll be better if you leave them alone as much as possible."

"I understand. And I'll be sure not to let him get out, either. I know how important that is."

"Good. Now come in."

Miss Fellowes opened the Stasis door for her and showed her in. Timmie and Jerry were busy with their games in the back room and paid no attention. She showed Mandy Terris what needed to be done in the next couple of hours, the requisition forms to fill out, the record-keeping.

As Miss Fellowes was about to leave, the girl called after her, "I hope you get a good seat! And, golly, I sure hope it works!"

Miss Fellowes did not trust herself to make a reasonable response. She hurried on without looking back.

But the delay meant that she did *not* get a good seat. She got no nearer than the wall-viewing-plate in the assembly hall. She regretted that bitterly. If only she could have been on the spot; if she could somehow have reached out for some sensitive portion of the instrumentation; if she were in some way able to sabotage the experiment—

No. That was madness. She summoned her strength and beat the foolish ideas back.

Simple destruction would accomplish nothing. They would simply rebuild and reconstruct and make the effort again. And she would have cut herself off from Timmie forever.

Nothing would help.

Nothing but the failure of the experiment itself—its irretrievable breakdown, its fundamental impossibility—something of that sort.

So she waited through the countdown, watching every move on the giant screen, scanning the faces of the technicians as the focus shifted from one to the other, watching for the look of worry and uncertainty that would tell her that something had unexpectedly gone wrong.

Watching—watching—

Nobody looked uncertain. No one seemed particularly worried. They had tested the equipment many times. They had run a thousand simulations; they had already satisfied themselves that a close-range temporal fix was feasible.

The count ran all the way out, down to zero.

And—very quietly, very unspectacularly—the experiment succeeded.

In the new Stasis that had been established there stood a bearded, stoop-shouldered peasant of indeterminate age, in ragged dirty clothing and wooden shoes, staring in dull horror at the sudden mad change that had flung itself over him.

And while the world went mad with jubilation, Miss Fellowes stood frozen in sorrow, jostled and pushed, all but trampled. Surrounded on all sides by triumph while she herself was bowed down with defeat.

When the loudspeaker began to call her name with strident force, it sounded three times before she reacted.

*"Miss Fellowes. Miss Fellowes. You are wanted in Stasis Section One immediately. Miss Fellowes. Miss Fell—"*

What had happened?

"Let me through!" she cried, while the loudspeaker continued its repetitions without pause. With wild energy she cut a path for herself through the crowds, beating at the people in her way, striking out with closed fists, flailing desperately, moving toward the door in a nightmare slowness.

*"Miss Fellowes, please—Miss Fellowes—urgent—"*

[53]

Mandy Terris was in tears in the corridor outside the bubble. "I don't know how it happened. I just went down to the edge of the corridor to watch a pocket viewing-plate they had set up. Just for a minute. And then before I could move or do anything—" She cried out in sudden accusation, "You said they wouldn't make any trouble; you *said* I should leave them alone—"

Miss Fellowes, disheveled and trembling uncontrollably, glared at her. "Where's Timmie?"

Mortenson had appeared from somewhere and was swabbing the arm of a wailing Jerry with disinfectant. Elliott was there; too, preparing an anti-tetanus shot. There was a bright bloodstain on Jerry's clothes.

"He bit me, Miss Fellowes," Jerry screamed in rage. "He *bit* me!"

But Miss Fellowes looked right through him.

"What did you do with Timmie?" she cried out.

"I locked him in the bathroom," Mandy Terris said. "I just threw the little monster in there and barricaded it with some chairs."

Miss Fellowes ran into the dollhouse, scarcely even noticing the ripple of disorientation as she entered Stasis. She pushed the chairs aside and fumbled at the bathroom door. It took an eternity to get it open.

At last. She looked down on the ugly little boy, cowering miserably in the corner.

"Don't whip me, Miss Fellowes," Timmie said huskily. His eyes were red. His lips were quivering. "I didn't mean to hurt him. You aren't going to whip me, are you?"

"Oh, Timmie, who told you about whips?" She drew him to her, hugging him wildly.

He said tremulously, "She did. The new one. She said you'd hit me with a long whip, that you would hit me and hit me."

"She was wicked to say that. You won't be whipped. —But what happened? What happened, Timmie?"

He stared up at her. His eyes looked enormous.

In a low voice he said, "He called me an ape-boy."

"What!"

"He said I wasn't a real boy. That he read it in the newspaper. He said I was just an animal." Timmie was fighting to hold back tears; and then they came, a flood of them. His words grew indistinct as he snuffled, and yet she could make out every syllable all too clearly. "He said he wasn't going to play with a monkey any more. I said I wasn't a monkey. I'm *not* a monkey. I know what a monkey is."

"Timmie—Timmie—"

"He said I was all funny-looking. He said I was horrible and ugly. He kept saying and saying and I bit him."

They were both crying now.

Miss Fellowes said, amid sobs, "It isn't true. You know that, Timmie. You're a real boy. You're a dear real boy and the best boy in the world. And no one, *no* one, will ever take you away from me."

She went outside again. Elliott and Mortenson were still bustling around, patching Jerry up. Mandy Terris was nowhere to be seen.

Miss Fellowes said, "Get that boy out of here. Take him to his father's office and finish whatever it is you need to do with him there. And if you see Ms. Terris, tell her she can pick up her paycheck and clear out."

They nodded. They backed away from her as if she had begun to breathe fire.

She turned and went back inside, to Timmie.

[54]

Her mind was made up, now. It had been very easy: the sudden awareness of what had to be done, the sudden resolve to do it right away, quickly, no hesitation possible. Maybe there were dangers in it that she didn't understand, but she had to take that chance. If she didn't act at all, Timmie would surely be sent back across time to die. If she did what she planned now to do, there was at least the hope that things would work out. On the one hand, the certainty of death—on the other, hope. An easy choice, that one. And there wasn't any time for considering and reconsidering, not now, not when Hoskins' own son had been mangled like this.

No, it would have to be done this night, *this* night, while the celebration over the success of Project Middle Ages still had everyone distracted.

She wished she could call Bruce Mannheim to let him know. But she didn't dare risk it. The switchboard computers might have some kind of security program in them; they might listen in and report what she was intending to do. She would have to get in touch with him after it was done. Mannheim wouldn't mind being awakened in the small hours of the night, not for *this*. And then he could get to work doing his part.

Midnight, she thought. That's the right time.

There would be no problem about her leaving and coming back that late. She often went there at night, even on nights when she had decided to sleep at her own apartment and had already left for the day. The guard knew her well and wouldn't dream of questioning her. He wouldn't think twice about why she happened to be carrying a suitcase, either. She rehearsed the noncommital phrase, "Some games for the boy," and the calm smile.

Games for the boy? Bringing them in at midnight?

But why should anyone doubt her? She lived only for Timmie. Everyone around here knew that. If she was bringing games for him in the middle of the night, well, that was the way she was. Why should he take any notice?

He didn't.

"Evening, Miss Fellowes. Big day today, wasn't it?"

"Very big, yes. —Some games for the boy," she said, waving the suitcase and smiling.

And went on past the security barrier.

Timmie was still awake when she entered the dollhouse.

"Miss Fellowes—Miss Fellowes—"

She maintained a desperate pretense of normality to avoid frightening him. Had he been sleeping? A little, he said. He had had the dream again, and it had awakened him. So she sat with him for a time, talking about his dreams with him, and listened to him ask wistfully about Jerry. She was as patient as she could force herself to be. There's no hurry, she told herself. Why should anyone be suspicious? I have every right to be in here.

And there would be few to see her when she left, no one to question the bundle she would be carrying. Timmie would be very quiet and then the thing would be done. It would be done and what would be the use of trying to undo it? They would let her be. They would let them both be. Even if what she was about to do blew every power line in six counties, there'd be no point afterward in bringing Timmie back to his place.

She opened the suitcase.

She took out the overcoat, the woolen cap with the ear-flaps, and the rest.

Timmie said, with a note of bewilderment and perhaps distress in his voice, "Why are you putting all these clothes on me, Miss Fellowes?"

She said, "I'm going to take you outside, Timmie. To where your dreams are."

"My dreams?" His face twisted in sudden yearning, yet fear was there, too.

"You don't need to be afraid. You'll be with me. You won't be afraid if you're with me, will you, Timmie?"

"No, Miss Fellowes." He buried his little misshapen head against her side, and under her enclosing arm she could feel his small heart thud.

She lifted him into her arms. She disconnected the alarm and opened the door softly.

And screamed.

Gerald Hoskins was standing there, facing her across the open door.

## [55]

There were two men with Hoskins and he stared at her, looking as astonished as she was.

Miss Fellowes recovered first by a second, and made a quick attempt to push past him into the corridor; but even with the second's delay Hoskins had enough time to stop her. He caught her roughly and hurled her back through the door of the bubble and up against a chest of drawers. Then he waved the other two men in and confronted her, blocking the door.

"I didn't expect this. Are you completely insane?"

Miss Fellowes had managed to interpose her shoulder so that it, rather than Timmie, had struck the chest. Now she turned, clinging to Timmie tightly and glaring defiantly at Hoskins. But the defiance went out of her as she began to speak. In a pleading tone, she said, "What harm can it do if I take him, Dr. Hoskins? You can't put something like an energy loss ahead of a human life."

Hoskins nodded to the others, and they stepped in alongside her, looking ready to restrain her if it turned out to be necessary. Hoskins himself reached forward and took Timmie out of her arms.

He said, "A power surge of the size that doing what you were about to do would black out an immense area. It would cripple the whole city all the next day. Computers would be down, alarms wouldn't function, data would be lost, all kinds of trouble. There'd be a thousand lawsuits and we'd be on the receiving end of all of them. The costs would run into the millions for us. *Way* up in the millions. We might even find ourselves facing bankruptcy. At the very minimum it would mean a terrible financial setback for Stasis Technologies, and a colossal public-relations fiasco. Imagine what people will say when they find out that all that trouble was caused by a sentimental nurse acting irrationally for the sake of an ape-boy."

*"Ape-boy!"* said Miss Fellowes, in helpless fury.

"You know that that's what the reporters like to call him," said Hoskins. "And ordinary people all think of him that way. They still don't understand what a Neanderthal actually is. And I don't think they ever will."

One of the other men had gone out of the bubble. He returned now, looping a nylon rope through eyelets along the upper portion of the wall.

Miss Fellowes gasped. She remembered the rope attached to the pull-lever outside the room containing Professor Adamewski's rock specimen so long ago.

She cried out, "No! You mustn't!"

But Hoskins put Timmie down and gently removed the overcoat he was wearing. "You stay here, Timmie. Nothing will happen to you. We're just going outside for a moment. All right?"

Timmie, white-faced and wordless, managed to nod.

Hoskins steered Miss Fellowes out of the dollhouse ahead of himself. For the moment she was beyond resistance. Dully she noticed the red-handled pull-lever being adjusted in the hallway outside. Odd how she had never paid attention to it before, never let it enter her consciousness.

The sword of the executioner, she thought.

"I'm sorry, Miss Fellowes," Hoskins said. "I would have spared you this if I could. I planned it for midnight so that you'd find out only when it was over."

She said in a weary whisper, "You're doing this because your son was hurt. Don't you realize that Jerry tormented this child into striking out at him?"

"This has nothing to do with what happened to Jerry."

"I'm sure it doesn't," Miss Fellowes said acidly.

"No. Believe me. I understand about the incident today and I know it was Jerry's fault. —Well, I suppose what happened today has speeded things up a little. The story has leaked out. No way that it wouldn't have, with the media crawling all over the lab today because of Project Middle Ages. And we'll be hearing stuff about 'negligence,' 'savage Neanderthalers,' all that nonsense, getting into the news, spoiling the coverage of today's successful experiment. Better to end the Timmie experiment right here and now. Timmie would have had to leave soon anyway. Better to send him back tonight and give the sensationalists as small a peg as possible on which they can hang their trash."

"It's not like sending a rock back. He's a human being, and you'll be killing him."

"Not killing. We've got no reason to think that the return trip is harmful. He'll arrive more or less in the same place we took him from, at a point in time that we calculate will be roughly ten weeks after his departure—plus or minus a couple of weeks, factoring in entropic drift and other little technicalities. And he won't feel a thing. He'll be back home—a Neanderthal boy in a Neanderthal world. He won't be a prisoner and an alien any more. He'll have a chance at a free life."

"What chance? He's seven years old at best, accustomed to be taken care of, fed, clothed, sheltered. Now he'll be alone in an ice age. Don't you think his tribe may have wandered off somewhere else in ten weeks' time? They don't simply sit still—they follow the game, they move along the trail. And even if by some miracle they were still there, do you think they'll recognize him? Three years older in ten weeks? They'd run screaming away. He'd be alone and he'd have to look after himself. How will he know how to do it?"

Hoskins shook his head. His expression was bleak, stony, implacable.

"He'll find his tribe again, and they'll take him in and welcome him back. I'm completely certain of it. Trust me, Miss Fellowes."

She looked at him in anguish.

"*Trust* you?"

"Please," he said, and suddenly there was anguish in his eyes too. "There's no way around this. I'm sorry, Miss Fellowes. Believe me, I am—sorrier than you'll ever give me credit for. But the boy has to go, and that's all there is to it. Don't make it any harder for me than it already is."

Her eyes were fixed on his. She stared steadily, in silence, for a long terrible moment.

At last she said, sadly, "Well, then. At least let me say goodbye to him. Give me five minutes alone with him. You can let me have that, can't you?"

Hoskins hesitated. Then he nodded.

"Go ahead," he said.

## [56]

Timmie ran to her. For the last time he ran to her and for the last time Miss Fellowes clasped him in her arms.

For a moment, she hugged him blindly. She caught at a chair with the toe of one foot, moved it against the wall, set it down.

"Don't be afraid, Timmie."

"I'm not afraid if you're here, Miss Fellowes. —Is that man mad at me, the man out there?"

"No, he isn't. He just doesn't understand about us. —Timmie, do you know what a mother is?"

"Like Jerry's mother?"

"Well—yes. Like Jerry's mother. Do you know what a mother does?"

"A mother is a lady who takes care of you and who's very nice to you and who does good things."

"That's right. That's what a mother does. Have you ever wanted a mother, Timmie?"

Timmie pulled his head away from her so that he could look into her face. Slowly, he put his hand to her cheek and hair and stroked her, just as long, long ago she had stroked him.

He said, "Aren't you my mother?"

"Oh, Timmie."

"Are you angry because I said that?"

"No. Of course not."

"Because I know your name is Miss Fellowes, but—but sometimes, I call you 'Mother' inside. The way Jerry does his mother, only he does it out loud. Is that all right, that I was calling you that inside?"

"Yes. Yes, it's all right. And I won't leave you any more and nothing will hurt you. I'll be with you to care for you always. Call me Mother, so I can hear you."

"Mother," said Timmie contentedly, leaning his cheek against hers.

She rose, and still holding him, stepped up on the chair.

She remembered what Hoskins had said, about objects that weren't anchored being swept along in time with the transit object. A lot of the things in the room were anchored; some were not. Such as the chair she was standing on. Well, so be it: the chair would go. That wasn't important. Other things might go, too. She didn't know which would be caught in the time field and which would not. She didn't care. It was no problem of hers.

"Hey!" Hoskins shouted, from outside the bubble.

She smiled. She clutched Timmie tightly and reached up with her free hand, and yanked with all her weight at the cord where it hung suspended between two eyelets.

And Stasis was punctured and the room was empty.

# EPILOGUE

# *Skyfire Face*

SILVER CLOUD walked over to Goddess Woman where she squatted drawing magical circles in the snow and said, "I need to talk to you."

She went on doing what she was doing. "Talk, then."

"Can you stop drawing the circles for a moment?"

"The circles protect us."

"Stop anyway," Silver Cloud said. "Stand up and look me in the eye. I have a serious matter to discuss."

Goddess Woman gave him a sour, scowling look and got slowly to her feet. He thought he could hear her bones creaking as she came out of her squat.

The snow had stopped, at least for a little while. The sun was shining weakly, a late-season sun, low on the horizon.

"Well?" Goddess Woman said. "Talk."

"We have to leave this place," said Silver Cloud.

"Of course we do. Everyone's known that for a long time."

"We're *going* to leave this place, is what I mean. Today."

Goddess Woman scratched her rump thoughtfully. "We still haven't been able to worship at the shrine."

"No. We haven't."

"We came here to do that. If we leave without doing it—after having failed to hold the Summer Festival—the Goddess will be angry at us."

Silver Cloud said, in irritation, "The Goddess *is* angry at us. We know that already. She sent the Other Ones to occupy the riverbank and keep us from using the shrine. All right, then we can't use the shrine. But we can't stay any longer, either. We have no real shelter here and not much food and we're right on the edge of winter."

"You should have admitted these things to yourself a long time ago, Silver Cloud."

"Yes. I should have. But at least I'm admitting them now. When we are finished talking, I will give the order to break camp, and you will perform the rites of departure, and we will leave. Is that understood?"

Goddess Woman stood staring at him for a time.

Then she said, "Understood, yes. But you can no longer be chieftain after this, Silver Cloud."

"I know that. The Killing Society will convene and do what has to be done. I can be left behind as an offering to the Goddess. Some other chieftain will lead us up the hill and out to the east to find shelter."

"Yes," Goddess Woman said. What he had just said didn't seem to perturb her in any way. "And who will be chieftain after you? Blazing Eye? Broken Mountain?"

"Whoever wants to be," said Silver Cloud.

"And if more than one wants to be?"

He shrugged. "They can fight it out, then."

"But this is wrong. You should make a choice."

"No," he said. "My wisdom is used up. My day is over. Go, get yourself ready for what happens next, Goddess Woman. I am done talking with you."

He walked away. She called his name, but he paid no attention. She hurled a snowball after him, and it struck his shoulder and snow ran down his back, but still he kept walking. He had no wish to talk with anyone now. This was his last day of life and he simply wanted to be calm, to be quiet, to pass the time peacefully until the Killing Society came for him with the ivory club. Tomorrow his leg would no longer hurt and someone else would bear his burdens of power.

He stood by himself, looking across the way to the shrine that his people had never been able to use.

Some Other Ones were stirring about down there, by the edge of the river. Warriors, they were, and armed. What were they up to? Young Antelope was on sentry duty near the shrine, and he was pacing back and forth in an uneasy way. An attack? Was that what they had in mind? Taking the shrine by force?

It would be just my luck, Silver Cloud thought. We sit here in stalemate week after week, each side afraid of the other, neither one willing to risk seizing the shrine by force. And the very day I decide to withdraw and give the place to them, they decide to take it from us in battle. And we have no way of communicating with them, so we will have to fight, and many of us will die. Needlessly. If they would wait until tomorrow, the shrine would be theirs without a fight, for we would be gone from here.

"Blazing Eye!" he called. "Tree of Wolves!"

The men came jogging over. Silver Cloud indicated what was going on down by the shrine.

"Are they going to start a fight?" Tree of Wolves asked.

"The Goddess only knows, boy. But you'd better get yourselves ready, just in case. Tell the others. Tell everyone. Even the old ones." Silver Cloud held up his own spear. "I'll be fighting right alongside you, if they attack."

Blazing Eye looked at him incredulously. "You, Silver Cloud?"

"Why not? You think I've forgotten how?"

Better to die in battle, he told himself, than to have to face the ivory club of the Killing Society. Though he would prefer no battle, and the peaceful departure of the People from this place.

Blazing Eye and Tree of Wolves ran off to sound the alarm.

Then, suddenly, the woman She Who Knows came leaping forward out of nowhere, as though she had been stung. She had gone off by herself this morning, as she often did: wandering back up the trail along the hill that led to the east. She grew stranger and stranger every day, that one did.

"Silver Cloud! Silver Cloud! Look!"

He turned toward her. "Look at what?"

"On the hill! The light!" She whirled, pointing back behind herself. "Do you see it?"

"What? —Where?"

He narrowed his eyes and peered upward. He saw nothing unusual up there.

"Along the path," She Who Knows said. "Where we came down. You see a light?"

"No. —Yes! *Yes!*"

Silver Cloud felt a strange chill. It was a light of a sort that he had seen once before. The air was sparkling up there, giving off dazzling flashes of red and green. Shining loops and whorls of color danced in a wild wreath-like shape. And at the center of it was a zone of fierce white light so brilliant he could barely stand to look straight at it.

There had been light like that when they had descended the hill into this place many weeks before. On the day when the Goddess had seized the boy Skyfire Face.

He muttered a hoarse prayer. He heard Goddess Woman chanting something behind him, and then the other two Goddess Women taking up the chant as well.

"What is that light, Silver Cloud?" someone asked him. "Tell us. Tell us!"

He shook the questioners off. Slowly, numbly, like a man who has walked too long in the snow and whose feet have turned to stone, he began to move toward the path that led up the hill. He had to get closer. He had to see.

"The Goddess is here again," a woman's voice whispered behind him.

He kept walking. He could hear the others following at his back. And, glancing down toward the shrine, Silver Cloud saw that the Other Ones too were aware of the apparition on the hillside, that they had halted whatever it was they were doing by the riverbank and were moving slowly toward it, drawn as irresistibly as he was by the urge to have a closer look.

"The Goddess is up there!" some woman moaned. "I see Her. I see Her!"

"The Goddess, yes!"

"The Goddess. And the Goddess is an Other One!"

"The Goddess is an Other One! Look at her! Look!"

Silver Cloud narrowed his eyes, straining to see what the others saw. But the light was too bright—that strange light, that bewildering whorl of color with the whirling whiteness at its heart—

Then the light began to fade. And Silver Cloud saw the Goddess.

She stood serenely on the hillside at the place where the strange light had glowed. She was of the Other Ones' kind, yes, very tall, very slender. Her skin was pale and her hair seemed fair and her lips were red, and her brow rose steeply and smoothly. She was wearing white robes of a kind that Silver Cloud had never seen before.

And she held a child in her arms. A child of the People.

Slowly, calmly, the Goddess descended the trail, coming down the hill to the group gathered at the base. Silver Cloud continued to go toward her. She Who Knows was at his left hand now, and Goddess

Woman on his right, and Keeps The Past just behind him. They clustered close to him, as if they were as mystified as he was and wanted the protection of the chieftain's sacred presence as they went toward Her.

She was very near, now.

How strange her face was! And—though it was an Other One face, unquestionably an Other One face—how beautiful, how tranquil! She was smiling and her eyes were shining with joy.

And the boy she was holding—half-grown, he was, and dressed in a strange kind of robe—his eyes were shining, too.

"The mark on his face—" She Who Knows said. "Do you see? The skyfire sign! You know who that child is. Where is Red Smoke At Sunrise? Look, Red Smoke At Sunrise, the Goddess has brought back your lost son Skyfire Face!"

"But Skyfire Face was only a little boy. And this one is—"

"The mark, though! The mark on his face!"

"Skyfire Face! Skyfire Face!" The shout went up on all sides.

Yes, Silver Cloud thought. Skyfire Face. It had to be him. How happy he looked! He was smiling, waving, calling out to them. In just a few weeks he had grown years older—some miracle of the Goddess, no doubt—but beyond question it was Skyfire Face, truly returned to them. Where had the boy been? Why had he been brought back now? Who could say? It was all some great and wondrous deed of the Goddess.

"Look," Keeps The Past whispered. "The Other Ones are coming."

Silver Cloud glanced around. Yes: the enemy was practically upon them, he saw. But not to make war: he could see that in their faces. Not only the warriors of the Other Ones were advancing up the hill, but all of them, the women and children and the old ones, too. And they all seemed as stunned by the appearance of the Goddess as were the People themselves—just as awed, just as humbled by this divine vision.

The Goddess stood waiting, holding the boy Skyfire Face still in her arms, and smiling. A golden light seemed to stream from them both.

Silver Cloud fell to his knees before them. Joy flooded from them in waves, bringing strange tears to his eyes, and he had to kneel to give thanks. Goddess Woman knelt also, and She Who Knows; and then he looked around and saw that the others too were dropping down to worship Her, both the People and the Other Ones. Everybody side by side, all thoughts of warfare forgotten, one by one kneeling in the snow, looking up with wondering eyes to pay homage to the shining figure with the smiling child in her arms who stood in their midst like a harbinger of springtime and peace.